# GODS & KINGS

Books by
# Lynn Austin
FROM BETHANY HOUSE PUBLISHERS

*Eve's Daughters*

*Hidden Places*

*Wings of Refuge*

REFINER'S FIRE

*Candle in the Darkness*

*Fire by Night*

*A Light to My Path*

CHRONICLES OF THE KINGS

*Gods and Kings*

*www.lynnaustin.org*

CHRONICLES
*of the*
KINGS

# GODS & KINGS

A NOVEL

## LYNN AUSTIN

BETHANY HOUSE PUBLISHERS

*Minneapolis, Minnesota*

*Gods and Kings*
Copyright © 2005
Lynn Austin

Cover design by The Designworks Group: John Hamilton

Published by Bethany House Publishers
11400 Hampshire Avenue South
Bloomington, Minnesota 55438

Bethany House Publishers is a division of
Baker Publishing Group, Grand Rapids, Michigan.

Printed in the United States of America

**Library of Congress Cataloging-in-Publication Data**

Austin, Lynn N.
    Gods & Kings / by Lynn Austin.
       p.   cm. — (Chronicles of the Kings ; 1)
    ISBN 0-7642-2989-3 (pbk.)
    1. Hezekiah, King of Judah—Fiction.  2. Bible. O.T.—History of Biblical events—
Fiction.  3. Israel—Kings and rulers—Fiction.  I. Title: Gods and Kings.  II. Title.
III. Series.
    PS3551.U839G63    2005
    813'.54—dc22                                2004019907

Dedicated to my husband,
Ken,
who never doubted


*The Lord is my strength*
*and my song;*
*he has become my salvation.*

EXODUS 15:2

LYNN AUSTIN is a three-time Christy Award winner for her historical novels *Hidden Places, Candle in the Darkness,* and *Fire by Night.* In addition to writing, Lynn is a popular speaker at conferences, retreats, and various church and school events. She and her husband have three children and make their home in Illinois.

# A Note to the Reader

Shortly after King Solomon's death in 931 BC, the Promised Land split into two separate kingdoms. Israel, the larger nation to the north, set up its capital in Samaria and was no longer governed by a descendant of King David. In the southern nation of Judah, where this story takes place, David's royal line continued to rule from Jerusalem. The narrative centers around events in the lives of two kings of Judah: Ahaz, who ruled from 732 to 716 BC, and his son Hezekiah, who ruled from 716 to 687 BC.

Careful study of Scripture and commentaries support the fictionalization of this story. To create authentic speech, the author has paraphrased the words of these biblical figures. However, the New International Version has been directly quoted when characters are reading or reciting Scripture passages, and when prophets are speaking the words of the Lord. The only allowance the author has made is to change the words "the Lord" to "Yahweh."

Interested readers are encouraged to research the full accounts of these events in the Bible as they enjoy this first book in the five-book CHRONICLES OF THE KINGS series.

Scripture references for *Gods and Kings*:
    2 Kings 16
    2 Kings 18:1–3
    2 Chronicles 28:1–8, 16–27
    2 Chronicles 29:1–14
See also:
    2 Chronicles 26:3–5, 16–23
    Jeremiah 26:18–19
    The prophecies of Isaiah and of Micah

# *Part One*

Ahaz was twenty years old when he

became king. . . . Unlike David his father,

he did not do what was right

in the eyes of the Lord.

———————

2 *CHRONICLES 28:1 NIV*

# I

THE RUMBLE OF VOICES and tramping feet awakened him. Hezekiah sat up in bed, his heart pounding, and for the first time in his short life he was terrified. Overnight his safe, quiet world in the king's palace had vanished, and he listened with mounting panic as the commotion in the hallway outside his room grew louder, closer. Men's voices shouted orders. Doors opened and closed. Children cried out in fear.

He turned to his older brother, Eliab, in the bed next to his and saw that he was also awake. Hezekiah scrambled off his bed and climbed in beside him. "Eliab," he whispered, "What's going on? Who's out there?"

Eliab shook his head, clutching the bedcovers. "I–I don't know." They huddled in the darkness, staring at the door, waiting.

In the distance, the mournful cry of a shofar trumpeted an alarm over the sleeping city of Jerusalem as the sound of footsteps thundered up the hallway, approaching Hezekiah's room.

"I'm scared," he said, swallowing back tears. "I want Mama."

Suddenly the door opened, and soldiers, armed with swords and spears, poured into the room, pulling Hezekiah and Eliab off the bed.

Hezekiah was powerless to stop them. His body went stiff with fear as they stripped off his nightclothes and forced a white linen garment over his head. The soldiers' hands felt cold and rough as they dressed him and tied on his sandals. The palace servants always treated him gently, smiling and making up little games as they helped him get dressed. But none of the soldiers spoke, and their cold silence terrified him. They dressed Eliab the same way, then hustled them out of the room.

More soldiers and a dozen priests in flowing robes crowded the hallway. In the flickering torchlight, Hezekiah saw his half-brothers dressed in the same white garments, huddled together, whimpering softly. His uncle Maaseiah stood over them, armed with a sword.

"These are all of the king's sons," he told the priests. "Let's get on with it. My troops have a long march ahead."

"Everything is prepared, my lord," a priest replied.

But before any of them had a chance to move, Hezekiah heard his mother shouting as she ran up the hall from the king's harem. "No, wait! Stop!" She was in her bare feet and was wrapping her outer garment around her as she ran. Her dark hair flowed uncombed down her back. Hezekiah tried to squirm free to go to her, but one of the soldiers held him back.

"What are you doing?" she cried. "Where are you taking my sons?"

"King Ahaz is holding a special sacrifice before the army marches," Uncle Maaseiah said. "Our northern border is under attack."

"What does that have to do with my children? They're only babies." She hugged her robes tightly around herself and shivered.

"Ahaz wants all of his sons to take part." Uncle Maaseiah signaled to his soldiers, and they quickly moved across the hallway to block her path. But not before Hezekiah saw all the color drain from her face.

"No! Wait!" she cried. "What kind of sacrifice?"

Uncle Maaseiah turned his back on her and motioned to his men. "Let's get on with it."

Hezekiah's mother began to scream, and the sound filled him with terror. He could hear her fighting desperately to get past the wall of men, to reach him and Eliab, but the soldiers held her back.

"Mama!" Hezekiah cried out. "I want Mama!" He struggled to go to her but one of the men picked him up as if he weighed nothing at all. Hezekiah wanted to fight but he felt limp with terror, and the soldier who held him was much too strong. His mother's screams faded in the distance behind them as the soldier carried Hezekiah through the maze of corridors and down the palace stairs to the courtyard.

Outside, the sky had begun to lighten as the sun rose behind the Judean hills. A huge crowd of people stood waiting in the palace courtyard, spilling over into the street outside the gate. A brisk wind whipped Hezekiah's tunic against his legs as the soldier lowered him to the ground. The thin fabric offered no warmth against the morning chill, and Hezekiah shivered with cold and fear. He had never seen so many soldiers before, lined up in even rows, their swords gleaming as they stood at attention before his father, the king.

King Ahaz wore the crown of Judah on his head and the royal robes embroidered with the symbol of the house of David. He was a large, round-bellied man, whose voice always sounded loud and angry. Everyone in the palace cowered before him, and Hezekiah had learned to fear him, too. He couldn't imagine why his father would order him and his brothers from their beds at dawn to stand with all these soldiers. As Hezekiah stood shivering in the windy courtyard, the tension in the air, the solemn look on every face, filled him with dread.

The assembly began to march, led by King Ahaz and Uncle Maaseiah. The city elders and nobles followed close behind, then the escort of soldiers and priests began to move. One of the soldiers gripped Hezekiah's shoulder and pushed him forward with all the other young princes of Judah. But instead of climbing the steep hill behind the palace to the Temple of Yahweh where the king usually offered his sacrifices, the procession wound down the hill through the narrow city streets.

They passed the spacious, dressed-stone mansions of the nobility, then marched through the market area, now quiet and deserted, the booths shuttered, the colorful awnings rolled up for the night. Hezekiah saw people watching the procession from their rooftops and peering from behind latticed windows. As the street narrowed, the soldiers squeezed closer and their swords pressed against Hezekiah's side. Where were they taking him? What was going to happen to him? Twice he stumbled as he missed a stair in the street, but the soldiers quickly gripped his arms and pulled him to his feet.

They finally reached the massive gate on the southern wall of Jerusalem and passed down the ramp, out of the city. Now the silent dawn began to echo with the beat of drums pounding in the distance. Hezekiah saw a craggy wall of cliffs, dark and foreboding, guarding the entrance to the Valley of Hinnom. As the procession turned into the narrow valley, he glimpsed a column of smoke billowing high into the air ahead of him, carried aloft by the wind.

The priests who marched beside Hezekiah began to chant, "Molech . . . Molech . . . Molech." The men in the procession joined in, chanting louder and louder to the throbbing beat of the drums. *"MOLECH . . . MOLECH . . . MOLECH!"*

Suddenly the wall of soldiers parted, and Hezekiah caught his first glimpse of Molech. He knew he wasn't dreaming. He knew the monster was real because he never could have imagined anything so horrible. Molech stared down at him from a throne of brass as the fire in the pit beneath the hollow statue blazed with a loud roar. Tongues of flame licked around the edges of his open mouth. His arms reached out as if waiting to be filled, forming a steep incline that ended in his open, waiting mouth.

Hezekiah's instincts screamed at him to run, but his legs buckled beneath him as if made of water. He couldn't move. One of the soldiers picked him up and carried him up the steps of the platform that stood in front of the monster's outstretched arms.

"MOLECH . . . MOLECH . . . MOLECH . . ." the crowd chanted to the pounding rhythm of drums. Hezekiah's heart throbbed in his ears as he huddled beside his brother Eliab. The billowing smoke made his eyes water. The heat burned his face.

The chief priest faced Molech with his arms raised, pleading with the god in a frenzied cry, but the chanting crowd and the noise of the flames drowned out his words. When his prayer ended, the priest lowered his arms and turned around. Hezekiah saw the cold, intent look on the man's face and he tried to back away, but one of Molech's priests gripped his arms. He couldn't escape.

"Which one is the king's firstborn?" the chief priest asked.

Uncle Maaseiah's signet ring flashed in the firelight as he laid his hand on Eliab's head. "This one."

The priest grabbed Eliab and lifted him high in the air. Hezekiah watched in horror as the man tossed his brother into the monster's waiting arms. Eliab rolled down the incline toward the open mouth, clawing at the brazen arms to try to stop his fall, but the metal was hot and polished smooth. He couldn't hold on. Eliab's pitiful screams wailed above the roar of the flames and the pounding drums, even after he had fallen over the rim and Molech had devoured him. His cries, coming from the depths of the flames, lasted only an instant though it felt like a lifetime.

Then a terrible stench, unlike any Hezekiah had smelled before, filled his nostrils and throat until he gagged. His stomach turned inside out, and he retched, as if trying to vomit out the memory, as well.

But the nightmare didn't end with Eliab's death. Other noblemen and city officials offered their sons to the priest and he tossed them, one after the other, into Molech's arms. They rolled helplessly, down into the flames as Eliab had. Hezekiah cowered in a heap on the platform and covered his face to escape the sight. But the horror of this day was engraved on his soul. He began to scream . . . and he didn't think he would ever be able to stop.

---

Abijah's son finally fell asleep, his small body warm and slack in her arms. For the first time all day, his grip on her loosened. But Abijah's clasp on Hezekiah didn't relax as she sat by the window and gazed into the evening sky.

Eliab was dead. Her son, her firstborn, gone forever. Her mind refused to comprehend it, even though her heart felt as if it had been torn out of her, leaving her body cold and hollow. Abijah's grief so overwhelmed her that she knew the pain would never fade as long as she lived. Her son never should have died. His life had been cruelly taken much too soon. And his own father had murdered him.

Her arms tightened protectively around Hezekiah. She wouldn't let him die the way Eliab had. She would protect him from Ahaz no matter what it took—but how? She had neither weapons nor the skill to use them.

Abijah had guessed where the soldiers were taking her children and what would happen to Eliab, but she had been powerless to save him. The guards had ignored her screams and pleas, restraining her long after the procession disappeared from the palace courtyard. She had heard Molech's drums in the distance, but she couldn't break free to help her child. When the sacrifice was over, Eliab was dead, and Hezekiah continued to scream, too young to comprehend the reason for the horror he had witnessed. Nor could Abijah comprehend it herself. All she could do was cling to her remaining son and weep, promising him that he was safe, that she would protect him. But she didn't know how she would keep that promise.

"Why don't you lay him down now, my lady?" her servant Deborah said. "You've been holding him all day." Deborah reached to lift Hezekiah from Abijah's arms, but she hugged him close.

"No—not yet. I need to hold him." Abijah longed for someone to hold and comfort her, to feel someone's loving arms surrounding her. But the only things that surrounded her were stone walls. They were warmed by fires in the brazier and on the hearth, decorated with tapestries and carpets that gave the appearance of comfort and warmth, but Abijah knew it was all a facade. Beneath their elegant surfaces, the walls, like her life, were as cold and hard as stone.

"Please, Lady Abijah—you need to eat something," Deborah begged. "There's some fruit here and some bread."

Abijah glanced at the tray, then shook her head. "I don't want food." She bit her lip and tasted salty tears. How could she eat when her life had been shattered like a bowl hurled to the floor? She would never be whole again.

"Starving yourself won't bring Eliab back, my lady."

Abijah's grief overflowed once again when she heard her son's name. "Oh, Eliab," she wept. "My beautiful child . . ."

Everything about her firstborn had been unforgettable: the first time she'd felt life moving inside her; the first time she'd given birth and held him in her arms; his first steps; his first words. Her son Eliab. He had been King Ahaz's firstborn as well, the future king of Judah. His young life had been so full of hope and promise.

"I never even kissed him good-bye. . . ." She bent to kiss Hezekiah, and her tears fell into his curly auburn hair.

"My lady, you should put him in his own bed now," the servant said. "You need to change your robe and comb your hair."

Abijah looked down at the front of her robe, which she had torn in her grief. She wouldn't comb her hair, wouldn't bathe or put on perfumes. How could she when Eliab was dead?

"No," she said quietly. "Let me mourn for my son."

"But you know you aren't allowed to mourn. It's not as if Eliab got sick and died, or—"

"I will mourn for my son!" she repeated. But there would be no mourners to wail with her, no funeral procession or prayers for the dead, no grave to mark the place where her child lay.

"His death was honorable, my lady—a glorious sacrifice to be celebrated," Deborah insisted. Abijah stared at her in disbelief.

"What kind of mother could celebrate her child's death? And what kind of father would kill his own child to save himself? Only a monster could do such a thing." She could see that her words had shocked the servant, but she didn't care. She looked down at her sleeping son again. "And only a monster would force his other children to watch."

"You'd better be careful what you say," Deborah said, her voice a near-whisper. "Your husband is the king."

"Oh, I know that well enough," Abijah said bitterly. "I was promised to the royal house of King David on the day I was born. All my life my father told me I would marry a king someday—as if that was a great honor. I would carry kings in my womb. I was blessed among women." She paused and fingered her torn garment. "But look at the price I've paid for that honor. My son is dead. And I'm married to a man I will hate until the day I die."

"Don't say such a thing. Someone might overhear and—"

"I don't care! I hate him! Nothing can change that."

"You don't mean it, Lady Abijah. It's only your grief speaking. You live a privileged life here in the palace."

"I live like a royal prisoner." Her rooms in the harem were among the best in the palace, with tall windows that overlooked the courtyard on one side, and a balcony with a magnificent view of the city on the other. Every furnishing in the room was beautiful: the tables and lampstands overlaid with ivory and gold, the couches beautifully carved and cushioned. Magnificent tapestries decorated all the walls, and her bed was perfumed and draped in silk. But the harem's splendor and luxury were for the king's sake, not hers. And like gilding over rotten wood, the decorations couldn't alter Abijah's unhappiness.

She had never questioned her destiny, never had any hopes or dreams of her own. Why should she dream when her life had been clearly laid out from birth and there was never a possibility that it could be different? Her father, Zechariah, had promised her to the house of David, and her life had proceeded in its orderly course toward that goal, like stars moving across the sky through their appointed seasons. Her wedding to Ahaz led to the purpose for which she'd been born; Eliab's birth fulfilled it.

Abijah remembered being glad to leave home. She had longed to flee from her father's melancholy, to escape the sight of him drinking himself into a stupor every night while her mother struggled to hide his secret. During the day, he had somehow managed to carry out his tasks—serving in the Temple, teaching students his vast knowledge of the Torah, debating the complexities of Yahweh's Law. He had hidden his drunkenness so well that few people ever guessed that his life had crumbled when King Uzziah died. Abijah had been relieved to leave home and move to the palace. But she'd had no idea that she had married an idolater. Or that one day he would sacrifice her son.

"I wish I had never married Ahaz," Abijah murmured. "I wish—"

She stopped, afraid to voice her wish out loud. But she knew that her life would have taken a different course if she had married Uriah. The high priest of Yahweh's Temple never would have sacrificed his firstborn son to Molech. Uriah had been a fixture in her household as she was growing up, her father's brightest pupil, studying for a future as high priest. When she remembered him now, she realized that Uriah had always loved her, had always treated her with tenderness. She had taken that love for granted, imagining that Ahaz would look at her the same way. But King Ahaz had never looked at her with anything but lust. Not long after she'd spoken her wedding vows, she'd given up hope for any love or companionship. She was Ahaz's property, to be used for his pleasure and to produce his heir—nothing more. Her sons had become her very life.

"My children came from my body, Deborah—my pain and blood and tears. When they took Eliab, they took part of me. And I couldn't stop them. My husband decided to kill my son, and there was nothing

I could do about it. But I won't let him take Hezekiah," she said, gripping him tightly. "I promised him I would protect him, and I'll die before I break that promise."

The servant knelt on the floor in front of her, pleading with her. "Please don't do something you'll be sorry for, my lady."

"I'm already sorry that I've let other people tell me what to do and think and feel all my life. It's time I decided for myself."

She turned to gaze through the window again but night had fallen and with it, darkness and fear. This night would never end for Abijah, even when the sun rose in the morning, unless she found a way to protect her child.

Deborah touched her hand. "You need to change your clothes, my lady," she said gently. "You can't let the king see you in mourning. What if he comes to your chambers tonight?"

Abijah would kill him. She hated him enough to do it. If Ahaz came tonight she would take a knife and plunge it straight through his heart. Let him suffer some of the pain she felt. But even though she wished it, Abijah knew it would be a foolish thing to do. She would forfeit her own life if she murdered the king, and then what would become of Hezekiah?

"Maybe I can make Ahaz hate me as much as I hate him," she murmured aloud. "Maybe then he'll banish my son and me."

"No," Deborah said. "The king would punish you by taking your son away from you. You would never see him again."

Abijah knew that Deborah was right. And if Ahaz took Hezekiah away from her, Abijah would have no reason to live.

"Let me comb your hair now," Deborah begged, "and change your gown. If King Ahaz comes tonight . . ."

Abijah recoiled at the thought of sleeping with Ahaz after he'd murdered Eliab. But then another thought occurred to her. Instead of earning Ahaz's hatred, maybe she should try to win his love. If her only weapons were her beauty and desirability, maybe she could use them to earn her husband's trust and influence his decisions. It might be the only way to protect Hezekiah from him. But how could she ever pretend to love Ahaz when she hated him so fiercely?

Hezekiah stirred in his sleep as a sob shuddered through him. Abijah looked down at him and rocked him gently. He was all she had left. Eliab was gone. And Abijah had promised Hezekiah that she would do whatever it took to save his life. If that meant feigning love for a man she hated, she would do it—for Hezekiah's sake.

"All right, Deborah," she said quietly. "I'll change my robe now. And you may comb my hair."

———

Zechariah stared at the empty wineskin through bleary eyes. He had consumed its entire contents in an effort to forget, but he hadn't forgotten. Vivid images of Molech's sacrifice played over and over in his mind, and they ended the same way every time. Innocent children burned to death in the flames, and Zechariah did nothing to stop it. He stood there, watching, and he didn't try to stop the king from sacrificing his firstborn son.

Zechariah had awakened to the sound of shofars that morning and had followed the procession to the Valley of Hinnom. But as he had watched the king and the city elders sacrifice their children to Molech, cowardice had paralyzed his limbs and sealed his lips. He knew God's Law. He was a Levite, responsible for teaching the Law to the king and to all the people. But Zechariah had remained silent.

When the carnage finally ended, he had wandered back to the city in a daze and stumbled into this inn, seeking refuge in the familiar, numbing power of wine. But even if he drank a reservoir full of wine he knew he could never erase the memory of those children—his own grandson, Eliab—being thrown into the idol's fire. And Zechariah had done nothing to save him. He covered his face with trembling hands, but the image refused to disappear. Why hadn't God's judgment fallen on him? He was the guilty one. He was the one who should have been punished, not an innocent child—not his own flesh and blood.

Night fell, customers came and went, but Zechariah ignored the noise and gaiety all around him. No one seemed to notice him, alone with his wine and his torment. Gradually the inn emptied as the other revelers went home. The innkeeper swept the stone floor and snuffed out the oil lamps for the night. Only Zechariah remained. He had tried to drink himself senseless, but the images had become more intense, not less. Now he was terrified to move. He couldn't go back and undo the mistakes he had made in his life, and he didn't want to compound his guilt by making still more. And so he sat, wishing he had died instead of Eliab.

"Zechariah . . . Zechariah, my friend."

He looked up to see his friend Hilkiah extending a hand to him, his eyes soft with pity. "Come on, Zechariah—the innkeeper wants to close. He asked me to walk you home."

Hilkiah didn't say *again,* but he could have. How many times, night after night, year after year, had the innkeeper sent for Hilkiah— Zechariah's only friend? Too many to count. Zechariah lowered his head until his forehead rested on the table.

"Leave me here," he said with a groan.

"You know I won't do that. You need to go home."

Hilkiah gripped him beneath his arms, grunting as he strained to lift him. The little merchant was short and plump, and he lacked the strength to get Zechariah to his feet. But that wouldn't stop him from trying. Zechariah braced his palms against the table and struggled to stand. The room whirled and swayed.

"Easy, now," Hilkiah soothed. "Take it slow . . ." Zechariah saw him leave a small pile of silver on the table and nod to the innkeeper. Then Hilkiah wrapped his arm around Zechariah's waist and guided him through the door.

Outside, a sliver of moon and a few faint stars provided the only light. The streets were shadowy and still as Hilkiah led him through the central market district and up the hill. The square stone houses lay clustered and stacked on top of each other, with one man's door looking down on his neighbor's roof. The houses, built from the native beige limestone, seemed gilded in the moonlight. Zechariah leaned heavily on his friend as they labored uphill, even though Hilkiah's balding head barely reached Zechariah's shoulders.

"Why are you doing this to yourself?" Hilkiah asked gently. "You're a servant of Yahweh—blessed be His name."

Zechariah halted as he tried to grasp Hilkiah's words. Why had he become a staggering drunkard? He was a servant in Yahweh's Temple, he wore holy garments, offered holy sacrifices. He was . . . Then, like a cloud blotting out the moon, the image of himself serving as a Levite vanished. He let out a soft moan.

"What happened to me? I was a holy man, but now . . . now . . ." He thought about the way he had once lived his life and the way he lived it now, and the gulf between the two seemed so enormous that he wondered how he had ever crossed it. Nor could he imagine crossing back and becoming, once again, a holy man. He lowered his head and tugged his beard in despair.

"I don't deserve to live anymore. I deserve to die!" His voice echoed through the quiet streets. Zechariah waited, yearning for God to strike him dead in payment for his sins, but nothing happened. "Why doesn't God punish *me,* Hilkiah? Why do little children have to die instead? I'm the one who deserves it!"

A dog began to bark, and someone lit a lamp in a nearby window. Hilkiah nudged him forward. "Come on. You'll wake up the whole city. You need to go home."

"I served in the Temple of Solomon," Zechariah said as they started walking again.

"Yes, I know, my friend. Come on."

"I'm a Levite. I can recite all of my ancestors back to Levi, son of Jacob."

"Not tonight," Hilkiah said, patting his shoulder. "It's late. Maybe another time."

"I was chief among all the other Levites. . . . I taught Yahweh's holy law. . . ." He suddenly felt a need to talk about his former life, as if it might help him discover how he had crossed the gulf to this other world, where kings sacrificed innocent children to idols.

"God gave me wisdom and understanding from the time I was very young," he rambled, "and so King Uzziah sent for me when he wanted to learn God's law. *Me!* I taught him to fear Yahweh and—"

He stumbled over a loose brick in the street and lost the flow of his thoughts. The night fell silent except for their labored breathing as they ascended the hill. The houses became larger and more lavish the higher they climbed, and Zechariah recalled that one of the largest was Hilkiah's. His family had supplied the fine linen for the Temple garments and rich embroidered cloth for royalty for many generations. But Hilkiah steered him past his own house, and they continued climbing until they reached the gates to King Ahaz's palace. Only the Temple of Yahweh on the hill above stood higher than the palace.

Zechariah halted to catch his breath. He remembered when he used to live in that palace. He'd been an important man, a man of power and authority. How many years ago was it? He had once commanded the nation, second only to King Uzziah.

"My daughter is married to the king," he said suddenly.

"Yes. Yes, I know." Hilkiah was trying to catch his breath, as well.

"King Uzziah told me—he promised me—if I ever had a daughter, she would marry into the royal house of King David. Can you imagine that? Before my daughter was even born she—"

Zechariah stopped. His daughter was Eliab's mother. Eliab had burned to death. It was all Zechariah's fault. "Yahweh, I'm so sorry!" he groaned. "Oh, Eliab, my child . . . I'm sorry!" He tried to sink to his knees but Hilkiah pulled him upright.

"No, no, my friend. Stand up. Come on." He kept Zechariah

moving, dragging him up the hill away from the palace, but the memories pursued him.

"I turned my back on God," Zechariah said with horror. "Slowly, slowly . . . year after year. Eating at the king's table, drinking his wine, listening to all the flattery . . . slowly . . . until one day . . ." He shook his head. "One day God was a stranger to me."

That was how he had crossed the gulf. Zechariah remembered now. Not in one great leap, but so gradually that he hadn't noticed the downward slope, hadn't realized how far he had separated himself from God until it was too late. He had lived to please himself instead of God all those years, giving little more than lip service to His holy laws. And now when Zechariah cried out to God, his numberless sins swallowed up his prayers before they reached heaven. His guilt filled the yawning gulf between him and God.

"I'm so sorry. . . ." he moaned.

"Shh . . . shh . . ." the little merchant soothed. "Never mind, now. You're almost home, my friend. See? There's the Temple."

"Leave me here, Hilkiah. I know the way."

The merchant clicked his tongue. "How can I leave you here? You'll never make it home by yourself. Come on."

They passed through the Temple gate and crossed the broad, deserted courtyard. Yahweh's Temple loomed ahead of them, the white stones bright in the moonlight. Zechariah halted again as another memory came to him with startling force. King Uzziah had wanted to go inside that Temple, into the holy place, where only the descendants of Levi were permitted to go. *The kings of other nations don't need priests to offer their sacrifices,* Uzziah had insisted. *Why should I need them?*

Zechariah closed his eyes, remembering Uzziah's arrogance, remembering with shame his own failure to act. He should have known what to tell the king. Zechariah was his trusted advisor, a teacher of God's holy law. But he didn't have an answer for Uzziah, didn't try to stop him. He had allowed the king to take a censer in his hand and walk into the Holy Place where he was forbidden to go. The priests had been the ones who had confronted the king, shouting at him as they ordered him to leave the holy sanctuary. In his pride, King Uzziah refused. But Yahweh saw him—and His judgment had fallen swiftly. There in the Holy Place, Yahweh cursed King Uzziah with leprosy. He fled from the Temple, an outcast for the rest of his life.

"It was my fault that Uzziah died a leper," Zechariah murmured. "I should have told him not to go inside. I should have stopped him. . . ."

"That was many, many years ago," Hilkiah said. "Every man in Judah has heard of the terrible fate of King Uzziah—may he rest in peace."

He nudged Zechariah until he started walking again, steering him in a wide arc around the outer perimeter of the Temple courtyard, away from the holy sanctuary. At last they reached the cluster of buildings on the north side that housed the storerooms, meeting rooms, and the living quarters that had been set aside for the Levites on duty. It was where Zechariah lived, even when he wasn't on duty. He remembered living in a house with his wife and family after King Uzziah died—after he'd moved out of the palace. But right now he couldn't recall what had become of his home or why he no longer lived there.

Hilkiah led him to his room and helped him remove his outer robe, then sat him down on his bed to untie his sandals. He gave Zechariah's shoulder a gentle squeeze. "Get some sleep, my friend."

"King Uzziah is dead," Zechariah mumbled.

"Yes. Yes, he is."

Zechariah remembered his funeral, his dishonorable burial outside the tomb of the kings. "His son Jotham is dead, too, and now his grandson, Ahaz, is king. He's married to my daughter. Did you know that?"

Hilkiah nodded. "Yes, you have told me that many times before.

Well, good night, my friend. I must go home now."

Zechariah clutched Hilkiah's arm to stop him. "Your children, Hilkiah! Where are your children?"

"My son Eliakim is at home," he replied, gently freeing himself from Zechariah's grip. "He's probably sound asleep already."

Zechariah had to make his friend understand, to stop him from making the same mistakes he had made. "You must diligently teach God's laws to your son—and to his children after him," he pleaded. "The Torah commands it. I failed to teach King Uzziah, and now . . . now King Ahaz is worse than all of the others. He has heathen altars on every street corner. He even sacrificed his son—" But that memory was too painful for Zechariah to bear, even through a numbing haze of wine. He covered his face with his hands. "It's all my fault!"

"God of Abraham, what can I do?" Hilkiah whispered.

"I have the answer for King Uzziah now! I know what to tell him!" Zechariah said. "I would tell him that Yahweh commanded us not to worship Him the way other nations worship their gods because they do all kinds of detestable things that the Lord hates. They even burn their sons and daughters in the fire as sacrifices to their gods!"

"You need to rest—" Hilkiah began, but Zechariah cut him off.

"I followed the procession to the Valley of Hinnom today."

"No, Zechariah . . . you would never take part in—"

"But I did! I went there!" He saw his friend's horror, but he forced himself to face Hilkiah and confess his sins. "I watched them sacrifice my grandson Eliab to a heathen god, and I remembered what else is written in the Torah: 'For I, the Lord your God, am a jealous God, punishing the children for the sin of the fathers to the third and fourth generation.' Eliab died because of me, Hilkiah. Because I sinned!"

Zechariah lowered his head to his knees, hiding his face in

shame. "Punish *me,* Lord!" he begged. "Not my children. Let me die for my own sins. Let me die!"

He felt Hilkiah's hand on his shoulder. "Ah, my friend, how can I ever comfort you?" he murmured. "God of Abraham . . . how can he ever find peace under such a burden of guilt?"

# 2

THE NIGHTMARE JOLTED HEZEKIAH awake. He had dreamed of Molech again, the image so vivid that he'd felt the heat of the flames. He lay awake in the darkness, breathing hard, his heart pounding until his chest hurt. He listened for soldiers and distant drums, but the palace hallways were quiet.

It was just a bad dream, he told himself. But when he gazed at Eliab's bed, he knew that Molech was real. He hadn't been dreaming on that terrible morning when they'd taken Eliab and thrown him into the fire. What if the soldiers came back for him?

It seemed to Hezekiah like a long time had passed since Eliab had died. Uncle Maaseiah and his soldiers had all marched away into battle, but what would happen when they returned? Hezekiah wondered if they would throw *him* into the monster's mouth the way they'd thrown Eliab. He remembered how the soldiers had picked him up as if he'd weighed nothing at all. He remembered their swords and spears. . . . A shudder passed through his body that jolted him upright. He was helpless. The servants who slept nearby wouldn't save him. They hadn't saved Eliab. Only Mama had tried to stop the soldiers. She would protect him.

Hezekiah climbed out of bed and ran down the darkened corridors to his mother's suite in the harem. Ever since Eliab died, she had allowed him to come and stay with her whenever he had a bad dream. And the nightmares had come nearly every night.

Her door was unlatched. Hezekiah pushed it open and ran to her. "Mama! Mama, I'm scared!" he cried. She sat all alone on the cushioned window seat, gazing into the night sky, but she turned at the sound of his voice and reached to gather him into her arms.

"Come here, my little one. Hush now, don't cry." Mama was warm and soft and very beautiful. Her dark hair flowed down her back in thick waves and smelled like flowers and myrrh. Hezekiah felt safe here. She would keep the soldiers away. She would stop the nightmares from coming. In the comfort of her arms, with his cheek resting against her shoulder, Hezekiah closed his eyes and fell asleep.

The sound of voices startled him awake. He cried out in fright, terrified that the soldiers had returned, but only his father stood alone in the doorway. He seemed huge to Hezekiah, his face scary in the flickering lamplight. Mama tightened her grip until Hezekiah could scarcely breathe. Her heart was beating as rapidly as his was.

"What is that boy doing in here?" Ahaz asked. He was wheezing from his climb up the stairs to the harem, and his forehead glistened with sweat.

"Good evening, my lord," Mama said, her voice almost a whisper. "I-I didn't think you would come tonight. Your son had a bad dream. He came to be comforted, that's all."

"Well, send him back to his room." Ahaz seemed so frightening that Hezekiah wished he could melt into his mother's arms. Instead, she slowly released him, lowering his feet to the floor as she stood. Then she tugged on his hand, urging him to bow down to Ahaz, as she was doing.

"Your father is our king," she told him. "We must bow to show respect to His Majesty." Hezekiah did as he was told. When he glanced up, his father looked pleased.

"Your son Hezekiah is much like you, my lord," Mama said, resting her hands on Hezekiah's shoulders. "He will make a fine choice to be your heir and successor one day."

Ahaz crossed the room until he stood in front of them. Hezekiah's heart raced so wildly as his father studied him that he was afraid it would burst. He wanted to run and hide.

"But you aren't my firstborn," Ahaz said. "I gave my firstborn as a gift to Molech."

Hezekiah began to tremble as the awful truth sank in. It wasn't the soldiers he needed to fear—it was his father. He was the one who had ordered the soldiers to throw Eliab into the flames. And Ahaz had the power to kill him the same way.

At last Ahaz looked away. He loosened the belt of his tunic as he turned to Hezekiah's mother. "Didn't you hear me, Abijah? I said send the boy away."

"Of course, my lord." She smiled, but Hezekiah knew it wasn't her real smile. She looked so different that a chill shivered through him. Mama was afraid of King Ahaz, too—almost as afraid as he was.

Hezekiah wriggled free and ran past his father, not stopping until he reached his own room. He slammed the door and leaned against it, as if to barricade himself inside. He felt sick with fear. His father had killed Eliab. The king was the most powerful person there was. Who could possibly protect Hezekiah from the king?

He was wide awake now, every muscle and nerve ending tingling. Where could he hide? His mother's room was no longer safe. He was afraid to stay here, but terrified to leave. He stood frozen in place, wondering what to do.

Gradually his eyes grew accustomed to the darkness and his breathing slowed to normal. The corridors outside his room were quiet and still. As the familiar contours of his room began to take shape, the shadows seemed less menacing. He could distinguish the bronze lampstands against the wall, the ivory table beneath the window, the charcoal brazier glowing faintly, his rumpled, empty bed. And Eliab's.

Tears filled his eyes and ran down his face as he remembered his brother. They had clothed Eliab in a tunic of white linen and forced him to walk in the procession to the Valley of Hinnom, sleepy and bewildered. Their father, dressed in royal robes, had led that procession. He had offered his firstborn to Molech. But what Hezekiah didn't understand was why. Why had his father killed Eliab?

Abijah moved forward into Ahaz's arms, desperate to hide her emotions from him. He seemed proud of what he had done, calling Eliab a gift to Molech. But Abijah remembered the holy laws her father had once taught, and those laws said that firstborn sons belonged to Yahweh. Their lives were to be redeemed with silver, not offered to idols. Yahweh wanted His children to serve Him with their lives, not their deaths. But Abijah didn't dare speak such thoughts out loud.

She leaned against her husband, forcing herself not to cry or yield to the grief that still consumed her. For Hezekiah's sake, she had to push aside her own revulsion as Ahaz's hands touched her. She must smile in spite of her pain.

"Do I please you, my lord?" she murmured as she returned his caresses.

"This is a good beginning," he said, bending to kiss her. She pretended to return his kisses, to act as if she enjoyed them. Then Ahaz stopped suddenly. "Why do you ask?" he said.

Her heart began to pound. She was afraid that she had overacted and made him suspicious. "B-because I want so much to please you." She hoped he wouldn't see through her clumsy reply, and quickly added, "I know you have several concubines, but I'm your only wife. Perhaps . . . perhaps I'm a little jealous of them?"

Ahaz grinned, and she hated him more fiercely than she ever

thought possible. She buried her face against his chest again to hide her loathing. "I want to be the one you come to each night," she said. "King David had a favored wife. I want to be yours."

"Shall I call you Bathsheba, then?" he asked as he kissed her neck.

She pretended to laugh. "If you'd like to, my lord."

Abijah knew that David had chosen Bathsheba's son to be his heir, even though Solomon wasn't his firstborn. If she could win Ahaz's favor above all the other women in his harem—if she was the one he came to for comfort and solace—she could ask him to designate Hezekiah as his heir someday. She loved her son enough to do that for him, to save him from Molech, even though she would have to sacrifice her own pride and dignity in order to do it.

This first night would be the most difficult, she told herself, coming so soon after Eliab's death. Maybe in time she would learn how to close off her mind and pretend she was somewhere else whenever Ahaz came to her. Maybe in time she would no longer be repulsed by him every time she held him. Abijah drew a deep breath and played her part, determined to do everything in her power to please Ahaz—for her son's sake.

But when someone interrupted them, pounding insistently on the door, Abijah felt immensely relieved.

"Who is it?" Ahaz shouted.

"Your Majesty, please forgive me for disturbing you," one of the chamberlains said from behind the closed door, "but a messenger just arrived with news of your army."

Abijah felt Ahaz grow tense. She looked up at him and saw his undisguised fear. She thought of Eliab and felt no pity for him.

"Just a minute," Ahaz called as he composed himself.

Abijah followed him as he crossed the room and opened the door. The chamberlain who waited outside looked very worried. "I'm sorry, Your Majesty. I never would have interrupted you if it hadn't been so urgent."

"What's the news?"

"It . . . it's not good, I'm afraid. And there are two other reports that I think you should see."

Ahaz turned to Abijah, and she saw how unsure of himself he was. He wanted to escape into her arms, not handle this crisis. She knew then that her plan to win his confidence would work. She could take advantage of his weakness and use her charms to influence him. If she could just push aside her revulsion and pretend that she loved him, she could find out what this crisis was about and what his plans were. Because if he was going to offer another sacrifice to Molech, she needed to hide Hezekiah from him.

She reached up to caress her husband's neck. "If you would like, my lord, I will gladly come and wait in your chambers until the meeting ends."

His eyebrows lifted in surprise. His face wore a vulnerable expression that she'd never seen before, as if her offer had touched him. Ahaz had always come to her rooms. She had never offered to go to his before.

"I would like that very much," he said.

He smoothed his thin, pale hair into place and wiped the beads of sweat from his forehead. Then he turned to his chamberlain. "Why does disaster always strike in the middle of the night?" he asked as they left together.

"I don't know, Your Majesty."

Abijah closed the door behind them and their voices faded as they hurried away. She felt filthy for playacting with him, for allowing her son's murderer to caress her, and she fought the urge to take a bath. This was just the first of many nights she would be forced to spend with him, and she wondered if she would ever get used to being with a man she despised. She sat down on the curtained bed for a moment and allowed the tears she had been holding back to flow.

When they were finally spent, she dried her eyes and steeled herself to go downstairs. She would wait for Ahaz in his bedchamber.

Hezekiah stood by his door for a very long time, listening to every sound: a cricket chirping in the courtyard below his window; an owl hooting softly in the valley near the spring; a shutter creaking as the wind blew past his window. Before long, the night sounds merged into a comforting rhythm and his legs grew weary, his eyes heavy with sleep. He was about to climb back into bed when he saw torchlight dancing through the crack under his door. Someone hurried down the hallway toward his room, then past it. Hezekiah opened the door a crack and peered out. He heard insistent pounding and urgent voices around the corner by his mother's room. He listened, ready to run, his heart thumping in his chest.

A moment later the light grew brighter as the man with the torch moved down the hall toward him again. He saw his father rounding the corner with a palace chamberlain. "I've summoned your advisors to the council chamber," the servant was saying. "You'll have a few minutes to read the reports for yourself before the counselors arrive."

Hezekiah stared through the narrow crack as his father hurried past. "What about my brother?" Ahaz asked. "Did the messenger say where Maaseiah is?"

Hezekiah didn't hear the reply. The voices grew faint as the men disappeared down the stairs. He stood shivering in the darkness, the floor cold beneath his bare feet. Why was his father asking about Uncle Maaseiah? Hezekiah stepped out into the hallway. For a moment he considered running back to the safety of his mother's room. But then a greater need, the need to understand why his father had sacrificed Eliab to Molech, overshadowed his wish for comfort. He crept down the stairs, following Ahaz to the council chamber.

A heavy curtain guarded the service entrance to the chamber, and Hezekiah slid past it, hiding in the anteroom where the servants usually waited to be summoned. The tiny room was empty, so he crouched behind a pillar and peered into the council room. His father's throne stood on a raised dais at one end of the room, with Uncle Maaseiah's empty seat beside it. Thick wool carpets and cushions were arranged in front of the dais for the king's advisors, and a servant scurried between them, lighting lamps and charcoal braziers. The room seemed gloomy, even with all of the lamps lit. When the servant finished, he left the council chamber, hurrying past Hezekiah without seeing him.

King Ahaz stood beneath a lampstand, reading from a scroll, his lips drawn into a thin line. Hezekiah heard him moan, and the parchment dropped to the floor as Ahaz tore the front of his robes. "I never should have let him go into battle," he cried out. "How can I run this nation without Maaseiah?" He gazed up at the thick cedar beams as if the answer to his question was written up there.

"Why don't you sit down, Your Majesty? You're upset." The chamberlain took Ahaz's arm and led him to his throne. "You've suffered a great shock. But your counselors are coming now. They'll know what to do."

Ahaz dropped into his chair as his advisors began hurrying into the room. They appeared groggy and confused, rubbing the sleep from their eyes. "Is it news of your army, Your Majesty?" someone asked.

Hezekiah stiffened, suddenly alert. He remembered the endless rows of soldiers that had lined up in the palace courtyard and forced him to walk down the hill to the Hinnom Valley. They had carried him up the steps to the monster's platform, then surrounded it so that he and Eliab couldn't escape. His father's army.

King Ahaz lifted a wine goblet from the ivory table beside his throne and took two quick gulps, then wiped his lips with the back of his hand. "Yes, disastrous news," he replied. "The army that I sent north to stop the invasion has been defeated. A hundred and twenty thousand soldiers have been slaughtered. My three commanders, Azrikam, Elkanah, my brother Maaseiah . . ."

He gestured to the empty seat beside his as his voice choked. The room grew so still that Hezekiah could hear the oil lamps hissing faintly as they burned, casting wavering shadows on the walls.

"All three men are dead," Ahaz said at last. He reached for the wineglass again and gulped two more mouthfuls. "The enemy alliance proved stronger than we thought. I've lost most of my army, and the invaders are still marching south, overrunning every village and town in their path. They've taken more than two hundred thousand people captive."

Hezekiah heard several of the advisors moan. Ahaz gulped another drink, then gripped the arms of his throne as if to steady himself. "The enemy is heading here. They're going to attack Jerusalem and try to overthrow my government."

Everyone started talking at once as a ripple of fear coursed through the room. When the shock wave reached Hezekiah, he began to shiver. He crouched lower in the shadows.

Ahaz drained his glass, then shouted, "Shut up and listen to me! There's more." Instantly the room fell silent. "I've had news from the south, as well. The King of Edom has taken advantage of this crisis to invade our only seaport. Elath is lost." Once again the meeting dissolved into chaos, and once again Ahaz shouted the men into silence. "There's still more! Our old enemies, the Philistines, have come against us, too. They've raided towns in the foothills and the Negev and have already captured Beth Shemesh, Aijalon, Timnah . . . three or four others I can't remember."

The men stared at Ahaz as if unable to believe what he was telling them. "We're being attacked on three sides?" someone asked.

"Yes."

Hezekiah didn't understand what was going on, but he could tell by the tense murmuring that these men were afraid. He listened breathlessly.

"What are we going to do?" another man asked.

"For the time being, we'll have to forget about the Edomites and the Philistines," Ahaz said. "Our most serious threat is from the northern alliance. The Aramean army will reach Jerusalem within a few days. They're organized and powerful, and we have very few soldiers left. So, you tell me—what are we going to do?" He gazed at his advisors for several long moments, but none of them replied. Ahaz's voice rose to a shout. "Doesn't anyone have a word of advice?"

A nobleman seated near the front finally stood. "Your Majesty, if Jerusalem is facing a lengthy siege, we must consider our water resources." The man wore several gold rings on his fingers, and whenever he gestured Hezekiah saw a pattern like fireflies on the ceiling above his head. "The rainy season is still months away," the man continued, "and the city's cisterns are getting low. Is there any way we can defend the Gihon Spring? Otherwise, once we seal the city gates we'll be cut off from our water supply."

"I know perfectly well where the spring is!" Ahaz shouted. "Everyone in Jerusalem knows that we don't have any fresh water inside our walls. But what can we possibly do about it now? The enemy will be here in a matter of days!" He glared at the man as if challenging him to answer. He shrugged and sat down.

"So. He has no advice for me," Ahaz said. "Do any of the rest of you?"

From the back of the room, almost against the rear wall, a lone figure rose to his feet. "I do, Your Majesty."

"Who are you? Come forward where I can see you."

"I'm Uriah, high priest of the Temple of Yahweh." He spoke in a deep, clear voice and, unlike Ahaz's other advisors, he appeared calm. He was tall and powerfully built, and he strode forward with such a commanding presence that Hezekiah curled up in the shadows where he was crouching, suddenly afraid.

He couldn't help comparing the high priest to Ahaz, and the king came up short on every point. Uriah had muscular shoulders and a broad chest, but Ahaz was flabby and round-shouldered, with no muscles beneath the fat. Uriah's black hair and beard looked full and thick, while the soft, reddish hair on Ahaz's face formed only a scraggly beard. The priest seemed to have no wasted motion, his every gesture sure and powerful, while Ahaz's hands fluttered and fidgeted nervously. Hezekiah was surprised to see his father lean forward in his seat as if in awe of the tall priest.

"You have permission to speak, Uriah."

"Your Majesty, our nation needs a strong ally to come to our defense in this crisis. I suggest that we quickly approach one of our neighboring nations for help."

"An excellent suggestion," Ahaz said, settling back on his throne again. "Now the question is, which nation would be most likely to help us?"

"I've given it a great deal of thought—" Uriah began, but Ahaz cut him off.

"Which nation does our enemy fear the most? I want to choose an ally that will fill the Arameans' hearts with dread."

"Your Majesty, it might be better if we—"

"I want an ally that will make them retreat out of Judah as soon as they hear the news of our alliance. Which nation would do that?"

The man with the many rings rose to his feet again. "Your Majesty, the Assyrians are the Arameans' greatest threat. The Assyrian empire is already vast and far-reaching, and I'm sure the King of Aram fears becoming the next target of their aggression."

"Perfect!" Ahaz shouted. "Would the Assyrians be willing to ally themselves with us?" he asked Uriah.

"An alliance with us would certainly give them a foothold in this region, which is what they're looking for," Uriah replied. "But I think we should consider a less dangerous ally first. The Assyrians are a vicious, violent, bloodthirsty nation, and I think it would be a mistake to ask them to—"

"Good! The more bloodthirsty the better," Ahaz said. "I want the men who killed my brother to suffer!"

His words jolted Hezekiah. He wanted to punish the man who killed his brother, too—but how? The man responsible was his father, the king.

"Uriah's right," Ahaz continued. "We must convince another

nation to come to our defense. We're in no position to defend ourselves without an army. The stronger that ally is, the better." He drew a deep breath. "We'll send a gift of tribute to Assyria and propose an alliance. This gift must be very lavish in order to convince them that we are a worthy ally. We'll need to send gold, silver, precious stones . . . and we'll need to act quickly, before the enemy lays siege to Jerusalem."

"But, Your Majesty," someone protested, "where will this gift come from? There's no time to levy taxes, and we've already emptied the royal treasuries to equip Maaseiah's army."

King Ahaz glanced all around the room, as if hoping that bars of gold would magically appear. Then his eyes fell on the high priest, still standing in front of him. "Uriah, you will remove the gold and other valuables from the Temple of Solomon."

Uriah looked distressed by Ahaz's plan. "But, Your Majesty, the Temple storehouses are nearly empty. The only valuables remaining are the sacred vessels that are used for worship. It's true that the Holy of Holies contains a wealth of gold, but it is part of the structure. There's no way to remove it without permanently damaging Yahweh's dwelling place."

King Ahaz didn't appear to be listening. "A wealth of gold . . ." he repeated. "I'm favorably impressed with your wisdom and counsel, Uriah. I'm putting you in charge of the gift to Assyria. If you do well, you will be the new palace administrator in my brother's place." He gestured to the empty seat at his right-hand side. "Tear the Temple down, if necessary, but this gift must be acceptable to the Assyrians."

Uriah nodded slightly, his expression unreadable. "Yes, Your Majesty."

"When everything is ready I will send a delegation to the Assyrian monarch, along with my personal appeal for a covenant with his nation." Ahaz looked confident for the first time that night. He rose from his chair and began issuing orders, gesturing to his advisors. "We'll need to raise another army for the defense of Jerusalem. You three are in charge of that. As for the rest of you, begin spreading word of the coming siege as soon as you're dismissed. Make sure the city and surrounding areas are prepared as quickly as possible. It may take some time for our new Assyrian allies to rally to our defense."

The task of making so many decisions seemed to exhaust Ahaz. He sank onto his throne again when he was finished. "That's all we can do for now. You're dismissed. Where's my servant?"

Hezekiah didn't move aside in time, and Ahaz's servant nearly tripped over him as he rushed into the anteroom to attend to the king. "What are you doing in here?" the man asked. He grabbed Hezekiah by the shoulders. "You don't belong in here."

"Let me go!" Hezekiah said as he struggled to break free. He needed to run upstairs and hide before his father saw him. But Ahaz had already heard the commotion.

"What's going on over there?" he asked. "Where's my servant?"

"I'm here, Your Majesty. I'm coming. Forgive me." He carried Hezekiah, still struggling, into the council room.

"I found this boy in the antechamber. I don't know how—"

"You again! What are you doing down here?" Ahaz demanded.

Hezekiah couldn't speak. He wanted to rush forward and strike his father for killing Eliab, but he couldn't seem to move. As he gazed up at Ahaz, a terrible darkness began building deep inside Hezekiah, growing moment by moment like a powerful storm. He was terrified of his father—that was certainly part of it. But this new feeling was much bigger, much more overwhelming than fear. It was hatred.

"Why are you looking at me like that?" Ahaz asked. "Get him out of here!"

The servant picked Hezekiah up and hustled him from the room.

During the brief disturbance with the king's son, Uriah had time to refocus his thoughts. He had been too astounded by his sudden promotion to palace administrator to think clearly a moment ago.

Now that the boy was gone, he strode to the front again. "One moment please, Your Majesty. I'd like to make one further suggestion."

"What is it?"

"I'd like to advise you to include a public sacrifice to Yahweh in your plans, my lord. We will need divine help in this crisis."

Ahaz sat up straight. "Another excellent suggestion, Uriah. I'm impressed with your wisdom. However . . ." Ahaz gathered the sparse whiskers of his beard together, looking thoughtful. Uriah heard the hesitation in the king's voice as he paused.

"However, I don't think it would be appropriate to sacrifice to Yahweh after emptying His Temple's storehouses," he finally said. "I'm uneasy about that. Surely you understand. No, we have already sought the help of Molech, the most powerful of all the gods. He won't desert us now, especially after I've personally sacrificed so much. So before the siege begins, we will hold another sacrifice to Molech."

Uriah's stomach turned over in horror at what he'd unwittingly initiated. He searched for a way to argue with Ahaz, to contradict him, but came up blank. Only a fool questioned the king's decisions.

Ahaz turned to the rest of his milling advisors, challenging them. "Perhaps those of you who withheld your sons from Molech the last time will consider the great danger this nation is in. We need Molech's great power in this crisis, and so we *all* must sacrifice a son this time. He's a demanding god, but surely we can father a dozen sons once Molech saves us from destruction."

Uriah reeled in shock at the king's words. Ahaz planned to kill another son, another of Abijah's children. As high priest, Uriah was sworn to fight against idolatry, not promote it. How had his advice to the king gotten so out of control?

"The sacrifice to Molech must take place as soon as possible, before the siege begins," Ahaz continued. He turned to Uriah. "I will leave all the preparations for it in your hands."

Uriah felt all the blood drain from his face as he stared at Ahaz.

For a long moment he was unable to speak. When he finally did, his voice didn't sound like is own. "I-I'm a priest of Yahweh, Your Majesty, not Molech."

"You're the new palace administrator!" Ahaz thundered, gesturing to his brother's empty chair. "Unless you don't want the job?"

Uriah stopped breathing. He had mere seconds to make the biggest decision of his life, a decision that would set the course of his future. He could sit at the king's right-hand side—or he could refuse.

"Of course, Your Majesty," he finally said, bowing slightly. "As you wish."

"Good. Then you're dismissed."

It took an enormous effort for Uriah to walk from the room on his trembling legs. Several of the other advisors tried to speak with him, to congratulate him as he left the council chamber, but he moved past them like a blind man. He needed to get out of the palace and find a place to sit down and think. Moving on instinct, he headed up the hill to the Temple.

Dawn was only an hour or two away, judging by the fading stars in the eastern sky. He needed to assimilate everything that had just happened before his many responsibilities as high priest crowded out all his other thoughts. He crossed the deserted outer courtyard and sank down on one of the steps that led to the inner court. The stones felt colder than the night air as he leaned against them.

It had been an astounding meeting. Uriah had seized the opportunity of Prince Maaseiah's death to catapult himself from the back row of the council chamber to the king's right-hand side. He had suddenly attained a position of enormous power in the nation, power he had worked hard to claim for over eighteen years. He should be overjoyed. Yet a gnawing unrest filled Uriah's soul as he thought of the price he would pay for that power.

He would have to desecrate Solomon's Temple, plundering its gold for the Assyrian tribute. He dreaded being responsible for that destruction, but he knew that King Ahaz would take whatever gold he wanted whether Uriah approved or not. At least he could try to hold the damage to a minimum.

No, the root of his unrest was the sacrifice to Molech. Uriah was Yahweh's high priest—how could he deliberately take part in idol worship? Yet if he refused to preside over the sacrifice he would forfeit his new position as palace administrator. Once again, he would be a powerless priest in the crumbling Temple of Yahweh, struggling to scratch out a living from meager offerings. One of Molech's priests would gladly do the king's bidding, and he would be the one to gain preeminence as high priest of the nation.

Uriah clenched his fists. Never! He would fight for what was rightfully his. Yahweh was the only God of Israel, and all the power belonged to His high priest, not Molech's. Uriah determined to do whatever needed to be done. After all, the palace administrator merely made all the arrangements for the sacrifice; he wouldn't have to officiate.

Uriah looked up at the holy sanctuary, looming above him in the darkness. The white stones appeared solid and substantial from where he sat in their shadows, but he knew that daylight would quickly reveal the truth of how badly the structure had deteriorated over the years. In its prime, Yahweh's Temple had been the pride of his nation. But now it stood forlorn, like a deposed queen, clothed in the remnants of her former glory. Uriah shook his head as if to erase the pitiful sight.

Ever since he'd inherited the priesthood, he'd watched helplessly as the institution that he served decayed from apathy. His countrymen had neglected the Lord's Temple and the required tithes and offerings for so many years that the priests and Levites could barely make a living, much less afford repairs to the building. Most of his brethren had deserted Jerusalem long ago, ignoring their regular terms of duty to pursue other means of supporting their families. Meanwhile, the worship of Yahweh had become stagnant, stuck in a routine of traditions and rituals that no longer had meaning for the people. Yet the priests and Levites who remained were opposed to change.

Uriah had deliberately pursued a position of power in King Ahaz's court, vowing to restore the Temple of Yahweh to its rightful place of authority in the nation. He had sat in the back row of the council chamber for nearly two years, watching for an opening, waiting for his chance at power. Now it had come. The only obstacle in his path was the sacrifice to Molech.

He sat on the cold step for a long time, watching the eastern sky grow lighter and lighter. When the sun finally peeked above the Mount of Olives, he shaded his eyes from it. He would have to leave soon. The priests and Levites would be arriving to begin their preparations for the morning sacrifice. But Uriah couldn't seem to move.

As a man of God, he knew that he should pray about a decision as big as this one, and he found it odd that he hadn't—that he couldn't. The longer Uriah sat, the more he longed for someone to confide in, someone who could appreciate the opportunity that King Ahaz had offered him and help put his conscience to rest. He thought of Zechariah the Levite. His former teacher and mentor was a brilliant man, well versed in the minutest letter of the Law. He was also an astute politician, setting the example Uriah had followed in pursuing political power. And although Zechariah had lost his position in court after King Uzziah died, Uriah felt drawn to him now. Zechariah was one of the few men who could understand the dilemma that Uriah faced and offer him advice.

He slowly rose to his feet, his body stiff with cold, and walked around the courtyard to the rusting door that led to the Levites' quarters. He paused in the dim corridor outside Zechariah's room. Seeing his former teacher always brought back memories of Abijah, and with those memories, a sense of hopeless frustration. Uriah had always known that she couldn't belong to him, but that knowledge hadn't stopped him from wanting her. He had loved Abijah since the first day he'd seen her, the first day he'd become her father's pupil . . . and his love for her was the only thing in his life that he'd never been able to control. He loved her still—the king's wife.

Uriah finally forced Abijah from his mind and rapped on her father's door. While he waited he thought of all the changes in his mentor's life—how Zechariah had fallen from political power, how he'd lost his home, his wife, his health. When no one answered the door, Uriah realized that he hadn't seen Zechariah in months. He nearly turned away, then decided to knock one more time.

"Go away," Zechariah called from inside. "Leave me alone."

Uriah stared at the closed door. He had put on a show of great self-confidence before the king a short time ago, but he suddenly felt inadequate before the man he had always admired and sought to emulate.

"Rabbi Zechariah, it's me, Uriah. May I have a word with you, please?"

Several minutes passed before Zechariah opened the door. He looked confused, his eyes bloodshot and unfocused, his robes rumpled and sour smelling, as if he'd slept in them. Uriah nearly turned away a second time. This couldn't be the respected Levite, the man who had once sat at the king's right hand. But it was.

The man Uriah remembered was tall and lean and strong, but now Zechariah's shoulders stooped as if bearing a heavy load. The spark of intelligence had vanished from his distinguished face and green eyes, and his pale features looked drained of life. He was barely fifty-five, but his unkempt hair and beard made him appear much older.

"Uriah . . . come in, come in," Zechariah stammered. He led the way into the room, staggering slightly, and cleared a place in the clutter for Uriah to sit.

"I'm sorry if I've disturbed you," Uriah began, "but I . . . I need to talk to you." He struggled to conceal his shock at the change in Zechariah. He could barely remember why he had come.

"I'll get some wine," Zechariah said. He tottered over to a shelf and produced a skin of wine and two goblets. Uriah winced with embarrassment.

"Uh, no thank you, Rabbi. It's too early for me. But, please . . . you go ahead."

He felt ashamed for Zechariah. Coming here had been a mistake. Uriah stared at the floor, groping for words, wishing he could leave. Zechariah took a few quick gulps from the wineskin. Then, with a pathetic remnant of his former dignity, he pulled up a stool and sat opposite Uriah.

"What did you need to talk to me about?"

Uriah saw the respected teacher he had come to seek as if through a dingy curtain. He cleared his throat. "Rabbi, I have just come from a meeting with King Ahaz. I wanted you to be the first to know— I've been appointed palace administrator."

"But—what about Prince Maaseiah?"

"Our army has been defeated. We've suffered enormous losses. The prince is dead."

"I–it's a great honor for you . . . but Prince Maaseiah . . . the . . ." Zechariah's confusion didn't seem to be caused by the news. His gaze darted all around the room as if he wasn't quite sure where he was.

"I want to accept this position, Rabbi. It's an extraordinary opportunity, but it would mean—" Uriah couldn't bring himself to admit that it would mean idolatry. He realized, suddenly, that he hadn't come for Zechariah's help in making a decision. Uriah had made his decision in the council chamber the moment Ahaz had offered him the prince's empty seat. He had come to win Zechariah's approval, as if his former teacher could somehow absolve him from guilt.

"It's just that some of my duties as palace administrator may go against the teachings of the Torah," Uriah explained. "But if I use this opportunity to establish myself as a close advisor to the king, I will be in a position to teach King Ahaz about Yahweh's law. And ultimately I can do a great deal of good."

He leaned forward on the edge of his seat, almost pleading for

Zechariah's approval. "All my life, all my ambition and striving has been with one goal in mind: to revive the role of the priesthood and make the Temple an influential force in this nation again. Now I can do that. I've worked my way up from the bottom, waiting for an opportunity like this. I'll be second in command to the king."

Zechariah stared at him blankly, as if wondering where he fit in.

"I know there are some priests and Levites who will object to what I'm doing," Uriah quickly continued, "and I'll need your help in winning them over. You're a man of influence here in the Temple. Surely you can understand what I'm trying to accomplish. You once held the same position in the palace, and you—" Uriah stopped, keenly embarrassed for reminding this broken, disheveled man of the power and position he had once held and lost. "I-I just wanted to ask if I could have your support," he finished.

"My support?" Zechariah echoed. He stared at Uriah for a moment, then a faint smile flickered briefly across his face.

"Yes, Rabbi, please support me in this. If I make a few concessions to Ahaz in order to gain his confidence, I can begin to teach him Yahweh's Law, the way you once taught King Uzziah."

Zechariah's head jerked backward at the mention of Uzziah as if Uriah had slapped him. Zechariah stared at him with watery eyes, then stood and shuffled to the shelf to retrieve the wineskin. "You're going to teach Ahaz? Make him stop his idolatry?" he asked with his back turned.

Uriah winced. "It may take some time, Rabbi, but that's what I hope to accomplish . . . eventually."

Zechariah raised the wineskin to his lips and swallowed, then wiped his mouth with his fist. Uriah waited.

"You've always had more ambition than any of the others," Zechariah said at last. "I won't oppose you if you decide to accept the position." His voice carried no enthusiasm.

"Thank you, Rabbi." Uriah stood and inched toward the door, eager to leave. "There are several announcements from the king that

I need to discuss with the chief priests and Levites, so I'm calling for a meeting at noon today. If you'll contact the chief Levites, I'll notify the chief priests."

Zechariah nodded but didn't face him.

"Thank you, Rabbi. Shalom." Uriah hurried from the room, closing the door quickly. His mentor's pathetic state had unnerved him, and he struggled to regain his composure as he wandered down the corridor. When he finally emerged into the sunlight again he stopped, closing his eyes to summon the image of himself that he had so carefully practiced, the one he had successfully portrayed before the king—the erect posture, the controlled gestures, the intimidating stare of a man of authority. Then he willed his body to conform to that image. Once he felt outwardly in control, Uriah battled to untangle his conflicting thoughts and feelings.

He couldn't imagine how a man as great as Zechariah had ended up in such a state. But now that Uriah had a chance to be as influential in the nation as Zechariah had once been, he was determined not to let the opportunity pass, even if it meant temporarily violating the Torah. A nagging voice tried to remind him of the price he would pay for disobeying the Law, but Uriah chose to ignore the voice.

Yahweh's Temple would regain the power and glory it once enjoyed in the days of King Solomon. Uriah would not let this institution crumble into obscurity. He would not.

# 3

ABIJAH WAITED IN KING Ahaz's private chambers for a long time, hating herself for what she was doing. She had never been in his rooms before—an opulent sitting room where he received visitors and a private bedchamber beyond—and she felt no better than a prostitute, giving herself in return for favors. But the payment was for Hezekiah's sake, not her own. If she kept thinking of Hezekiah, she could do this.

Abijah quickly brushed away a tear. She couldn't think of him without remembering Eliab, but she couldn't descend into grief tonight. She had to forget that this man she would pretend to love had killed him. She sat down on the sofa as the hours passed, and dozed.

At last the door opened and King Ahaz entered. He didn't seem to see Abijah at first, and she glimpsed, in his expression, all his unguarded feelings. He was afraid, unsure of himself. Then Ahaz noticed her and his expression changed to one of surprise—and relief. He seemed glad not to be alone and pleased that she had come to him.

Abijah went to him quickly, not allowing herself time to think.

She stroked her hands down his arms. "What's wrong? You look so unhappy, my lord. Is there something I can do for you?" He pulled her to himself, gripping her as if to keep from falling.

"My brother Maaseiah is dead."

"Oh no. I'm so sorry." It was a lie. Abijah felt no grief for Maaseiah. She had begged him not to take her sons away, but he had turned his back on her. Eliab's death had been Maaseiah's fault as much as it had been Ahaz's, and she was glad that he was dead. She stayed in Ahaz's arms, resting her face against his chest so she wouldn't have to face him. She couldn't let him see through her lies.

"How you must mourn," she murmured as she caressed his back.

"Yes. I relied on Maaseiah. And now he's gone." The grief she heard in his faltering voice made her angry. He had shown no grief for Eliab.

"I never should have sent him into battle," he continued. "I should have led the army myself."

But Abijah knew that the idea was preposterous. Ahaz had inherited the fair, ruddy coloring of his famous forefather King David, but unlike David, Ahaz was no soldier. His indulgent lifestyle had made him so unfit that he could barely walk up a flight of stairs without pausing for breath—let alone lead troops into battle.

"How can I even begin to comfort you?" she soothed.

"My brother's life wasn't our only loss," he said shakily. "My army has been nearly wiped out. The Arameans are invading us even now, taking thousands of prisoners. They're going to lay siege to Jerusalem."

His words frightened Abijah. If he had sacrificed his son at the threat of an invasion, what would he do now that the situation had grown so much worse? Would he offer a second son? She had to learn his plans—and try to stop him.

"What have you decided to do, my lord?"

He sighed, and his arms went slack as he released her. She saw how deeply worried he was. "It's so hard to know if I've made the right decision," he murmured.

"I'm sure you have. Tell me."

"I'm going to seek an alliance with the king of Assyria and ask him to come to our defense. It was the only worthwhile piece of advice that my counselors had to offer, and it came from Uriah, the high priest of Solomon's Temple."

Abijah's heart speeded up as she pictured Uriah. He was everything that Ahaz was not—strong, disciplined, a devout follower of Yahweh. Something stirred inside as she imagined herself in Uriah's arms. If Eliab had been Uriah's son, he would have lived to serve Yahweh instead of dying as a sacrifice to Molech.

Ahaz seemed to notice her distraction and leaned toward her. "Do you know him?"

"Yes, I know Uriah. He was my father's student. And of course I've seen him serving as high priest at the Temple."

"He was the only one of my advisors that had any common sense. I've offered him my brother's job as palace administrator."

A rush of relief flooded through her. Uriah would never advise Ahaz to sacrifice his sons to Molech. In fact, he would argue strongly against it. Abijah knew she had an important ally.

"You've made a very wise choice, my lord. Uriah will be a strong, capable advisor."

"I hope so," Ahaz mumbled. He looked forlorn, and Abijah knew him well enough to appeal to his self-pity.

"My poor husband. What a terrible strain you're under. Why don't you lie down and get some rest?" She led him into the bed-chamber and helped him remove his outer robe. She could see that he was too deeply shaken for his desire to be stirred, and she was grateful. He was clinging to her for comfort, nothing more. He sank into bed and closed his eyes.

"You shouldn't be alone in your grief," she said as she snuffed out the oil lamps. "I'll stay with you, if you'd like." She lay down beside him without waiting for his answer, and he clung to her. But Abijah lay wide awake beside him for a very long time.

Ahaz awoke after dawn, all alone. Abijah had gone, and he felt the ache of loneliness. He had been so surprised—and grateful—for the comfort she had given him last night. He wished she were still here.

He was exhausted, but sleep eluded him. He tossed and twisted in bed for over an hour, battling with the ensnaring bedcovers and his doubts and fears. Everything had been taken care of, he assured himself. He had done the right thing. Hadn't he?

The decision to call on the Assyrians for help had made sense in the council chamber, but now that he was alone he wasn't so sure. What if they didn't come to his defense? He suddenly recalled what Uriah had said about the Assyrians—that they were a vicious, violent nation—and he wondered if an alliance with them was truly the only solution.

He cursed his father for dying so suddenly, leaving him in control of the nation at the age of twenty. Ahaz had enjoyed being a prince, indulged and spoiled by his father and all the court, but now he found the pressures of his reign intolerable, the burden of decisions and responsibilities unbearable.

At last he kicked the bedcovers onto the floor and gave up his attempt to go back to sleep. He had no other choice but to call on the Assyrians. Maaseiah was dead, and the thought that he might die as well made him weak with fear. He rose and crossed to the window, peering out through the lattice as if from a prison cell. The sun had risen above the Mount of Olives, and the streets below him bustled with activity. People were flocking to Jerusalem from nearby villages and towns to take refuge behind the city's massive walls as news of the invasion spread.

A hot, dry breeze blew up from the Judean wilderness and rustled through the branches of the tree outside Ahaz's window. He stared at the quivering leaves, and it seemed to him that the whole city trembled as the leaves did. Fear, like a starving animal, gnawed at his insides, slowly consuming him.

He stepped away from the window, afraid to watch the bustle of activity, feeling helpless. He remembered his counselor's warning about the city's inadequate water supplies, and his anxiety increased. A long line was probably forming down by the Gihon Spring as slaves and servant girls made their way through the Water Gate and down the steep ramp, balancing clay jars on their heads. Water would be as crucial to his nation's defenses as swords and spears, yet Jerusalem had no source of fresh water within its walls. The Gihon Spring and aqueduct lay outside of them—but a solution to the problem eluded him.

Maybe he shouldn't remain idle, hiding in his rooms as his nation prepared for the siege. He needed to make a public appearance, to be visible to the people of Jerusalem, to convince them that he was confident and unafraid. After all, that was a great king's duty in a time of crisis. And maybe he could convince himself, as well. He decided to take an inventory of his water supplies himself, and he rang for his servant.

The man entered with his head lowered, bowing like a dog about to be beaten. "Forgive me, my lord," he muttered as he touched his forehead to the floor. "I don't know how the boy managed to slip past me."

At first Ahaz had no idea what his servant was talking about. Then he recalled his son's outrageous appearance in the council room and his anger flared. "You should have been at your post. It could have been an intruder instead of my son. You know my enemies are plotting to kill me."

"I swear to all the gods that it will never happen again, my lord. Please, have mercy."

"I should have you beaten, or maybe I should beat you myself, but there's no time for it. Get up. We have a siege to prepare for."

"Thank you, my lord. Thank you." The man scrambled to his feet, bowing repeatedly.

"What did you do with him?"

"With your son, my lord?"

"Who else are we talking about? Yes, my son!" The word sounded peculiar to Ahaz, as if he'd spoken of his son for the first time. His sons had never seemed like real people to him, merely faceless infants, possessions under his sovereign control—until last night, that is. Twice he had seen his son face to face and looked into his accusing eyes.

"I took the boy to his room, Your Majesty."

"Bring him here."

"But . . . but, he's only a child, my lord. He didn't mean any harm."

"I said bring him here."

Ahaz stared out the window as he waited for the servant to return, and he felt pleased when his son bowed properly in respect when he finally entered. Abijah's son had been well trained. Ahaz suddenly recalled her request to be his favorite wife and knew she undoubtedly wanted her son to be chosen as his heir instead of one of his concubines' sons. But there was plenty of time for that, wasn't there? This boy was a mere child. And he was a fine-looking boy, with Abijah's wide brown eyes and tawny skin. His dark hair had a coppery cast, inherited from Ahaz's own family line—the House of David.

"You are Eliab?" he guessed.

The boy looked startled, then shook his head. "I'm Hezekiah."

Ahaz remembered then. Eliab had been his firstborn—his gift to Molech. He recalled the way Eliab's small body had tumbled helplessly into the flames, and he shuddered. He stared down at Hezekiah, trying to determine what emotion he read in his dark eyes. Fear? Yes, certainly fear—but something else, as well.

"So. I find you everywhere it seems—sleeping in my wife's chambers, inviting yourself to my council meetings. Maybe you would like to be the king in my place?"

Hezekiah didn't answer. He stood very still, staring up at him, his gaze never wavering. Suddenly Ahaz deciphered the look in Hezekiah's eyes and his jaw dropped in astonishment. It was hatred.

"How dare you!" Ahaz barely restrained himself from slapping him. "Someday you'll be in my place. Someday you'll see what it's like to face one crisis after another. You'll be the one who has to make decisions, regardless of the cost. Do you think it's so easy?"

Hezekiah's eyes filled with tears, but he remained in control of himself. Ahaz had to admit that his son had courage, and he suddenly felt foolish for losing his temper.

"Why am I wasting my breath on a child?" he muttered. "So. You enjoy following me around? Get dressed. You can accompany me on my inspection tour. Get him ready," he told his servant. "He's coming with me."

An hour later, with his son by his side, Ahaz walked down the long main street of Jerusalem with his entourage, inspecting the levels of rainwater in the city cisterns. The fact that most of them were barely half full distressed him. Swarms of curious citizens joined in the procession—children and servant girls and farmers fleeing the surrounding countryside, along with city elders and noblemen who were hoping to be noticed and acknowledged by the king.

At first Ahaz tried to appear dignified and older than his years, but soon the sight of so many people looking to him for strength and trusting him for deliverance began to heighten his anxiety. He felt the weight of his responsibility like an enormous burden, as if he were required to carry everyone on his shoulders. The load exhausted him and the siege hadn't even begun yet.

When he finished examining the cisterns, he led the procession out of the city through the southeast gate to the Shiloah Pool, a man-made reservoir built to hold the overflow from the Gihon Spring and supply the southern section of the city with water. From there he followed the aqueduct up the Kidron Valley, coming at last to the spring. But once he reached it, Ahaz found that there was little for him to do except stand and stare into the water, in spite of his grand procession.

The city's protecting walls on the cliff above his head receded in the distance like a fading mirage, and the gap between the walls and the spring seemed infinite. He could see no way to defend the spring against the enemy, and he wondered how long Jerusalem could survive without fresh water. Long enough for the Assyrians to come to his defense—if they came at all? Ahaz's plans seemed useless to him now, like a dream that makes sense during the night but turns absurd in the light of day.

The waters of Gihon were black and cold and deep, as if no bottom existed. Ahaz stared at the spring, not really seeing it, and saw, instead, the defeat of his city and his own certain death. This inspection tour had been a mistake. He felt worse than before. What's more, he no longer had his brother by his side, but his son, a mere child. With Maaseiah dead, Ahaz had no one to turn to with his doubts and fears. He could only hold his feelings inside, turning them around and around in his mind until they sucked his soul down into the darkness of depression. He stood immobilized. The crowd grew still. The procession waited in awkward silence.

Dimly, he heard the rustle of robes and footsteps approaching on the path. Ahaz looked up as the crowd parted, and he recognized the slender, aristocratic man walking toward him, holding a small boy by the hand. His distant cousin's regal bearing and reddish beard confirmed his kinship to Ahaz and the royal line of King David. Father and son bowed in respect, then stood before Ahaz and his son.

"What do you want, Isaiah?" Ahaz asked.

"This is my firstborn son, Shear-Jashub," Isaiah answered quietly. His eyes bored into Ahaz, and he knew it was an accusation. His own firstborn son was dead. The strange name Shear-Jashub meant "a remnant will return," just as a mere remnant of Ahaz's army would return.

"You think you're so clever, don't you?" Ahaz said. "What do you want?"

"I have a word of advice for you."

"Advice? I might have known. You'd like a position in my court now that I've lost my three top men."

Isaiah shook his head. "No. I've renounced my kinship to the house of David because—"

"You were *thrown* out of the palace," Ahaz interrupted. "And for good reason. My father didn't want to listen to your radical opinions, and neither do I."

Isaiah took a step closer. "How can I remain silent when my nation is rushing toward disaster? Unless Judah reforms—"

"Reforms? If we listened to you, we'd end up living in tents like Abraham."

Isaiah held his head high, meeting Ahaz's gaze without flinching. He repeated quietly, "Unless this nation repents—"

"That's enough." Ahaz held up his hands. "We don't need a doomsayer, Isaiah. The people are already worried. You can't get an audience in my court, so you force your views on the common people and call it prophecy. Well, I don't want to listen to you, and neither do they."

"I have a word for *you*, King Ahaz—from Yahweh." Isaiah's tone changed, and there was something in his manner, an unmistakable authority in his voice, that made Ahaz keep silent. "Be careful, keep calm, and don't be afraid," Isaiah told him. "Don't lose heart because of these kings who have come against you."

"What are you talking about?" Ahaz exploded. "Their armies are rapidly approaching Jerusalem!"

"Yes, but the Lord God says their plan will not succeed. You must stand firm in your faith in Yahweh—or you will not stand at all."

"I don't know where you get your bizarre ideas, and I don't care. I've already made plans to deal with this crisis, and I'm not changing them now."

Isaiah's eyes narrowed. "You don't believe that Yahweh can deliver you from the enemy, do you? You'd rather ask the king of Assyria for help than put your trust in the Lord."

Ahaz glared at him, wondering how he had learned of the

planned alliance so quickly. "The gods belong in the temples, not in the streets," Ahaz said. "And certainly not in government."

Isaiah took another step forward. "Ask Yahweh for a sign. Let Him prove that He will crush your enemies as He has said. Ask anything you like, in heaven or on earth."

"No. I won't put Yahweh to the test." Isaiah's confidence shook Ahaz. If his cousin somehow produced a miracle in front of all these people, Ahaz would have to abandon his plans and trust in the sign. He couldn't afford to take that risk.

"Hear now, you house of David!" Isaiah said angrily. His quiet voice grew and surged as he spoke, like water rushing down a dry riverbed, until it seemed to thunder. "You're not satisfied to exhaust my patience—you'll exhaust the Lord's patience, as well! Very well then, Yahweh himself will choose the sign—a virgin shall conceive and give birth to a child. And he shall be called Immanuel."

"That's ridiculous. How can a virgin bear a child?"

"The lands of the kings you dread so much *will* be laid waste," Isaiah continued. "But Yahweh will bring a terrible curse on you and on your nation and on your family, too. The mighty King of Assyria will come with his great army. Yahweh will take these Assyrians you've hired to save you and use them to shave off everything you have: your head and the hair of your legs, and your beard also."

Ahaz didn't want to hear any more. He turned his back on Isaiah and strode toward the steep ramp that led up to the city, anxious to escape his cousin's words. They were too horrible to consider. What if Isaiah was right? What if the Assyrians decided to invade him instead of rescuing him? He glanced over his shoulder to see if Isaiah had followed him and saw Hezekiah behind him, gazing up at him with accusing eyes. Ahaz quickly turned away.

He led his procession back to the palace as quickly as he could, refusing to acknowledge the gawking crowds who clamored for a glimpse of their king. Then he sent Hezekiah away with a servant and returned to his own bedchamber, deeply depressed. Outside his window the frantic preparations for the siege continued, but Ahaz no longer sought comfort in activity. The hole inside where fear gnawed at him felt even larger.

He didn't want to be king anymore. He wished that someone else could rule instead of him. But his brother Maaseiah was dead and Ahaz was alone. There was no one else. He lay facedown on his bed and wept.

---

Uriah sat in the Temple council chamber and planned his strategy, ignoring the arguing priests and Levites. His head pounded from tension as the meeting dragged on and on. The overcrowded room, a smaller version of the king's council chamber, felt charged with emotion.

He had asked his uncle Azariah, the retired high priest, to preside over the meeting from his place on the raised dais; the others sat in a semicircle around him. But after the announcement of King Ahaz's decision to raise tribute for Assyria, the meeting had quickly reached a stalemate as the priests argued over which section of the Holy Place should be dismantled for its gold. Uriah closed his eyes and squeezed his throbbing temples with his fingertips.

"This is what I hate," he mumbled to the priest seated beside him. "These fools can't even reach a simple consensus. No wonder the people have deserted the worship of Yahweh."

The priest yawned. "Do you suppose they'll finish in time for the evening sacrifice?"

"Not at this rate. I don't know how the Temple has managed to survive this long, but I can see how it will end." Uriah sighed and tried to concentrate on the discussion again. He hadn't mentioned his promotion yet, or Ahaz's decision to offer another sacrifice to Molech. He would need to handle those subjects with great care. Let the men exhaust their energy arguing over the Assyrian tribute first.

After what seemed like hours, the priests finally reached an agreement. Like a proud noblewoman taken captive, the Temple would be stripped of her finery to pay for the tribute to Assyria. Azariah divided the work among the men and was about to dismiss the gathering when Uriah rose from his place.

"Just a moment, gentlemen. There is one more matter we need to discuss." The men groaned with fatigue, but Uriah took his time, choosing every word, every gesture with care. He must win their support. There was no other option.

"At the emergency council meeting this morning, King Ahaz asked me to replace Prince Maaseiah as palace administrator. I have decided to accept the position."

His words were met with stunned silence. He had expected applause or at least words of congratulations, but the room grew very still. He decided to lay everything before them at once, while they were still in shock, and get it over with quickly.

"One of my first duties as palace administrator is to organize a public sacrifice before the siege begins."

"Here at the Temple?" Azariah asked.

"No. Ahaz plans to offer another sacrifice to Molech."

Conaniah jumped to his feet as if he might strike Uriah. "Have you lost your mind? How can you possibly organize a sacrifice to idols? You're the high priest of Yahweh!"

"He's right," Azariah said. "I don't see how you can possibly serve as palace administrator to a king who worships Molech. It's out of the question. You've gone too far, Uriah."

Their protests opened the floodgate, and everyone began talking and shouting at once. Uriah's head felt as if it would burst.

"Let me finish!" he finally shouted above the noise. "At least listen to me before you condemn me!"

Azariah began calling for silence and eventually restored the meeting to order. When everyone was seated, Uriah began to slowly circle the men, his voice calm and authoritative. As he spoke, he fixed his intimidating gaze on each priest and Levite in turn—a silent warning not to defy him. Most of the men would respect him enough to follow his lead if he could make his words persuasive enough—and if he could silence his opponents.

"We serve a dead institution," he began. "Look around you. Even the building is crumbling down on us, and we don't have the resources to repair it. It's time we faced the truth: the men of Jerusalem are no longer willing to support this Temple or its priesthood with their tithes. Like the king, they go elsewhere for spiritual help, to the idols and shrines in the groves. Meanwhile, we barely take in enough offerings to keep our families alive. It's time to make some changes."

"How can you talk about change?" Azariah interrupted. "Yahweh *never* changes. He ordained all the laws and the sacrifices, even the pattern for the Temple itself. You don't have the authority to change what the Almighty One has commanded."

"I have not finished speaking!" Uriah shouted, forcing himself to take authority over his elderly uncle. "You'll have a chance to speak when I'm through." Azariah sat down but his face was white, his lips taut with anger. The tension in the room swelled as Uriah continued.

"Our Temple worship must change as the world changes or it will eventually die out altogether. We're so bound to tradition that we no longer listen to the people. I'm not talking about changing Yahweh's laws, I'm talking about examining our traditions. If the men of Judah are drawn to the religions of the nations around us, then we need to ask ourselves why. It's time we consider changing our outmoded traditions to fit the times instead of blindly clinging to the old ways."

Azariah could no longer restrain himself. "That's outrageous!" he shouted. "Don't listen to him!"

The room erupted into chaos. Uriah watched helplessly, wondering how he would ever restore order again. After several frustrating minutes he began to shout, "Quiet, all of you! Be quiet and listen to me! Are you going to think for yourselves or let a few closed-minded extremists think for you?"

Eventually, most of the men quieted. Uriah ignored the few scattered objections and continued speaking, his voice hoarse from the strain. "If this Temple is going to survive, it's essential that we have the king's support. The people follow his leadership in spiritual matters—you know that. Some of you can remember how it was when Uzziah was king. This Temple was the focal point of the nation because of him." He turned to Zechariah. "Tell them how you won Uzziah's confidence and were able to influence the entire nation."

Zechariah made a shaky attempt to stand and speak, but Uriah quickly realized from his glazed eyes and swaying legs that he was drunk. Uriah hastily resumed his speech.

"My esteemed colleague has already assured me of his full support," he said as he waved Zechariah away. "My point is that King Ahaz is very young and has no understanding of Yahweh's law. It's up to us to teach him and draw him back to the worship of Yahweh. Then we'll be able to draw back the people, as well. King Ahaz trusts me. He has made me second in command of the nation. I'm merely using this sacrifice as a first step to revive the worship at this Temple."

"By worshiping idols?" Conaniah shouted. "You want to revive the worship of Yahweh by sacrificing to Molech? That's insane! The only way to revive Temple worship is through repentance. The men of Judah must give up their idolatry and turn their hearts back to God!"

Uriah swiftly crossed the room and stood before Conaniah, towering over him in an unspoken threat. "This Temple has been trying to operate under your narrow-minded, archaic views long enough. Repentance! Where has that gotten us? The whole purpose of this Temple is to serve the spiritual needs of the people. Obviously our traditions aren't meeting those needs or the people would come back. First we must draw them back to worship. Later we can wean them from their idolatry."

"No, you're wrong!" Azariah said. "The purpose of this Temple is to serve Yahweh, not the people. We sin against Him if we lead the people into idolatry."

"We're not leading them into idolatry!" Uriah shot back. "They're already worshiping idols! We can sit here and starve to death from lack of offerings, or we can change and reclaim some of our former power and strength in this nation. This is our chance! I have the king's trust and support. If I don't take a leading role in this sacrifice, then Molech's priests will. Look, I'm simply making all the arrangements. Molech's priests will perform the ritual. But the people must be convinced that our priesthood is supreme over all the others."

"Absolutely not!" Azariah answered. "We're priests of the one true God. We can't give our consent to idolatry."

"Our consent isn't an issue!" Uriah shouted. "Ahaz is stripping the last of the Temple's wealth—don't you understand that? There's nothing left! Are you going to sit here clinging to the past while the building crumbles down around you?" He slammed his fist against the wall with such force that bits of plaster and dust fell from the ceiling as if to prove his words. The room was silent for a moment.

"It's getting very late," Uriah said, his voice calm and controlled. "We've debated long enough. We have to carry out the king's orders today. The tribute must be sent to Assyria before the siege begins. And the sacrifice must be held immediately. We can't waste any more time arguing. It's time to vote."

He ignored the scattered murmurs of dissent and scooped up the container of pebbles used for voting. As he passed it around, each man took one black and one white stone.

"If you wish to support me as high priest and revive our Temple worship, put in the white stone," he ordered. "If you wish to tie my hands with your antiquated traditions and wait for the Temple to fall down around you, put in the black stone."

"Don't listen to him!" Azariah pleaded. "He's giving us no choice!"

"That's because there *is* no choice—don't you understand that?

We're the dying custodians of a dying institution. We need change. Now vote."

"No!" Azariah hurled his stones at Uriah's feet. "I refuse to accept your leadership. I refuse to have any part in a vote for idolatry. The very idea is an abomination to God himself!" He strode from the room. Conaniah and a few others followed.

Uriah held his breath, waiting to see how many more would leave. When enough men remained for their decision to be legally binding, he exhaled. He quickly passed the box for the vote, listening to the dull thud of the stones as they hit the bottom. When it came around to him, he tossed in his white stone, then turned the box over and dumped its contents in the middle of the circle.

"Count them," he ordered.

He could tell by the mixture of black and white that the vote would be close. Uriah watched tensely as two scribes separated and counted the stones. If the vote went against him, he would have to resign as high priest. His authority over the priests and Levites and his power to make changes in the Temple would come to an end. But if he won, today would bring a new beginning.

"Twenty-three black," the first scribe announced.

"And twenty-eight white," the second one added. "The vote has gone in your favor, Uriah."

They passed the container to collect the unused stones, and the men silently filed out, exhausted from the emotional strain of the meeting. When he was alone, Uriah sank onto his uncle's seat on the dais, staring at the stones still piled in the center of the room.

He had won. He had a new position of power with the king, and now the priests and Levites supported his leadership, as well. His whole life had shifted in the past few hours and had finally come into focus.

Uriah knew he should be elated, but his victory left him with a hollow feeling inside that he was afraid to examine too closely. He would wait until the sacrifice to Molech was over, he told himself. Maybe then he would feel differently. Maybe then he could silence the nagging voice that haunted him.

# 4

HIS MOTHER'S SCREAMS JOLTED him awake. Hezekiah opened his eyes and the nightmare returned. Like the rumble of an approaching storm, the soldiers poured down the hallway toward his room. They were coming again—for him.

The last time they came, Hezekiah hadn't known the horror that awaited Eliab. But this time he knew. He needed to run, he needed to hide, but there was no place to hide. His mother's screams grew louder, closer.

Maybe this was just a dream. Maybe he would wake up. But when he saw his brother's empty bed next to his, he remembered the stench and the roar of the flames, and he knew it wasn't a dream.

The soldiers flung his door open and pulled him from his bed. Strong hands tried to force the tunic over his head. Hezekiah remembered Molech's gaping mouth and how his brother had fallen, head-long into the flames, and he fought against the soldiers with all his strength. But they picked him up effortlessly, almost amused at his struggle, and carried him out of his room.

The hallway was shadowy and dim, but he saw dozens of soldiers in the flickering torchlight. The high priest was there, too—the tall, broad-shouldered man Hezekiah had seen in his father's council room. Mama was on her knees, clinging to his feet, pleading with him.

"Uriah, please! I beg you! Please don't take my son!" Her eyes were wild and frantic, her face chalky with fear.

"Mama, help me!" Hezekiah cried. "Help me!" He struggled to go to her, but the soldier held him tightly.

"Please, Uriah, please!" she begged.

"Abijah, don't . . ." The high priest tried to take her arm and help her stand up, but she clung to his legs.

"They've already killed my Eliab. Isn't that enough?" she asked. "Please don't kill Hezekiah, too! I beg you! For my father's sake! For my sake, have mercy on my son! He's all I have left!"

"Take her out of here," Uriah said quietly.

"No—Uriah, no! You have to help me!" A knot of soldiers surrounded her. She screamed helplessly as they pried her hands from Uriah's feet. Hezekiah fought and kicked with all his strength, crying in terror as he struggled to go to his mother. But she disappeared from sight as the men dragged her away, her agonized screams fading in the distance.

Then the high priest turned to Hezekiah. He gripped Hezekiah's shoulders in his huge hands and shook him. "Be quiet!"

The power of his thundering voice stunned Hezekiah into silence. He gazed up at Uriah, and the man seemed like a giant to him. Hezekiah pleaded wordlessly for his life, too terrified to speak, but Uriah turned away.

"Let's get this over with," he said.

The soldiers made Hezekiah join the other children, the sons of Ahaz's concubines. Hezekiah and his half-brother Amariah were nearly the same height and only a few months apart in age. But he knew that he was older than Amariah. As the eldest son of King Ahaz, Hezekiah knew he was next in line on the royal throne of King David. He was also next in line to die in the fire.

He couldn't walk. One of the soldiers bent to pick him up, and he fought desperately to break free. But the more he struggled the tighter the soldier gripped him. Hezekiah kicked and flailed, clawing at the arms that encircled him, crying out in terror as he was carried through the halls and down the darkened stairways. By the time he reached the courtyard and the waiting procession, Hezekiah felt bruised and numb, too exhausted to struggle anymore.

The early morning sun hurt his eyes when he emerged from the dimly lit palace corridors. But as his eyes adjusted, he could see that everything was nearly the same as the last time—the huge crowds of people, the waiting priests and nobles, the white-robed children. Only the endless rows of soldiers were missing. And in the middle of them all was his father, King Ahaz.

The procession started down the hill through the city streets to the Valley of Hinnom again. The soldier who was carrying Hezekiah set him down and ordered him to walk, but Hezekiah's legs trembled so violently with fear that the soldiers had to support him on either side. The two men pushed and dragged him through the streets until they finally reached the southern gate.

Hezekiah froze when he saw the jagged cliffs that marked the entrance to the valley of death. Once again, a thin column of smoke snaked into the sky in the distance. He couldn't move.

"No . . . no . . ." he whimpered. But the soldiers jerked him roughly by the arms and propelled him forward against his will, his feet dragging.

Some of the other children started to wail, and the priests began their chant to drown out the pitiful cries: "Molech . . . Molech . . . Molech . . ." The throbbing cadence echoed off the cliffs and city walls, swelling as the procession inched closer to the site of the sacrifice. Each beat of the priests' drums felt like a fist in Hezekiah's stomach. They were almost there. He couldn't escape.

Suddenly the man Hezekiah remembered meeting at the Gihon Spring pushed his way through the crowd, stepping in front of King Ahaz to block his path. Isaiah's eyes flashed with anger, and his whole body shook with rage until he seemed about to burst apart. He shouted above the pounding drums in a voice that penetrated to the soul.

"Hear, O heavens! Listen, O earth! For Yahweh has spoken: 'I reared children and brought them up, but they have rebelled against me. The ox knows his master, the donkey his owner's manger, but Israel does not know, my people do not understand.'"

"Get out of my way!" Ahaz said, shoving him aside. The king continued walking, his eyes fixed on the fire god ahead of him. But Isaiah stayed with him, walking backward to face him, shouting to be heard above the din.

"Ah, sinful nation, a people loaded with guilt, children given to corruption!" He spread his arms wide to include the entire crowd. "They have forsaken Yahweh. They have spurned the Holy One of Israel and turned their backs on him."

Again, Isaiah tried to stand in Ahaz's path, and Hezekiah felt a glimmer of hope for the first time since he'd been awakened that morning. But the king shoved him aside—harder than before. Isaiah stumbled and nearly fell.

"Oh, my people, haven't you had enough punishment?" Isaiah cried, fighting to regain his balance. "Must you forever rebel? Your country lies in ruins, your cities are burned, foreigners are plundering everything they see while you stand here helpless and abandoned!"

Hezekiah saw Uriah elbowing his way to the head of the procession to stand beside the king. He towered over Isaiah, but the prophet showed no fear as he met the high priest's gaze.

"Your hands are full of blood," Isaiah accused. "Wash and make yourselves clean. Take your evil deeds out of God's sight! Stop doing wrong; learn to do right!"

Uriah signaled to two of the soldiers. "Keep this man out of our way," he told them. Then he turned, joining Ahaz and the priests of Molech as the procession moved, step by step, toward its destination.

Isaiah made no more attempts to follow the king as the two soldiers held him back. But he stood by the edge of the road and pleaded with the people as they filed past him. "'Come now, let us reason together,' says Yahweh. 'Though your sins are like scarlet, they shall be as white as snow; though they are red as crimson, they shall be like wool. If you are willing and obedient, you will eat the best from the land; but if you resist and rebel, you will be devoured by the sword.' For the mouth of the Lord has spoken."

Isaiah's efforts seemed futile. The chanting crowd followed the king's example, ignoring Isaiah's words, turning away from him. The last door of escape seemed to slam shut in Hezekiah's face. All hope was gone. He was going to die.

But as the soldiers dragged Hezekiah forward, he turned to see Isaiah looking directly at him, staring straight into his eyes. His gaze seemed to penetrate deep inside Hezekiah, stripping him naked.

"Don't be afraid," Isaiah told him, "for Yahweh has ransomed you. He has called you by name. You belong to Yahweh. When you go through deep water, Yahweh will go with you. And when you ford mighty rivers, they won't overwhelm you. When you pass through the fire, you won't be burned. The flames will not hurt you. For Yahweh is your God. The Holy One of Israel is your Savior."

The soldiers tightened their grip on Hezekiah's arms, propelling him forward once again. He turned his head, trying to keep Isaiah in sight, waiting for Isaiah to rescue him from the soldiers' grasp, but the prophet couldn't move.

Over and over Isaiah's words throbbed in Hezekiah's ears to the pounding beat of the drums. *"When you pass through the fire, you won't be burned . . . for Yahweh is your God. . . ."* Over and over he repeated the words to himself, as if they possessed the power to protect him from what lay ahead.

The mob formed a circle around Molech, as close as the billowing heat allowed. In front of Hezekiah, the priests and their attendants mounted the steps of the platform, carrying the children. Molech waited with outstretched arms, his brazen image glowing, his mouth open wide. Hezekiah's legs buckled and he collapsed, paralyzed with fear. He tried to fight back as one of Molech's priests scooped him up, but the priest pinned his arms to his sides as he carried him up the steep steps and set him down on the platform. Once again Hezekiah faced the fiery monster.

The high priest of Molech began to chant the ritual of sacrifice, but Hezekiah heard none of the words. He was only aware of the intense heat on his face and the outstretched arms reaching for him. Isaiah's words still echoed over and over in his mind to the rhythm of the drums and the pounding of his heart. *"When you pass through the fire . . . Yahweh is your God. . . ."* The priest holding Hezekiah's shoulders tightened his grip, as if sensing that his instincts screamed for him to flee.

Now the chanting crowd reached a frenzied, deafening pitch. The moment of sacrifice was near. Hezekiah could no longer hear his own screams above the noise of the crowd, the beating of the drums, and the roar of the flames. The words of Isaiah that he had repeated to himself began to blur, and in his terror he remembered only one word: *Yahweh.*

The monster's huge brass eyes stared down at him, tongues of flame darted from his gaping mouth. Molech's priest finished his prayer and turned toward Hezekiah.

*"Yahweh!"* Hezekiah screamed in terror, over and over again.

"Which one is the firstborn?" Molech's priest asked.

Uriah looked down at Hezekiah. Their eyes met. But when he stretched out his hand, it rested on Amariah's head. "This one."

Molech's priest reached past Hezekiah and grabbed Amariah. Hezekiah saw the wrong son being hurled into the fire god's arms. He heard his half-brother scream as he rolled toward the open mouth. He watched Amariah die in the flames instead of himself.

As the roaring crowd continued its cry for more, Hezekiah felt dazed. Another child was thrown into the flames, and another and another until the nauseating stench filled the air, stinging his eyes, burning his throat, gagging him.

Then it was over.

Isaiah's words resounded in Hezekiah's mind once again: *"When you pass through the fire, you won't be burned . . . for Yahweh is your God."*

And Hezekiah fainted in a heap on the platform.

---

The throbbing cadence of drums faded and died with the last of Molech's victims. The crowds returned to their homes in somber silence to finish preparing for the siege. As Uriah walked beside King Ahaz through the city gates and up the hill to the palace, he wondered how the king felt about what he had just done.

Uriah had been a priest all his life. He had sacrificed thousands of animals and was no stranger to bloodshed. But none of his sacrificial victims had ever looked at him the way Ahaz's son had. No dumb beast had ever shown such terror.

Uriah had told himself it would be just an empty ritual—another sacrifice like all the many others he had presided over. But he had never witnessed human sacrifice before, and he was not prepared for the overwhelming revulsion he now felt.

For a brief moment, when Isaiah had blocked the king's path, Uriah had found himself praying that Ahaz would listen to him, that he would stop the terrible slaughter before it began. But the king had ignored the prophet's words and carried Uriah's carefully laid plans to their deadly conclusion.

It was still early morning, but Uriah stumbled wearily through the city streets and up the hill as if he had worked a full day of heavy labor. He reached the palace numb and exhausted. As he accompanied Ahaz down the corridors to his chambers, he heard anguished cries of grief and mourning coming through the open windows of the king's harem, and Uriah shuddered. What had he done? He had managed to save Abijah's son, but what about the other child? He had condemned another mother's son—another innocent child—to death.

"She'll get over it," Ahaz grumbled, as if reading Uriah's mind. "As soon as the next one is born, she'll forget."

Uriah fought the urge to punch him. Ahaz talked about his concubine as if she were a cow that quickly forgot her weaned calf. But Uriah remembered how desperately Abijah had pleaded for her child's life, and he knew she would never forget. Nor, he guessed, would Zechariah. Suddenly his teacher's pathetic condition made sense. The first victim had been his grandchild.

When they reached the king's private chambers, Uriah waited for Ahaz's orders, struggling to keep his features unreadable, his emotions hidden from view.

"Well, it's over," Ahaz sighed. "I think everything went well, don't you? And I was glad to see that more of the city elders have finally realized how serious our situation is and have offered up their sons, too."

Uriah mumbled a vague reply, unable to meet Ahaz's gaze.

"I believe Molech will hear us this time," Ahaz said, as if trying to convince himself. "He's a very powerful god, you know. He asks for a great sacrifice, and so his power must surely be very great in return."

Uriah didn't reply. His anger at the king's superstitious ignorance came close to the flash point. He had little patience with the stupidity of idolatry and was eager to begin the monumental task of teaching Yahweh's laws to Ahaz, beginning with the first commandment. But not today. Today Uriah was too physically and emotionally drained to do anything.

"I guess there's nothing more we can do except wait for the invasion," Ahaz said. His confidence in Molech seemed to abruptly vanish, and his fear became transparent in his trembling voice. "How long do we have, Uriah? How long before the siege begins?"

"A few days perhaps. Certainly no more than a week." Uriah tried to sound calm, to instill a measure of confidence in the panicky king.

"Are we prepared? Can we withstand it?" Ahaz's face wore the pathetic look of a beggar pleading for alms. Uriah battled his revulsion as he recognized the king for what he was—a coward. Only a coward would send his children to their deaths in order to save his own life.

"Yes, Your Majesty," he replied. "Defensively, our city is well situated. The enemy will grow tired of the siege long before we will."

But Ahaz didn't look convinced. He paced the length of the sitting room, wringing his hands. Uriah longed to escape from him, to run as far from the palace as he could and never return. He would have to support Ahaz and be his strength through this crisis, and he wondered where he would find the energy. He already felt exhausted.

"Your Majesty, if I may be excused, I need to oversee the Assyrian tribute payment," he said, grasping at any excuse.

"Yes, I suppose so," Ahaz replied.

Uriah hurried away before the king changed his mind. He knew he really should supervise the Levites as they collected the gold, but he felt numb and sick, as if he had swallowed a heavy stone. He left the palace through the royal portico and headed up the hill to the Temple.

When he reached the outer courtyard, he stopped to catch his breath. The scene was a stark contrast to the narrow valley where Molech sat enthroned. The Temple courts felt open and spacious, the view of the surrounding mountains unhindered by jagged cliffs. Everything seemed peaceful, the silence welcome after the noise of Molech's ritual, the air sweet after the stench of burning flesh.

Uriah paused at the gate to the inner courtyard to steady himself and gazed up at Yahweh's sanctuary. It was as familiar to him as his own face. Yet for some reason, it seemed alien and remote, like a scene from a dream. A faint breeze rippled the water in the huge brass sea where the priests washed, and the water gleamed like molten silver in the sunlight. Isaiah's words rippled through Uriah's mind: *"Wash and make yourselves clean. . . . Your hands are full of blood."*

Uriah gazed down at his hands. When he ministered in Yahweh's Temple, they would become stained with the blood of the sacrifice.

Today they had remained clean—yet they felt filthy. He looked up at the huge brass altar that dominated the center of the courtyard, its fires slowly burning as they consumed the lamb from the morning sacrifice. But as Uriah stared at it, the lamb seemed to take the form of a child in the shimmering heat.

He shuddered and shook his head to clear away the image. When he turned to leave, he nearly collided with Zechariah, who had staggered blindly into the courtyard. Zechariah lost his balance, and as Uriah grabbed him by the shoulders to steady him, he smelled wine on his breath.

"I have to stop him," Zechariah murmured. He appeared frantic, his bloodshot eyes wild with fright.

"Stop who, Rabbi?" Uriah feared that Zechariah meant him— that he was coming, too late, to stop Molech's sacrifice.

"King Uzziah . . . I must stop Uzziah!"

"King Uzziah is dead," he said, shoving him away in disgust. "And you're drunk." Uriah's anger and self-loathing boiled over, and he lashed out at Zechariah. "I admired you so much. I wanted to be just like you. You had the most brilliant legal mind the priesthood had seen in generations, and now you're talking to a king who's been dead for years. You're a disgrace, Rabbi. How could you turn your back on everything you believed in?"

Zechariah didn't answer. He stared into the distance, watching the birds fluttering around the roof of the Temple.

"I'm taking you back to your room," Uriah said. "Stay there until you're sober." He spun Zechariah around and led him back to his chambers. Pity, guilt, and grief raged inside Uriah, but he carefully hid them behind his anger, the only emotion he dared express without losing control and breaking down.

"Look at this place!" he cried when they reached Zechariah's room. "This entire building is falling apart! I'm tired of begging for the tithes that are rightfully mine, tired of going hungry year after year, tired of scraping and pleading. I swear to God I'll win back the power and recognition our priesthood deserves and restore this Temple to its former glory, no matter what it takes. I was counting on your help to do it, Zechariah, but if all you want to do is drink, then stay out of my way!"

He gave Zechariah a shove, and the older man stumbled, losing his balance and collapsing in a heap on the floor. Several moments passed as he lay without moving.

Finally Zechariah looked up. His eyes were no longer vacant but filled with despair, the weaker man looking to the stronger one for answers. "Uriah . . ." he moaned. "Can I ever find forgiveness for what I've done?"

A chill passed through Uriah's veins as he remembered the sacrifice to Molech—as he remembered what he had done. Then the room seemed to grow colder and colder as Zechariah's agonized cries filled the air.

"Yahweh, please let me die . . . let me die . . . let me die!"

# 5

ABIJAH WEPT WHEN THEY brought Hezekiah to her and placed him in her arms. His hair and clothing reeked of smoke, but she held his sooty face between her hands and kissed him over and over, the grime mingling with her tears. Hezekiah clung to her, and she saw in his eyes all the horrors he had witnessed.

How had he been miraculously spared? She wondered if Uriah had intervened. Abijah had been stunned to see the high priest assembling the king's sons for the sacrifice. She had hoped that, as Ahaz's advisor, Uriah would oppose his idolatry, not help him. But if Uriah had heeded her pleas and saved Hezekiah, that was all that mattered.

"Yahweh," Hezekiah whispered, his voice hoarse from screaming. "Yahweh!"

Abijah didn't understand why he repeated the word again and again. Yahweh was the God that her father worshiped. How had her son heard His name at Molech's sacrifice?

"Hush, baby. You're safe now," she murmured. "Everything's going to be all right."

But as she gazed at her trembling child, she wondered if he ever would be the same. The winsome, curious boy who had brightened the palace corridors with his laughter was slipping away like fine silk through her fingers. Watching Eliab die had changed Hezekiah into a terrified child who awoke screaming night after night, afraid to sleep again and risk the nightmare's return. But today's sacrifice had severed the last cords of his reason and trust. He'd chosen to escape from the reality of a world that included Molech, retreating to a safer place within his own mind. And Abijah didn't know how to reach him. She clung to his body as if the force of her love could bring him back.

Part of her wanted to retreat from reality, as well. Her life had veered so far from its natural course of marriage and family that it seemed to descend on a path to Sheol. She had married royalty, a descendant of King David . . . a man capable of killing his own children.

"They will never take you away from me," she said, crushing Hezekiah to her. "Never." But she knew it was an empty vow that she was powerless to keep.

Maybe she should pray. Maybe she should call on Yahweh, the God Hezekiah asked for. But wasn't He the God who had married her to Ahaz? Hadn't her father's devotion to Yahweh won her the honor of marriage to the royal family? Abijah had never asked God for anything before. She had learned early in life not to have any wishes and desires of her own.

"You want nothing," her mother had told her, "except what your father wants for you. What you want doesn't matter." Abijah had accepted that, had grown up knowing it would always be so.

She remembered a warm afternoon, shortly before her marriage, when Uriah had come outside to the courtyard of her father's house where she sat, daring to talk to her alone. "Do you want to marry Prince Ahaz?" her father's student had asked her.

"My choice doesn't matter," she had replied. "Surely you know that."

"Because King Uzziah made a promise to your father?"

"No, because I'm a woman. I will be given in marriage—given, like a present. Do presents have the luxury of choosing who will receive them?" She had felt no bitterness, she had merely stated the truth.

"And you accept that, Abijah?" Uriah asked.

"Of course," she replied.

Uriah had stared off into the distance for a moment, gazing at the golden roof of the Temple, barely visible above the trees and rooftops. When he turned to her again, she saw the tender concern written on his face. "Haven't you ever wanted something so badly that you were willing to fight for it?" he had asked.

Abijah hadn't answered his question. She hadn't understood it then. But now she did. And something inside her, an inner strength she didn't know she had, told her to fight for Hezekiah. She couldn't let him slip away. She had already lost one son, and she couldn't bear to lose another.

"Come back to me, sweetheart. Please, come back," she begged. She took Hezekiah's stiff little hands in hers and clapped them together, singing one of the rhyming songs he had once loved so much. He didn't respond.

"Yahweh," he sobbed.

For the remainder of the day Abijah fought for her son, trying every means she could think of to draw him back to a world he no longer wanted to be part of, a world he feared and mistrusted. The hopelessness of her battle exhausted her. His body remained rigid with fear, his eyes stared sightlessly.

As the afternoon waned she carried him to the window, but he wouldn't look out. It was nearly time for the evening sacrifice. Then darkness would fall, and the long, terror-filled night would begin for both of them. She rocked Hezekiah gently and felt a sob shudder through him.

"Yahweh . . ."

Where had he learned that name? What part did the ancient God of her father play in this nightmare? She might never know.

Abijah's maidservant entered the room with a tray of food, setting it on the small table beside the window seat. Her eyes were filled with compassion "My lady, you've been holding him all day. You need to eat something. Let me hold him for a while."

Abijah shook her head. The food held no appeal. Her stomach churned with dread at the possibility that her son might never be whole. Hezekiah didn't seem to hear the maid enter the room or speak, but when a shofar sounded in the distance, announcing the evening sacrifice, he jumped.

"Yahweh!"

Abijah decided in that moment what she must do for her child. If Hezekiah called for Him then she would call on Him, too. Yahweh held the key to his mind for some reason, so she would find that key and unlock it.

"Hezekiah, Mama has to leave you," she told him, kissing his forehead, "but I'll come back in a little while, I promise. Deborah will take you now."

The maid looked surprised as Abijah stood and beckoned to her. "But . . . where are you going, my lady? You aren't allowed—"

"I'm going to the evening sacrifice at the Temple," she said firmly. "That's allowed."

Abijah nearly changed her mind when she tried to lift Hezekiah into Deborah's arms and he clung to her, screaming. But Abijah pried his hands loose, promising him that she would return. Then she covered her head with her shawl and hurried out of the palace, nearly running up the royal walkway to the Temple.

Very few worshipers had gathered for the evening sacrifice—a dozen men, a handful of women. Abijah scanned the Levites' faces, looking for her father, then searched among the priests for Uriah. She didn't see either man. As the worshipers fell to their knees in prayer, Abijah fell to hers, as well, crying out to Yahweh for the first time in her life.

"Lord, you know I've never asked you for anything before," she cried. "And I'm not asking for myself now, but for my son. He cries for you, Lord. Please help him . . . please show me what to do to bring him back. I'll come here to worship you every day—twice a day! I'll do anything, Lord, if only you'll hear my prayer and help my son."

She stayed on her knees for a long time, praying, never noticing that the service had ended. Nor did she notice that a white-robed priest had approached until his voice startled her. "Would you like to make an offering, my lady?"

Abijah hastily wiped her tears. "No . . . I . . ." She didn't know what to say. She had asked Yahweh for help, but she didn't understand what she was supposed to do next. The priest crossed his arms and glanced around the courtyard as if impatient to complete his duties.

"My . . . my father is Zechariah, the Levite," she said. "Do you know where he is? Could you take me to him?"

The priest frowned slightly, then nodded. "Come this way."

Abijah didn't know why she had asked for her father. She only knew that her son needed Yahweh's help and Yahweh was her father's God. She would do whatever Yahweh required if only He would save Hezekiah. She hurried to keep pace with the priest as he led her inside the Levites' quarters. She only hoped that King Ahaz would never discover what she was doing.

---

When Zechariah opened his eyes, he was alone, sprawled on the floor of his room. He had no memory of how he got there. What hour was it? What day? He couldn't recall. Then he saw the empty wineskin and remembered praying to die. Yahweh hadn't answered his prayer.

Zechariah slowly pulled himself to his feet, leaning against his bed for support. Through the cracks of his shuttered window he could see that the sun was low in the western sky. He had slept in a drunken stupor all day, and now he was sober again. The numbing effects of the wine had worn off, leaving him powerless to face his guilt and failure, powerless against the memories of Molech's sacrifice. He searched his disheveled room, desperate for a drink, but the wineskins were all empty. He was too shaky to go buy more. He sank onto his bed and covered his face.

If he could go back and unravel all the mistakes he had made, he would gladly do it. But Zechariah could never go back. And now Eliab had paid for those mistakes with his life. It was just as the scriptures said—*"He punishes the children and their children for the sins of the fathers to the third and fourth generation."*

"No . . ." he moaned. "No, please . . . no more! Have mercy, Lord. Have mercy!"

When the trumpet blast suddenly announced the evening sacrifice, it startled Zechariah as if the voice of God had called out in accusation. Then the distant music of the Levites' choir began to drift into his room. Zechariah mumbled the words aloud as the choir sang, desperate to drive away the painful images of Molech's sacrifice: "'Out of the depths I cry to you, O Lord; O Lord, hear my voice . . . If you, O Lord, kept a record of sins, who could stand? But with you there is forgiveness. . . .'"

Zechariah stopped. He had sung the words of this psalm all his life without hearing them. Could they be true? Would the Almighty One really stoop down to where he lay and forgive him? Molech's image suddenly reared before Zechariah, and it seemed to mock the psalmist's words. He continued reciting to drive the image away: "'I wait for Yahweh, my soul waits, and in his word I put my hope . . . for with Yahweh is unfailing love. . . .'"

Zechariah remembered once serving a God of unfailing love and forgiveness. If only Yahweh's forgiveness could end this bitter cycle of sin and punishment and death for Zechariah's children and his children's children. His soul wanted that, longed for that, more than life itself. He shut his eyes, reciting with the choir: "'O Israel, put your hope in Yahweh . . . with him is full redemption. He himself will redeem Israel from all their sins.'"

Full redemption. Zechariah suddenly realized that redemption was the bridge that would lead him back across the chasm of sin, back to God. And Yahweh himself would provide that bridge. Zechariah fell on his face before Him, pleading with God to forgive him for what he had done.

"'Have mercy on me, O God, according to your unfailing love . . . Wash away all my iniquity and cleanse me from my sin . . . Against you, you only, have I sinned and done what is evil in your sight. . . .'"

Zechariah understood now. His life had been dedicated and consecrated to Yahweh, yet he had lived only for himself. That was his greatest sin—wasting the life that belonged to God. Zechariah cried out, praying King David's prayer of repentance from the depths of his heart and soul. "'Wash me, and I will be whiter than snow. Let me hear joy and gladness . . . Hide your face from my sins and blot out all my iniquity. . . . Restore to me the joy of your salvation. . . . Then . . . then . . .'"

Zechariah paused, stumbling over the words. Outside, the sun was rapidly sinking below the western hills. The light was fading, the shadows lengthening. He felt as though time was running out.

"Then . . . then . . ." What came next? What could Zechariah possibly promise God in order to make restitution for all of his sins? "'You do not delight in sacrifice, or I would bring it; you do not take pleasure in burnt offerings . . .'" The blood of a thousand lambs and goats could never bring Eliab back or give Zechariah another life to live over again. He struggled against the pain in his heart to remember the rest of the psalm. "Then . . . 'Then I will teach transgressors your ways, and sinners will turn back to you.'"

"O God, forgive me!" he pleaded. "Forgive me and give me another chance. Let me make up for the wrong I have done. I *will* teach transgressors your ways, Yahweh. Please give me another chance to serve you. Please!"

The shofar sounded again in the distance, signaling the end of the sacrifice. As Zechariah opened his eyes and looked around, he realized that the images of Molech had all fled. He remained where he lay on the floor, reveling in the peace he now felt, afraid to disturb it—until he heard a soft knock on his door. He rose to his feet and stumbled across the room. Had he forgotten something? Was he supposed to be on duty at the Temple?

He opened the door to find his daughter, Abijah. Her lovely face was streaked with tears, her eyes red with grief. Zechariah drew back, expecting hatred and reproach for his part in Eliab's death, but Abijah fell into his arms.

"Abba, please help my son Hezekiah," she begged. "Night after night he dreams about the sacrifice to Molech. And now that he's witnessed it for a second time, he . . . I don't know if he'll ever be the same."

Zechariah shuddered. Images of the fire god had tortured his own mind for weeks. How much worse it must be for a child.

"His mind isn't the same," Abijah said. "Fear is destroying him. Please help him, Abba."

"H-help him?" Zechariah stammered. "I don't know how."

"I don't know, either! But he cries for Yahweh, your God, over and over again, and I don't know why."

Yahweh—his God. The God of forgiveness and unfailing love. Zechariah felt so helpless, so unworthy. He couldn't help his grandson. He didn't know how. And he desperately needed another drink. "What do you want me to do?" he asked, releasing Abijah from his arms.

"I don't know. Just sit with him, talk to him. Maybe you can find out why he asks for Yahweh and what he wants from Him. Please come and talk to him."

"Come? Come where?"

"To the palace."

"No," Zechariah said abruptly. "No, I can't go back to the palace." Everything in his life had begun to go wrong when he'd lived in the king's palace.

Abijah began to weep, and her grief tore at Zechariah's heart. "I have no one else to turn to, Abba. My son Eliab is dead, and I don't know how I'll go on living if I lose Hezekiah. *Please* help me!"

Zechariah looked into his daughter's eyes and realized that she wasn't blaming him for his part in Eliab's death—or for arranging her marriage to an idolater. It was as if she had already forgiven him for all his past wrongs and wanted only his help. And Zechariah knew, then, that Yahweh had heard his prayer. Yahweh was offering His forgiveness, too. Zechariah could make restitution for all the wrong he had done by helping Hezekiah. The journey back to the palace stretched before him like a slender bridge, reaching back across the gulf, back to God.

"I'll come," Zechariah said hoarsely. "I'll do what I can." His hand trembled as he gripped Abijah's and followed her out of the room, closing the door behind him.

Zechariah walked down the hill to the palace, down to where his life had veered off course, as if unraveling a tapestry that had gone awry. He would return to where his first mistake had been made and start all over again, with the twisted mess he had made of his life coiled at his feet like a tangled pile of wool. He would begin anew, not seated beside King Uzziah in the splendor of the royal throne room, but with his grandson in the palace nursery.

As the guard admitted them inside, Zechariah wondered how long it had been since he'd last been here. It had been many years, yet the bitter memories seemed as fresh as yesterday. He had failed both his God and his king.

Abijah led Zechariah through the familiar corridors, then up a flight of stairs that were unknown to him. He'd never been near the forbidden harem or the palace nursery before, and he wondered if he would be stopped and sent away. King Ahaz certainly wouldn't welcome his interference if he learned of it. Zechariah slowed his steps as he considered turning back, but then he heard a child crying in the distance and he followed Abijah as she ran the last few yards to her son's bedchamber.

The servant girl was exhausted from struggling to soothe Hezekiah, and Abijah quickly lifted him from her arms. The boy clung to his mother, staring straight through Zechariah with wide, frightened eyes as if he wasn't even there. The only word he spoke was "Yahweh," whispered in a hoarse voice.

*I've done this to him,* Zechariah thought. *This is all my fault.* The Torah said don't be like the other nations—they sacrifice their children to idols. But he hadn't heeded the warning. He sank down on the bed across from Hezekiah's and prayed for forgiveness as Abijah rocked her son in her arms to soothe him.

It took a long time for the boy to fall asleep, and Zechariah could see how weary Abijah was from her efforts to comfort him. "I'll stay and watch over him," Zechariah said when she finally laid him in his bed. "Why don't you get some rest?"

At first she was reluctant. "We need to help him, Abba. He's terrified."

"I know. He'll be safe with me."

"What if he wakes up again?"

"I'll send a servant to fetch you if he calls for you."

Zechariah finally convinced her. But after Abijah left he sat down on the empty bed again, wondering what he could possibly do for his little grandson. He certainly wasn't strong enough to fight off Ahaz's soldiers if they came back—although he knew he would sooner die than let Ahaz sacrifice this child.

Gradually the oil lamps burned lower and the room darkened. A gentle breeze blew through the open window, bringing cooler air after the hot, dry day. The room was quiet except for the sound of Hezekiah's breathing. But Zechariah wasn't sleepy. He needed a drink. He knew where the palace wine cellars were and where to find the chief steward. If he just slipped downstairs for a moment, he could return with a skin of wine. He rose to his feet and shuffled to the door.

Suddenly Hezekiah's cry shattered the stillness. It startled Zechariah so badly that he feared his heart would leap from his chest. For a moment, he couldn't think what to do. Then he turned and saw Hezekiah sitting up in bed, screaming in terror, and Zechariah quickly gathered him into his arms. The boy clung to him, sobbing.

"Yahweh! Yahweh!"

He seemed so small, so vulnerable, that Zechariah's eyes filled with tears. He felt a heavy weight of guilt for the part he played in Hezekiah's nightmare, but he didn't know how to help him. "Shh . . . shh . . ." he soothed as he stroked Hezekiah's curly hair. "Yahweh's here with us. Yahweh's here. . . ."

Then, not knowing what else to do, Zechariah began reciting from the Psalms, stirring up the nearly forgotten words from somewhere in his memory. "'Yahweh is my light and my salvation—whom shall I fear? Yahweh is the stronghold of my life—of whom shall I be afraid?'"

Almost imperceptibly, Hezekiah began to relax. His sobs died away to soft whimpers. Zechariah swallowed the lump in his throat and continued reciting: "'For in times of trouble, Yahweh will keep me safe in his shelter. Yahweh will hide me in the secret place where he dwells and will set me up on a high rock . . .'"

Eventually, Hezekiah fell asleep in Zechariah's arms. The oil lamps flickered, then burned out. But Zechariah continued to recite throughout the long night until the first soft rays of sunlight lit the room. "'Yahweh is my shepherd, I shall not be in want. . . . Even though I walk through the valley of the shadow of death, I will fear no evil, for Yahweh is with me.'"

# 6

URIAH STOOD ATOP JERUSALEM'S walls and gazed down at the enemy troops encamped in the valley below. The sun would soon dip below the rim of the western hills, and he realized that he had been listening unconsciously for the trumpet to announce the evening sacrifice. But there would be no trumpet. It hadn't sounded for more than six weeks, since the day the Aramean armies poured into the valleys surrounding Jerusalem and the siege had begun. So far the city's thick walls and steep cliffs had withstood the enemy's attacks, but supplies and tempers were growing short. And with no wood for the altar fire, no lambs for the offering, the daily sacrifices in Yahweh's Temple had ceased.

Uriah turned away and descended the long flight of stairs from the wall to the street. He felt tense and exhausted as he made his way to the palace throne room, dreading his meeting with King Ahaz. Every day the king sent him to the top of the walls to survey the enemy encampments, but the king refused to look for himself. Messengers raced in and out of the throne room with news of the latest attempts to breech the gates, but Ahaz wouldn't observe the fighting or offer words of encouragement to his meager troops. He had vowed not to leave the palace until the siege was over. Uriah had been forced to act as a buffer between the king, isolated in his palace, and the real conflict taking place outside.

A palace chamberlain opened the door for Uriah, bowing to him, then ushered him into the king's presence. The leisurely splendor of the throne room was a stark contrast to the noise and confusion of warfare outside. Uriah had difficulty adjusting to the change. He entered wearily and bowed low before the king.

Ahaz appeared bored as he slouched on his massive ivory throne. He acknowledged Uriah's presence with a limp wave of his hand. "This cursed weather," he said with a groan. "I can't take this heat." The servants who were fanning the king with palm branches began waving them faster.

Uriah glanced at his smaller throne beside the king's, wishing he could sit down, but Ahaz offered no invitation. The afternoon heat pressed against Uriah like a wall. He longed for a cup of cold water from the Gihon Spring, but the only water available came from the city's cisterns and tasted warm and stale.

"Yes, it's very hot, Your Majesty," Uriah said. "I've come to report that—"

"I'm tired of just sitting here, tired of this stifling throne room, tired of watching all these useless advisors of mine scurry around all day whispering and arguing." The knots of men scattered around the throne room froze, eyeing the king with alarm. But Ahaz made no effort to move off his throne, in spite of his claim to boredom. "I'm sick of this cursed siege," he said. "Six weeks already! Six weeks of sitting cooped up in this city waiting for help to arrive. When are the Assyrians going to come to our rescue?"

Uriah was tempted to reply that he was a priest, not a prophet, but he forced himself to be patient. "I'm certain that help will come any day now, Your Majesty. The tribute we sent has surely reached the Assyrian emperor by now." He recalled the long, winding caravan that had been hastily sent to Tiglath-Pileser, loaded with the last of the Temple's wealth. Uriah had stood on the tower of the north gate with Ahaz and watched the camels depart, nodding their way slowly down the road, calmly chewing with their crooked jaws. That was the last time that Ahaz had left the palace. A day and a half later, thousands of enemy troops had arrived and the siege had begun.

"Well, what's taking the Assyrians so long?" Ahaz grumbled. "I'm cut off from the rest of the world. I don't even know what's happening to my nation—or if I have a nation left."

Uriah saw the king slipping into one of his foul moods, and he searched for an excuse to get away from him. It seemed as if he spent more time trying to keep the king from becoming depressed than he did helping him run the country. Today Uriah had no energy to spare for either task.

"Your Majesty, the fighting is over for the day," he said. "With your permission, it's time for your other advisors and me to prepare our daily reports."

Ahaz nodded, blotting the sweat off his face with a linen towel. "The fighting is over for today," he repeated to his advisors. "Everyone go and prepare your reports." The counselors filed from the throne room, whispering among themselves. Uriah quickly turned to follow them, eager to escape from the gloomy king, but Ahaz called him back. "Stay behind, Uriah. You will join me for dinner in the banquet room."

Uriah bowed slightly, gritting his teeth. "As you wish, Your Majesty."

The king's servants scurried around Ahaz, adjusting his robes as they escorted him with exaggerated pomp from the throne room. Uriah followed him along the covered walkway toward the banquet hall, dreading the task of trying to lift his spirits. The air was slightly cooler in the open courtyard as the evening breezes blew in from the Judean hills, but they carried the scent of smoke from the valley below, a reminder that the nation was at war.

The banquet room had been built to serve hundreds of guests, but only one table had been prepared for the evening meal. It seemed lost in the vast, echoing space. When Uriah saw Abijah waiting to dine with her husband, he drew in his breath. She was so beautiful that he had to look away, afraid that his longing for her would be plain for anyone to see.

"Good evening, my lady," he murmured as he bowed in respect. He kept his eyes lowered, avoiding Abijah's gaze.

She bowed to her husband, then hovered close to him, fussing over him and plumping the cushions for him as she helped him get comfortable at the table. Uriah couldn't watch. Abijah was much too lovely and intelligent to be married to a crude man like Ahaz. She should belong to a man who truly loved her—a man like himself.

The king motioned for Uriah to sit at his right-hand side and Abijah at his left. Uriah sank onto the cushions, staring in amazement at the exquisitely embroidered tablecloth, the shimmering silver bowls and plates. Servants glided in and out, bringing platter after platter heaped with delicacies: roasted lamb, cooked lentils and beans, cucumbers, melons, pomegranates, fig cakes, olives, grapes, cheese, and bread. Uriah would consider such a meal extravagant in prosperous times, but with his nation suffering, his city under siege, the meal seemed grotesque. He fingered his silver goblet, wondering why Ahaz had plundered the silver from the Temple if the king owned all of this. But he knew better than to question him. Ahaz could strip him of his new position as easily as he had awarded it.

When the meal had been spread before them, Uriah bowed his head to recite the blessing over their food. But before he could begin, Ahaz interrupted. "Go ahead, eat!" he said, gesturing to the table. "What are you waiting for?"

Uriah hesitated, wondering if he should remind the king of Yahweh's law. He had promised himself that he would use his position as palace administrator to instruct Ahaz, but he had found very few opportunities so far. As Uriah searched for the right words, Ahaz reached across the table for a handful of olives and stuffed them into his mouth.

"Is something wrong?" the king asked.

"No, Your Majesty." Uriah whispered a hasty prayer under his breath, then looked around for the pitcher of water for the ritual hand-washing. Ahaz stopped chewing and glared at him.

"Now what are you looking for?"

Uriah glanced at Abijah, hoping to take his cue from her. She had been raised in a devout home and certainly knew what the law prescribed. But she seemed as unconcerned about the required washing as Ahaz did. Maybe it was because of the siege, he told himself. All of the city's water supplies were being rationed.

"It's . . . it's nothing," Uriah mumbled. Surely the ritual didn't matter during wartime.

A servant appeared at Uriah's side with a platter, heaped with juicy chunks of lamb. Since no daily sacrifices were being offered at the Temple, Uriah knew that the animal had been slaughtered as one of Ahaz's many sacrifices to Baal. And judging by the blood pooling along the edges of the platter, it hadn't been slaughtered according to the Law, either. As the high priest of Yahweh, he was forbidden to eat such defiled food. But as if in a dream, Uriah found himself grimly piling several slices of the meat onto his plate.

This was how sin took hold, his conscience tried to warn him. First with a drop, then a small trickle, and finally in a flood, all the laws and precepts he had faithfully followed all of his life would be washed away before his eyes if he wasn't careful. But Uriah pushed the warning aside as he tried to remember his larger goals—restoring the Temple, empowering his priesthood, preserving his newly-won authority in the nation. Nothing else mattered—certainly not vain, empty rituals that had lost their meaning centuries ago.

"Eat, Uriah, eat," Ahaz urged. "You've put in a full day's work. You deserve it." He turned to Abijah, boldly caressing her in front of

Uriah and all the servants. "How about you, my lovely one? Are you enjoying the meal?"

Uriah risked a glance and saw Abijah's flushed cheeks as she answered the king.

"Yes, my lord. It's an honor to dine with you, as always. Here—have you tried one of these figs?" She leaned close to feed one to Ahaz, and Uriah had to look away. He remembered all the times she had dined with him at her father's table, how her witty conversation and sparkling laughter were the highlights of his evening. To see her this way—little more than a beautiful servant to Ahaz—was unbearable. Uriah picked at his food for several minutes, pushing it around on his plate to make it appear as though he was eating.

"I want to ask you something, Uriah," Ahaz said suddenly. "The other advisors aren't here now, so tell me the truth. How are we really holding up against the siege?" The king continued to stuff food into his mouth as if he had asked about the weather instead of the state of his nation. Uriah studied him for a long moment, wondering if he should tell him the truth or lie to him, cheering him with half-truths and false hopes as he'd been doing for the last six weeks. Uriah decided that he was sick of the charade. Ahaz needed to hear the truth.

"Your Majesty, our greatest threat isn't the enemy on the outside," he said slowly. "Jerusalem's walls and steep slopes are a formidable barrier. They can withstand a great deal."

"Good." Ahaz grunted and spat three olive pits onto his plate.

"The greatest threat in siege warfare is always morale. The people are starting to panic as they see their water supplies diminishing, and—"

"I thought I said to post guards at the cisterns and ration the water supplies," Ahaz shouted, spitting small bits of food from his overfull mouth.

"That's being done, Your Majesty, but—"

"By all the gods in heaven, this is the limit! Defending this city from the enemy is bad enough, but now you're telling me I have to use my precious manpower against my own people? Curse them all!" He threw down his bread and pushed away his plate.

Abijah quickly moved to soothe Ahaz, kneading his shoulders as she whispered something in his ear. The king ignored her. He grabbed his wine goblet and drained it, then signaled for more. Too late, Uriah realized that it had been a mistake to give him the truth.

"I'm sick to death of this siege!" Ahaz said. "We should have sent the tribute to the Arameans instead of to Assyria. Maybe they would have gone home and left us alone. We could have thrown in a few thousand slaves, too, if that's what they're after. Do you think it's too late to buy their favor?"

Uriah tried to hide his irritation at Ahaz's stupidity. "The Arameans never would have been happy with tribute, Your Majesty. They want the whole nation of Judah. Besides, there's no tribute left to send." He deliberately kept his gaze on Ahaz, ignoring the silver-laden table in front of him.

Ahaz grunted and returned to his meal, downing another glass of wine. He ate in silence for several minutes, then asked abruptly, "How do you like your new living quarters, Uriah? Is everything satisfactory?"

Uriah suppressed his astonishment at the sudden change of topics. "Everything's more than satisfactory, Your Majesty." In fact, his rooms were luxurious compared to his old quarters on the Temple Mount where everything was falling into disrepair. He had moved to the palace a week ago, but Uriah still struggled to adjust to all his privileges as palace administrator.

"Good, good," Ahaz said, biting into a chunk of bread. "I wanted you here in the palace, close at hand in case I need you. They were my brother Maaseiah's quarters. . . ." Ahaz stopped eating. Uriah looked away as the king battled his emotions. "I never should have let Maaseiah go into battle," he said in a trembling voice. "I should have sent somebody else. He didn't even get a decent burial."

Uriah knew how much Ahaz still mourned for his brother, and he silently marveled at the fact that the king had never shown remorse over the death of his sons. The memory of those children huddling together, gazing up at the priests in terror, made Uriah shudder. He glanced at Abijah again and saw the depth of her grief in her unguarded expression. He knew then that her hovering concern for Ahaz was an act, just as his own conduct was. They were both playing parts in this drama, with Ahaz as the central character—both pretending to be someone they weren't. But Uriah had chosen his role deliberately; Abijah had never been given a choice.

"You've suffered a great loss, Your Majesty," Uriah forced himself to say. "I am honored that you chose me, although I know I can never replace Prince Maaseiah."

Uriah's words seemed to pacify Ahaz. He grunted and began eating again. "By the way," he said with his mouth full of bread, "I understand you're not married. How did you manage that?"

Uriah was at a loss for words. How could he explain that he had loved only one woman, and that he loved her still? Abijah should have been his wife, not Ahaz's. He wondered if Ahaz ever took the time to talk to her. Did he know anything at all about her? Did he know that lilies made her sneeze or that she was afraid of spiders? Did Ahaz notice the way the corners of her mouth turned down slightly just before she smiled? Or didn't Abijah smile anymore?

"I'm not sure, Your Majesty," Uriah said, shrugging as if it didn't matter. "No time to look for a wife, I guess."

"Well, if you ever get lonely, just let the servants know," Ahaz said. "They'll arrange to have a few concubines sent to your quarters." Ahaz reached to caress Abijah again, and Uriah nearly choked. Everything about this dinner disgusted him: the lavish opulence, the wasted food, the inane small talk. Ahaz was a fool, discussing concubines when his city was under siege. Uriah could no longer stand the sight of him. He studied his plate, toying with his food, wishing he had an excuse to leave.

The sudden crash startled him. He looked up to discover that Ahaz had just hurled a plate to the floor. "You're lying to me!" the king said. "All my advisors are lying. The Assyrians aren't coming and we're all going to die, aren't we?"

Uriah wondered how much longer he could disguise the hatred he felt toward his king. "It will all work out, Your Majesty," he said calmly. "The Assyrians will come."

"But that's the trouble! Remember what Isaiah said? What if they don't come as allies? What if they attack us, too?"

"They will come to help us, Your Majesty. I'm sure of it. Don't listen to Isaiah. He's a fool."

Ahaz pushed his plate away and rose ponderously from his seat. "I don't want any more food. I'm going to the council chamber and wait for the reports." When Abijah rose to help him, Ahaz boldly kissed her. "Wait in my chambers," he said.

Uriah couldn't bear to see them together. He stood, doing his best to ignore Abijah, and followed the king out of the banquet hall and across the open courtyard. The air felt cooler now that the sun had set and the first few stars appeared in the sky above their heads. Uriah wished he didn't have to go inside. He longed to walk slowly up the hill to the Temple Mount and enjoy the stars' dazzling brilliance from the highest point in the city. Instead, he followed the king into the council chamber and sat down on the dais at his right-hand side.

Ahaz waited to start the meeting until a servant filled his wine-glass. He drained it in one gulp and wiped his lips with the back of his hand. Uriah tried to recall how many times Ahaz had drained his cup during dinner, but they were too many to count. When the king finally spoke, his words came out slurred. "Let's get this over with. Somebody start."

The army chief rose to his feet, shuffling through his scrolls with quick, nervous gestures. "Our casualties have been light today—only 24 men killed and 17 wounded. But our supplies of weapons are getting dangerously low, and we don't seem to be recovering very many weapons from the enemy. They make sure every shot hits its mark. None are wasted."

As he droned on in a boring monotone of statistics, Uriah noticed that Ahaz wasn't listening. When the chief finished his report and sat down, several moments passed in silence as Ahaz gazed unseeingly into space. Uriah decided to take over, nodding to Ahaz's defense minister.

"We'll hear your report next."

"The enemy concentrated their assault against our most vulnerable area, the northwest gate," he began, making no attempt to disguise his anxiety. "We sustained only minor damage, but their repeated attempts to set the gates on fire were almost successful. We managed to douse the flames, but our water supplies are becoming critically low. In fact, there was nearly a riot at Solomon's Temple today when a mob tried to break through the gates to draw water from the bronze laver."

King Ahaz shouted a curse. "Do I have to take a sword and guard every cistern in this city myself? Doesn't anyone ever listen to me? I told you from the start of this cursed siege to post guards at all the cisterns and to ration the water!"

The defense minister spread his hands. "But, Your Majesty, every available soldier is needed to defend the walls."

Ahaz shouted another curse. "No wonder we're in such a sorry state! I give orders that nobody bothers to follow!" He turned on his defense minister in a rage. "Get out! Get out of my sight right now!"

The atmosphere was tense as the minister gathered up his things and hastily left the room. Uriah knew it was his job to appease Ahaz. And for the good of the country, he shouldn't allow the king to make any decisions when he was this drunk.

"Your Majesty," he said soothingly, "you shouldn't have to listen to this. It's upsetting you. I'll finish hearing the reports for you, and we can decide what measures need to be taken in the morning, after you've rested. A weary king will be no help to his nation, my lord."

He took Ahaz's arm and pulled him to his feet, then led him to the door as if he were a child. It didn't take much to convince Ahaz. He stumbled from the room, allowing Uriah to steer him to his chambers. Too late, Uriah remembered that Abijah was waiting inside.

"Send my servants in here with some more wine," Ahaz said, slurring his words. "You have no idea what unbearable pressure I'm under."

"Get some rest, Your Majesty. I'll take care of everything." But as Uriah turned to leave, Ahaz suddenly clutched his arm.

"Are sacrifices being offered night and day?" he asked. "To Baal . . . Asherah . . . Molech? *All* the gods?"

Uriah felt his patience being strained to its limits. He drew a deep breath. "Listen, Your Majesty. There is very little wood, and we can't spare many animals because of the siege—"

"Check on it!" Ahaz ordered. "I want sacrifices! Make sure none of the gods is being offended!"

"I'll see to it, Your Majesty. Rest well."

Uriah hurried away, wondering what he would do if Ahaz ordered another sacrifice to Molech. It was impossible at the moment with enemy troops camped in the Hinnom Valley. But what about when the siege ended? He remembered how Ahaz's sons had cowered in fear, and his revulsion for the king was so great that Uriah wanted to keep walking, past the council chamber, out of the palace, back to the Temple of Yahweh on the hill above the city. But the king's advisors were waiting for him in the council room. Uriah was second in command of the nation.

He passed a trembling hand over his face and straightened his shoulders, then strode into the council chamber to take his place as head of Judah's royal court.

————

When Ahaz opened his eyes, slivers of sunlight were streaming through his shutters, intensifying the pain that throbbed behind his eyes. He could remember nothing of the night before, but he found himself on the couch in his sitting room. His body ached from sleeping in such a cramped position. He groaned, and when he tried to sit up, his stomach churned as the room spun.

"Your Majesty?"

The voice startled him, echoing loudly through his head. He tried to focus on a blurred figure standing in his doorway.

"Who is it? What do you want?"

"It's Uriah, Your Majesty."

Ahaz groaned and covered his eyes to stop the pain. "More bad news of the siege, no doubt," he mumbled, remembering the unfinished reports from the night before. "Just go away. I can't take this anymore."

But as Uriah approached the couch, his stony features, usually unreadable, were curiously cheerful. "Your Majesty, they're leaving!"

"Who's leaving? What are you talking about?" Ahaz's mouth tasted sour and dry. He searched for a drink of wine and spied a half-empty goblet on the table beside his couch.

"The armies outside the walls have broken camp. They're retreating."

"What?" Ahaz forgot about the wine and struggled to his feet, trying to comprehend Uriah's words. As they slowly penetrated his foggy mind, he wondered if this were a cruel joke designed to send him over the brink of sanity. "Are you telling the truth?" He grabbed the front of Uriah's tunic with both hands and tried to shake him, but the brawny priest didn't budge. "Are they really leaving?"

"Yes, Your Majesty," he replied calmly. "It's the truth. Come to the wall and see for yourself."

Ahaz released his grip and eased down onto the edge of his couch. "So. They've come at last. My plan worked. The Assyrians came to our defense."

"Yes—they're probably attacking Aram from the north. The Arameans obviously received word of an invasion and have gone back to defend their own land. It's over."

Ahaz breathed a sigh of relief as he felt some of the strain lift from him for the first time in months. It was over. He had survived. Now he could return to his accustomed lifestyle and leave all the day-to-day decisions to Uriah.

"No one will dare attack my country now that Assyria is our ally," he said. "Molech answered my prayers, Uriah. I paid a great price for Molech's favor, but it was worth it, wasn't it?"

Uriah remained silent. Ahaz never could decipher the high priest's thoughts, and his stony silences made Ahaz nervous. He waved his hand, dismissing Uriah. "Thank you for the news. You may go."

When he was alone again, Ahaz slumped back on his couch, silently planning the feast of celebration he would hold. He smiled as tantalizing visions of revelry danced before him. But his smile faded as he recalled his cousin Isaiah's words: *"Your hands are full of blood . . . you will be devoured by the sword."*

Ahaz's mood darkened. He glanced at his hands as he reached for his wine goblet, as if expecting to see blood on them. He took a gulp, but the warm wine tasted like vinegar, and he spewed it out in disgust, cursing Isaiah for intruding on his thoughts like an unwanted guest.

Gradually, Ahaz became aware of shouts coming from the courtyard below his window. He crossed the room and cautiously peered between the wooden slats. News of the retreat seemed to be spreading like a grass fire throughout Jerusalem, and the relieved citizens emerged from their homes into the streets to celebrate.

The siege was over. Nothing was going to spoil his mood today, least of all Isaiah, whose prophecies of doom had obviously proved worthless. He rang for his servants. It was time to get dressed. He must lead his nation in a celebration of victory.

----

The shofar sounded, announcing the morning sacrifice as Abijah left the palace and hurried up the hill to the Temple. The long siege of Jerusalem was finally over, and she was eager to attend the daily worship services again. This morning her heart overflowed with praise to God for answering all of her prayers. Her nation's crisis had ended and Ahaz wouldn't need to offer any more sacrifices to Molech. But more than that, Abijah wanted to thank Yahweh for healing her son.

Hezekiah was fully recovered—his fears forgotten, his nightmares a thing of the past. He had grown very close to Zechariah over the past few months, almost as if he imagined that his grandfather was Yahweh and would protect him from any danger. Zechariah still lived in the palace, still slept in Eliab's bed every night. Abijah didn't know how Ahaz would respond if he ever found out, but she had taken care to keep her father's presence a secret.

As Abijah made her way to the women's courtyard to watch the sacrifice, she was surprised to see that the Temple grounds looked nearly deserted. The invading armies had just retreated, the city had been spared—why hadn't more people come to offer their thanks to God? In fact, why hadn't her husband, the king of Judah, come?

It seemed to Abijah that worship at Yahweh's Temple had declined very rapidly since she was a child coming to watch with her mother—and that idolatry had flourished since Ahaz had reigned. She felt a stab of guilt, knowing that she had also neglected to worship God after her marriage. But that would change from now on. Yahweh had answered her prayers, saving Hezekiah from Molech and restoring him to normal again. Abijah would praise God for that as long as she lived.

She heard a lamb bleating and saw one of the Levites leading the animal toward the altar where the priest stood waiting. But she had to close her eyes as the priest slit the lamb's throat, her stomach too queasy to witness the bloodshed. Years ago, her father had recited the story of Abraham offering his son, Isaac, to Yahweh—and how Yahweh had provided a ram in Isaac's place. *"Every time you hear the sound of the ram's horn,"* Zechariah had told her, *"remember that God himself will provide a sacrifice for our sins."*

She opened her eyes in time to watch the priest sprinkle the blood on the altar, and she remembered Moses and the story of the first Passover. The lambs had died in place of Israel's firstborn sons, the blood marking the doorposts so that the Angel of Death would pass over those houses. Abijah wondered how her nation could have forgotten the stories of Abraham and Isaac and Moses so quickly. How could they offer their sons to Molech in order to save themselves?

"Give thanks to the Lord for He is good," the priest chanted, and Abijah murmured the response out loud: "His love endures forever."

"Give thanks to Him who struck down the firstborn of Egypt and freed us from our enemies."

"His love endures forever." This morning Abijah felt God's love shining down on her as warmly as the sun, blessing her and her son.

The priest ascended the ramp and placed the sacrifice on the altar. The aroma of roasting meat reached Abijah a few moments later, and she recalled yet another reason to give thanks to God: She was going to have another baby. The child could never take Eliab's place, but he would be someone for Abijah to hold and love, offering her a new reason to hope.

"Thank you, Lord, for this new life," she whispered as the priest lifted his hands in prayer. "May all of my children live to serve you."

# 7

ZECHARIAH PULLED THE HEAVY curtains into place over the window of Hezekiah's bedchamber and lit the oil lamp. It sputtered to life, casting flickering light in the darkened room. He watched Hezekiah settle into bed and pull up the covers.

"Grandpa, will you sing for me?" he asked sleepily. Hezekiah gazed up at him with solemn brown eyes, and Zechariah felt his heart constrict. How he had grown to love this child in the past few months!

At first they had clung to each other, each one needy in his own way. But in time, with the siege over and the threat of Molech a mere memory, bonds of love had replaced the cords of need. Zechariah bent to smooth the covers into place around him.

"Yes, of course. Close your eyes now, and I'll sing until you fall asleep."

"Okay," Hezekiah yawned.

Zechariah sat on the edge of the bed and closed his eyes. He hummed softly for a moment, his body swaying slightly in rhythm, then he began to sing the slow, haunting melody.

"'I love you, O Lord, my strength. The Lord is my rock, my

fortress and my deliverer; my God is my rock, in whom I take refuge—'"

"Grandpa?"

Zechariah stopped short when Hezekiah interrupted. "What is it, son?"

"Can Yahweh close His mouth?"

"What? Why do you ask about Yahweh's mouth, child?"

Hezekiah sat up in bed, peering intently at Zechariah. "Because Molech never closes *his* mouth. I think he must get tired of holding it open all the time." Hezekiah spread his mouth wide and made a menacing face in an imitation of the fire god. "Is Yahweh's mouth like that, too? Can Yahweh close His mouth?"

Zechariah couldn't help smiling. His delight in his grandson and his deep love for him welled up inside until it burst forth in laughter. Zechariah's life had been arid for so long that he couldn't recall the last time he had laughed. He only knew that it felt good, like the first cup of cold water from the Gihon Spring after the long siege had ended.

"No, son," Zechariah replied at last, "Yahweh's mouth isn't open all the time like Molech's."

"Well, what does Yahweh look like? Can you show me His statue sometime?"

Zechariah stroked Hezekiah's curly hair. It felt thick and silky beneath his hand. "There is no statue, son. One of Yahweh's commandments is that we must never try to make an image of Him."

"Why not?"

"Well, because Yahweh is so . . . so. . . ." He gestured helplessly as he searched for the right words to describe God. "We could never put all of Yahweh's greatness into a mere statue. Besides, no one has seen God. No one knows what He looks like. We only know that we are made in His image."

Hezekiah fidgeted, as if struggling to comprehend. "But,

Grandpa, how do you know that Yahweh is real if you can't see Him?"

The simple question struck Zechariah like a hammer blow. He was speechless. The joy he had felt a moment ago vanished, replaced by fear. He was a Levite. He had once instructed priests and counseled the king. Now he couldn't even answer a child's simple question. He was terrified to try.

"Hezekiah," he said softly, "you need to go to sleep now. You would like to keep me up all night with your questions, wouldn't you?"

Hezekiah tugged on Zechariah's sleeve. "But, Grandpa—"

"No, son. Go to sleep, and I promise . . . I promise we'll talk about Yahweh in the morning." He motioned for Hezekiah to lie down, then smoothed the covers into place around him again. Zechariah turned away to avoid his grandson's probing eyes, ashamed of his cowardice. "Good night," he mumbled.

"Good night, Grandpa."

Zechariah cleared his throat to continue singing, but suddenly Yahweh seemed very far away again, the gulf between them unbridgeable. His voice trembled slightly as he began.

"'Yahweh is my shield and the horn of my salvation, my . . . my—'" He stumbled over the words, momentarily confused. Hezekiah's question still haunted him. How could he prove the existence of a God he couldn't see? "'My stronghold. I call to the Lord, who is worthy of praise, and I am saved from my enemies.'"

He continued singing in the darkness, his body rocking gently in rhythm with the verse. Because it was a nightly ritual he knew the words, but they were empty words to him. He no longer knew the answers. His inadequacy and failure shamed him.

Before long he became aware that the pattern of Hezekiah's breathing had changed as he'd fallen asleep.

"'In my distress I called to the Lord; I cried to my God for help. . . .'" Zechariah sang.

*O Yahweh, I'm calling to you for help now,* Zechariah prayed silently. *Hezekiah asks how I know you are there. What shall I tell him? O Yahweh, help me!*

"'. . . From his temple he heard my voice; my cry came before him, into his ears . . .'"

*God? Do you really hear my cry? Please help me,* he prayed.

In the fading lamplight, Hezekiah's dark hair had a coppery cast. As Zechariah tenderly brushed a curl away from his face, he felt his love for Hezekiah like a deep ache in his heart. The boy's soul had been healed, his nightmares forgotten. But he had never asked questions about Yahweh before.

As he sat in the silent darkness, Zechariah's love for Hezekiah twisted into a knot of pain inside him, and he fell on his face to the floor in desperation.

"Almighty God, have mercy on this small boy. Send someone to teach him about you. Please don't let him walk in the ways of Ahaz. Don't punish him for the sins of his father—and grandfather. Mold him into your servant, Lord. Hear me, I pray."

The stars moved silently across the heavens as the city slept. A breeze rustled past the curtain, and the oil lamp sputtered, then died. Zechariah never noticed. With his forehead pressed to the floor, he cried out to God throughout the night, praying as he hadn't prayed for many years.

"Please send someone to teach him, Lord. I can't do it. You had mercy on me before and answered my prayer. I asked for forgiveness, and you gave it to me. Now I ask for your help again, even though I'm not worthy to call on you. Please, please, teach him your laws. Let him grow up to serve you, I pray."

At dawn, as the sun inched from behind the Mount of Olives in the east, Zechariah lay exhausted and still. He had no words left to pray. The knotted burden in his heart had been unbound. In the darkened room he could barely see Hezekiah's bed a few feet in front of him, but he heard him breathing softly.

Then in the silence, from somewhere deep inside Zechariah's soul, Yahweh spoke.

*"You will teach him, Zechariah."*

"No, I can't, Lord, I can't! I failed with Uzziah, and I don't want to fail again. Not with Hezekiah. Not with him. I love him, God. I love him, and I can't . . . I can't."

But the voice of Yahweh spoke in his heart once again to still his protests.

*"Sing the rest of the psalm."*

That was all.

Zechariah began to tremble. His heart raced as he struggled to recall which psalm he had sung to Hezekiah earlier that night.

"'My God turns my darkness into light,'" he whispered, remembering. "'With your help I can advance against a troop; with my God I can scale a wall. . . . It is God who arms me with strength and makes my way perfect.'"

Tears slipped down Zechariah's cheeks. Yahweh had spoken to him again! Zechariah tried to remember the last time he had heard that powerful, tender voice speaking to his heart. It seemed like a lifetime ago. He, like Uriah, had been newly appointed to be palace administrator. Zechariah's first love had been the Law—God's holy, precious Torah. But through the years another mistress slowly took its place: his pride—pride in his own achievements and in the recognition he received before the entire nation.

Suddenly he understood why he had failed with King Uzziah. He had relied on his own knowledge, his own strength, and it hadn't been enough. He had stopped seeking God's strength and wisdom. Zechariah covered his face in shame.

"Forgive me, Yahweh. Forgive my foolish pride."

The sun rose steadily to the top of the Mount of Olives and crept over the ridge, flooding around the edges of the curtains. Hezekiah stirred slightly and sighed in his sleep. Zechariah rose to his feet and gazed down at his grandson.

He resembled his mother so much, with Abijah's dark hair and eyes. Ahaz was ruddy and fair, like the house of David, but Hezekiah wasn't like him. Zechariah closed his eyes again in prayer. "Make him different in spirit, too. Help me to teach him about you. Help me, give me wisdom!"

Fear began to knot his stomach again, but Yahweh's wisdom spoke louder than Zechariah's fear as he recalled the words of the Proverbs: *"Trust in the Lord with all your heart and lean not on your own understanding; in all your ways acknowledge Him, and he will make your paths straight."*

"Thank you," Zechariah prayed softly. "We will teach Hezekiah. You and I, Lord—we will teach him."

When Hezekiah awoke, blinding sunlight was streaming into his room. He sat up, rubbing his eyes, and saw that his grandfather had thrown open the curtains that covered his window.

" 'The heavens declare the glory of the Lord!' " Zechariah shouted. He gestured toward the sun and sky, the green and brown hills outside the window. " 'The skies proclaim the work of his hands!' " He folded his arms across his chest as if nothing more needed to be said. Hezekiah stared at his grandfather in surprise, too sleepy to comprehend.

"Listen, son, last night you asked how we know that Yahweh is really there. All we need to do is open our eyes and see all the marvelous things He has created. The *heavens* declare His glory!" Zechariah crossed the room and gently urged Hezekiah out of bed, dressing him in his robe and sandals as he talked.

"The sun, the moon, the stars, the rolling hills and valleys around us—they all speak to us of God's glory. Yet the greatest miracle of all is that we are made in His image. Come on, son. Today I will teach you about Yahweh, our God."

Hezekiah remembered how his grandfather had seemed unwilling to talk about Yahweh last night—almost as if he was afraid. But this morning Zechariah's face glowed with excitement. Hezekiah couldn't imagine what had brought about such a change in him, but he sensed that they were about to start on a great adventure, and he ran to open the door, eager to begin.

He skipped ahead of Zechariah, running down the stairs and through the palace hallways, wishing his grandfather would walk faster. But he stopped to wait for him by the main doors, and as he watched him striding forward, he decided that Yahweh must look like his grandfather—tall and strong, with a flowing beard. Yahweh's eyes must be just as wise and kind, his face noble and dignified like Zechariah's. As his grandfather walked toward him he smiled and reached to take Hezekiah's hand.

"Where are we going, Grandpa?"

"I want to take a walk outside the city where we can see Yahweh's creation."

"Okay." Hezekiah would follow his grandfather wherever he led him. He felt safe and happy when they were together.

The city had just awakened from sleep as they left the palace hand in hand and walked down the hill through the streets. The air was smoky with the first fires of the day and filled with the sounds of grinding hand mills and crowing roosters. In the marketplace a merchant shouted threats at his servant as they hastily piled goods for their first customers. Zechariah stopped at a market stand and bought two barley buns and a handful of dates. Hezekiah ate them while they walked, spitting out the pits.

As they approached the Valley Gate, Zechariah pointed to a little shrine that had been set up along one of the streets. It was a statue of a fierce-looking man holding a lightning bolt. Offerings of food and flowers lay spread at his feet.

"See that?" he asked Hezekiah. "People make altars like these to worship their idols. But idols aren't gods at all—they're only statues made by human hands and human imaginations. There is only *one*

God, Hezekiah. You know Him by the name of Yahweh, the God of salvation."

The little image was half as tall as Hezekiah and looked harmless enough. But he shuddered at the thought of facing Molech's blazing image again and gripped Zechariah's hand a little tighter.

When they reached the Valley Gate, they left the walled city, following the course of the aqueduct up the Gihon Valley to the spring. Hezekiah recognized it as the route he had taken with his father the first time they had met the prophet Isaiah. Terraced olive groves and vineyards swirled down the rocky slopes of the mountains to the east, the tree branches drooping under the weight of ripening fruit. A herd of goats clambered over the rocks beneath the city walls, scrambling to find the sparse clumps of grass that grew among the stones. When Zechariah reached the spring, he stopped.

"Have you ever seen the wind, Hezekiah?"

He shook his head. "Nobody can see the wind, Grandpa."

"Then how do you know it's there?" Zechariah folded his arms across his chest and smiled.

Hezekiah looked up at him, puzzled by the question. "Because I can feel it blowing on me," he said with a shrug.

"Ah! You've never seen the wind, but you know it's there because you see evidence of what it does—how it ripples through the golden seas of wheat and rustles through the tree branches. And you can feel it cooling you on a hot summer day. Well, it's the same with Yahweh. You and I have never seen Him, but we can see evidence of where His hand has touched our lives—like when He saved you from Molech. And we can hear Him speaking to our hearts—the way He spoke to you through His prophet Isaiah. And if you reach out to Him, Hezekiah, you will feel His touch on your life and on everything that you do. He's the Creator of life, the Creator of everything there is."

Zechariah spread his arms wide and shouted to the hills and fields, "'Hear, O Israel! Yahweh is God—Yahweh alone! Love Yahweh your

God with all your heart and with all your soul and with all your strength!'"

He looked down at Hezekiah, and they grinned at each other as the goats on the hillside bleated in response to Zechariah's shouts.

"Those words are the *Shema,* our covenant with Yahweh," Zechariah told him. "You must learn those words and never, ever forget them: 'Hear, O Israel. Yahweh is God—Yahweh alone.'"

They sat down together on a low stone wall near the spring and watched as serving girls stooped to fill their jugs with water, then carried them up the ramp, balanced on their heads. Hezekiah looked up at the steep cliffs and city walls that towered above him. They formed a powerful stronghold against the enemy, and he felt vulnerable outside them. Molech lived in the valley outside those walls.

Hezekiah inched closer to his grandfather for reassurance, then closed his eyes and tilted his face toward the sky. As he felt the sun warming his cheeks, he remembered the heat of Molech's flames. The fire god's strength and power could be seen and felt; Yahweh, who was unseen, offered no such evidence of strength. Hezekiah felt safe beside Zechariah, but he longed to be certain that Yahweh's power was greater than Molech's. He looked up at Zechariah again.

"Grandpa, is Yahweh strong?"

"Yes, son. Of course He is."

"But is He really, *really* strong?"

"Yahweh has all the strength you'll ever need in your life. That's what your name means in Hebrew, Hezekiah—'the Lord is my strength.'"

Hezekiah wanted to believe him, but he also wanted a strength he could see and touch. "But if you can't see Yahweh," he persisted, "how do you know how strong He is?"

Zechariah drew a deep breath, pausing before he answered as if searching for the right words. "Don't be fooled by strength you can see," he said at last. "Yahweh often hides His power in the simple things, the weak things, and so His strength seems foolish in man's eyes. Shall I tell you a story about Yahweh's power?"

"Yes!" Hezekiah loved to hear stories. He nestled close to his grandfather, leaning against him.

"Our enemies once had a champion warrior," Zechariah began, "a giant man named Goliath who stood more than nine feet tall. All of our soldiers were terrified of him."

Hezekiah remembered the huge high priest who had led the sacrifice to Molech. As Zechariah told the story, Hezekiah pictured Uriah as the giant Goliath.

"Now your ancestor King David was just a boy like you," Zechariah continued, "but he volunteered to fight the giant."

"Did David have a sword, Grandpa?"

"No, he was too little for a sword and armor. All he had was a shepherd's sling and five smooth stones."

"Was he scared?"

"Not at all! The king and all of the soldiers in Israel's army were afraid of Goliath, but David had faith in Yahweh, his God. That's because when David worked as a shepherd, guarding his father's sheep, Yahweh had helped him kill a lion one time, and a bear another time. David knew all about Yahweh's strength. He shouted to Goliath, 'You come against me with a sword and a spear, but I come against you in the name of the Lord Almighty!'"

Hezekiah could barely sit still as he imagined the lop-sided contest—a giant like Uriah against a small boy like himself. "Who won, Grandpa? Who won?"

"Yahweh won, of course! David put a stone in his slingshot and hurled it at Goliath before the giant even had a chance to draw his sword. The stone hit Goliath right in the middle of the forehead, and he crashed to the ground. You see, Goliath made a mistake when he sneered at the size of his opponent. David was just a boy, but he had Yahweh on his side—even though no one could see Him—and Yahweh's power can help you conquer even the strongest enemy!"

Hezekiah smiled as he pictured himself defeating the huge high priest with Yahweh's help. "What else did Yahweh help David do? Tell me another story!" he begged.

Zechariah laughed and hugged him. "Well, now, let me think. Do you see how tall and strong those city walls are above us?" he finally asked, pointing to them. "When David grew up, he wanted to conquer the city of Jerusalem so he could build a temple for Yahweh. But Jerusalem was a strong fortress, and it belonged to the wicked Jebusites. They taunted David, saying, 'You'll never get inside these walls!' But—"

"David got in, didn't he, Grandpa!"

"Yes, he did," Zechariah replied, laughing again. "You see, Jerusalem has one weak spot—the water supply. This Gihon Spring is outside the city walls. Remember how we had to ration water during the siege?"

"It tasted bad," Hezekiah said, making a face. "I didn't like it."

"You're right, it did taste stale. Well, the Jebusites had decided to dig a secret water shaft from the city down to the spring so they could draw water from it during a siege. But Yahweh led David to the secret tunnel, and some of his men climbed up it. That's how David's army got into the city."

"Is the tunnel still there, Grandpa?"

"I don't think so. That was hundreds of years ago. David probably sealed it up so his enemies wouldn't crawl through it the same way he did."

The day was growing hotter as the sun climbed higher in the sky. Hezekiah didn't mind, but he saw Zechariah mop his brow as he rose to his feet. "I guess we'd better head back, son."

Hezekiah hesitated. He needed to know one more thing about Yahweh, and he summoned all his courage to ask it. "Grandpa, does Yahweh want sacrifices, too?"

Zechariah squatted down to face him. "Yes, Yahweh also asks his people for sacrifices. But He forbids us to kill our own children. We sacrifice lambs or—"

"Does Yahweh eat the lambs like Molech eats people?"

"No, son, He doesn't eat them."

"Then why does Yahweh want them?"

Zechariah drew a deep breath. "Because when we sin, we deserve to die. But Yahweh allows us to sacrifice a lamb to pay for our sins, instead. The lamb dies in our place."

Hezekiah felt tears burning in his eyes as he remembered Molech's sacrifice. "Amariah died instead of me," he said softly. "I was really the firstborn son."

Zechariah drew him into his arms. "Yes, your brother is gone. But I thank God that you're alive."

Hezekiah clung to his grandfather for a long moment, feeling safe and content. "Will you tell me more stories about Yahweh tomorrow?" he asked.

"Yes, I'll tell you dozens of stories tomorrow—and the next day and the next." Zechariah took his hand again as they started walking up the steep path toward the Water Gate. "Come on, Hezekiah—say the Shema with me this time. 'Hear, O Israel . . .'"

"Say it louder, Grandpa," Hezekiah begged. "Make the goats bellow again."

" 'HEAR, O ISRAEL," Zechariah shouted. "YAHWEH IS GOD—YAHWEH ALONE!'"

# 8

ABIJAH STOOD AT THE window in her husband's chambers, staring down at the figures waiting in the courtyard below. The Judean soldiers looked hot and disgruntled after standing in the courtyard fully armed for almost an hour waiting for King Ahaz to descend the palace steps so the journey could begin. The horses stamped the ground impatiently and strained at their bits, while behind them, the caravan of slaves and pack mules stood loaded and waiting, the mules tossing their heads and pulling at their tethering ropes.

The Assyrian soldiers heading up the caravan seemed the most restless of all as they waited silently in their ranks. They had arrived in Jerusalem without warning to summon King Ahaz to a meeting with their emperor, Tiglath-Pileser. Ahaz's enemy, Aram, had been destroyed, and Tiglath-Pileser's message ordered Ahaz to follow the Assyrian soldiers to the ruined capital of Damascus immediately. Abijah didn't really care about all of the politics—she couldn't wait to be rid of Ahaz for a few months, to be free from the need to pretend to be his loving wife.

She heard Uriah clear his throat and turned to study him, wondering if he was as eager for Ahaz to leave as she was. Uriah appeared calm and serene as he stood with his arms folded across his chest, watching the king, but she could tell by the way he clenched his jaw that he was losing patience. Ahaz's dawdling seemed deliberate as he took his time choosing robes and finery for his trip, changing his mind every few minutes and ordering his servants around in circles. Whenever Uriah managed to catch the attention of one of the servants, he would glare at him as if hoping to frighten him into moving faster. But his efforts were useless. Ahaz simply wouldn't be rushed. Finally, Uriah seemed to reach the end of his patience.

"Your Majesty, the caravan has been waiting—"

"Let them wait. I'm not ready."

"But the journey to Damascus will be a long one, and you should make the most of the daylight hours."

Ahaz turned on him angrily. "I am about to leave on a very important diplomatic mission. I'll be meeting with the great emperor Tiglath-Pileser. I will *not* be rushed." He turned back to finish primping in front of his bronze mirror.

"But, Your Majesty, the Assyrian ambassadors arrived more than a week ago to summon you. You really should—"

"Don't you see?" Ahaz interrupted. "I'm finally getting the international recognition I deserve. The emperor of the most powerful nation on earth wishes to meet with me." He smiled at himself in the mirror. "We're allies. We'll be sitting in counsel together—discussing the nations of the world, signing treaties as equals, pledging our support to one another. I must look my best." He adjusted the folds of his embroidered robe and turned sideways, admiring himself.

Uriah stared at the king in disbelief. Abijah could guess what he was thinking. Ahaz was a fool to imagine that he would sit as an equal with the king who had just rescued him from a bloody invasion and siege. Even she could see that. She heard Uriah draw a deep breath as if steeling himself before he spoke.

"Your Majesty, you've formed an alliance with Assyria, but that doesn't mean—"

"You've heard the reports of what our Assyrian friends have done for us, haven't you, my dear?" Ahaz asked, turning to Abijah. "They've conquered Aram and deported their population. The Arameans' allies have surrendered rather than meet the same fate. And now the Assyrians want to meet with me."

"That's my point, Your Majesty," Uriah said. He took a step toward Ahaz, gesturing as he pleaded with him. "With such obvious power and military strength, surely you can't possibly think—"

But Abijah could tell that Ahaz wasn't listening. He interrupted Uriah to bark a new set of orders at his exhausted servants, then added, "I will always be remembered as one of Judah's greatest kings."

Uriah gave up trying to reason with him and turned away. Abijah forced herself to go to her husband's side, reminding herself that for a few blessed weeks she would be free of him.

"You look magnificent, my lord," she said as she smoothed the folds of his robe, "and as regal as any king in the world." Even as she said the words, Abijah felt like a hypocrite. It embarrassed her to have Uriah see her with Ahaz, even though she knew it was foolish—she was Ahaz's wife. And lately the king had wanted her with him as often as possible, relying on her for comfort and companionship. With her father helping Hezekiah, it had become more important than ever for Abijah to remain close to Ahaz, distracting him. She only wished that she could tell Uriah it was all an act. Instead, she felt humiliated every time Ahaz caressed her in front of him.

At last Ahaz decided he was ready. "Come outside with me, Uriah, and see my procession off," he said. "You come, too, my dear."

Abijah followed him outside, standing with Uriah on the palace steps as trumpets announced the king's appearance. Nobles and elders bowed before him in obeisance as Ahaz surveyed the waiting caravan with pride. The Assyrian soldiers, sent to escort him to Damascus, stood in tight, well-disciplined ranks, ready to lead the procession.

Behind them, Ahaz's personal chariot stood harnessed to a team of six horses. It would carry Ahaz, his driver, and the valet who would attend to his personal needs. Pack mules and slaves carried equipment for the journey, as well as more gifts for the Assyrian king. The remainder of the Judean army, meager as it was, served as a rear guard.

The crowd greeted Ahaz, shouting, "Long live the king!" Abijah knew how much her husband loved all the regal trappings and splendor. He was probably savoring every moment. But as the king mounted his chariot, a voice suddenly shouted above the murmuring crowd.

"Your Majesty! King Ahaz, wait!"

She saw the king's good mood turn to rage as Isaiah pushed his way through the crowd, hurrying toward the chariot. She heard Uriah groan, and he bounded down the steps, elbowing his way through the mob toward the prophet.

"No! I refuse to listen to you," Ahaz shouted. "I won't let you ruin this day with your useless cries of doom and ruin. Is Jerusalem destroyed? Has the enemy defeated us? No, because your words were nonsense. I've entered into a covenant with Assyria. I've made an agreement with Tiglath-Pileser. Nobody can defeat us now. You're nothing but a false prophet."

"Therefore hear the word of the Lord, you scoffers who rule this people in Jerusalem," Isaiah cried. He stood beside the king's chariot with dignity, his voice steady as he mimicked Ahaz's words. "You boast, 'We've entered into a covenant with death, we've made an agreement with the grave. When an overwhelming scourge sweeps by, it can't touch us, because we've made a lie our refuge and falsehood our hiding place.'"

"I told you I don't want to hear any more!" Ahaz's face was flushed with rage. He signaled to his driver, but the chariot couldn't move until the ranks in front of it moved.

"This is what the Sovereign Lord says," Isaiah continued, shouting loud enough for the gathered crowd to hear. "'Hail will sweep away your refuge, the lie, and water will overflow your hiding place. Your covenant with death will be annulled; your agreement with the grave will not stand.'"

Uriah finally reached Isaiah's side, and he grabbed the prophet by the arms, trying to drag him away from Ahaz's chariot. But they made little progress in the crowded street, and Isaiah continued to shout as they struggled.

"The understanding of this message will bring sheer terror, King Ahaz. The bed will be too short to stretch out on, the blanket too narrow to wrap around you."

"You're a *fool*!" Ahaz shouted. "You don't know what you're talking about—beds that are too short! I have an important journey ahead of me, a trip that will have lasting significance for this nation long after you're gone."

"Stop your mocking," Isaiah shouted back, "or your chains will become even heavier. The Lord Almighty has told me of the destruction decreed against this whole land."

His words sent a chill through Abijah's veins. She had hoped that her nation was finally out of danger, her children safe. But what if Isaiah's words proved true and their troubles were only beginning? What would happen to Hezekiah—and to the baby who would be born in a few months? She rested her hands on her stomach and closed her eyes for a moment, praying as she did every day that Yahweh would keep her children safe.

Ahaz's signal to start finally reached the head of the caravan, and the black-bearded Assyrian soldiers set off at a brisk pace. The crowds parted to let them pass, the people cheering their king and drowning out Isaiah's warnings. But the prophet's words echoed in Abijah's heart long after the procession disappeared from sight.

---

A cold, damp rain fell over Jerusalem and low-hanging clouds hid the surrounding hills from view. But Hezekiah didn't care about the chilly morning weather as he skipped through the wet streets, splashing his sandals in all of the puddles, splattering muddy water over his ankles and feet.

"Watch where you're walking," his mother scolded. "You're getting your feet all wet." But she was smiling, and Hezekiah knew that she wasn't really angry. He ran back to where she and Zechariah had halted as they paused to catch their breath.

"Please hurry up," he begged as he ran in circles around them. "We're going to be late and miss the morning sacrifice."

"We'll be on time, son. Don't worry," Zechariah said.

"I want to see all of it, Grandpa."

"I know. We're almost there now. See that wall?" he asked, pointing. "That's the top of the Temple enclosure."

Hezekiah took each of them by the hand and tugged them forward. "Please hurry!"

"I can't climb any faster," his grandfather said. "This damp air makes my bones ache."

"You promised to take me to the Temple a long time ago."

"I know, I know. But we had to wait for the right time, son."

"I'm not sure your father would approve if he knew that we were taking you to Yahweh's Temple," his mother added. "But he left for Damascus yesterday."

Hezekiah felt a delicious thrill at the thought of sharing a secret with his mother and grandfather. The fact that his father might not approve made it even more exciting. "Why doesn't he want me to come here?" he asked. "Because he worships Molech?"

"Well, yes. That's part of it," Zechariah replied.

"Doesn't he worship Yahweh, too?"

"Your father can't do both, remember? 'Hear O Israel. Yahweh is our God—Yahweh alone.'"

Hezekiah remembered. It was the first thing that Zechariah had taught him. "Will you take me inside the Temple after the sacrifice, Grandpa?"

"Well, remember now—only the priests can go into the holy sanctuary."

"I know. But we can go inside where you live, can't we?" Zechariah had told him that Yahweh's Temple was the most wonderful place on earth, and Hezekiah was eager to see all of it.

"I'll show you everything I can," Zechariah promised.

Hezekiah dropped their hands again. They were walking much too slowly. His mother ruffled his hair, and Hezekiah darted off in search of another puddle.

"Don't get your feet all wet," she called. But it was much too late to heed her warning. Hezekiah's feet were already wonderfully drenched.

At last they reached the top of the hill and passed through the gate into the Temple's outer courtyard. Hezekiah could see the roof of the sanctuary up ahead. His mother left them to go into the women's court, warning him to stay with his grandfather. But as he and Zechariah walked around to the front of the building, which faced east, Hezekiah was shocked to see ugly wooden scaffolding covering the front of it. Yahweh's Temple didn't resemble the magnificent structure he had expected to see.

"Those are the bronze pillars I told you about," Zechariah said, pointing to the two massive columns that supported the porch of the sanctuary. "Do you remember their names?"

Hezekiah squinted his eyes as he tried to recall what Zechariah had taught him. "One is Boaz, and the other is . . . um . . . what is it again, Grandpa? I forgot."

"The other is Jakin: 'Yahweh establishes.' And Boaz means 'In Him is strength.'"

"Why are they all covered up with ugly boards?"

Zechariah gave a sigh that was almost a groan, and Hezekiah looked up at him. "Because your father wanted the bronze metal-work. I wish you could have seen those pillars before your father stripped them. They used to be overlaid with bronze and covered with magnificent carvings."

"Why did he take them all apart, Grandpa?"

"Because he needed presents to give to the king of Assyria, and he knew that the most beautiful treasures in the nation were here in Yahweh's Temple."

Hezekiah looked around and was surprised to see that only a handful of people had come to the sacrifice at the Temple. Thousands of people had followed the procession to the Valley of Hinnom to worship Molech, and he had expected at least as many people—even more.

"Where is everyone?" he asked Zechariah. "Why didn't they come to see Yahweh's sacrifice?"

Zechariah sighed again. "Because the people of Judah have turned away from worshiping Yahweh. They worship many false gods now, and they don't seem to know the difference. It's up to the king to lead the way, and the people will follow his example. But your father has turned his back on Yahweh."

"Why did he do that?"

Zechariah shook his head. "I don't know, son. I guess, in a way, I'm to blame, and I'm sorry."

Hezekiah didn't understand how his grandfather could be to blame. He was about to ask him about it when a plump little man hurried over to them, followed by a boy who was a few years older than Hezekiah and a head taller.

"Zechariah, my friend! Oh, praise the name of the Lord," the little man gushed. "It's so good to see you!" His brown eyes beamed with joy as the two men embraced. "This is my son, Eliakim," he said, gesturing to the boy. "I've been so worried about you, Zechariah. But you look wonderful! Wonderful!"

"I am a new man, Hilkiah—thanks be to God. I want you to meet my grandson, Prince Hezekiah."

Hilkiah immediately dropped to his knees to bow, pulling his star-

tled son down beside him. Their actions surprised Hezekiah. He
rarely left the palace and wasn't used to having people bow to him the
way they bowed to his father.

"Eliakim and I are honored to meet you," Hilkiah said. The two
stood up again, and the adults were soon deep in conversation, ignoring the boys. Hezekiah saw Eliakim studying him from head to toe.

"Are you really a prince?" he asked.

"Yes."

"Then King Ahaz is your father?"

"Yes."

"Why didn't he come to the sacrifice with you?" Eliakim fired his
questions so rapidly that Hezekiah barely had time to think before
answering.

"Um . . . he went to Damascus."

"Why did he go there?"

"To see another king, I think." Hezekiah turned away to watch
the activity in the courtyard, wishing that his grandfather would hurry
up and finish talking. A handful of priests and Levites had emerged
from a side door and were gathering beside a huge bronze altar.

"What does it feel like to be royalty?" Eliakim asked.

"I don't know," Hezekiah said with a shrug.

"Abba says that kings and princes have royal blood. Do you?"

"I guess so."

"Well, what does it look like?"

The only time Hezekiah had seen his own blood was when his
nose had bled a little. "It's dark red," he said, remembering.

"So is mine. How is royal blood any different, then?"

"I don't know," Hezekiah said, shrugging again. He had never
thought about being different before. But then, he had never met any
other children besides his brothers. And he'd never met anyone who
asked as many questions as Eliakim did.

"Are you going to be the king someday?" Eliakim continued.

Hezekiah hesitated, unwilling to admit that he was now Ahaz's firstborn son. "I don't know. Maybe."

"You'll get to stand on that platform over there by the pillars, if you do," Eliakim said, pointing to it. "What are you going to do when you're the king?"

Hezekiah answered with another shrug, hoping it would discourage more questions.

"I've never seen you here before," Eliakim said. "Is this your first time?"

"Yes."

"Are you going to come to the evening sacrifice, too?"

"Maybe."

"Abba and I come every day, morning and evening. I have to watch from out here because I'm not old enough to go into the men's court, yet. But after my next birthday I can worship with Abba and all the other men."

Zechariah had explained to Hezekiah that he would have to wait until he turned twelve before he'd be allowed to participate in the ritual, and now he found himself envying Eliakim because he was almost a man. He wondered what it would be like to have a father like Hilkiah who brought him to Yahweh's Temple twice a day. Suddenly one of the priests blew the shofar from high atop the temple wall. Hilkiah said good-bye and hurried off to join the other men in the inner court. Eliakim followed his father as far as the gate.

"We'll have to watch from out here, too," Zechariah reminded Hezekiah. He squatted down beside him and rested his hand on his shoulder, pointing to the activities taking place. The men had gathered around a huge basin of water, fifteen feet across and taller than his grandfather.

"First the men have to cleanse themselves at the Bronze Sea," Zechariah explained. "They confess their sins to Yahweh and wash to make themselves symbolically clean. The Sea used to stand on a base of twelve oxen made of brass, one for each tribe of Israel. Ah—they were so beautiful! They stood taller than you, and three faced east, three west, three north, and three south. They were magnificent!"

"What happened to them?"

"Your father took them, to give to the Assyrian king. Look now. See how the men are washing? They must cleanse their feet so they can walk uprightly before God, and their hands so that all their works will be clean in His sight, and their lips so that they will speak only words that are pure. Now they can go before the altar. Come on, let's move over here so we can see better."

He took Hezekiah's hand as they walked to the other side of the courtyard. There was no statue, no open mouth or waiting arms—only a huge, square altar looming in front of them, twice as high as a man's head. The air above it shimmered. When a gust of wind suddenly blew in his direction, Hezekiah felt the heat and smoke on his face, and he drew back in fear.

"I want to go home," he said.

"It's okay, son," Zechariah assured him. "You don't have to be afraid."

Hezekiah gripped his grandfather's hand tightly, fighting his fear and the strong memories that the sacrifice stirred.

One of the priests led a lamb over to the altar and Hezekiah saw the blade of a knife glinting in his hand. As the lamb twisted and strained against the rope, Hezekiah remembered the weight of the soldier's hands on his shoulders, preventing his escape. He remembered his brothers, Eliab and Amariah, and he blinked back tears.

"I want to go home," he said again.

Zechariah knelt to face him and took Hezekiah's hands in both of his. "Yahweh isn't like Molech, son. There's nothing to fear in His Temple. See how the men are laying their hands on the lamb's head? The lamb will take their place and bear all their sins. Blood has to be shed in order to pay for our sins, but the lamb's blood will be shed, not yours and mine."

When the last man lifted his hand from the animal's head, the priest swiftly slit its throat. The lamb stopped struggling and went limp as the bowl that the Levite held slowly filled with blood. Hezekiah felt sick. He closed his eyes so that he wouldn't have to watch.

Then above the murmur of voices and the hissing and crackling of the flames, Hezekiah heard his grandfather's familiar voice, singing along with the Levites' choir. The deep, rich tones comforted Hezekiah, and he opened his eyes and looked around. The Levite musicians had assembled on the steps of the sanctuary with their instruments, and Zechariah sang along with them: "'O Lord, how many are my foes! How many rise up against me! Many are saying of me, "God will not deliver him."'"

When Hezekiah looked at the lamb again, not much remained. The priest had swiftly skinned and gutted it, and as the men gathered around the great altar, one of the priests walked up the ramp with the offering. Another priest sprinkled the lamb's blood all around the base of the altar as the Levites sang: "'But you are a shield around me, O Lord; you bestow glory on me and lift up my head. To the Lord I cry aloud, and he answers me from his holy hill.'"

Hezekiah watched as the worshipers dropped to their knees, then fell forward together, their foreheads touching the wet pavement's stones. It was the same way people sometimes bowed before his father.

"'I lie down and sleep; I wake again, because the Lord sustains me. I will not fear the tens of thousands drawn up against me on every side.'"

When the men finished bowing, they looked up at the priest who stood ready to present the sacrifice. "'Arise, O Lord! Deliver me, O my God!'"

The priest placed the offering on the altar and stepped back as a pillar of flame soared high into the air. Hezekiah jumped back in surprise. No wonder Yahweh had power over Molech. He was also a God of fire.

"He is here!" all the men shouted. "He answers!"

Zechariah had assured him that Molech wasn't real, but Hezekiah still feared the monster that had killed his two brothers. But after seeing Yahweh's power in the pillar of fire, he was nearly convinced that this unseen God was every bit as strong.

The priests placed the remainder of the lamb on the altar, but there was no pillar of flame this time—only a plume of smoke and the sound of hissing coals. The aroma that drifted from Yahweh's fire smelled wonderfully sweet.

The worshipers all began to leave, and within minutes the courtyard stood deserted. The morning sacrifice was over, and now Hezekiah remembered his long-awaited tour of the Temple.

"Can we see the doors made of gold now?" he asked as Zechariah rose to his feet.

"Ah—the golden doors to the Holy Place. Yes, come on, then."

They went through the gates as the last of the worshipers came out and crossed the silent courtyard to the porch of the sanctuary. They had to squeeze past the wooden scaffolding in order to see the huge double doors to the Holy Place. But when Hezekiah finally reached them, the doors weren't golden at all. They stood stripped and bare, the wood gouged and scarred.

"They're not gold!" he said. "They're just plain old wood!" He felt Zechariah's hand on his shoulder.

"I'm sorry, son. I didn't know. I guess King Ahaz took that, too. Ah, Yahweh, forgive him."

Hezekiah felt cheated, his disappointment hitting him like a fist in the stomach. He followed Zechariah back across the courtyard and into the maze of Temple storerooms on the north side of the mount, but his enthusiasm for the tour had vanished. Zechariah tried to point out a few things along the way, but everything appeared dingy and drab to Hezekiah, with crumbling plaster and stringy cobwebs. When they came to a large storeroom, Zechariah seemed shocked to discover that the shelves were nearly empty. He looked around as if in a dream, then picked up a tarnished silver cup and tried to polish it against his sleeve.

"This was the treasury for the sacred vessels used in all the sacrifices," he said. "This room used to be full, but now . . . I guess every-thing was sent to Assyria." Zechariah stared blankly at the empty shelves as if forgetting that his grandson was there. Hezekiah tugged on his grandfather's sleeve to draw him back.

"What will the other king do with all of it, Grandpa?"

"I'm not really sure. Melt everything down, I suppose. I've also heard that heathen kings sometimes use holy vessels like these for drinking wine at feasts to their false gods. It hurts me to think of Yahweh's sacred things being used in such a way." He sighed and closed the door to the storeroom, then led the way down the hall. "I saved my favorite place for last—the Temple library."

They entered a long, narrow room with a row of deep windows set high on one wall. Below the windows and on the opposite wall, dozens of niches had been carved into the thick, plastered walls. They were filled with hundreds of scrolls, the wooden handles protruding into the room. More shelves filled with scrolls were arranged in rows in the middle of the room, and between them were benches and tables where scribes and scholars could work. But only one scribe sat at his desk, copying the faded Hebrew letters from an ancient scroll. The other storerooms had smelled damp and musty but this room had the fragrant smell of parchment and wood.

"These scrolls contain all the laws that Yahweh gave our nation," Zechariah said. "And they also tell the history of our forefathers all the way back to Adam and Eve. Yahweh's truth is one thing that your father can never change or destroy."

Hezekiah couldn't understand why his grandfather seemed so proud of this room. There was nothing valuable here, no silver or gold—only dusty, yellowing scrolls.

"You're disappointed in the Temple, aren't you, son?"

Hezekiah shrugged and stared at his mud-spattered feet. Zecha-riah rested his hand on Hezekiah's shoulder.

"I'm very sorry for misleading you about the glory of this Temple. I've been blind to how badly it has deteriorated, until today. I was remembering how magnificent it all was during the golden age of King Uzziah. But that was long ago. I'm sorry, Hezekiah. Today I'm seeing it through your eyes—how it really is, not how it used to be."

"I wish it was still beautiful, Grandpa. Why did my father have to wreck everything?"

"Come. Sit down over here." Zechariah led Hezekiah to one of the worktables, and he watched as Zechariah scanned the stacks of scrolls. When he found the one he wanted, Zechariah sat down beside him and carefully unrolled it.

"You know, Yahweh isn't surprised that your father's enemies attacked him all at once. In fact, Yahweh caused it to happen. This scroll is from the Torah and was written before the children of Israel moved to this land. May I read you some of it?" Hezekiah nodded but didn't look up as he idly kicked his sandal against the table leg.

"'After you have had children and grandchildren and have lived in the land a long time,'" Zechariah read, "'if you then become corrupt and make any kind of idol, doing evil in the eyes of Yahweh your God . . . you will quickly perish from the land that you are crossing the Jordan to possess.'"

Hezekiah didn't understand. He looked up at Zechariah, waiting for him to explain.

"The reason your father had to strip the Temple," he said, "is because our enemies attacked us from every side. They destroyed entire cities and carried thousands of people away as captives. It happened just as Yahweh said it would, because the people have turned away from Him to worship idols. Your father gave Yahweh's gold to the Assyrian king so he would save us from our enemies. We're supposed to be servants of Yahweh, but now we're servants of Assyria instead."

Hezekiah felt a shiver of fear. "Will Yahweh go away and stop being our God?" he asked.

"Well, let me read the rest of this to you, and maybe you can answer that question yourself: 'But if from there you seek Yahweh your God, you will find him if you look for him with all your heart and with all your soul. When you are in distress and all these things have happened to you, then in later days you will return to Yahweh and obey him. For Yahweh is a merciful God; he will not abandon or destroy you.'

"He'll forgive us, Hezekiah," he answered softly. "Yahweh loves us, and He'll forgive us if we'll only turn back to Him. I know with all my heart that this is true."

Hezekiah stopped kicking the table leg, and they sat in silence for a moment.

"You know, son, someday you'll be the king of Judah and—" Zechariah stopped. "No. You're much too young to understand the responsibilities that lie ahead. We've talked enough for today."

Hezekiah struggled to understand all that his grandfather had said, but his disappointment was too great.

"Grandpa?" he asked at last, "couldn't Yahweh kill all our enemies and save us? Then my father wouldn't have to spoil His Temple. Couldn't Yahweh do that?"

"Certainly He could! Don't you remember the story I told you about how Yahweh helped David defeat Goliath?"

Hezekiah nodded.

"And remember Joshua and the battle of Jericho? And how Yahweh caused the sun to stand still so Joshua could defeat the five Amorite kings? Yes, of course Yahweh could defeat *all* of Judah's enemies."

"Then why didn't He, Grandpa?"

Zechariah's face looked sad as he shook his head. "Because our nation no longer believes in Him . . . and so no one bothered to ask Him to."

# 9

THE DESERT WIND SWIRLED across the road, raising a cloud of soot and dust. King Ahaz closed his eyes to shield them from the dirt and to block out the scene of utter desolation lying before him. The escort of Assyrian soldiers had halted Ahaz's procession a short distance from Damascus and left him to wait in the searing heat with only the canopy of his chariot to protect him from the sun. Ahaz rubbed the grit from his eyes and opened them again, but the dismal view hadn't changed.

The magnificent city of Damascus stood in ruins. Thick stone walls that had once offered protection now displayed gaping holes. Ahaz glimpsed jackals scavenging through the debris. As far as he could see, black Assyrian tents spread like a low-hanging cloud across the charred plain, revealing no trace of the rich vineyards and olive groves that once graced the fertile river valley. Where thick forests of sycamores and carob trees once stood, only blackened stumps remained.

The Assyrian soldiers had set a brisk, exhausting pace and the long journey had wearied Ahaz. Every bone and joint in his body ached from the jolting ride, and he desperately wanted to bathe and lie down in a cushioned bed. But as he gazed at the desolate city in front of him, he knew that his accommodations couldn't possibly be luxurious. Ahaz sank back in his chariot with a groan.

"This heat is intolerable! Don't just stand there—fan me!" he told his valet. He closed his eyes as the servant waved a palm frond back and forth through the suffocating air. Several minutes passed before the valet roused him.

"Your Majesty, someone is coming."

Ahaz stood up, watching nervously as three chariots approached, then halted amid a choking cloud of dust. The warrior who emerged from the lead chariot was Assyrian, armed with a sword, bow, and spear. His tunic was embroidered with golden threads, and he wore his black hair and squared-off beard in the style of royalty. Ahaz climbed from his chariot and bowed before him, certain that this was the great monarch, Tiglath-Pileser, greeting him as a friend and ally.

"I am Ahaz ben Jotham, King of Judah and Jerusalem," he announced. The Assyrian responded with a few mysterious sentences, then motioned to a man in the chariot behind him to come forward and translate.

"You needn't bow down," the translator explained. "He is only the Rabshekah—the Assyrian emperor's representative."

"Oh. I see." The mistake embarrassed Ahaz, and he felt his cheeks flush.

"The Rabshekah will deliver the tribute that you've brought to the emperor's storehouses. He will also take command of the Judean soldiers and weapons that you have brought the emperor as a gift."

"Wait a minute," Ahaz said in alarm. "There must be some mistake. These soldiers are all that's left of my army. I didn't intend them as a gift. Can you explain that to the Rabshekah?"

The translator gave a short laugh. "I don't think you want me to do that. The vassal nations of Assyria aren't allowed to have armies. You won't need one. You're under Assyrian protection now. Tell your troops to follow the Rabshekah, King Ahaz. Then you must follow me." He gave a smirking grin, and Ahaz fought the urge to slap him.

Helpless rage flooded through Ahaz as he relayed the order to his captain, then he watched in numb silence as his army marched away with the Assyrian escort. He had departed Jerusalem with a grand procession; now he would be disgraced when he returned with only his personal chariot and a handful of servants and bodyguards. He wondered if his soldiers would ever be allowed to return to their homes and families again.

When the dust settled once more, the interpreter broke the uneasy silence. "I will take you to your tent now."

"Tent? My *tent*?" Ahaz repeated, his humiliation turning to outrage at being accorded only a tent for his accommodations. But he quickly suppressed his anger, realizing that without an army he was scarcely in a position to protest. He mounted his chariot with an angry groan, and the interpreter crowded in beside him, pointing the way for the driver. Ahaz stared glumly at the distant ruins of Damascus as the chariot jolted down the dusty road.

"I'm Jephia, son of Shemaiah, of the tribe of Naphtali," the interpreter said. "Your tent isn't too far."

"Naphtali?" Ahaz asked. "You're an Israelite?"

"Of course. That's why I was chosen to interpret for you."

"How did you end up in Damascus?"

Jephia stared at him. "How did I end up in Damascus?" he repeated incredulously. "You're obviously very naive when it comes to the Assyrians, King Ahaz ben Jotham. The Assyrians captured me when they invaded Israel. I'm their slave, their property. They can bring me to Damascus or anywhere they please. And it pleased them to make me your interpreter."

Ahaz looked away so he wouldn't have to see Jephia's mocking grin. "I saw evidence of the Assyrian invasion on my journey through Israel," Ahaz mumbled.

"Yes, our king wisely surrendered and paid tribute in order to spare Israel from the total destruction that Damascus received. Most of my countrymen won't suffer deportation—at least for now. But my nation is a vassal state of Assyria, and that means—" Jephia paused and laughed with contempt. "That means we are *all* slaves. Here's your tent, King Ahaz."

The chariot drew up to a small encampment outside the ruined city walls. Ahaz's tent, consisting of four large rooms, was much bigger than he had expected and well supplied with food, wine, and to his great amazement, a portable bath.

"When will I have an audience with the Assyrian emperor?" Ahaz asked. He saw Jephia suppress a smile, and it infuriated him. "That's the reason I've traveled here!" he shouted. "We have a treaty to sign. We're allies."

Jephia responded to his outburst calmly. "When all of the other vassal kings have arrived, Tiglath-Pileser will summon all of you at once. You must stay here until then. I will stay with you and see to your needs." He bowed slightly.

Ahaz was accustomed to servants who cowered before him in fear, and Jephia's lack of servility angered him. The man's manners were outwardly correct, but every time he spoke the word "vassal" his contempt was ill concealed. Ahaz didn't want Jephia's assistance. He turned his back on him and summoned his own valet.

"I would like to bathe and then rest awhile," he said. He smiled with satisfaction as his servants leaped into action, bustling around the tent to wait on him. "You're excused," he told Jephia.

Several tedious days passed as Ahaz rested from his journey, and he quickly became bored. He had plenty of excellent food and wine but nothing to do except grow more nervous and impatient as he waited for the Assyrian monarch to summon him. Yet he was determined not to ask Jephia about the delay, hating the translator's mocking smile and the way he explained everything as if Ahaz were a child.

When a message finally arrived at Ahaz's tent, he called Jephia to interpret it. The slave read it through silently, and his eyebrows lifted in mild surprise. "The Rabshekah has sent for you. All the other vassal kings have arrived. I'm to conduct you on a tour of Damascus, then you'll meet your *ally,* Tiglath-Pileser."

"Finally," Ahaz sighed. "I'll need some time to get ready and—"

"No," Jephia said, shaking his head. "The Rabshekah has summoned you. You must come at once." There was a stern note of warning in his voice that Ahaz didn't miss. He glared at Jephia for a moment, then hurried into his tent, changing his robes as quickly as he could.

He reappeared a few minutes later, and they mounted his chariot riding in silence to the ruined city. Ahaz struggled to conceal his shock and horror as he saw evidence of the Assyrians' atrocities. On either side of the road that led to the main gate, row after row of bodies hung from tall stakes.

"The emperor would like you to meet the chief elders of Damascus," Jephia said. "They were impaled alive and left to die, watching the destruction of their city."

Ahaz gazed straight ahead, holding a linen handkerchief over his mouth to keep from vomiting. A sign above the gate read: *This is the fate of the enemies of Assyria.*

"The scribes take a head count," Jephia explained, pointing to a grisly mound, "and the soldiers are paid accordingly."

"They could have picked a better route for visitors to take," Ahaz said. "We shouldn't have to look at all this."

Jephia stared at him, shaking his head. "You still don't understand, do you, King Ahaz ben Jotham?"

"Understand what?"

"Why do you think all these corpses were left here? Why do you think you were invited to Damascus in the first place?"

"The emperor and I are allies—"

"No," Jephia said sharply. "This isn't going to be a meeting of 'allies,' as you so naively believe. This summons was carefully planned as a warning to all the vassal nations like yours. Tiglath-Pileser knows that you'll never dream of rebelling against him after you've seen what happened to Damascus. He doesn't want your friendship, King of Judah. He wants your fear and submission."

Ahaz shook his head as if he could shake aside Jephia's words. "No . . . I don't believe . . ."

"He wants your tribute, King Ahaz—now and for the rest of your life. He knows that no matter how much he demands, you'll beat it out of the backs of your people rather than see Jerusalem end up this way."

Ahaz stood paralyzed. He wanted to call Jephia a liar, but as he stood before the gate, watching the other vassal kings approach, he knew that Jephia was telling the truth. He felt like a fool for not realizing it before. He leaned against the side of his chariot, shaken and dazed. Then, with agonizing clarity, he recalled Isaiah's parting words: *"The Lord Almighty has told me of the destruction decreed against this whole land."*

"I've seen enough," Ahaz said quietly. But Jephia shook his head. "You'll see it all."

Ahaz rode through the rubble-strewn streets of Damascus in gloomy silence, the sights around him a vague blur. But Jephia continued with his grim narration, pausing to point to a group of naked men and women with shorn heads, picking through the wreckage.

"These are the survivors of another city in a distant part of the Assyrian empire, deported here to rebuild Damascus while their own land is rebuilt by strangers. That's the Assyrian way."

"The Assyrian way," Ahaz repeated softly. He was beginning to understand the full extent of Assyria's brutal power and military might. His nation would become a puppet kingdom in the vast Assyrian Empire, and there was nothing he could do but pay homage.

"That mound ahead is where the temple once stood," Jephia said, gesturing to a man-made hill, the highest point in the city. "We'll have to walk from here. The streets are choked with debris from the temple."

Ahaz climbed from the chariot and followed Jephia, weaving

around massive stones that had once been part of the Aramean temple. He was grimy with sweat and with the sooty dust that seemed to cover the entire land. When he paused to catch his breath and mop his face, he saw the other vassal kings making their way up the slopes of the temple mound behind him.

"Why are we all assembling here?"

"You must all pay homage to the Assyrian gods, confessing that they're superior to your own nation's gods."

Ahaz nodded, too numb to argue, and followed Jephia to the top of the hill. Not one stone of the former temple remained upon another, and the paved courtyard was bare except for a massive bronze altar standing in the center. Pictures of Assyria's gods decorated all four sides of it, but the central figure on each panel was the god Assur—a warrior armed with a bow and riding a winged sun. Ahaz and the other kings gathered around the altar while the Assyrian priests led the animals forward to be sacrificed. Jephia translated the priests' incantations for him:

"All praise to Assur, who has led us to victory over our enemies. All praise to Assur, who has wielded his judgment over them. All praise to Assur, who has made Assyria the most powerful nation in all the earth. All praise to Assur and his representative among us, Emperor Tiglath-Pileser."

Dread overwhelmed Ahaz as he bowed in homage with the other kings to proclaim Assur's sovereignty over his own God. He remembered how Yahweh had punished his grandfather, King Uzziah, and he was terrified of angering Him. But he was every bit as terrified of the Assyrians. He had no choice but to kneel in the dust beside the others and proclaim, "Yahweh, the God of Judah, bows before Assur."

The ceremony continued in a dizzying whirl of chanting and bloodshed until the combined heat of the sun and the giant altar nauseated Ahaz. He wished it would end. He wanted to lie down alone in his tent and try to weave the fraying strands of his life back together.

But when the ritual finally ended, Jephia turned to him with a mocking smile.

"And now you'll finally meet your *ally,* Tiglath-Pileser."

Ahaz looked down at his robes, filthy with sweat and dust. "Dressed like this?"

Jephia merely smiled and led the way through the rubble to the former king's palace, one of the few buildings in the city that was still intact. The emperor's canopied throne stood on the palace steps, and the visiting kings were ordered to assemble on the street below it. The Assyrian emperor wore a long purple tunic of richly embroidered silk and a tall conical cap decorated with golden threads. The jewels that adorned his fingers and wrists glinted in the sun. A dozen slaves fanned him with palm fronds.

Ahaz stood below the throne in the dizzying heat, wishing he could lie down somewhere with a glass of wine to cool his thirst. "What happens now?" he asked Jephia.

"First, there will be a procession of captives. Then all the vassal kings will take part in a ceremony to pledge their submission." Jephia had pronounced the word *vassal* with his usual contempt, but it no longer bothered Ahaz. He understood the reality of what it meant, and he knew that he'd been a fool to believe himself the emperor's equal.

The procession began with squadrons from the Assyrian army. Ahaz watched as row after row of black-bearded warriors passed before him, their weapons flashing in the sun. Then the cavalry followed, with more horses than he'd ever seen together in his life. Still more warriors rode past in chariots, then the battering rams and siege towers paraded past. Ahaz remembered the fierce beating Jerusalem's walls had suffered during the siege a few months before, yet the weapons the Arameans had used against him were child's toys compared to the Assyrians' arsenal. Jerusalem's aging walls would topple in a matter of months under their assault.

Wave after wave of Assyrian soldiers marched past, until it seemed to Ahaz that the entire population of Judah must have paraded before him. Then came the plundered treasures of Damascus, heaped in golden piles on hundreds of wagons. Ahaz had never seen so much wealth, and it made his own gift to the Assyrian monarch seem worthless. The Aramean prisoners of war staggered behind the riches that had once belonged to them, led by the king and his nobles and princes. They wore only chains around their ankles as their captors led them through the streets by bridles that pierced their nostrils and lips.

When the captives reached the palace steps, the Assyrian emperor rose and unsheathed his sword to begin the long punishment of the defeated king. Ahaz watched in horror as the Assyrians staked the captives to the ground by their wrists and ankles and slowly tortured them to death. Clearly, the Assyrians were skilled at prolonging their victims' suffering as long as possible. Shock and fear overwhelmed Ahaz as the agonized screams went on and on. When he was unable to endure another moment, he pushed to the rear of the crowd, fell to his knees, and vomited.

More than ever, Ahaz longed to be back in his palace in Jerusalem and away from the Assyrians' horrible butchery. He wished he had never called upon this bloodthirsty emperor for assistance. As his nausea finally subsided, Ahaz remembered Isaiah's warning: *"You have entered into a covenant with death."*

Ahaz wiped his eyes and mouth and struggled to his feet, aware that he had to return and watch the rest. He looked up and saw Jephia waiting for him, and for the first time he saw a hint of compassion in the interpreter's eyes. The tortures finally ended, but the cries of the dying men resounded in Ahaz's mind for a very long time.

"Now the vassal kings and their attendants will line up to pay homage to Tiglath-Pileser," Jephia told him, "assembling in order of importance and power." Ahaz was humiliated to find himself among the least important. As he waited in line, trembling with fear, he wondered how he had ever imagined himself sitting with the Assyrian emperor as an equal, signing treaties and discussing the nations of the world.

At last he walked forward, his knees threatening to buckle beneath him. "I am Ahaz ben Jotham, King of Judah and Jerusalem—Your Majesty's humble servant and vassal." He fell before the king with his forehead pressed to the ground, as all the other kings had bowed. The dust of Damascus filled his nostrils and throat. When he felt the touch of the royal scepter, he rose again, resisting the urge to wipe the dirt from his forehead and robes. He understood what he was—a pathetic puppet king, sworn to serve the Assyrians for the rest of his life. And if he rebelled or failed to send tribute, his punishment would be the same as the tortured king's had been.

"Is it over now?" he asked Jephia. "May I return to my tent?"

Jephia shook his head. "The king has invited you to a banquet in his honor. You can't refuse his invitation."

They followed the others inside the palace, into a huge banquet hall decorated with tapestries depicting the many nations in the Assyrian Empire. Dancers whirled across a platform to the music of an orchestra while hundreds of slaves stood beside the tables, ready to serve the kings. Ahaz was led to his seat at the lowest-ranking table where meat dishes, breads, vegetables, and fruits of all kinds lay spread before him. The food repulsed him. He felt only an unquenchable thirst.

Near his table slaves poured wine into a huge bowl, then ground a mixture of leaves and seeds into a fine powder and stirred it into the wine. When they finally served it, Ahaz gulped it down. The slaves replenished his cup as quickly as he emptied it.

It was meant to be an extravagant feast, but Ahaz couldn't enjoy it. He couldn't forget the horrors he had witnessed that day or the withering dread he'd felt as he'd bowed before the Assyrian king. He swallowed another cupful of wine and stared at the linen tablecloth as the noise and merriment roared in his ears.

Gradually, Ahaz felt the wine taking effect, and it seemed as though the room began to sway with the music. He liked the sensation at first, but as he looked up at one of the tapestries on the wall, he was startled to see that the figures on it had somehow come to life and were dancing in front of him. He shut his eyes to blot out the strange image, but swirls of light and color appeared before him in the darkness, spinning crazily. His head felt as if it might shatter into a thousand pieces.

He quickly opened his eyes but had trouble focusing them. As he fumbled for his glass of wine, his hand seemed to suddenly detach from his wrist and float through the air. Ahaz grabbed the glass with both hands and gulped another drink as he fought to control his splintering mind. When he tried to set down the empty glass, it slipped from his grasp and crashed to the floor.

"What's happening to me?" he cried, clutching his head.

"It's the wine," Jephia told him. His voice seemed to come from a distant corner of the room. "The Assyrians mix powerful drugs with their wine and allow the gods to take them on a journey into the world of the spirits. It's part of their worship."

Ahaz moaned. He didn't want to journey to the spiritual world. If he could journey anywhere, he would like it to be home. He covered his face with his hands, trying to envision Jerusalem's familiar sights: his palace, Yahweh's Temple, the terraced hillsides surrounding the city. But Isaiah appeared before him, instead: *"You will be devoured by the sword!"*

Ahaz uncovered his eyes, and the prophet vanished. He reached for the new glass of wine that the servants had brought him, and took another drink. "I'm losing my mind!" he told Jephia.

"It's useless to fight the power of the drugs, King Ahaz. Let the spirits carry you away."

Ahaz knew Jephia was right. He was too sick and exhausted to fight, and so he yielded to the control of the drugged wine. As he did, his mind suddenly came into focus, and it seemed as if he could think more clearly than he ever had before. In a blinding flash of revelation, he realized what Isaiah's words really meant: the wealth of Judah would be devoured as Ahaz struggled to meet the Assyrian tribute demands, tribute that would fund the Assyrian sword.

He closed his eyes and the prophet reappeared in a swirl of flashing lights. *"The understanding of this message will bring sheer terror,"* Isaiah warned. *"The bed will be too short to stretch out on, the blanket too narrow to wrap around you."* Ahaz knew what that prophecy meant, too. He had faced the truth about himself today, and he could no longer blanket it with lies. He opened his eyes, seeking to escape from the prophet's words in the only way he could: he drank the remaining contents of his cup.

For several minutes—or maybe it was hours—the room spun in circles around Ahaz as the potent mixture took effect. Then the motion gradually slowed, and all the horrible events of the day began to fade and blur into a past that he could scarcely remember. His fears shrank and then dissolved entirely, as a wonderful feeling of euphoria overwhelmed him. Ahaz wanted that feeling to last forever. He wanted more wine.

As the servants refilled his glass again and again, the only fear that troubled Ahaz was the fear that his cup might run dry.

# IO

ZECHARIAH AWOKE FROM A DEEP sleep to find Hezekiah standing over him, shaking him. "Grandpa . . . Grandpa, wake up."

He blinked his eyes, trying to focus them. "What is it, son?"

"What's that noise? Listen . . ." The sound of hammers ringing against stone drifted into the room from the courtyard below the bedroom window.

"It sounds like they're building something," Zechariah replied. "It sounds nearby, too." He yawned, his mind still fuzzy with sleep, and swung his feet to the floor. He saw Hezekiah eyeing his slow movements with the impatience of youth. "You don't have to wait for me, child. Go on—open the window and have a look. Tell me what you see."

Hezekiah darted across the room and tugged on the heavy curtains until they opened. He stood on his tiptoes peering down into the courtyard.

"Grandpa, you're right. They're building something down there. Come and see." Zechariah shuffled to the window and boosted Hezekiah for a better view. "What are they making, Grandpa?"

"I have no idea."

They watched as workers removed paving stones from the center of the palace courtyard to dig a foundation. More workers labored to haul huge limestone blocks to the site. The base of the cleared area was small, but judging from the number of stones, the finished building was going to be tall. A tower, perhaps? Was Ahaz preparing to worship the heavenly bodies in addition to all the other gods he worshiped?

Zechariah suddenly realized how bright the room was. "Oh, my—look how high the sun is already," he said, pointing toward the Mount of Olives. "We'll have to hurry, or we'll be late for the morning sacrifice." He put on his robe and smoothed down his hair and beard, then helped Hezekiah finish dressing.

"Can we go see what the men are building, first?" Hezekiah asked.

"There's not enough time. We're late as it is."

"Don't forget this," Hezekiah said as he handed him his prayer shawl. Zechariah smiled.

"You're learning, aren't you, son? You'll make a fine man of God, one day, just like King David." Zechariah draped his prayer shawl over his shoulders, and they hurried through the palace hallways and out to the street.

The sound of ringing hammers should have receded in the distance behind them, but as they climbed the hill, Zechariah was surprised to hear hammers pounding in the Temple courtyard, as well. It was a sound that definitely didn't belong there. He began to walk faster, a trickle of fear running like sweat down his spine. As soon as he passed through the Temple gates, it was as if the earth had shifted from under him and the familiar landscape of the Temple's inner court had tilted askew.

"What are they doing, Grandpa?" Hezekiah asked, but Zechariah was too shocked to reply. Overnight, the altar of Yahweh had been moved from the middle of the courtyard using sledges and pulleys and teams of oxen. A huge new altar was being constructed in its place.

Zechariah hoped he was dreaming. But as he moved closer, Zechariah was horrified to see that the changes were much worse than he'd imagined. The brass side panels for the new altar were covered with graven images.

"No . . ." he murmured. "No, that can't be—not here in Yahweh's Temple!" But in the center of each panel, the Assyrian god, Assur, stood astride a winged sun. Zechariah stared in horrified disbelief.

The presiding Levites and priests emerged from the Temple's side door in a frightened huddle, as if fearful of the wrath of God. They gathered around the altar of Yahweh that now stood on the north side of the courtyard.

Zechariah felt Hezekiah tugging on his sleeve. "Grandpa, why is it all changed?" he asked.

"I don't know, but I intend to find out. Wait right here." He left Hezekiah standing by the gate to the inner court and hurried over to speak with the priest who was preparing for the morning sacrifice.

"What is that abomination doing here in Yahweh's Temple?" Zechariah asked, pointing to the new altar that was being built. "It's idolatry! What's it doing here? Who ordered this?"

The priest glanced around before answering in a hushed whisper. "King Ahaz ordered it. He sent the plans for it from Damascus and told Uriah to have it built before he returns."

"And Uriah agreed to this?" Zechariah asked in astonishment.

The priest gestured helplessly. "What could he do? It was the king's command. We're supposed to offer all of the sacrifices on the new altar when it's finished. Yahweh's altar will only be used for seeking guidance."

"He can't do that!" Zechariah shouted. The handful of men who were gathering to worship turned to stare at him. "Where's Uriah?" he demanded.

"Probably still at the palace. He doesn't come here every day—"

Zechariah strode back across the courtyard, through the gates, and down the hill to the palace. With every step he took, his shock transformed into anger. He was only vaguely aware of Hezekiah trotting behind him.

"Grandpa . . . Grandpa, wait. What about the sacrifice?"

"Not now, son. Go back to your room." He hurried through the palace hallways to Uriah's chambers, his anger burning hotter every minute. But when he stopped to catch his breath, he noticed Hezekiah staring up at him. "Go upstairs and wait for me," he said again, as he pounded on Uriah's door. It opened a crack and a servant peered out. Zechariah barged past him.

"Where's Uriah? I need to speak with him. Where is he?" He was trembling with rage.

Uriah emerged from an inner chamber, followed by another servant. "What are you doing here, Rabbi?" he asked.

"You can't let Ahaz do this!" Zechariah shouted. "You must put a stop to it!"

Uriah looked him over then muttered to his servants, "He's probably drunk. Take him back up to the Temple." The two men moved toward Zechariah.

"I'm not drunk, Uriah! Call them off," he said as he tried to free himself.

The high priest stared gravely at Zechariah, then motioned to his servants. "All right—let him go. Give us a few minutes alone."

Zechariah waited until the servants disappeared, his gaze never wavering from Uriah's. "You have no right to do this!" he shouted. "And neither does King Ahaz! Make them stop!"

"You'll have to calm down, Rabbi, and tell me what you're talking about." Uriah spoke to him as if he was a child. Zechariah struggled to contain his anger.

"I'm talking about that . . . that . . . abomination you're building!"

"That 'abomination,' as you call it, is actually quite ingenious," Uriah replied. He gestured to the construction in the palace courtyard, just visible outside his window. "The Babylonians invented it to keep track of time. The tower will have stairs that spiral down the side, and as the sun moves higher or lower in the sky, the tower will cast a shadow on the stairs. Each stair represents an increment of time—"

"I don't care about that! I'm talking about the heathen altar you're building in Yahweh's Temple!"

"I don't need to explain my decisions to you," Uriah said coldly.

"Yes, you do! I'm still a Levite, Uriah. And what you do in Yahweh's Temple is still my concern." He stared up at the tall priest and saw Uriah's expression soften slightly, with respect.

"Listen," he sighed. "I'm trying to centralize our national religion at the Temple. The king has altars all over the city, and it confuses people. This new altar will draw everyone back to the Temple—"

"Draw them back? You want people to come to Yahweh's Temple to worship idols? That's insane! This time you've gone too far. You're bringing idolatry right into God's house!"

"No, listen to me. Only at first." Uriah spread his huge hands as he attempted to reason with Zechariah. "You know as well as I do that hardly anyone ever comes to the Temple anymore. The morning and evening sacrifices are very poorly attended. But if we can draw people back, eventually they'll view Yahweh as supreme over all their idols. I'm doing it for the good of the Temple."

Zechariah slowly shook his head. "Maybe you can convince all the others to believe you, but not me. No, Uriah. You're lying to them and to yourself." He glared at Uriah until the younger man finally looked away.

"I can't tell King Ahaz what to do," he said quietly. "He ordered me to build the altar, and I have to do what he says."

"I thought that was why you took this position—so you could teach him Yahweh's laws?"

"I'm trying to. But I need more time."

"You'll never change Ahaz by working *for* him. You have to fight *against* him. Take a stand, Uriah. Show him he's wrong. You must resign as palace administrator."

"Resign?" Uriah gave a short laugh as he began pacing in front of Zechariah. "Resign—and then what? He'd make me resign as high priest of the Temple, too. Then maybe I could take up farming? Or serve as a priest in some remote village out in the desert somewhere? No. I'm not going to resign. Not now—"

"Not after you've had a taste of power and luxury," Zechariah finished for him. Uriah stopped pacing and glared at him.

"That has nothing to do with it."

"Doesn't it? You can't lie to me, Uriah. I know better than anyone else what temptations you're facing. I've lived here, too—remember?"

Uriah looked away. "Yes, I remember."

"And we're very much alike, you know—the same drive, the same burning ambition to succeed. Yes, I understand you very well. You've worked long and hard to get where you are, and now that you're at the top, you sometimes have to do things that compromise your faith. Believe me—I know. But you can't go back. It's a long way down to where you've crawled up from, isn't it? A long way down. And when you hit the bottom again, you're afraid you'll shatter into a thousand pieces, like I did. So rather than fall, you'll make a few concessions to your faith. A little here, a little there, and every time you compromise, something inside your spirit dies a little."

"This is nonsense." Uriah folded his arms across his broad chest, but he wouldn't look at Zechariah.

"Is it? Can you honestly stand there and tell me you didn't die inside when you watched those children burn to death? Because if you can, then it's already too late. You're already dead."

Uriah turned away to stare out the window. When he spoke again, his voice was so soft Zechariah could barely hear him. "Go away and leave me alone."

"Uriah, resign!" Zechariah begged. "Do it now, before it's too late. Make them stop building this altar. Help me oppose Ahaz's idolatry. Because that's what I have every intention of doing from now on."

Uriah swiftly turned to face him. "Are you forgetting that Ahaz is the king? If you oppose him he'll have you executed."

"Yahweh dealt with King Uzziah when he sinned, and He'll deal with Ahaz, too. But you'll face Yahweh's judgment along with the king if you cooperate with him. Believe me, I know what I'm talking about."

As Zechariah gazed at Uriah's troubled features, he sensed the conflict raging in his heart. But even as he watched, Uriah's face hardened again. His jaw locked as he thrust his chin forward, and he seemed immovable, as if carved from stone.

"I'm not going to turn into a religious fanatic, Zechariah. Not even for you. I can serve Yahweh much better if I stay here, in a position of authority. I know how to handle Ahaz. That's where you went wrong. You didn't know how to control King Uzziah."

"If you have so much control over him, then put a stop to this altar."

"I've already explained it to you," he said coldly. "The altar will draw the people back to the Temple, back to Yahweh. I don't see it as a threat. Why are you so resistant to change?"

It seemed to Zechariah that the high priest's conscience had also turned to stone. He shook his head. "I thought I could reach you. I thought I could make you see the truth. But I guess it's too late. All of this has blinded you," he said, gesturing to the luxurious room. "Power is intoxicating, isn't it? I'm not sure I would have listened to the truth, either."

As they stared at each other for several moments, Zechariah knew Uriah would never give in. Zechariah turned to leave and saw Hezekiah standing outside the open door, listening—and his anger at Uriah returned. If he and King Ahaz continued to rebel against the God of their fathers, Hezekiah would have no future, no nation to reign over. Zechariah knew it was up to him to stop Ahaz—for his grandson's sake. He reached for Hezekiah's hand, then turned to point an accusing finger at the high priest.

"You're serving the wrong king, Uriah."

For a week after his confrontation with Uriah, Zechariah wrestled over what to do—how to stop the heretical changes that were taking place in Yahweh's Temple. When he heard that King Ahaz had returned and that he would preside over a dedication ceremony on the new altar, Zechariah knew that the time had come for him to act. He must do the will of God regardless of the consequences to himself.

On the evening before the ceremony, he walked up the hill to his old quarters in the Temple and retrieved his Levitical robes. Before the shofar announced the sacrifice the next morning, he put them on for the first time in many months.

"Grandpa, why are you wearing that robe?" Hezekiah asked as he watched him dress.

"I'm going to assist the priests in the Temple this morning."

"But you said we wouldn't go to the Temple anymore until they got rid of the new altar."

"I know I did. Come here, Hezekiah. We need to talk." Zechariah crouched beside Hezekiah and put his arm around his shoulder. "The men who put that altar in Yahweh's Temple have done a very evil thing. And I made a promise to Yahweh that I would speak out against such evil. It's my job to teach men God's laws, so that's what I need to do. Do you understand?"

"I guess so."

"Now that your father is home from Damascus, he's planning a special sacrifice this morning on the new altar. What he's about to do is wrong. So I must keep my promise to Yahweh and tell the king and all the other men of Judah that it's wrong."

"Can I come, too, Grandpa?"

"No, son—not this time."

"Please? I'll be real quiet. No one will even know I'm there."

"No. You must promise me that you'll stay here. Promise?"

"Okay," he answered reluctantly. "I promise."

"Good boy."

"Grandpa? When you're done telling them, will you come back here to teach me my lessons?"

Zechariah hesitated. "Well, your father is very unpredictable. I'm not sure how he'll react."

"Please, Grandpa?"

Zechariah hugged him tightly. "Yes, of course I'll be back. I may be a little bit late, but I'll be back."

"I love you, Grandpa."

Zechariah held him close a moment longer. "And I love you, too." He slowly rose to his feet and caressed Hezekiah's hair. "I must go now, or I'll be late."

The dew covering the pavement stones dampened the hem of Zechariah's robes as he hurried up the hill and through the gates to the inner courtyard. The other Levites and priests bustled around, making sure everything was in order, while Uriah, dressed in the mitre and ephod of the high priest, supervised them. Zechariah was careful to avoid him, skirting around the perimeter of the courtyard to where the Levite choir had assembled on the Temple porch. They stared at him in surprise as he approached in his ceremonial robes.

"Zechariah—what are you doing here?"

"I'm taking part in the sacrifice today."

"But aren't you past the age of retirement?" his friend Shimei asked.

"Yes. But I'm going to sing anyway." He offered no other explanation, and no one pressed him further.

The blast of trumpets signaled the approach of King Ahaz. He arrived by the processional route through the main gate, and a great crowd of people swarmed behind him, filling the courtyards. A hushed whisper crackled through the assembly like a grass fire as they caught their first glimpse of the magnificent new altar. Then the whisper died away as the Levites began to sing.

While Ahaz led the way to the Bronze Sea, Zechariah watched the ritual closely, waiting for the right moment. He continued to sing the litany as the priests slaughtered the sacrifices and the men assembled around the new heathen altar. At first Zechariah saw no major changes, aside from the fact that it was a pagan altar. Uriah conducted the ritual the same way he had on Yahweh's altar.

But when the time came for the high priest to ascend the ramp with the sacrifice, King Ahaz stepped forward from the crowd and walked to the top of the altar, followed by Uriah and the priests.

"Yahweh, help us all!" someone beside Zechariah whispered. "Is the king going to make his own offering?"

Zechariah stopped singing. "No, he isn't," he told them calmly. "Because I'm going to stop him."

Shimei grabbed his arm. "Have you lost your mind?"

"No, I made a promise to Yahweh."

He shook free of Shimei's grasp and pushed his way to the front of the Temple porch. Zechariah knew that he should have spoken out years ago. He should have stopped King Uzziah from entering the sanctuary. He should have stopped Ahaz from sacrificing his sons to Molech. The knowledge that God had forgiven him and had offered him a second chance fueled his courage.

"King Ahaz, stop!" The choir stopped singing as Zechariah's voice carried across the courtyard with authority. "What you're about to do is a grave sin. Only the anointed priests of Yahweh can come before Him to present sacrifices. They are the intermediaries between God and man. That's why Yahweh brought judgment on your grandfather, King Uzziah. And He'll bring judgment on you, too, if you commit this act."

He saw King Ahaz's face turn red with rage. "Get him out of here!" he told Uriah.

The high priest quickly descended the altar stairs, signaling to the

Temple guards, but Zechariah continued to shout.

"Yahweh will not tolerate this blasphemous altar in His Holy Temple. His commandment says, 'You shall not make for yourself an idol in the form of anything in heaven above or on the earth beneath or in the waters below. You shall not bow down to them or worship them. . . .'"

The guards seized Zechariah's arms. He tried to fight them off as they dragged him down the steps of the porch. "What are you doing? Let go of me! You should be helping me!"

But before they were able to remove him from the courtyard, Isaiah suddenly pushed his way through the crowd and stood at the base of the altar.

"I will call on Uriah the priest and Zechariah the Levite as witnesses," he shouted as he unrolled a large scroll. He held it aloft for everyone to see. On it were the words *Quick to the Plunder—Swift to the Spoil.*

"When my wife conceived and gave birth to a son," Isaiah said, "the Lord told me, 'Name him *Quick to the Plunder—Swift to the Spoil.* Before he can say papa or mama, the riches of Damascus and the plunder of Samaria will be taken away by the King of Assyria.' These two witnesses—Uriah and Zechariah—can testify that they heard me speak this prophecy on the day I brought my son here to the Temple for his circumcision. My son is still just a baby, and you have seen with your own eyes, King Ahaz, the fulfillment of that prophecy."

Ahaz didn't move or speak. As Zechariah watched, the king seemed to melt with fear where he stood, like a piece of fat in the fire.

"Now Yahweh is speaking another prophecy to His people: Because these people have rejected His words, the Lord is about to bring against them the mighty floodwaters of the River—the king of Assyria with all his pomp. It will overflow all its channels, run over all its banks and sweep on into Judah, swirling over it, passing through it and reaching up to the neck." Isaiah pointed his scroll at Assur's image on the new altar and said, "Its outspread wings will cover the breadth of your land!"

The courtyard was silent except for the crackling of the altar fire as Isaiah rolled up the scroll again and strode away. Ahaz, who had stood stunned, suddenly shook himself, as if coming to his senses.

"Stop him! Somebody stop him!" he shouted as he quickly descended the altar steps. But Isaiah vanished into the crowd before any of the guards could move.

Zechariah was relieved to see that the disruption to the king's ceremony was irreversible. The milling crowd began drifting out of the courtyard in stunned confusion, as if frightened away by Isaiah's words. Ahaz drew his robes around himself like a protective shield and stormed across the courtyard, out of the Temple gates.

"Your Majesty, wait!" Uriah called. "We haven't finished the sacrifice!" He raced after the king, shoving people out of his way.

"It's all over now," Zechariah told the two guards who still gripped his arms. "Let me go." They released him, and he felt a sense of satisfaction and victory as he watched the people leave. He had done the right thing this time. Yes, Yahweh had won.

King Ahaz heard Uriah calling to him as he hurried down the royal walkway to his palace, but he didn't stop. He didn't want anyone to see that he was shaking uncontrollably. But when Uriah finally caught up to him outside his chambers, Ahaz turned on him angrily.

"The next time my sacrifices are interrupted, I'm holding you responsible. I never want to see Isaiah or hear his words again. Do you hear me? Never again!"

"I'm sorry—"

"And you'd better get your Levites under control, too, or I'll be looking for a new high priest!"

"I'm sorry, Your Majesty. I don't know why Zechariah—"

"Get rid of him!"

Ahaz shuddered as he recalled Zechariah's warning. He had been a child when his grandfather, Uzziah, had been stricken with leprosy, but he remembered that day and his grandfather's grief and anger very well. Ahaz had been afraid of Yahweh's power ever since—and of men like Zechariah and Isaiah who claimed to speak for Him. It was one of the reasons why Ahaz had wanted Yahweh's high priest on his side.

"Zechariah's a dangerous fool," Ahaz said, "and I never want to see him again."

"But he's your father-in-law—"

"I know who he is! And I know what he's up to. He's trying to regain the political power that he had with my grandfather—that's what this is all about. It's treason! Kill him!"

"Yes, Your Majesty. I'm sorry about what happened today. I'll take care of everything, and we'll hold another sacrifice tomorrow. I assure you that nothing will go wrong."

But Ahaz was barely listening. Isaiah's vivid description of the deluge of Assyrian soldiers had overwhelmed him, and he felt as if he were drowning. He had rejected Isaiah's advice at the Gihon Spring and ignored his warnings before leaving for Damascus. Both times Isaiah's prophecies had been fulfilled. What if he was right this time?

Fear paralyzed Ahaz. In a nightmare vision, he saw Jerusalem besieged by thousands of Assyrian troops, battering rams pounding the city walls, his nobles and advisors impaled on stakes in the Gihon Valley. And he saw himself being slowly tortured to death by the Assyrian emperor. Ahaz knew of only one way to escape from this vision. He fled to his chambers and ordered some wine, mixed the Assyrian way . . . to help him forget.

---

Abijah awoke that morning with cramps, and she wondered if her baby would be born today. Eliab's birth had taken all day, Hezekiah's half that time. The midwife had assured her that each successive birth would be quicker than the last, and Abijah was eager to get it over with.

"Maybe I'll be holding my baby in my arms by nightfall," she told her servant.

"Then you should stay in bed, my lady. I'll send for the midwife."

"No, Deborah. It could be nothing. I want to get up and get dressed."

She struggled out of bed, and her servant helped her get dressed and fix her hair. When breakfast arrived, Abijah sat near the window to eat it, watching the worshipers climb the hill to the Temple Mount for the morning sacrifice. There seemed to be hundreds of them this morning—many more than usual—and she wondered why. Then she saw her father leave the palace and hurry up the hill; Hezekiah wasn't with him. She understood that it wasn't wise to take him to the Temple now that King Ahaz had returned from Damascus. But why was her father wearing his Levitical robes? Abijah suddenly felt afraid.

"Is something going on at the Temple this morning?" she asked Deborah.

"I don't know, my lady. Would you like me to ask someone?"

Abijah hesitated, unsure whom she could trust. With her husband worshiping numerous gods, she didn't want to draw attention to the fact that she had become a regular worshiper at the Temple—or that her father was living in the palace, teaching Hezekiah about Yahweh.

"No, it doesn't matter," she said. But she pushed her breakfast tray aside, no longer hungry.

A few minutes later, Abijah's anxiety increased when she saw King Ahaz leave the palace and ascend the royal walkway with a small procession. He rarely attended the daily sacrifices at the Temple. Why was he going this morning? She heard trumpets announce his arrival in the Temple courtyard, and when the wind blew just right, she could faintly hear the Levites' choir singing the liturgy. Her cramps seemed stronger now, but she wasn't sure if they signaled the beginning of her labor or her growing unease.

Abijah was still gazing out of the window, worrying, when she saw King Ahaz hurrying down the walkway from the Temple, alone. It was much too soon for the sacrifice to have ended, but he was returning to the palace, walking very fast. Now she was sure that something was wrong, and she needed to find out what it was.

Modesty had confined Abijah to the harem during the last months of her pregnancy, and the king hadn't sent for her since his return from Damascus. But she threw caution and convention aside as she went downstairs to try to intercept Ahaz before he reached his chambers. As she neared the last corner, she heard voices—Ahaz and Uriah, arguing. She halted, unseen, to listen.

"Zechariah's a dangerous fool," she heard Ahaz say, "and I never want to see him again."

"But he's your father-in-law—"

"I know who he is! And I know what he's up to. He's trying to regain the political power that he had with my grandfather—that's what this is all about. It's treason! Kill him!"

"Yes, Your Majesty."

Abijah had to lean against the wall as her knees went weak with fear. What had her father done? And why would Uriah agree to kill him? Uriah respected Zechariah. He had once loved him like a father.

"I'm sorry about what happened today," Uriah continued in a soothing voice. "I'll take care of everything, and we'll hold another sacrifice tomorrow. I assure you that nothing will go wrong."

Abijah remained hidden from sight until she heard the king's door slam shut, then she stepped out into the hallway—and into Uriah's path. "Please don't kill my father," she begged him. "Please, Uriah!"

He glanced around in alarm, then pulled her away from Ahaz's doorway. "Are you crazy?" he asked in a hushed voice. "What are you doing down here?"

"I heard what King Ahaz just said. Don't let him kill my father! Please, Uriah—please!"

"Do you want to get yourself killed along with him? Go back upstairs."

"Not until you tell me what's going on? Why does Ahaz want him dead?" She saw Uriah glance around again and knew that he was afraid of being seen or overheard. But Abijah's need to know was greater than her fear. She pulled him down the hall a few steps to his own private chambers and opened his door.

"Are you out of your mind, Abijah? We can't be alone together."

"Tell me what's going on—quickly—and then I'll leave." She went inside ahead of him, ignoring the sharp, stretching pain she felt in her groin. Uriah finally stepped through the door behind her and closed it.

"The king ordered an Assyrian altar to be built in the Temple," he told her. "Today was the dedication ceremony, but your father and Isaiah disrupted it."

"But that's a good thing, isn't it? If Ahaz is bringing his idolatry into God's Temple, weren't they right to speak out against it?"

Uriah didn't reply. He turned away from her and closed his eyes as if wishing that she and her question would disappear before he opened them. She could see that he was fighting an internal battle, but she couldn't understand what it was. Uriah was Yahweh's high priest. Why would he even consider compromising with idolatry?

"The crowd at the Temple this morning was the biggest I've seen in years," he said softly. "I've been trying for so long to draw the people back—and today they came."

"But you said Ahaz built a foreign altar. You're God's high priest, Uriah. You know that my father was right. Why are you on Ahaz's side?"

He turned on her, suddenly angry. "Why do *you* do everything Ahaz says? I see you acting like a devoted wife—is that genuine, Abijah? Or are you playing a part, too—doing whatever is necessary to please the king and accomplish your goals?"

"I obey him because he's my king and my husband," she said

calmly. "But if Ahaz commanded me to do something that was a sin against Yahweh—I'd choose to obey God, not him."

"At the cost of your life?" His eyes held hers, challenging her. She drew a deep breath for strength but refused to look away.

"Yes—even at the cost of my life. Because if I denied my God, I would have nothing left that mattered. And I believe that God would give me the strength to make that choice if I had to, the same way He has given me the strength to show love to my son's murderer day after day. My faith in God has been rekindled these past months as I've worshiped Him. I've seen evidence of His answers to my prayers. He saved my son—"

"*I* saved your son," Uriah said coldly.

"Yes . . . thank you." She was suddenly afraid of Uriah. He was no longer the man she had once known, the man who was devoted to God, the man who had always gazed at her with tenderness. The anger she saw in his eyes and heard in his voice was directed at her—and perhaps at God, too. "Don't be angry with me, Uriah," she begged.

"You should have been *my* wife, not Ahaz's. But your father had other plans."

Abijah reached for Uriah's arm—to soothe him and to steady herself as the cramping pains in her abdomen grew worse. She needed to return to the harem. But she needed to appease Uriah, first. Her father's life was in his hands, just as Hezekiah's had been on the day of Molech's sacrifice. She could see that Uriah didn't care about doing the right thing—the moral thing. He no longer seemed concerned with Yahweh's laws. But maybe he would spare Zechariah for her sake.

"You're right, my devotion to Ahaz is an act," she said, moving closer to him. "I would have chosen to marry you—not Ahaz. And I think my father would have chosen you, too. He admires you, Uriah, and he loves you like a son. But King Uzziah planned my marriage to the royal family to reward my father. Believe me, *Ahaz* is your enemy, not my father. We need to fight him together—you and I."

Uriah grabbed her suddenly and pulled her close, then bent to kiss her. But his kiss was rough and possessive, and Abijah knew that the emotion that drove him was anger, not passion. She yielded to him for her father's sake, for Hezekiah's sake, aware that she and Uriah would forfeit their lives if they were caught. When Uriah tried to draw her closer, her unborn child became a barrier between them, and he pushed her away as suddenly as he had grabbed her, staring resentfully at her pregnant belly.

"Get out," he said.

"Uriah, please don't kill my father!" she begged. She felt another stab of pain, so sharp it made her gasp. Uriah opened the door.

"I said, get out!"

---

Zechariah returned to his rooms in the Temple to change his clothes. As he folded his ceremonial robes and placed them on his bed, he knew that today was probably the last time he would ever wear them. But he had stopped the king. He had kept his promise to God. That was all that mattered.

He sighed as he thought about his long career as a Levite. There were many things he was ashamed of, many things he regretted. But Yahweh had forgiven him, entrusting him with other duties now. He must continue to teach Hezekiah—to make sure that he would be a king after God's own heart like King David. That was the most important task Zechariah could possibly do to serve his God and his nation.

He would say good-bye to all his friends, then move out of the Temple for good. He couldn't serve Yahweh in a Temple that was polluted with idolatry. He left his robes on the bed and quickly rummaged through the room, hurriedly packing his personal belongings. As he stuffed the last of his scrolls and keepsakes into a small wooden chest, he glanced around, dismayed at the mess he had made with his hurried packing. But he had no time to straighten the room. He had promised Hezekiah that he would return for his lessons, and Zechariah would keep that promise.

Suddenly his door flew open and Uriah filled the doorframe. Zechariah knew by his expression that Uriah's anger was raging dangerously out of control.

"Your actions at the sacrifice have outraged the king!" he shouted. "Maybe you were once a highly respected rabbi, but you have no right to interrupt the sacred observances whenever you feel like it!"

Uriah towered over him like a stone giant, but Zechariah remained calm. "I have sworn an oath to be faithful to Yahweh, and I will keep that oath, speaking out whenever my God is blasphemed."

"Why now? Why all of a sudden? You didn't protest when Ahaz sacrificed to Molech—and you were there, Zechariah."

"I know. And I'm ashamed of what I've done—and haven't done—in the past." He stepped closer to Uriah in an act of defiance. "But my past is forgiven. And I will no longer stand by while you and Ahaz lead the entire nation into idolatry. I won't let you do it. I'll join with Isaiah to preach against it every chance I get."

The muscles in Uriah's face rippled as he clenched his jaw. "You'll never get that chance. And neither will your friend, Isaiah," he said with quiet control.

"Is that a threat?" he asked in surprise. Uriah didn't answer. Zechariah sensed the struggle that was raging in the high priest's soul. "When did we become enemies, Uriah? You were my finest student. My protégé. When did you join the opposing side?"

"This is very hard, for I have great respect for you, Rabbi. Look, we don't have to be enemies. You're entitled to hold opinions that are different from mine. Promise me that you won't cause any more public disruptions, and you'll be free to believe whatever you like in private."

Zechariah heard something in Uriah's tone that sounded like an ultimatum. For the first time that day, Zechariah felt a tremor of fear. "And if I don't promise?"

"Then you'll be in rebellion against the king." They stared at each other for a long moment before Uriah spoke again. "Look, the king holds me responsible for what my priests and Levites do. He has ordered me to silence you—any way that I have to."

Zechariah knew that Uriah was begging for a promise of silence. And he knew that Ahaz would go to extreme measures to guarantee that silence. But he also knew that he could never turn his back on God's forgiveness. He remembered watching his little grandson die, and knew that he feared the wrath of God more than he feared Ahaz's threats. He slowly shook his head.

"I can't promise to be silent."

"Then you're a *fool!*" Uriah's stony efforts to control his rage began to crack. "I'm warning you, the king won't stand for it!"

"He'll have to kill me to silence me."

"That's what he's planning to do! Don't you understand? He sent me here with orders to get rid of you. Ahaz is accusing you of treason—of making a grab for political power. Why are you being so stubborn, Rabbi? Give up! You can't possibly win against the king."

"Maybe not, but at least I'll die with a clear conscience. Will you?" He stared up at the high priest without flinching, and Uriah's rage boiled over.

"Curse you, Zechariah! Why can't you forget your holy crusade for Yahweh and go back to your wine?" He had scooped up an empty wineskin lying on the littered floor and shoved it into Zechariah's hands, then stalked from the room, slamming the door behind him. A cloud of dust filtered down from the plastered ceiling.

The confrontation left Zechariah shaken. He sank down on his bed and sat there for a long time, staring at the wineskin and replaying the scene as if he could somehow alter it and convince Uriah of his error. Then he remembered Hezekiah. Zechariah had promised to return to the palace hours ago. He lifted his trunk by one end and dragged it across the room. But when he opened the door, two Temple guards stood outside.

"What are you doing here?" he asked in surprise. "Can you give me a hand with this trunk?"

"I'm sorry, Rabbi, but we have orders to make sure you remain in your rooms."

"Orders? What are you talking about? I have business to attend to." He tried to push past them, but they stood firm.

"Uriah's orders. Rabbi, please, you must cooperate with us. We can't let you leave."

Zechariah stared at them in disbelief, then finally went back inside and closed the door. He had never expected Uriah to carry out his threat so soon. He felt dazed, unable to grasp what was happening to him. God had given him a second chance, and he had been obedient. Surely God would honor that obedience and protect him for his faithfulness. Why was he being held prisoner?

He thought again of Hezekiah. He had scarcely begun teaching him God's Law. There was so much the boy had to learn. And he loved him. Dear God, how he loved him!

But with two guards outside his door, there was no way Zechariah could go to Hezekiah. He picked up the empty wineskin and hurled it against the door in frustration. It burst at the seams, splattering the remaining dregs of crimson wine across the floor and walls. Then Zechariah sank to his knees and buried his head in his hands.

"Why, Yahweh?" he cried. "You told me to teach Hezekiah and that's what I'm trying to do. How have I failed you?"

Zechariah was still praying hours later when he heard the door open. He looked up to see his friend Hilkiah standing in the doorway, his jovial face furrowed with concern. The guards loomed behind him in the passageway.

"Zechariah? How are you feeling, my friend?"

Zechariah scrambled to his feet. "Hilkiah, please come in, come in."

Hilkiah eyed the guards briefly. "All right—but they told me I can only stay for a minute." He closed the door and glanced around uncomfortably at the disheveled room and the puddle of splattered wine. "Zechariah, I think you should know . . . Uriah has told everyone that you've gone insane."

Zechariah was stunned. "Insane? Is that what he's saying? Because I dared to speak out against his idolatry? You don't believe him, do you?"

"No, no, no. Of course not. You're my friend. I should believe Uriah? May the Holy One strike me dead! All my life I've been faithful to Yahweh—blessed be His name. I hate what they've done to His Holy Temple, and I'm proud of you for speaking out. I'm just sorry that you're being held here. Such a place! I've come to ask how I can help you. Is there anything you need?"

"Yes, please!" Zechariah clutched Hilkiah's arm in desperation. Then, forcing himself to stay calm, he loosened his grasp. "Please— my grandson Hezekiah is waiting for me at the palace. I told him I'd come back, but I don't know how long Uriah is going to keep me here. Can you deliver a message for me?"

"You want me to go to the palace? Ah, my friend, I don't know how I can do that. I don't have the right to speak to the prince. And who can I trust there to deliver your message? I could end up getting you into even worse trouble. Please, I can't promise something like that."

Zechariah sighed and rubbed his eyes. "You're right. Never mind." He would have to wait a while longer and hope that Abijah would be allowed to come and see him.

"I'm sorry. I'm so sorry," Hilkiah murmured.

"No, it was an impossible request. I guess there's nothing else you can do for me. Go home, my friend, before they lock you up, too."

"Are you sure?" As Hilkiah reached to open the door, Zechariah suddenly remembered what else Uriah had threatened to do.

"Hilkiah, wait a minute!" He quickly crossed the room and leaned against the door to close it. "Listen," he whispered urgently. "You must get a message to Isaiah. He's in danger, as well. Have they arrested him yet?"

"I don't think so. He disappeared before they could."

"Then you must reach him and warn him. He has to leave Jerusalem. They'll silence him the next time he tries to prophesy."

Hilkiah looked doubtful. "Well, I'll try——"

"Hilkiah, please! Swear to me that you'll do it!"

"Very well, my friend. With the Holy One's help, I will go to Isaiah and warn him—somehow."

"Thank you, Hilkiah. May God go with you."

"And also with you. Shalom, my friend."

They quickly embraced, then the door closed behind Hilkiah with a hollow thud. Once again, Zechariah was alone with his doubts.

"Why, Yahweh?" he whispered. "Why?"

# II

HILKIAH ROLLED OVER ON his bed, changing positions for what seemed like the hundredth time that night. His body craved sleep, but his mind refused to be silent. The night air felt as hot as noontime and both his tunic and his bedding were soaked with sweat. But it wasn't the heat that kept him awake. Every time he closed his eyes he saw his friend Zechariah pleading with him to warn Isaiah. Hilkiah had promised to do it, and he knew he would never get to sleep until he did. Yet how could he?

At last he gave up trying to sleep and crept up to the roof of his house, hoping for a breeze. Hilkiah's house stood high on the city mount among the wealthiest homes, just below the king's palace. It clung to the hillside, and from his rooftop he could look down on the roofs of the other houses from a dizzying height. A full moon shone above the surrounding mountains, and as Hilkiah slowly turned to view them, he saw the outline of the Temple wall on the hill above him. He groaned and looked away, pulling his beard in frustration.

"Ah, God of Abraham, how I can I do it?" he whispered.

He wondered if Zechariah realized what a dangerous thing he had asked him to do. Visiting Zechariah at the Temple had been a risk in itself, but if he was seen with Isaiah now, he could be accused of conspiracy. His own life would be in danger.

Hilkiah truly believed that Zechariah and Isaiah were right. The heathen altar didn't belong in Yahweh's Temple. And he knew that he should have the courage to fight idolatry the way those two men did. But how would his young son Eliakim survive if his father were imprisoned in the Temple—or executed as a traitor to the king?

A year ago during the sultry summer months, a fever had crept through the city from house to house, stealing away Hilkiah's wife and two youngest children. All that he and Eliakim had left were each other.

He looked up at the Temple again. In a few hours it would be time for the morning sacrifice on the new altar. Imprisoned in the Temple, Zechariah couldn't stop the ceremony this time or prevent King Ahaz from presenting his own offering. But Isaiah would probably try to intervene, and the guards would be waiting for him when he did. He wouldn't slip away this time. Hilkiah thought of his son sleeping peacefully in the house below and shuddered. Then he had another thought. Isaiah had a family as well—two small sons with strange prophetic names. What would become of them if Isaiah was arrested? Hilkiah took a deep breath and exhaled slowly.

"God of Abraham, help me." He turned to descend the stairs that led from the roof to the street, determined to warn Isaiah.

"Where are you going, Abba?"

"Oh, Eliakim!" he gasped. "What are you doing up here in the middle of the night?"

"I couldn't get to sleep." Eliakim's thick black hair was tousled and damp with sweat. He was a slender, handsome boy, nearly as tall as Hilkiah was. Hilkiah rested his hand on his son's shoulder, and his heart swelled with love.

"I know. I know. It's hot, isn't it? Why don't you get a mat and come up here to sleep?"

"It's not because of the heat!" Tears sprang to Eliakim's dark eyes, and he twisted away to hide them.

"What's wrong, son?"

Eliakim exhaled angrily. "I'm mad about what happened yesterday. They ruined my birthday and it wasn't fair. I'm finally a man, finally old enough to watch the sacrifices in the men's court with the others, and everything got ruined."

"I'm sorry, son. I didn't realize you were so upset." Hilkiah tried to draw him into his arms, but Eliakim pulled away.

"Those two crazy men who stopped the sacrifice ruined everything."

"Now wait just a minute," Hilkiah said. "Those two men did the right thing. They *should* have stopped the sacrifice. What the king was about to do was *wrong*. He's not supposed to offer his own sacrifice. According to the Torah, only the priests can do that."

Eliakim looked skeptical. "Well, none of the other priests tried to stop him—not even the high priest."

"Grown-ups don't always do the right thing, Eliakim—even when they know what the Torah says." Hilkiah recalled his own indecision a few moments ago and winced. "Anyway, I was going to tell you in the morning, but I may as well tell you now. We won't be going to the sacrifices at the Temple anymore."

"Abba, no! Why not?"

"I'm sorry, Eliakim. I know how much you looked forward to being old enough to go, but they've brought idols into the Temple and we won't take part in idolatry."

"But aren't the sacrifices important? Aren't we supposed to go?"

"Of course they're important. But we're supposed to go out of love for the Eternal One—blessed be His name—and to worship Him as the one true God. Otherwise, it's just an empty ritual. When they put that pagan altar in His Temple, the Holy One of Israel had to withdraw His presence from that place. It's a heathen ritual now, a meaningless ceremony to false gods. We have no reason to go anymore."

"But I want to go! It's not fair!"

Hilkiah knew how much his son longed to be a man, but at the moment he was acting like a disappointed child. "We will continue to say our morning and evening prayers," Hilkiah soothed, "but we'll say them at home from now on—just you and me."

"It's not the same thing. Can't we please go once in a while? Just so I can see what it's like?"

"No, son. We can't," Hilkiah said sternly. "Don't even ask such a thing." Eliakim's reaction crushed him. He had tried to teach him what the Torah said, had tried to instill in him a love for God, but Eliakim seemed interested only in the outward rituals at the Temple. Hilkiah wondered where he had failed.

"Eliakim, listen to me. It takes more than a birthday to make you a man. If you always go along with the crowd, even when they're wrong, then you're a coward, not a man, no matter how old you are. But if you really believe that something is wrong, that it goes against God's teachings, then you must have the courage to stand up for what you believe. That's what those two men did yesterday, and that's what I'm trying to do. Do you understand?"

Eliakim didn't reply. He kicked at the packed clay rooftop with his toe. Hilkiah tried again to explain.

"Listen, son, the Levite who spoke out yesterday is my friend Zechariah. Do you know what happened to him after the sacrifice? He's being held under arrest at the Temple, and they're telling everyone he's crazy. Zechariah could probably promise to keep quiet about his beliefs and maybe they'd let him go free. But I know my friend and he won't do it. That takes courage, son. That's being a man."

Eliakim looked up at him. "Are you going to start protesting, too, Abba?" he asked. His voice trembled.

"No. I don't have the authority and influence that Zechariah has. It would do no good at all for me to protest." Hilkiah felt ashamed of himself, even though he could justify his reasoning. "But there is something else that I can do to help," he said, remembering.

"What, Abba?"

"The other man who spoke out yesterday is Isaiah. He was born to the house of David, but I believe he is also an anointed prophet of the Eternal One. His prophecies have been a thorn in the king's flesh for a long time, but today Ahaz reached the end of his patience. They're going to arrest him the next time he prophesies. Zechariah begged me to warn Isaiah. He must leave Jerusalem immediately."

"Let me warn him, Abba."

"Absolutely not! It's too dangerous."

"Then it's dangerous for you, too."

"Yes, but I'm an adult—"

"So am I!" Eliakim shouted.

Hilkiah felt trapped. If he convinced his son of the risk involved, the boy might beg him not to go. But he couldn't let Eliakim take such a risk, either. "I'm the one who promised to go," Hilkiah said at last.

"Abba, I'm not afraid. Please, let me show you that I'm a man. Let me do something as an adult. You said I should have courage, right? Let me warn Isaiah."

"I don't think—"

"I'm smaller than you, and I can run faster and hide in the shadows better. Besides, they wouldn't arrest a boy, would they?"

Hilkiah knew that his son had a point. And he knew how badly Eliakim longed to prove he was a man. He hesitated until his son made his final, decisive argument.

"Abba, you taught me that the God of Abraham would always protect me if I did His will. Won't He protect me now?"

Hilkiah drew his son into his arms. Maybe he hadn't failed after all. Maybe Eliakim had learned about faith instead of ritual.

Eliakim walked at a brisk pace, afraid that his courage would melt away if he didn't hurry. He had never walked alone through the city at night, and every strange sound startled him, every familiar landmark looked eerily unfamiliar. He jumped when a dog barked in a nearby courtyard, certain that his pounding heart could be heard. But once he grew used to the sound of his sandals slapping against the paving stones, a sense of pride filled him. He was finally proving that he was a man.

The moon lit the narrow, twisting streets as he followed his father's directions to the quiet alley where the prophet lived. It didn't look at all like a street where royalty should live. Eliakim wondered why Isaiah didn't live in the palace or at least among the noblemen's houses high on the hill if he was born into the house of King David. Instead, Isaiah lived in a neighborhood where the stone houses were stuffed so tightly against each other that they couldn't even catch a cool breeze.

Eliakim paused in the shadows to catch his breath, then crept up to Isaiah's house, the last one on the street. He saw the faint glow of an oil lamp inside and wondered why it had been left to burn all night. He rapped lightly on the gate and waited, hoping someone would answer before his knocking awakened the neighbors. A moment later the door opened, and Eliakim recognized the man who had read from the scroll at the sacrifice.

"I'm Eliakim, son of Hilkiah, the merchant," he said breathlessly. "And I have a message for you from Zechariah the Levite."

Isaiah didn't seem surprised to see Eliakim. He nodded in greeting and led the way through the gate, crossing a tiny courtyard and entering the one-room house.

A small cooking hearth stood on one side of the room, cluttered with clay pots. Beside it was a homemade table littered with scrolls and the dimly burning oil lamp. Isaiah's wife slept on a straw mat across the room with a baby nestled close to her. Another child slept on a mat by her feet. Eliakim thought of his own mother and two younger brothers who had all died, and he swallowed hard.

"Please sit down," Isaiah said. He motioned to a wooden stool beside the table and Eliakim sat. "Can I offer you anything?" He gazed so intently at him that Eliakim felt naked.

"N-no, thank you, Rabbi. I've only come to bring you a message from Zechariah." He felt breathless and tongue-tied, awed by the presence that seemed to surround the prophet. He swallowed again, hoping that his words would sound coherent. "Zechariah is under arrest at the Temple because of what happened yesterday at the sacrifice."

Isaiah frowned slightly but said nothing.

"Zechariah says that you're in danger, too, and that you shouldn't prophesy anymore. He said you should leave Jerusalem right away."

Isaiah nodded slowly. "Yes, I believe he's right. I think my work here is finished for now."

Isaiah's reaction puzzled Eliakim. After his father's speech about standing up for what you believed in, he'd expected Isaiah to reject the warning. He was disappointed that the prophet had given in so easily.

Isaiah rested his hand on Eliakim's shoulder. "You were sent by Yahweh, and I thank you for coming. I heard the voice of God warning me to leave tonight, but I've been sitting here arguing with Him. I'm not afraid of King Ahaz. And I'm willing to face imprisonment like Zechariah for Yahweh's sake."

Eliakim glanced at Isaiah's sleeping family.

"Yahweh knows every breath they take," the prophet said, as if reading his thoughts. "If I left now, I would appear to be a coward, wouldn't I? Afraid that God couldn't protect my family or me? But I'm not afraid. That's why I've been wrestling with God all night. A few minutes ago I asked Him to show me that leaving Jerusalem was His will. And then you came."

Eliakim stared, amazed at Isaiah's intimacy with Yahweh. Hilkiah talked to the God of Abraham all the time, but as far as Eliakim knew, God had never talked back. Isaiah made it sound as if he had regular conversations with the Holy One, and Eliakim wondered how he'd attained such a relationship with Him. He remembered pouting about not being allowed to go to the Temple to see the heathen rituals, and he felt ashamed.

"So I guess I'll be leaving Jerusalem," Isaiah said with a sigh. He glanced around the room as if mentally starting to pack. "But it isn't fear that makes me leave. Yahweh has other plans for me. I know that I'll be starting a community of prophets to teach some of the younger ones, but beyond that . . . well, Yahweh will show me."

Eliakim stood and edged toward the door. It seemed as though hours had passed since he'd left home. "Rabbi, I should go now. Abba will be worried."

"I understand."

Isaiah led him through the door and across the small courtyard again. Eliakim felt certain that the next time Yahweh talked to Isaiah, He would tell the prophet exactly what kind of a boy he really was. He longed to apologize for wanting to go to the Temple for the wrong reasons, but he couldn't find the right words to say.

When they reached the street, Isaiah rested his hand on Eliakim's shoulder and fixed his searching gaze on him once again. "Eliakim . . ." He pronounced the name slowly, respectfully. "Your name means 'Yahweh will establish.'" Then the tone of Isaiah's voice changed to one of authority and power, and Eliakim's heart began to pound.

"In that day I will summon my servant, Eliakim son of Hilkiah. He will be a father to those who live in Jerusalem and to the house of Judah. I will place on his shoulder the key to the house of David; what he opens no one can shut, and what he shuts no one can open. I will drive him like a peg into a firm place; he will be a seat of honor for the house of his father. All the glory of his family will hang on him."

Then, much to Eliakim's surprise, the prophet embraced him. "Shalom, Eliakim. May Yahweh's peace go with you."

"And with you, Rabbi," he breathed.

# 12

HEZEKIAH SAT CROSS-LEGGED on the carpet, gazing out of his window at the new Babylonian clock tower in the palace courtyard. He idly counted the steps that spiraled up the side until they disappeared from view behind the tower, then counted them as they spiraled down the other side again. He had been waiting here for his grandfather to come back for his lessons and had watched as the shadow inched its way up to where it now stood on the top step. Another lonely morning had come and gone, and still his grandfather hadn't returned.

How long had it been, now? Hezekiah's baby brother, Gedaliah, had been born on the day that their grandfather went away, and the servants said that the baby was forty days old today. The servants had been keeping Hezekiah away from his mother's room, telling him he was a big boy who no longer needed his mama. Hezekiah was lonely, especially at night when he saw the empty bed beside his own. First his brother had gone—and now his grandfather.

He was trying to picture his grandfather's face when he heard a knock on his door. Hezekiah jumped up and ran to open it, certain that Zechariah had returned at last. Instead, a tall, lanky stranger stood gazing down at him.

"Hello there. Are you Hezekiah?" he asked, smiling pleasantly.

The man had wavy black hair and dark skin, and his clothes were in a style Hezekiah had never seen before. He appeared to be in his early thirties, yet he had no beard or mustache. He carried an untidy pile of scrolls that threatened to topple from his arms any minute, and Hezekiah remembered all the scrolls in the Temple library. Maybe his grandfather had sent this stranger.

"Yes, I'm Hezekiah," he answered hopefully.

"My name is Shebna, and I am very glad to meet you," he said with a strange accent. "I have been hired by King Ahaz to be your tutor." He smiled broadly, showing a straight, even row of white teeth. Hezekiah was too disappointed to return his smile. Shebna had been sent by King Ahaz, not by his grandfather after all.

"I already have a teacher," he said at last.

"You do? But the king assured me that I was your very first tutor."

"No, my grandpa is teaching me. I'm waiting here for him to come back." He turned away and went to sit on the floor by the window again. Shebna followed him across the room.

"Oh? The king never mentioned anything about your grandfather. What is it that your grandfather teaches you?"

"About Yahweh and His Torah. I learned to recite the Shema. Do you want to hear it?" Hezekiah wanted to impress this stranger with what a good job his grandfather was already doing.

"All right," Shebna replied, nodding slightly.

Hezekiah sat up very straight, concentrating on the words. "'Hear, O Israel. Yahweh is our God—Yahweh alone. Love Yahweh your God with all your heart and with all your soul and with all your strength.'"

"Your grandfather taught you that?"

"He's a Levite," Hezekiah said proudly. "He wears a special robe and a turban when he helps the priests in Yahweh's Temple."

He had worn them on that last day—the day his grandfather had gone to tell the king that the new altar shouldn't be in Yahweh's Temple. Zechariah had hugged Hezekiah good-bye, saying, *I'll be back. I may be a little bit late, but I'll be back."* Hezekiah had promised to wait here for him, and he had kept his promise. Why hadn't his grandfather kept his?

"So has your grandfather taught you about anything else besides Yahweh and the Torah?" Shebna asked, interrupting his thoughts.

The question puzzled him. "Well, no . . ." Those were the most important things to learn, weren't they?

"Good. I like to teach my students in my own way, from the very beginning. And from now on, I am going to be your teacher."

"Will we learn about Yahweh?"

The tutor looked uncomfortable. "No. I am not a Jew, I am Egyptian. I do not believe in Yahweh."

Hezekiah stared up at him in fear. "Do you worship Molech?"

"No, I do not worship Molech, either. How did we ever get into this?" he muttered under his breath. "Look, I am going to be very honest with you right from the start. I do not believe in any gods at all, even the gods of my own nation, Egypt. I think they are all up here," he said, tapping his high forehead. "In the minds of men. People make up gods to explain all the things they cannot understand. For example, if there is a drought, they say, 'The gods must be angry.' But I believe that there are droughts simply because it has not rained. That is all. I do not believe in the supernatural. I seek knowledge, not myths."

Hezekiah turned away from him to stare out of the window. He didn't like Shebna. He wanted his grandfather.

"What is the matter?" Shebna asked him. "Why did you make that face?"

"Yahweh is *real*!" he replied angrily. "He's like the wind—that's why you can't see Him. My grandpa didn't make him up!"

"Very well. We will not talk of Yahweh anymore. King Ahaz knows all about my views on religion, but I am not here to teach you about that." He smiled his broad, even smile again. "Would you like to start your lessons today? I am eager to see what kind of a student you will be. Can you read?" Hezekiah shook his head. "Would you like to learn how?"

"I want my grandpa." He felt tears stinging his eyes, and he quickly rubbed them away.

Shebna gave a forced smile and sprawled on the floor beside him, dumping his scrolls in a heap. "I will make you a bargain, Hezekiah. We will take turns—first, you answer a question for me, and then I will answer one for you. Is that fair enough?"

Before Hezekiah could reply, Shebna pulled a scroll from the pile and unrolled it. "This scroll tells a story. Once I teach you to read, you will know what that story is about." He produced a small clay tablet and began carving on it with a stylus. "This is the word for *house*. See? Now, why don't you look at this story and see if you can find *house* anywhere on the scroll." Shebna pushed the scroll and the tablet across the floor in front of Hezekiah.

For a moment he wasn't sure if he should read it or not, afraid of being disloyal to his grandfather. But the Temple library had been his grandfather's favorite place, and its rows of scrolls had captured Hezekiah's imagination. He longed to unlock their mysteries and read about all his favorite heroes. In the end his curiosity won, and he began to study Shebna's scroll. It was a jumble of strange markings, and he nearly pushed it away when suddenly he spotted the word Shebna had drawn on the tablet. Then he saw it again and again, and he felt the power of unlocking a secret. He could read!

"There . . . there . . . there and there," he replied, pointing to several places on the scroll.

Shebna smiled broadly. "That was very good. You found all of them. You have learned to read one word already. Soon you will be able to read the entire story. Now, what about numbers? Do you know your numbers?"

"I can count. And I can name the twelve tribes of Israel. Want to hear them?"

"Not now." Shebna scraped the tablet clean and began drawing circles in the soft clay. "Suppose you had six figs and you ate two. How many would—"

"Four." Hezekiah answered before Shebna finished, and the tutor's thick black eyebrows rose in surprise.

"And suppose I had five figs. How many would we—"

"Nine."

"Have you done this before?"

Hezekiah thought the question was ridiculous. "I've eaten figs lots of times."

"That is not what I meant. Anyway," Shebna quickly continued, "if we wanted to divide up all the figs between us—"

"You'd have to cut one in half," Hezekiah said, already picturing them in his mind, "or it wouldn't be fair."

Shebna's eyes widened in surprise. "I did not realize my division problem worked out unevenly, but you solved it anyway. You seem quite bright."

"Can I ask you a question now?" Hezekiah asked.

Shebna smiled weakly. "Certainly. That was the bargain."

"Why do you smile all the time if you're not really happy inside?"

Shebna's smile faded, and he looked at Hezekiah in surprise. "And what makes you say I am not happy?"

"Because your eyes aren't happy."

Shebna leaned back on his elbows as he studied him. "You seem quite perceptive, as well as bright. Tutoring you could be a tremendous challenge. But you do not like me very much, do you?"

Hezekiah shrugged. "I don't know . . ." He gazed down at the scrolls on the floor in front of him, feeling sad again. Then he remembered that it was his turn to ask Shebna another question. "Where's my grandpa? He said he'd come back for my lessons, but it's been days and days."

And for the first time Hezekiah formed the question in his mind that he had tried so hard not to think about. If his grandfather had abandoned him, would Yahweh abandon him, too?

"I do not know where your grandfather is," Shebna sighed. "That is the truth. I will try to find out for you. But in the meantime, the king has hired me to teach you. Is there something you would like to learn about?"

Hezekiah thought of all the soldiers who had come for his brothers and him. The men had been armed with swords and spears, and he'd been helpless against them. If his grandfather and Yahweh could no longer protect him, then Hezekiah needed to protect himself. "I want to learn to be a soldier, like King David," he said.

"Really? Do you like to read about warriors and battles?" Shebna shuffled quickly through his scrolls. "I have many stories about brave warriors and the battles they fought. Perhaps we can read one of them."

"Do you have the one about David and Goliath?" For the first time, Hezekiah was almost interested.

"Maybe . . . somewhere . . ." The scrolls rustled noisily as Shebna rifled through the pile. "Let me see. There must be one here . . ."

"My grandpa has lots of stories about King David in the Temple library. He'll let you borrow some."

"Yes, I am certain he would," Shebna said. For some reason, he sounded annoyed. He abruptly pushed his scrolls aside and studied Hezekiah again. "So, you want to be a soldier, yes? Can you shoot a bow and arrow? Fight with a sword? Throw a spear? Can you ride a horse?"

Hezekiah shook his head to each of these questions.

"Would you like to learn how?"

"Yes!" Hezekiah couldn't help feeling excited. If he had his own sword and learned to use it, he could save himself from Molech. He wouldn't have to wait for Yahweh or his grandfather, who might never come back again.

"Follow me, then," Shebna said as he stood. "First we will go to the stables and find you a horse, then to the armory to get a sword. . . ."

Hezekiah scrambled to his feet, hurrying to keep up as Shebna strode from the room.

Zechariah walked down the long hallway from his room to the door, each step slow and deliberate. He knew he had to keep his aching joints moving in spite of the pain, or eventually he would be unable to walk at all. The sun glared off the golden roof of the Temple, blinding him momentarily as he stepped outside, and he shielded his eyes from it. Then he slowly crossed the deserted courtyard, aware of the gatekeepers who were watching him from their posts.

As his eyes adjusted to the bright light, a sudden movement in the middle court caught his attention. He shaded his eyes from the glare and drew closer for a better look. Someone seemed to be beckoning to him.

"Abba—Abba, it's me!"

"Abijah? Is it really you?" Zechariah hobbled to the gate that separated the courtyards and embraced his daughter, blinded now by tears.

"Abba! Thank God you're all right! I've been praying and praying. . . ."

"Yes, I'm fine, just fine," he assured her. "A little stiff in my joints maybe, but that's what happens when you live in a crumbling old building." Abijah was the first person from the outside that he had seen in more than a month, and she looked lovelier to him than ever before. "So, tell me your news. You've had your baby, I see."

"Yes, another son. Ahaz named him Gedaliah. He's forty days old already, and I came to the Temple today to make the offering for purification." She smiled as she spoke, but then Zechariah saw her eyes fill with tears.

"What's wrong?" he asked gently.

"I've been so worried about you, Abba. I overheard Ahaz telling Uriah to execute you, and I've been so afraid. . . . I begged Uriah not to do it. . . ."

He drew her into his arms again. "I'm fine, Abijah. Uriah put me under house arrest to keep me quiet—that's all. We've had a major disagreement, you might say, about his new altar, and I think my living arrangements here will be quite permanent."

"Then you're a prisoner?"

"It's not so bad. I spend a lot of time reading and studying the Torah. And I can walk around the courtyard when there aren't any sacrifices being held. It's not so bad."

"How can you be so calm about it? You're being held prisoner for no reason, without even a trial."

"It's all right, Abijah. Yes, at first I questioned God throughout the long, boring days and sleepless nights. I kept waiting for Him to vindicate me and to punish my enemies. And when He didn't, I immersed myself in the Holy Torah, always questioning, demanding answers.

"But then I read the Book of Job, and I discovered another victim of injustice who demanded answers from God. And do you know what I learned from Job? Yahweh doesn't owe us an explanation for what He does. He's sovereign over all: 'Can you fathom the mysteries of God? Can you probe the limits of the Almighty? They are higher than the heavens—what can you do? They are deeper than the depths of the grave—what can you know? . . . If he comes along and confines you in prison . . . who can oppose him?' So you see? I don't need to know why anymore."

"Things have gotten worse in Jerusalem since you've been imprisoned here," Abijah said. "King Ahaz worships every new god he hears of, and it seems as if Uriah is encouraging him. The servants told me that Ahaz consults witches and mediums."

"I've seen the changes here, too. The quiet orderly rhythm of the Temple is no longer the same. Ahaz even had the doors of the holy sanctuary closed. Can you imagine that? The golden candlesticks in the Holy Place have gone out. And Uriah has instituted an entirely new order of rituals and sacrifices in Yahweh's Temple. I wouldn't worship here even if they allowed me to."

"It scares me, Abba. What's going to happen to our nation?"

"I'm afraid that we're rushing headlong toward ruin, plunging deeper and deeper into sin. I don't suppose there are too many godly people left anymore. I questioned Yahweh about that, too, but He showed me in His word that He's still in control of the nation, the king, and even Uriah. 'If he holds back the waters, there is drought; if he lets them loose, they devastate the land. . . . Both deceived and deceiver are his. . . . He silences the lips of trusted advisors and takes away the discernment of elders. . . . He deprives the leaders of the earth of their reason; he sends them wandering through a trackless waste. They grope in darkness with no light; he makes them stagger like drunkards.'"

"I came to comfort you, Abba, and instead you're comforting me," Abijah said.

"How is Hezekiah?" Zechariah asked quietly. "How I miss him!"

Abijah's face looked troubled. "They haven't allowed him to visit me since Gedaliah was born. The servants told me that the king hired an Egyptian scholar to tutor him."

"An Egyptian? What can a foreigner teach him? Hezekiah should be studying the Torah, and learning about—" He stopped when he saw the fear in his daughter's eyes. Zechariah drew her close again.

"There is a reason for everything that happens," he said in a trembling voice. "Hezekiah is in Yahweh's hands now, and we have to trust Him. I pray many, many times each day for Yahweh to be with Hezekiah. And Yahweh hears. He'll watch over him."

"I'm afraid for you, Abba," Abijah murmured. "What's going to happen to you?"

"Don't be afraid. Yahweh has given me peace. That doesn't mean that I'll never have struggles or questions. Our lives will always be filled with those. But the peace of God comes from knowing that there's an order in the universe and there is a reason for whatever happens, even if only Yahweh can see it. We must trust His sovereign will. 'To God belong wisdom and power. Counsel and understanding are his. What he tears down cannot be rebuilt; the man he imprisons cannot be released.'"

"Then they'll never let you go free again?"

"It doesn't matter, Abijah. It doesn't matter at all. I have Yahweh's peace—and that makes me free."

Abijah returned from the Temple immensely relieved. Her father was alive, and although he was a prisoner, his unwavering faith in Yahweh—his certainty that God was in control—had convinced her to trust Him, too. Zechariah had changed so much during the months since Molech's sacrifice—and especially since he'd come to the palace to help Hezekiah. He was no longer the pitiful alcoholic she'd known growing up, but the man of God who had once counseled kings. She knew that those changes—and his newfound strength and courage—had come from God, and his faith fueled her own.

Once inside the palace, Abijah passed the hallway that led to Uriah's quarters. She wished she could send a message to him, thanking him for sparing her father's life. But Uriah would be angry with her for taking such a risk.

She hurried up the stairs to Hezekiah's room, eager to explain to him that his grandfather still loved him, that he longed to come back but couldn't. But when she got there, Hezekiah's room was empty. Disappointed, she returned to the harem, certain that baby Gedaliah would be awake by now and crying to be fed. But when Abijah opened the door, the room was strangely quiet, the cradle empty.

"Where's my baby?" she asked Deborah.

"They came and took him."

A tremor of fear went down Abijah's spine when she recalled Ahaz's sacrifices to Molech. "Took him? Where? Why?"

"They moved him to the palace nursery, my lady." Deborah seemed nervous for some reason, and Abijah followed her gaze; Ahaz's chamberlain stood in the corner with his arms folded, waiting.

"Why are you here?" she asked him.

"His Majesty has summoned you to the throne room." He gestured to the door and waited for her to lead the way.

Abijah's heart began to race. Ahaz had never summoned her to the throne room before. "Perhaps . . . would he like to see his new son?" she asked.

"The king said nothing about his son. He sent for you."

*Lord, help me,* she prayed, and she remembered her father's words: *"There is a reason for whatever happens, even if only Yahweh can see it. We must trust His sovereign will."* She drew a deep breath for courage and walked through the corridors to the throne room.

King Ahaz's anger was apparent as soon as she entered, his expression one of slowly simmering rage. She bowed low on shaking knees, wondering what she had done to cause his displeasure and how long he had been waiting for her. When she rose again, she noticed that Uriah wasn't in the room, and her heart seemed to stop beating. Had someone seen them together, kissing? A tall, lanky man in Egyptian robes stood below the throne, but Abijah was certain that he wasn't one of the palace servants. Could he have seen her with Uriah? She whispered another prayer, then said, "You sent for me, Your Majesty?"

"Where have you been? I sent my servant to the harem for you an hour ago, and you weren't there."

"I'm sorry, my lord. I went up to Yahweh's Temple to offer the sacrifice of purification that's required by the Torah. It has been forty days since the birth of our son."

"Without my permission?"

The question stunned her. "Yes . . . I–I'm sorry. I didn't know that I needed your permission to fulfill one of Yahweh's commandments."

"*I'm* the one who decides which gods my family will worship and *when* they will worship them. You will consult *me,* not some outdated rulebook, when you want to know if it's time to give an offering."

"I'm sorry, Your Majesty."

"But that's not why I called you here." Once again, Abijah was afraid that he had found out about her visit to Uriah's chambers. She risked glancing up at Ahaz and noticed how strange his eyes looked. They had a frenzied, manic appearance that she had never seen in them before, and his pupils looked abnormally large. This was not the man she had married.

"By whose authority did you invite your father into my palace to brainwash my son with myths and lies?" Ahaz shouted.

For a long moment, Abijah was speechless. This wasn't about Uriah at all—it was much, much worse. It involved Hezekiah. And her father. And Yahweh. Abijah silently asked God for help and heard the words that came out of her mouth as if someone else spoke them.

"I-I wanted Hezekiah to learn some of our nation's history and traditions. I thought he should hear the stories of Yahweh that I grew up with. He's my son—"

"No! You gave birth to him and to this new child—that's all! You have no other part to play in any of my sons' lives. How dare you try to influence what he learns?"

"But Yahweh is—"

"You'll never see any of my sons again—ever!"

It was Ahaz's most vicious blow, more painful than any beating—and one she hadn't bargained for. Tears filled her eyes when she remembered the baby's empty cradle, and she longed to cling to Ahaz's feet and plead with him not to take her children away from her, to at least let her hold them one last time and kiss them good-bye. But she knew what Ahaz's answer would be.

"And now you will tell Shebna, my son's tutor, exactly which lies your father taught him."

For a reason she couldn't explain, Abijah felt no fear. She had already lost her sons, and she had nothing else to lose except her life. Without her children, Abijah's life with Ahaz wasn't worth living.

"My father didn't teach Hezekiah lies," she said calmly, wiping her tears. "He taught him about Yahweh, the God of our ancestors, and how He delivered our people from slavery in Egypt. He taught Hezekiah the truth—that there are no other gods but Yahweh, the God of Abraham and Isaac, the God of our fathers—"

"Your father is dead," Ahaz said coldly. "I ordered Uriah to execute him for treason." He studied her closely, as if hoping to enjoy her reaction. Abijah prayed that he would never find out that Zechariah was still alive.

"He and Isaiah were plotting against me," Ahaz continued when she didn't respond. "And I think you're part of it. I think that's why you've played the dutiful wife these past few months. It's why you've been running up to the Temple every day. And it's why you brought your father into my palace."

"No, Your Majesty. It isn't true. I—"

"You and Zechariah have been conspiring to brainwash my heir. And once you control his mind, you'll murder me while I sleep."

"Please—there is no conspiracy," Abijah said.

"You're a liar!" Ahaz's face grew red as his anger mounted. "Ever since I sent Yahweh's gold to Assyria, his so-called spokesmen have been plotting to get rid of me. Your father and Isaiah invoke Yahweh's name every time they threaten me. They disrupted my sacrifice in front of the entire nation, hoping to trigger a revolt. Isaiah has royal blood in his veins, and I know he wants my crown. If there's no plot, how did he manage to disappear as soon as he heard that I was about to arrest him?"

Abijah scrambled to think of a reply, desperate to reason with him. "Your Majesty, Uriah is Yahweh's high priest. He can explain to you why my father and Isaiah—"

"You leave Uriah out of this. He has already proven his loyalty to me by his obedience. He didn't threaten me with Yahweh's wrath when I ordered him to make sacrifices to Molech and Assur—Uriah obeyed me. But we'll soon see whose side you're on. You will bring an offering to Asherah's sacred grove—right now. *She's* the goddess of fertility, and you need to thank *her* for the gift of my new son. If you refuse, it will prove that you're part of the conspiracy. You'll be executed for treason like your father."

Abijah could scarcely breathe. She didn't want to die. Offering a sacrifice to Asherah would be a simple way to escape the death penalty. It was just a meaningless ritual. Abijah could appease Ahaz and perhaps win back his trust if she did it. Maybe he would relent and let her see her children again. But she also knew Yahweh's commandments—thou shalt not make a graven image; thou shalt not worship or bow down to it. She might buy time here on earth if she pretended to worship Asherah, but she would face God's judgment for all eternity.

"I can't take part in idolatry," she said, her voice barely a whisper. "I won't worship any other God but Yahweh."

Ahaz's eyes turned as cold and gray as granite. "You'd rather die than obey me?"

Abijah had to choose between her life and her soul. She had nothing more to lose. Her father was imprisoned, and she would never see her children again. "I can't disobey God," she said in a trembling voice.

Ahaz gestured to his guards. "Very well. Grant her wish."

Two of them moved forward and gripped her arms. Abijah's heart pounded with terror. What had she done? She was going to die! Her children would grow up without a mother. She needed to kiss her baby good-bye and urge Hezekiah to remember what Zechariah had taught him—to never betray his God. What would become of her sons? Abijah's limbs seemed to melt with fear. She couldn't move or walk.

*Lord, help me!* she prayed.

And suddenly Yahweh's peace washed over her, filling her. It was the same peace she felt up on the Temple Mount when she was in His presence; the same calm she'd felt when her father assured her that God was in control. Yahweh held her in His arms. Death wouldn't separate her from Him, it would draw them closer. In the few minutes she had left before she died, she would put her children into God's hands, knowing that they were safer there than in her own arms.

But before the soldiers had a chance to lead Abijah from the throne room, she felt God giving her the courage to say one final word. She turned and met her idolatrous husband's gaze, repeating the words he loathed and feared: "Hear, O Israel. Yahweh is God—Yahweh alone."

Uriah hurried down the hill to the palace, worried that he had been absent from Ahaz's side for too long. The king's emotions had been extremely unstable since he'd returned from Damascus, and Uriah couldn't bear to be in his presence for extended periods of time. Ahaz had developed such an obsessive fear of doing something to anger his Assyrian masters or to insult their gods, that he imagined plots and conspiracies everywhere.

Uriah had said that he needed to meet with the Levites, but he had walked up to the Temple to be alone. He had stood on the mountaintop, breathing the familiar aroma of sacrifices and incense, enjoying the courtyard's spaciousness after the dark confines of the palace, savoring the peace and quiet. The city of Jerusalem lay far below him, and so did its problems and concerns. He had gazed at the distant, unshakeable hills and had drawn strength from them.

But he had lingered longer than he'd planned. Now, as he hurried toward the throne room, he hoped that his absence hadn't angered Ahaz. But the throne room doors stood open, and the king was no longer holding court. Shebna, the Egyptian tutor Ahaz had recently hired, stood outside the chamber with his shoulders hunched, his head bent low, his hands on his thighs as if in distress.

"Are you all right?" Uriah asked.

Shebna gave a start of surprise and looked up. Uriah could see that the man was deeply shaken, his dark face as pale and gray as a dead fish. "It is all my fault," Shebna mumbled. "I mean, I may have caused . . . I didn't mean to, but how was I to know that the king would respond in such a drastic way?"

Uriah took Shebna's arm to steady him and felt his body trembling. "Can you calm down and speak clearly?"

"I need to know what I have done. Have I truly uncovered a plot or . . . or caused a terrible tragedy?"

The mention of a plot made Uriah uneasy. "We can't talk here," he said. He glanced around to see if they had been seen or overheard, then led the tutor down the hall to his own quarters. After dismissing his servants, Uriah once again asked Shebna what was wrong. The Egyptian drew a deep breath.

"As you know, I began my tutoring duties with Prince Hezekiah yesterday. But when we spoke, the prince told me that he already had a tutor. It was my understanding that I was to be the first one."

"You are the first one," Uriah said impatiently. "Hezekiah is barely old enough to start lessons."

Shebna shook his head. "No, my lord. Prince Hezekiah said that his grandfather has been teaching him."

Uriah felt a ripple of fear. "Zechariah?"

"I do not know his name—but he is a Levite."

"Go on."

"But it is too terrible—!"

Uriah saw Shebna's horror and his own fear began to multiply. He wanted to shake the story out of him, but he forced himself to wait until the man was in control.

"I am sorry," Shebna finally said. "I should have come to you, first. I made the mistake of asking King Ahaz about the grandfather. If only I had known. . . ."

"Known what?"

Shebna swallowed. "King Ahaz sent for his wife this morning while I was present. It was her father who has been teaching the prince, and she was the one who gave him access to the palace."

Uriah had to sit down. "Wait a minute—what are you saying?"

"The king accused his wife of treason along with her father. He said they and another man who is of royal blood were conspiring to assassinate him once they had brainwashed his heir. The king's wife denied everything, but he . . . he ordered her to be executed."

"Not Abijah!" Uriah sprang to his feet, the cry out of his mouth before he could stop it.

"The king gave her a chance to prove her loyalty—the same way that you have proven yours, my lord. He demanded that she worship Asherah. But she refused . . . and . . ."

"*No!* I need to stop this!" Strength surged through Uriah as he ran toward the door. He jerked it open so violently he nearly tore it from its hinges.

"Wait, my lord!" Shebna called from behind him. "Wait! It is too late! They already took her out to be executed."

"*NO!* You're lying!" Uriah whirled around and grabbed the tutor's shoulders, nearly shaking the life from him before regaining control of himself.

"I am sorry," Shebna murmured. "It is true, and I am so very sorry."

"No, forgive me," Uriah said, releasing him. "Did I hurt you?"

"Just tell me, my lord, for my own peace of mind—did I do the right thing?"

Uriah was too distraught to offer reassurances to this man. *Abijah—executed?* It was too horrible to grasp. He wanted to break down and cry, but he didn't dare weep in front of Shebna. His eyes burned with the effort of holding back his grief. "I-I don't know," Uriah finally said. "I'll find out and—and I'll let you know. You may go now."

Uriah covered his face and collapsed to the floor as soon as Shebna was gone. Why hadn't he been there? If only he had remained in the throne room. If only he hadn't stayed at the Temple so long. He had saved Abijah's father and her son—why hadn't he been there to save her?

*Abijah . . . gone?* Uriah recalled his last conversation with her, when she had begged for her father's life. She had insisted that if Ahaz ever commanded her to sin against Yahweh she would choose to obey God, not him. *"At the cost of your life?"* he had asked her.

*"Yes—even at the cost of my life. Because if I denied my God, I would have nothing left. He would give me the strength to make that choice."*

Uriah covered his mouth, fighting the urge to be sick. At that moment he hated Ahaz enough to murder him. The king had married the only woman Uriah had ever loved—and now he had killed her. Uriah scrambled to his feet. He couldn't serve Ahaz for one more day—one more hour!

He would resign. That's what Zechariah had asked him to do months ago. *"Help me oppose Ahaz's idolatry,"* he had begged. *"You're serving the wrong king."*

But Uriah knew what would happen if he resigned now. Ahaz had no qualms about executing his supposed enemies—Zechariah, Isaiah, his own wife! Uriah would be next.

And he didn't want to die.

"Oh, God!" he moaned as he sank to the floor again. But it was a cry of despair, not a prayer. Uriah couldn't recall the last time he had prayed. *"Every time you compromise, something inside your spirit dies a little,"* Zechariah had warned him. Was that why God seemed so far away now? Was that why Uriah couldn't bring himself to make the same choice that Abijah had made, to die for her faith?

No. Uriah still believed in Yahweh, still served Him. He could do more good for God if he remained alive and served at the king's side than if he died a martyr. He had already saved Hezekiah's life and Zechariah's. And he might have saved Abijah's life, too—if he had been there. Oh, God, if only he had been there! But he hadn't been—and Abijah was dead.

Abijah was dead.

Grief suddenly overwhelmed Uriah. He buried his face in a pillow so no one would hear his bitter sobs, and wept.

---

Hezekiah was surprised to see Shebna in his bedroom the next morning when he woke up. He had enjoyed the hour that he'd spent with him yesterday, visiting the royal stables and watching the soldiers sparring. But Shebna could never replace his grandfather.

"Why are you here?" Hezekiah asked as he climbed out of bed.

"Your father says that you are no longer a baby. Now that you have begun your studies with me, it is time you moved out of the nursery."

Shebna had brought half a dozen servants with him, and they began packing all of Hezekiah's things and removing them from the room while he got dressed and tied on his sandals. Shebna wasn't smiling his phony grin the way he had yesterday. His face, like his eyes, was very somber.

Everything seemed to be happening too fast. Hezekiah didn't want to move out of his room. What if his grandfather came back, looking for him? He wanted to stay here, near his mother, even if she was busy with the new baby all the time. He fought back tears as he watched the servants carry away his things.

"Are you ready to go?" Shebna asked, gesturing to the door.

Hezekiah nodded, but he wanted to see his mother first, to tell her that they were making him move away from her. He needed to hug her and say good-bye. He ran through the door ahead of Shebna and turned down the hall toward the harem, knowing that Shebna wouldn't be allowed to follow him. He burst through the door to his mother's suite without knocking—but she wasn't there. The room looked huge and empty, stripped of all her things. Even his baby brother's cradle was gone.

"Mama?" he called as he searched the vacant suite. "Mama, where are you?" The rooms were so empty his voice echoed.

"You don't belong in here. You need to get out."

Hezekiah whirled around. The harem eunuch stood in the doorway.

"Where's my mama?"

"She's . . . she's gone." The eunuch's voice sounded strange, as if something was choking him. "Come here," he said, beckoning to Hezekiah. He backed away.

"Where did she go?" he asked warily. Wherever it was, no matter how far away, he would find her and go to her.

"Hasn't anyone told you?" the eunuch asked.

"Told me what?"

The man swallowed. When he spoke his voice was very soft. "Your mother is dead."

"No, she isn't!" Hezekiah shouted. "It isn't true! She isn't dead!"

But the eunuch closed his eyes and nodded. "I'm sorry. I wish it wasn't true. Your mother was a beautiful woman . . . and we will all miss her."

Hezekiah bolted past the man and ran from the room, blinded by the tears he could no longer hold back. He wanted to keep running forever—he didn't care where. But Shebna grabbed him as he sprinted past his old bedroom and pulled him inside the room. It was empty, just like his mother's room. Even his bed was gone.

"Let me go! Let me go!" he cried as he struggled with Shebna. The tutor released him, but he stood in front of the door, blocking the way out.

"I am sorry, Hezekiah. I wanted to tell you about your mother in a much kinder way, but you did not give me a chance."

"It isn't true! She didn't die!"

Shebna sighed. "I know how difficult it must be for you to accept it—but it is true. Do you understand what it means when someone dies?"

Hezekiah understood all too well. It meant she wasn't coming back—ever. He would never see her again. He had watched his brothers die, and they were gone forever. Hezekiah sank down on the bare floor and sobbed. Too many things were changing. He was losing all of the people he loved. He didn't even get a chance to see Mama one last time or say good-bye! Now he was alone—so alone. Hezekiah buried his face in his arms and cried until his whole body ached.

After a while, he was aware of Shebna sitting down beside him. The tutor laid a comforting hand on Hezekiah's shoulder. "I am sorry," he murmured. "I am truly sorry."

Shebna had known all about his mother. Maybe he knew about his grandfather, too. Hezekiah lifted his head. "Do you know where my grandpa is? You said you would find out."

The tutor hesitated for such a long time that Hezekiah wondered if his grandfather was dead, too. At last Shebna drew a deep breath. "I am sorry if I misled you when I agreed to find an answer to your question yesterday. I can teach you to read and to work with numbers. I will gladly teach you everything I know about nature and about history and geography. But if you have a question about your family or about religion, you must ask your father."

His father.

Hezekiah's grief hardened into hatred at the mention of his father. He was the one who was making everything in Hezekiah's life change. His father had ordered the sacrifices to Molech. His father had built a pagan altar in Yahweh's Temple, and Zechariah had gone up there to tell him it was wrong. *Your father is very unpredictable,* his grandfather had said. *I'm not sure how he will react.* His father was the reason Zechariah had never returned.

Hezekiah lowered his head again, weeping with grief and helpless rage. His father was the cause of all his sorrow. But he was the king of Judah, and Hezekiah was powerless against him.

After a long time, he felt Shebna's hand on his shoulder again. "You are not alone," he said quietly. "I am your friend. If you want to talk, perhaps it will help you feel better."

Hezekiah wanted his terrible pain to go away. It was too hard to feel this way. He hurt so much he could scarcely breathe. But he didn't want to talk to Shebna.

"When the rainy season comes," Shebna continued, "it seems as if it will never end. But then one day the clouds part and the sun shines again. It will be that way with your sadness, too. There is so much I want to teach you about the world. And believe me, the sunlight of knowledge is a wonderful healer. When you are learning something new, you will begin to forget your loss for a little while. I can help you forget your terrible sadness, if you will let me."

Hezekiah wanted to believe him. But then he remembered his mother's empty room, remembered that she was dead, and he began to cry all over again.

"Would you like to be alone for a while?" Shebna asked. "Or shall I stay?"

Hezekiah didn't think he could bear it if one more person left him. "Stay," he whispered.

"Very well."

Hezekiah sobbed until he had no tears left. When they finally died away, he felt empty inside. Shebna rose to his feet, stretching his lanky body.

"When you are ready, Hezekiah, I have selected a horse for you. A trainer is waiting to teach you to ride it. And I have another surprise. The armory is crafting a sword just your size, for you to practice with."

Hezekiah raised his head and wiped his face on his sleeve. "Will it be sharp?" he asked in a hoarse voice.

Shebna smiled. "Would you like it to be?"

Hezekiah nodded.

"Then let's go tell them, shall we?" He extended a hand to help Hezekiah to his feet.

# Part Two

Ahaz . . . shut the doors

of the Lord's temple and set up altars

at every street corner in Jerusalem. In every

town in Judah he built high places to burn

sacrifices to other gods and provoked the

Lord, the God of his fathers, to anger.

2 CHRONICLES 28:24–25 NIV

# 13

HEZEKIAH GLANCED AT THE clock tower in the courtyard outside the window of his study. It was time for his appointment with King Ahaz. He rose from his seat beside Shebna and straightened his robes, then raked his fingers through his beard to smooth it. He wished he could avoid this meeting altogether.

"I'm a grown man, Shebna. Why does being summoned by my father always make me feel like a child?"

"He is the king," Shebna replied, rolling up the scroll they had been studying. "It is his job to make everyone feel belittled."

"No, it's more than that. No matter what I do, he makes me feel like I've failed to measure up to his expectations. And I never know what to expect when he summons me. He never tells me the reason beforehand."

Shebna set down the scroll and leaned back. He was now in his late forties with silver streaks through his dark hair. His lanky body was thinner than ever, as if every morsel he ate fueled a mind that was always at work, analyzing, reasoning. "Did the king summon you to the throne room or to his private chambers?" he asked. "That should give you a clue."

"Private chambers. A personal matter, I presume."

"Hmm. Relationships between fathers and sons can be notoriously difficult, especially for two men who are as different as you and your father are."

"Yes, and he's also the king—that makes our relationship impossible." Hezekiah started toward the door, but Shebna touched his sleeve, stopping him.

"A word of advice? Be careful. King Ahaz has an unpredictable temper. Whatever happens, do not make him angry." The worried look on Shebna's face surprised Hezekiah. He'd never realized that his tutor was so afraid of Ahaz. But now was not the time to ask him why.

"Thanks for the advice," Hezekiah said. He hurried away to face whatever surprises lay ahead.

King Ahaz aroused a broad range of emotions in Hezekiah, from fear and hatred to pity and revulsion. But those emotions rarely included respect—and never, that he could recall, had they included love. His bitterness extended back as far as he could remember, though the exact cause of it was long forgotten. He avoided Ahaz as much as possible and dreaded being summoned to see him.

A servant opened the door for him to his father's opulent chambers. Thick carpets warmed the stone floors and Assyrian tapestries decorated the walls. The scent of incense filled every corner of the room, sticking in Hezekiah's throat. He bowed low, steeling himself for a possible confrontation and remembering Shebna's warning. Regardless of what happened, he would not arouse Ahaz's anger.

"You wanted to see me, Your Majesty?"

"Yes. I may have some interesting news for you." Ahaz reclined on his divan among a clutter of silken cushions, his expression one of boredom. Hezekiah wondered if he had been summoned to be Ahaz's entertainment. His father didn't offer him a seat but left him standing while he took his time coming to the point. "Pour my son some wine," he told his servant.

"No, thank you," Hezekiah said, holding up his hand. He hoped that his refusal wouldn't irritate his father, but it wasn't even noon. He saw Ahaz eying him narrowly.

"How old are you now?" he said at last.

"I'm twenty-five, sir."

"Twenty-five . . . is that so? Well, I'm fairly pleased with your education so far. You've done well in your studies and your military training." He rose ponderously from his seat to wander around the room, occasionally picking up some trinket and examining it casually.

"Tell me—has Shebna taught you how to conduct yourself at formal ceremonial proceedings?"

Hezekiah considered how to answer. He knew that his father conducted frenzied sacrifices at altars all over the city, and they disgusted him. "If you mean taking part in formal religious rituals, I really don't have much interest in—"

"No, no," Ahaz said impatiently. "I don't mean religious sacrifices. I know you never participate in those." The truth was that Ahaz rarely allowed Hezekiah to join him at public ceremonies or even at the Temple's worship services. The physical contrast between father and son was great, and it was almost as if Ahaz didn't want his heir to compete with him in the public eye. He kept Hezekiah in the background as much as possible.

"No, what I meant was, how much do you know about formal diplomatic protocol?"

"I'm fluent in a few languages," Hezekiah said, trying to sound patient. He was already tired of his father's games and wondered where these questions were leading. "And I've studied the customs of international diplomacy, if that's what you mean."

"Yes. That's exactly what I mean. And do you like to travel?"

"I've traveled throughout most of our nation, Your Majesty, and it was quite enjoyable." The prospect of leaving Jerusalem's confining walls excited Hezekiah, but he pretended indifference, unwilling to give Ahaz any leverage over him.

"Good, good," Ahaz replied, and for no apparent reason he began to laugh. But his laughter triggered a coughing fit that left the king wheezing and flushed. Hezekiah hesitated, unsure how to react. Should he express his concern—or would sympathy only highlight his father's weakness? In the end he said nothing, and Ahaz's servant helped the king back to his divan and refilled his wineglass. Ahaz took a few sips.

"Tell my cupbearer to send something stronger than this," he said. When the servant was gone, Ahaz looked up at Hezekiah again. "It's time I arranged a marriage for you. Would you like that?"

Ahaz's condescending manner infuriated Hezekiah, and he had difficulty hiding it. His father was toying with him, hinting at travel, then tossing in a marriage. He knew the danger of contradicting his father, but he couldn't stop himself from saying, "I already have several concubines, sir. A legal wife doesn't interest me at all."

"Well, you'd better get interested," Ahaz growled. "My trade minister is negotiating an agreement, and if he's successful, I've decided that his daughter will be wed to you."

The idea of being used as a prize, a reward for doing the king a favor, enraged Hezekiah. For a moment he couldn't speak.

"The girl's name is Hephzibah," Ahaz continued. "She sounds *delightful*, doesn't she?" He laughed at his own joke, a pun on her name, which meant *my delight is in her*. Hezekiah nodded mutely, knowing that his opinion didn't matter. Ahaz had already made up his mind. He would be commanded to marry her.

"Hephzibah's father is negotiating a trade agreement with Tyre. Are you interested in traveling with him as an envoy?"

"Yes, of course. But Tyre? Why would—" Hezekiah stopped short, catching himself. As much as he liked the idea of travel, the trade agreement made no sense to him.

"But—*what*?" Ahaz asked impatiently.

He hesitated, aware of the danger in questioning Ahaz's decision. But Shebna had taught him to think logically, and Hezekiah couldn't help speaking his thoughts. "Why would we want a trade agreement with Tyre, since we have no direct access routes to their territory?"

Ahaz looked at him blankly. "What are you talking about?"

"When the Philistines conquered our territory in the foothills, they took control of all the northern passes through the mountains to the coastal trade route. In order to trade with Tyre, we'd have to go through Philistine territory and pay duty or else go farther north and—"

Hezekiah stopped when he saw his father's face slowly reddening. Too late, he realized the mistake he'd made in demonstrating his superior knowledge to Ahaz.

"But you're aware of all this, sir," he mumbled. "I didn't mean to imply . . ." But Hezekiah knew from his father's expression that Ahaz had been ignorant of the situation.

The king sprang from his couch to confront him. "You have all the answers, I suppose? Maybe you think you'd be a better king than I am?"

"I wasn't trying to—"

"Don't interrupt me! I'm still the king of this nation, not you! Although you'd jump at the chance to take over, wouldn't you?"

Hezekiah didn't reply.

"*Wouldn't* you?" Ahaz demanded, glaring up at him.

"No, sir. I don't want to take over. But I do feel that I'm capable of holding a position of responsibility in your government, and I'm willing to serve in any—"

"I'm sure you are, just like Absalom served *his* father, King David, by staging a rebellion!" Ahaz looked him over accusingly, as if Hezekiah had chosen to be tall and lean and muscular in order to spite his overweight father. "I know the fickleness of the masses. The last thing I need is for you to persuade them that you'd make a better ruler than I would."

His father's accusations angered Hezekiah, and in spite of his resolution, he lost his temper in self-defense. "I never said I wanted to take over! But since I *am* going to be the king someday, why can't you at least allow me to attend the Advisory Council meetings once in a while so I can get acquainted with how the nation—"

"No! How dare you?" Ahaz turned his back and stalked across the room. "Next thing I know you'll be poisoning me in my sleep."

"What?"

"Silence!" The rage that Hezekiah saw in his father's eyes stunned him into silence more than the command did. He watched Ahaz gulp some wine, and it seemed to cool his father's temper. Hezekiah waited.

"You're not ready to take responsibility yet," Ahaz finally said. "Maybe once you settle down with your new wife I'll have more for you to do—if you deserve it, that is. Now get out!"

Hezekiah brushed past the royal cupbearer on his way out and strode down the palace corridors, furious with Ahaz. But he was angrier with himself for losing his temper. It would probably cost him the opportunity to travel with the trade mission—as useless as it was. He only wished that Ahaz had changed his mind about the marriage, too.

As soon as Hezekiah reached his study, Shebna read the anger on his face and sighed. "Your father did not have good news for you, I gather?"

Hezekiah groaned and sank onto a pile of cushions near the window. "I don't know—it might have been good news if I hadn't lost my temper. My father was about to make me an envoy on a trade mission—to Tyre, of all places. But when I pointed out the futility of a trade agreement without trade routes, it infuriated him to discover that I knew more about geography than he did."

"Oh, dear," Shebna said, wincing.

"It gets worse. I asked him for a chance to learn more about running the nation, and he accused me of plotting to overthrow him."

Shebna slowly lowered himself onto a bench, his dark face turning pale. "Plotting. . . ?"

"Yes. That's when I lost my temper and he threw me out. Oh, I almost forgot. My father has arranged a marriage for me."

"You did not refuse, I hope."

"He's using me, Shebna, like . . . like some kind of trophy. I'm to be a reward for some trade minister or other. I'd like a more useful function in the kingdom than that."

Shebna shook his head in dismay. "Do you realize how dangerous it is to make him angry, my lord? If only you would hold your fiery temper when you are with him, be patient, and listen to him without comment."

"I honestly tried this time, but it was all so idiotic—a trade agreement with Tyre!"

"Well, idiotic or not, it was an opportunity to prove yourself to him, and—"

"And I ruined my chance."

"You will have to get back in his favor, my lord. Perhaps it would help to show interest in the wife he has chosen."

"I don't want a wife that my father has chosen."

"See? Your stubbornness always gets you into trouble."

Hezekiah looked at Shebna, then managed a smile. "You're right, as usual. Do you have any other advice I need to hear?"

"You have finished your education, as far as I am concerned. You already know more than I do. If the king were to ask me, I would suggest that he allow you to gain practical experience in running the nation. He could make you a lower court judge or civic administrator. At the very least, you could sit in on his advisory meetings and find out what is going on in the nation."

"I agree, Shebna, but unfortunately my father doesn't. In fact, I asked for a seat on the Advisory Council just now, and that's when he accused me of plotting to overthrow him."

"Then, now is not the time for me to discuss it with him. We would both be wise to wait."

Hezekiah heard the note of fear in the tutor's voice, and for the second time that morning he was aware that Shebna was deeply afraid of King Ahaz.

"I'm afraid of him, too," Hezekiah said quietly. "He's too impulsive. He lets his emotions rule him. And he doesn't have to make me his successor. He has no shortage of heirs, as he's always quick to remind me. My brother Gedaliah gets along with him much better than I do."

Shebna looked thoughtful. "But you say he hinted at making you an envoy?"

"He said *maybe*. But my father has hinted at a government position before and nothing ever came of it. So I'll just have to wait and see this time, too. My father is not an old man, Shebna. I could be waiting years to inherit the throne."

"That is true, my lord," Shebna said with a sigh.

"Then maybe you'd better start giving me lessons on how to be patient."

# 14

HEPHZIBAH LAY ON A PILE of cushions beneath the fig tree in her family's courtyard, dreaming of the man she would marry. Her father told her she had several suitors, and she paraded them through her mind as she gazed up at the shiny green leaves, considering each of them as a husband. Her opinion wouldn't matter of course, but she loved to dream all the same.

Hephzibah knew she would command a high price when her father negotiated her bride price, not only because he was a prominent government official, but also because she was very beautiful. She had been told that it was so all her life, but she recently had become aware of the effect she had on men, even with her face discreetly veiled. She was petite and fine-boned with a fragile quality that made men desperate to possess and protect her. And Hephzibah also had the natural grace and elegance that spoke of her social standing among Judah's nobility.

The afternoon sun warmed her as it dappled through the trees, the tranquil afternoon and quiet hum of insects made her drowsy. She closed her eyes, then awoke to see her father smiling down at her.

"Is this any way for the prince's future bride to spend the afternoon?" he said, laughing. He was dressed in the ornamental robes that he wore when he attended the king's court, and she knew he had just returned home from the palace. Beads of perspiration dampened his forehead and his face was flushed, not only with heat but also with excitement. Hephzibah quickly sat up, not sure if she was dreaming.

"What did you say, Abba?"

"I suppose I shouldn't tell you about it until the arrangements are final," he said. "But I can't keep quiet about a secret this big."

"What, Abba? Please tell me." She grabbed both his hands and pulled him down beside her onto the cushions.

"I've been working on a special project for King Ahaz for the past several months, and he's been very pleased with what I've accomplished. This morning he told me that once my trade agreement is finalized, you will be married to his son, Prince Hezekiah."

The news astonished her. "Oh, Abba! You mean, I'll live in the palace? Me? Married to a prince?"

"Yes, my dear girl. And your future husband is also the heir to the throne. He'll be the next king of Judah."

The news overwhelmed Hephzibah. Her shock, combined with the afternoon heat, made her feel dizzy. This had to be a dream. It couldn't possibly be true.

"Oh, Abba," she whispered.

"What's the matter? I thought you'd be thrilled, but you look as if you've seen King Uzziah's ghost."

Hephzibah knew she should be overjoyed but terror gripped her instead. "I never dreamed . . . I never thought . . . Abba, I don't know what a king's wife is supposed to do."

Her father laughed. "She's supposed to bear him sons—many, many sons. It's what every man expects from his wife, whether he's a king or a slave."

Hephzibah knew that he was right. As her terror slowly began to subside, replaced by the excitement of this unexpected betrothal, her

mind teemed with questions. "What does he look like, Abba? Have I
ever seen him? How old is he?"

"Slow down—one question at a time," he said, laughing again.
"Besides, does it really matter what he looks like? He's going to be
the king someday."

Hephzibah had seen King Ahaz in processions and at royal ceremonies, and she remembered him as grossly fat. Not even the aura of
royalty or his fine robes could disguise that fact. The thought of being
married to him, being held against his doughy belly, made her shudder. Once again she was afraid.

"Yes, Abba—of course it matters. Is Prince Hezekiah pale and fat
like his father?"

"Hephzibah!"

She clapped her hand over her mouth. Her outspokenness had
shocked her father.

"That's the king of Judah you're talking about," he said. "How
can you be so disrespectful?"

"I'm sorry, Abba." She lowered her eyes and tried to look repen-
tant, but she shuddered at the thought of being married to someone
like Ahaz, whether he was the king or not.

"Ah, I forgive you. You're bound to be a little jittery before your
betrothal." He brushed her dark hair from her face affectionately. "To
tell you the truth, I don't know much about your future husband. I've
seen several princes, but I don't know which one is Hezekiah. They
never come to council meetings. I've heard that they study under an
Egyptian tutor, a genius of a man, so they say. And they spend a lot
of time with the captain of the palace guard for their military training.
I promise I'll try to find out more once you're betrothed, all right?"

"Yes, Abba," she answered quietly.

For the rest of the evening Hephzibah alternated between joy and
terror as she dreamed of being wed to an unknown prince. The pam-
pered life appealed to her, with elegant clothing and jewels and hundreds of servants. But her dream man was supposed to be handsome

and strong, not flabby and pale. What would she do if Prince Hezekiah resembled his father? How could she hide her revulsion every time he held her or pressed his bloated cheek to hers?

Long after the household retired for the night, Hephzibah tossed and turned in bed, unable to sleep. Her father said it might be weeks before she would be certain if the betrothal would take place, and Hephzibah decided that she could never cope with the terror of the unknown that long. She had to find out whom she was marrying and stop the betrothal, if necessary, before it was too late.

All night Hephzibah watched the stars sweep slowly past her window and the silver moon rise and set. By the time she had formulated her plan, it was nearly dawn. She rose from her disheveled bed and crept into her younger sister's room.

"Miriam, wake up," she whispered as she shook her awake.

"Hephzibah? What are you doing here?" she asked sleepily.

"Shh. Be quiet and listen to me. You've got to help me. I'm going to go out of my mind if you don't."

"What's wrong?"

"Abba's betrothing me to a prince."

"I already know that," she said in a cranky voice. "You woke me up to tell me what I already know?"

"Shh. Listen to me. I've got to find out what he looks like before it's too late. What if he's really horrible? What then?"

"You'll marry him anyway, like a dutiful daughter should. Now let me sleep." She closed her eyes and rolled over with her back to Hephzibah.

"Will you please listen to me?" Hephzibah begged. "If I really hate him, maybe I can pray to all the gods to cancel the betrothal or . . . or take a vow or something. Please, Miriam. Suppose it was *your* betrothal. Wouldn't you want to know what he looked like? You've got to help me."

It required no effort on Hephzibah's part to plead desperately. She merely had to think of sitting beside the fat, pompous king, and helpless panic overwhelmed her. Miriam rolled over again to face Hephzibah.

"It depends. What do you want me to do?"

"I have a plan. We'll stuff cushions in our beds so it looks like we're sleeping. Then we can sneak out and try to get a look at Prince Hezekiah."

Miriam sat up straight. "Are you crazy? We can't wander around the city by ourselves. If Abba catches us, he'll have us stoned."

"Shh. We're going to dress up as servant girls and pretend we're on our way to the spring for water. Listen—I have it all figured out. Abba said the prince spends a lot of time drilling with the captain of the palace guards. I know where the guardhouse is. It's close to the Water Gate. The men practice there every morning."

"You're really crazy!" she said, shaking her head. "Go back to bed."

"Miriam, name your price. I'll do any favor you ask if only you'll help me." She gripped her sister's hand between hers.

Miriam studied Hephzibah as if she were a stranger. "You're actually serious about this, aren't you?"

"Yes. Very serious. I'll give you anything you want."

"I sure hope I don't act this crazy when it's *my* turn to get betrothed." She pulled her hand from between Hephizbah's and swung her feet to the floor.

"Then you'll help me? Oh, thank you! Thank you!" Hephzibah wrapped her sister in a hug.

Miriam held up her hand in warning. "For a price, remember? First of all, swear to me that you'll help me find a royal husband, too."

"I swear it."

"And you'll give me those golden earrings that Abba bought you in Beersheba."

Hephzibah hesitated, then agreed. "Okay. Done."

"And . . ."

"Don't get greedy, Miriam. I think that's more than enough, don't you?"

"No, swear to me that if we get into trouble, you'll say I was innocent but you forced me to do it."

"We won't get into trouble."

"Swear?"

"Okay, I swear. By Asherah and Baal: I forced you to do it. Now, please—let's hurry!"

They padded their beds with cushions and crept down to the kitchen, where Hephzibah bribed two servant girls into lending them their clothes. Then, with their faces discreetly veiled, Hephzibah and her sister hurried down the back lanes to the Water Gate, balancing water jugs on their heads.

The sun had not quite reached the top of the Mount of Olives yet, but it bathed the streets with hazy, golden-pink light. Hephzibah shivered in the servant's thin gown, and Miriam's hand felt icy as Hephzibah towed her through the streets behind her. Curiosity propelled Hephzibah forward at a rapid pace, but Miriam, who didn't share her motivation, dragged her feet as if wishing she had never come.

As they neared the Water Gate, Hephzibah heard hearty shouts coming from the courtyard near the guard tower and the metallic ring of sword against sword. "See?" she whispered. "I told you they practice here every morning."

They followed the wall of the courtyard until they came to an open gate and peeked inside. Dozens of men stood around the perimeter of the yard, cheering two guardsmen who were engaged in a duel. Some of the observers wore the tunics of the palace guard, some wore ordinary clothes, and a few wore the embroidered robes of the nobility.

"Great. So how are we going to know which one is your prince and future husband?" Miriam asked.

"Let's listen for a minute. Maybe we can find out."

"I don't like this," Miriam said nervously.

"Shh."

Hephzibah scanned all the faces of the young noblemen, searching for one who resembled King Ahaz. The task seemed hopeless, so she turned her attention to the duel. The older of the two sparring guards seemed to be winning, and as he pressed his advantage, his young opponent finally threw down his sword in defeat.

"You win, Captain Jonadab," he conceded. The watching men cheered.

"Psst—we can't stay here forever," Miriam whispered. "We're going to get caught."

"Please. One more minute."

"Who's going to challenge me next?" the victorious captain asked, scanning the crowd. "How about you, my prince?"

Hephzibah froze as the captain nodded toward a young dark-haired man in his early twenties. The prince shrugged off his embroidered robe and tossed it aside, striding forward amid a chorus of shouts and cheers. Hephzibah's heart began to pound, not with excitement but with fear. He had a trim, compact build, very different from King Ahaz's, but there was something in his swagger, a hint of arrogance or cruelty in his eyes that frightened her.

*Oh, please, Lady Asherah. Don't let it be him.*

The young prince seemed to have more self-confidence than skill, and the captain repeatedly cut short his attempts to show off before his audience. Before long the prince seemed to realize that he was making a fool of himself, and he angrily sheathed his sword.

"I'm not in the mood for a real fight," he said. His eyes flashed dangerously.

The captain gave a respectful bow. "Another time, then."

"Is he Prince Hezekiah?" Miriam whispered.

"I don't know."

"Come on. We've been gone too long already. Let's get the water and go home." Miriam tugged on her arm until she reluctantly turned away.

Hephzibah felt frustrated and disappointed as she headed through the gate and down the steep slope to the spring. A long line of servant girls and slaves waited beside the spring, chattering happily as they filled their jugs. The water was cold, the work harder than Hephzibah had bargained for, and even with her jug only half full she could barely lift it.

"That's full enough, Miriam—let's go," she whispered, and they headed back up the ramp to the city. As they neared the guards' courtyard again, Hephzibah decided that she had to try once more to see Hezekiah.

"Just one more minute," she pleaded with her sister. "That's all—I promise."

They peered through the open gate and saw that the captain had a new opponent—another nobleman. He was tall and strongly built, yet amazingly agile for his size, darting out of the captain's reach, then lunging to take the offensive. His skill with the sword was breathtaking, and Hephzibah's pulse raced as she watched him sparring.

He was poised, confident, handsome. His curly brown hair and beard looked coppery in the morning sun. Hephzibah began praying to every god that she could think of that this nobleman would turn out to be Prince Hezekiah. It was too much to hope for, but if she learned who he was, maybe her father could arrange a betrothal to him instead.

Suddenly Miriam cried out. Icy water drenched Hephzibah's legs as her sister's water jug crashed to the ground. A strong hand clamped down on Hephzibah's shoulder and swung her around. Four guardsmen had moved up unnoticed behind her and her sister, and now the men surrounded them, leaving no escape.

"I've never seen you two girls before," one of them said, pawing at Hephzibah's veil. "Let's have a look at you."

"Yeah—I want to see what I get for my money," another said as he snatched Hephzibah's water jug from her hands.

"No! Leave us alone!" Hephzibah cried. She twisted away from the soldier, and her veil tore partly away from her face.

"Hey now! She is a pretty one," the soldier said. "Remember, I saw her first." He moved behind her and pinned her arms to her side, his hands bruising her arms.

"No, please! Let me go!" Hephzibah begged as she struggled to break free. "Stop!"

As the men closed in around them, Miriam began to scream. One of the soldiers grabbed her and clamped his hand over her mouth. Hephzibah struggled with all her strength, crying out in terror, but the soldier was much too strong.

"Let them go."

The command was spoken with authority. The knot of soldiers parted, and Hephzibah saw the handsome nobleman standing before her. He was breathless from the duel, the front of his tunic wet with sweat. He sheathed his sword and spoke again.

"These girls are terrified, can't you see that?"

"They're just common serving girls, my lord," one of the soldiers replied. "They come around here for only one reason—to meet soldiers."

"Resisting is part of their game, sir," the soldier holding Hephzibah added.

"N-no, please . . ." she stammered. "We weren't playing a game. We didn't want to meet soldiers. . . ."

The nobleman studied Hephzibah's unveiled face as if trying to determine if she was telling the truth. His deep brown eyes were somber, almost melancholy, and the intensity of his gaze unnerved her. Finally he turned his attention to the four men.

"Soldiers under my command will never misuse their power on defenseless people," he said. "Do you understand?"

"Yes, my lord," they muttered. The soldier holding Hephzibah released his grip. The nobleman retrieved her water jug from the man who'd taken it and handed it to her.

"Go home," he said. "And don't come around here again."

Hephzibah nodded and gripped her sister's hand. When she tried to walk, the street felt unstable beneath her shaking legs. She had completely forgotten about her betrothal or finding the prince, when she suddenly heard a voice from the crowd shout, "Prince Hezekiah, I'll challenge you next."

She froze at the name, then risked a glance over her shoulder. As if in a dream, she saw the tall nobleman acknowledge the offer.

"I'll accept that challenge," he said, and a smile flickered across his solemn features.

Hephzibah closed her eyes, afraid she would faint. Then she felt Miriam tugging angrily on her hand and she turned toward home again, clutching her water jug.

"It's all your fault," Miriam said, still weeping as they climbed the hill. "I never should have come with you."

"Miriam, I'm sorry. But it's all right now—we're fine."

"We were nearly raped!"

"Shh—not so loud. And stop whimpering, we're almost home. If Abba finds out what happened, we'll be disgraced. We'll both die old maids."

By the time they reached the servants' entrance at the rear of the house, Miriam had composed herself. But when Hephzibah reached the safety of her bedroom, all her pent-up fear and excitement finally caught up with her. She collapsed onto her bed and began to weep. Miriam shook her angrily.

"What's the matter with you? We made it home safely. You saw your stupid prince; why are you crying now?"

"Yes, I saw him—and now I want to marry him more than anyone else in the whole world. If Abba doesn't get him for my husband, I know I will surely die."

Hephzibah paused for breath when she reached the sacred grove of Asherah on the hill outside Jerusalem the following afternoon. The day was blistering hot, and the servants who led the young bullock and carried her grain and wine offerings sweated from the exertion of their climb and the size of their loads. They gazed at her expectantly when they reached the top of the hill, as if hoping she would offer them a share in the feast after the sacrifice.

Hephzibah felt a sense of awe as she considered the enormity of her mission and its importance for her future. She must please the goddess, must somehow win Lady Asherah's favor and secure her betrothal to Prince Hezekiah. Her other suitors no longer interested her, nor was she content to leave her destiny in the hands of others. Hephzibah had decided to appeal to the ultimate source—Asherah, goddess of love and fertility.

The high priest of Asherah looked impressed when he glimpsed the extravagant offering Hephzibah's servants bore. He hurried over to greet Hephzibah, bowing slightly. She could tell by his clothing that he was one of the many foreign priests that King Ahaz had brought to Jerusalem. They seemed to be multiplying throughout the land, growing in boldness as well as in numbers.

"How may I help you?" the priest asked.

"I wish to make an offering to the goddess," she told him, "and pour out a drink offering and burn incense."

The priest's brows arched slightly. "The goddess will be pleased with such devotion. Do you have a petition to make?"

"Yes, and also a vow."

"Very well." He smiled faintly and led the way into the grove. An altar and several incense burners stood inside the stone enclosure. An Asherah pole stood beyond them in an inner grove.

As the priest lit Hephzibah's incense and prepared to slay the bullock, she knelt before the golden image of Asherah and closed her eyes in prayer.

"Queen of heaven," she prayed silently, "I bring my offering to you, asking that you would please grant my petition. Please let me be married to Prince Hezekiah."

Tears sprang to her eyes as she remembered the glint of sunlight on his sword, the sheen of sweat on his tanned arms and legs, the burnish of copper in his dark hair and beard. She imagined being held in his arms, becoming his wife.

"If you'll answer my prayer, Lady Asherah, and bring about our marriage, I vow this day to give the first daughter from our union to you."

She never doubted her ability to fulfill her vow. Kings were interested only in sons. A daughter would be hers to do with as she pleased.

Hephzibah kissed the little statue reverently. Then, suddenly overcome with emotion, she hurried from the sanctuary to preside over the sacrificial feast with her family and friends.

# 15

"HEPHZIBAH, MY DARLING, HOW beautiful you look! Fit for a king!"

Hephzibah saw a glow of pride in her father's eyes. "Oh, Abba, do you really think so? Do you think the prince will be pleased to have me for his wife?"

"When he sees you, he will faint for joy. Turn around and let me look at you."

Hephzibah's embroidered wedding gown had been fashioned by the finest craftsmen in Jerusalem. She wore golden bracelets on each arm, loops of gold in each ear, a chain of gold around her neck with a ruby pendant the size of her thumbnail—her betrothal gifts from the palace. Her maids hadn't pinned up her dark, wavy hair yet, and it flowed loose down her back. Hephzibah did a small pirouette in the center of the room, and her father sighed, slapping his arms to his side in a gesture of helpless awe.

"You're too beautiful to cover with a veil. The whole kingdom should see Prince Hezekiah's beautiful bride. Let's leave the veil off."

"Abba, you're teasing."

"I have a right to be proud of my beautiful daughter," he said, kissing her forehead.

"Hephzibah, why are you standing around?" her mother asked as she bustled into the room. "Fix your hair. Put your veil on. You should be down in the courtyard with your bridesmaids already. The prince could come for you any minute."

"Mama, there's lots of time. We'll hear the groom's procession coming. It's still early." She felt surprisingly calm and happier than ever before in her life. She had dreamed about Hezekiah for months, sacrificed and prayed and made vows to Asherah in order to reach this day, and now the goddess had answered her prayers. Today he would come to take her for his wife.

"Is your sister ready? Have you seen her?" Mama fussed. "What's taking her so long? I'm going to check on Miriam. Papa, go watch for the procession."

"I'd better do what I'm told," her father said with a wry smile, but there was love in his eyes as he watched his wife hurry off.

Hephzibah felt a tingle of excitement spread through her. Her husband would look at her with love, too. "Thank you, Abba! Thank you for this wonderful day!" she said, hugging him.

"May the goddess bless you with many, many sons," he murmured. As he turned to leave, Hephzibah saw a tear in his eye.

She knew she should go downstairs and let her maids pin up her hair, then take her seat in the flower-strewn chair beneath the fig tree, but her heart was too full of joy for her to sit quietly and wait. She wanted to dance and leap and sing. She ran to her window, listening for the music of the groom's procession, but heard only the usual city sounds. Servants and slaves and merchants went about their affairs as if it were an ordinary day. Didn't they know that today would mark the beginning of a love so deep and strong that it would outshine the love of Solomon for his Shulammite maiden?

Hephzibah smiled as she picked up her lyre, singing the beautiful song of Solomon to herself: "'Listen! My lover! Look! Here he comes, leaping across the mountains, bounding over the hills. . . . My lover spoke and said to me, "Arise, my darling, my beautiful one, and come away with me." ' "

---

Hezekiah stood before a tall bronze mirror as his servants dressed him in his wedding robes and placed a small golden crown on his head. He saw Shebna's reflection as he stood behind him, nodding his head in approval.

"You're looking very pleased with yourself," Hezekiah told him. "I hope you realize this is all your fault. The only reason I'm getting married is because you said I should appease my father."

Shebna grinned. "You look magnificent, my lord—like a king."

"Well, I don't feel like a king; I feel trapped. My life is controlled by a man I despise."

"Try to smile anyway. It is your wedding day."

His wedding day. Hezekiah knew he should try to act pleased, but instead he brooded over the fact that months had passed and King Ahaz hadn't said another word about giving him a government position. Hezekiah still regretted losing his temper and wished he had kept quiet about Ahaz's trade agreement, but maybe Shebna was right. Maybe after his wedding he would regain his father's favor.

At last everything was ready—even if Hezekiah wasn't. He followed the dancers and musicians as his groom's procession journeyed down the hill from the palace. Crowds of people thronged the streets to join in the revelry, cheering and scattering branches and flowers at his feet. Hezekiah felt as if he were on display, like an article in the marketplace under a gaudy striped awning. He wished he could do something to earn cheers besides get married. His heavy wedding garb seemed to suffocate him.

Mercifully, Ahaz's trade minister lived close to the palace, so Hezekiah didn't have to parade through the entire city. The procession waited in the street while he and his brother Gedaliah, who was his groomsman, went inside.

His bride was waiting for him in her father's courtyard, seated in a chair beneath a fig tree, surrounded by bridesmaids. He couldn't see her veiled face, but she looked like a mere child to him, too young to be given in marriage. She was clothed in layers of embroidered linen, and Hezekiah wondered if she felt as hot and miserable as he did. But when he took her hand it was cold, and he felt a rush of pity for the girl. Perhaps she was as unwilling to endure this charade as he was.

Hezekiah spoke his wedding vows without paying attention to them. He wished the day was over, but he knew it was just beginning. After saying their vows, he and his new bride would return to the palace to preside over the lavish wedding banquet that Ahaz had ordered.

The feasting and drinking lasted all evening and far into the night. Long before the moon rose the king was drunk, his bellowing laughter heard in every corner of the banquet hall. He could scarcely walk without help, and his eyes were glazed and bleary as he made the rounds of his guests. His behavior disgusted Hezekiah, and he barely touched his own wine. He managed to avoid his father for most of the evening, but close to midnight Ahaz staggered up to him and pulled him aside.

"I think you'll enjoy my delightful little gift, tonight. Picked her out for you myself. Delicate little child, isn't she?"

Suppressed anger and hatred surged through Hezekiah. He didn't want to accept any gift from Ahaz, and if his father had personally chosen Hephzibah, then he didn't want her. As Hezekiah struggled against the urge to lash out, his father said, "Don't wear yourself out too much, because I've decided to send you to Tyre with your new father-in-law when your wedding week is over."

At that moment Hezekiah hated Ahaz more than he thought possible. Even more, he hated his own helplessness and the power his father held over his life. He was about to tell Ahaz to keep his gift and his worthless trip when Shebna gripped his arm, squeezing it until Hezekiah winced in pain.

"Your son is speechless with gratitude, Your Majesty," Shebna said smoothly. "I thank you on his behalf."

Hezekiah silently willed Ahaz to leave before he lost control, but instead his father inched closer, nudging him like a conspirator. "But maybe you won't want to go away and leave her when the week's over. Such a pretty little child. I should have kept her as my own concubine."

Another rush of anger swept through Hezekiah. He was about to tell Ahaz he could take back his gift, when Shebna gripped his arm again and spoke before Hezekiah could.

"Thank you for your generosity in giving away such a lovely woman. Will you excuse your son now? There is something he needs to attend to."

"Very well. He's excused."

Hezekiah pushed his way through the crowd and out to the palace courtyard, where the chilly evening air would cool his fury.

---

For Hephzibah, the long day of wedding festivities seemed endless as she waited for Hezekiah to take her away to their bridal chamber. There were dancers and music and unending courses of food, then a rambling speech by King Ahaz that seemed to honor her father. It was followed by more music, more dancing, more food. The opulence of the palace dazzled her; the attention lavished on her by everyone except her husband overwhelmed her. She had been in such a state of excitement all day that she felt exhausted.

But suddenly Hezekiah appeared beside her and reached for her hand, drawing her to her feet. The room fell still for the space of a heartbeat when the wedding guests saw them, then the hall rang with clapping and cheering. Her face grew warm, and she was grateful for the veil.

Hezekiah stared straight ahead as he led her away from the din, up the stairs, through the maze of hallways. She felt the pressure of his hand on her arm but had no sensation of her feet touching the floor. At last he led her inside their wedding chamber and closed the door. The sound of her own heart pounding in her ears drowned out the noise of the wedding feast below.

Neither of them spoke as Hezekiah unfastened her veil to see her for the first time. She hoped her father was right, that he would find her beautiful. But as he studied her face, she saw an unspoken question in his eyes. He frowned as if deep in thought, then his brows arched in surprise.

"Is your father paid so poorly that you have to fetch the water every day?" he asked.

Hephzibah's heart stood still. She had never considered that he might remember her or recognize her from that day. But he had—and she didn't know what to say. The marriage wouldn't be official until it was consummated. He could still change his mind. She began to shiver as he stared at her, waiting for her answer.

"No, he isn't poorly paid, my lord," she said.

"I didn't think so. Then maybe you can explain why you were standing by the guard tower several months ago with a jug of water in your hands. Or am I mistaken?"

"No, my lord. You're not mistaken."

Hephzibah's heart pounded so loudly she was certain he could hear it. Would he annul their marriage and expose her shame before the entire wedding party? She felt a cry of despair rising from deep inside her, but she held it back along with her tears. She looked down, afraid to face him and see rejection on his face, but he put his hand under her chin and gently lifted her head until she had to look at him again.

"You must have had a very good reason to venture out unescorted like that."

Hephzibah saw no anger in his eyes, only curiosity as he waited for her explanation. Her words tumbled out in a rush. "When my father told me I would be married to a prince I was terrified. I didn't know what you looked like, and so I had to find out before it was too late because I was so afraid that you'd look like your—"

She stopped, horrified at what she had almost said.

"Like my father?" he finished for her.

Hephzibah felt the blood rush to her face and knew it betrayed her guilt. She had committed a grave mistake. How many times had Abba scolded her for being outspoken? How many times had he said it was unladylike? What would happen to her now for insulting the king?

The silence between them seemed endless. Then Hezekiah laughed out loud. It was the most welcome sound Hephzibah ever heard. Still, she knew she must apologize.

"I-I'm sorry, my lord. I didn't mean to say it. I didn't mean to insult the king."

He smiled, dismissing her protests with a shake of his head. "I like your honesty, Hephzibah. It's very refreshing. But tell me, now that you've seen me—do you think I resemble my father?"

He stood before her with his hands on his hips, smiling broadly as he waited for her appraisal. He was so handsome that Hephzibah's chest tightened until each breath hurt.

"No, my lord. You don't resemble the king."

"I see. And what if you'd gone to the guard tower that day and discovered a resemblance? Would it have made a difference to you?"

Hephzibah panicked. She could see no way to answer his question without insulting either Hezekiah or his father. She groped for words, aware that she had to say something.

"I did a very foolish thing, my lord. I never should have left my father's house. Thank you for rescuing me."

His smile faded, and his eyes grew serious once again. "I'm sorry, Hephzibah. It wasn't fair of me to put you on the spot like that. It's just that I was curious to know what would motivate a beautiful young woman like you to take such a risk. I suppose I was vain enough to believe that any woman in the nation would be honored to marry a prince, no matter what he looked like."

"Oh yes, my lord! It's true! Most women would!"

"But not you?" His smile returned, and she managed to smile back weakly.

"I would marry whomever Abba arranged for me, my lord." And as difficult as it was to take her gaze off him, Hephzibah looked down at her feet again.

"Your honesty is refreshing, Hephzibah, and so is your daring, although I think your father would be outraged if he ever found out about it."

"Yes, my lord."

"And I hope you won't be fetching water any more now that you're a married woman?"

She felt a glimmer of hope and looked up at him again. "I promise, my lord."

He reached for her, drawing her into his embrace. The top of her head barely reached his chin. She felt the hard strength in his arms, the warmth of his body, and she clung to him, unable to believe it was real, that her prayers had been answered. Then, still holding her close, Hezekiah gave a heavy sigh.

"I guess a nobleman's daughter has a lot in common with a king's son. Neither one of us has anything to say about who we will marry."

Hephzibah's panic returned as she puzzled over his words. Was he unhappy about his father's choice? Was there someone else he had wished to marry instead? She longed for the day when she would understand him completely and would be able to read his heart in his eyes. She would learn what each sigh and gesture meant, understand his half-spoken thoughts, and communicate with him without words as her parents often did. More than anything else, Hephzibah longed to be truly his wife, his lover, his friend.

His beard brushed her cheek as he bent to kiss her for the first time. And as she kissed him in return, Hephzibah prayed to the goddess Asherah that she would win Hezekiah's complete devotion, his trust, his undivided love.

But when Hezekiah left the bridal chamber after their week together, he didn't return to Hephzibah again.

# 16

KING AHAZ SLOUCHED ON his throne, browsing through a pile of documents. Uriah said they required only his seal to levy more taxes to meet the Assyrian tribute demands, but they were written in such heavy official language that Ahaz couldn't make sense of them. The stiff, tightly rolled parchment curled in his hands, exhausting his limited patience. He finally tossed the scrolls onto the table beside his throne.

The tedious morning routine of signing documents and listening to petitions bored Ahaz. He sipped his wine and allowed his mind to wander to the more pleasurable activities he had arranged for later in the day.

A small commotion near the door to his throne room interrupted his thoughts. He looked up to see Uriah arguing with one of the chamberlains. Ahaz smiled. A good quarrel always made an interesting diversion.

"Tell Uriah and the chamberlain to come here," he told his servant. He drained his wineglass as the arguing men approached and bowed before him.

"What's the problem, Uriah?" he asked.

"There's no problem, Your Majesty. I've given the chamberlain my decision, and he has defied me." The chamberlain huffed in protest but Uriah ignored him. "I was about to summon another chamberlain—that's all. I'm sorry if we disturbed you. We'll continue our discussion outside." Uriah seemed anxious to leave. He bowed and slowly backed away as if he had something to hide.

"Just a minute. Why did you defy my palace administrator?" Ahaz asked the chamberlain. The man glanced uncertainly at Uriah, then back at the king.

"I was trying to deliver a message to you, Your Majesty, but Uriah wouldn't let me."

"That's because all messages and petitions must be cleared through me first," Uriah said angrily.

"But that's exactly the problem," the chamberlain insisted. "They won't give the message to you. They asked to speak directly to the king, and unless you let them, we'll never find out what they want."

Uriah glared at the chamberlain, as if demanding his silence. The priest was hiding something, Ahaz was certain of that. He sat up, no longer bored.

"Who wants to see me? Tell me what's going on," he ordered.

"Your Majesty, envoys have arrived in Jerusalem from the northern kingdom of Israel," the chamberlain explained. "They've requested an audience with you to present a petition from their king."

"There can be no audience with King Ahaz unless they explain their petition to me first," Uriah interrupted. "That's standard diplomatic courtesy."

Ahaz's interest grew. He hadn't received a foreign emissary in many years, except from Assyria—and they came each year only to collect the annual tribute payments. He shifted in his seat with excitement, then leaned forward to announce his decision.

"Bring the envoys to me. Tell them I'll hear their petition."

"No, Your Majesty, wait," Uriah pleaded. "We need to take our time and think through all the implications of this. I advise you to postpone a hearing of their petition until tomorrow. Take time to consider—"

"I don't want to wait. I want to know why they've come."

"But receiving diplomats from another nation is a very serious decision, Your Majesty. If word reaches Assyria that we received them, they could interpret it as an act of rebellion. They might think we're plotting to form an alliance with Israel."

"That's ridiculous. I want to know why they've come, and I want to know now." He waved Uriah away and nodded to the chamberlain. "Bring them here."

"Wait!" Uriah grabbed the chamberlain's arm to prevent him from leaving. "Your Majesty, I must advise you that the Assyrians—"

"I know what you've advised. You just told me. And your advice is nonsense. Besides, Emperor Tiglath-Pileser is no longer a threat to us because he's dead."

News of the Assyrian emperor's death had reached Ahaz a month ago. He had lived in mortal fear of the man for years, never forgetting the emperor's brutality and ruthlessness or how he had tortured the leaders of Damascus. But at last Ahaz was free from his fear. The monarch who haunted his dreams was dead.

"Yes, he's dead, Your Majesty. But that's precisely why we need to be even more cautious," Uriah insisted. "His death doesn't mean that we're no longer an Assyrian vassal. In fact, the emperor's successor will probably act swiftly to quench any fires of rebellion that flare up in order to confirm his authority."

"My mind is made up," Ahaz said. "I will receive the envoy right now."

Uriah's shoulders sagged in defeat. He released the chamberlain and took his seat beside Ahaz. "I hope this doesn't end in disaster," he mumbled.

The chamberlain returned a short time later, followed by King Hoshea's emissaries and a dozen slaves bearing gifts for Ahaz. They paraded into the carpeted throne room and bowed low before him, giving Ahaz a feeling of power and authority he hadn't experienced for a long time. He remembered the humiliation he had suffered when he'd been forced to bow before the Assyrian monarch, and he silently vowed that he would never bow to any man again.

"Your Majesty, King Ahaz ben Jotham, Great and Mighty King of Judah, we are your humble servants." They bowed again, touching their foreheads to the floor. Ahaz allowed them to remain in that posture for several moments before stretching out his scepter to acknowledge their obeisance.

"You may rise and state your petition."

"Thank you, Your Majesty," the leading delegate said. "We bear gifts and a message from our lord, King Hoshea of Israel."

"The last emissaries from Israel were soldiers who besieged my city," Ahaz reminded them. "I'm pleased to see that your new king has decided to treat me with respect. State your petition."

"Your Majesty, our lord King Hoshea would like to meet with your representatives at a conference in Samaria. He wishes to discuss a united approach in our relations with the new Assyrian monarch, Shalmaneser."

Uriah leaped from his chair. "Do you know what you're proposing? Has your king gone insane?" He turned to Ahaz, pleading urgently. "Your Majesty, you must send them away at once to let it be known that Judah would never consider joining such a conspiracy. The Assyrians have spies everywhere!"

"Oh, sit down," Ahaz said, waving him aside. "When I want your advice I'll ask for it. You may continue," he told the envoy.

"As you know, the Assyrians annexed our northern-most territories as provinces fourteen years ago. But lately they've begun raiding many of our border towns and villages, carrying our people away as captives and plundering our land. This is in addition to their heavy tribute demands. Now that Tiglath-Pileser is dead, our king has decided to throw off the heavy Assyrian yoke that has crippled us for so long. He's sending envoys to the Egyptian pharaoh, as well, asking him to join with us in putting an end to Assyrian domination."

Uriah sprang from his seat again to confront the Israeli representative. "Has your king forgotten what happened the last time your nation tried to form an alliance against Assyria?" He turned to Ahaz. "Your Majesty, please. You saw what happened to Damascus. Do you want to risk the same punishment for Jerusalem?"

Once again, Ahaz recalled the torture and devastation he had witnessed. But his old adversary was dead. He had no reason to fear. The prospect of meeting with the Egyptian pharaoh and the kings of other nations excited him. It was time he took his place as a world leader again.

"Your petition is very interesting," he told the emissary. "I will need some time to consider it."

"But there's nothing to consider!" Uriah said. "They're proposing treason and suicide! Please, you must stop this discussion before it goes too far—"

"Enough!" Ahaz silenced him with a shout. "I'll do whatever I please. As I was saying," he told the envoy in a calm voice, "you will accept my hospitality as royal guests and dine with me tomorrow night. I will have an answer for King Hoshea by then. You are dismissed."

Ahaz watched as they paraded from the throne room, leaving their gifts spread at his feet. Then he turned to Uriah who sat stiffly beside him. "I want you to assemble the men who took part in my trade delegation to Tyre and have them join me for dinner tonight. We'll send them to Samaria with this delegation. Make sure you include my son, Hezekiah. He'll be my personal representative. I shall return to my chambers now."

Ahaz was aware of Uriah following him across the courtyard, his face creased with frustration, even despair. His distress gave Ahaz a rare feeling of power over the intimidating priest, and he liked the feeling. He hoped that Uriah would plead with him further so he would have the pleasure of refusing him again. When Ahaz reached his chambers, Uriah granted his wish.

"Your Majesty, please listen to me, I beg you. You're endangering the safety of our entire nation. I urge you to have the emissaries stripped and beaten immediately and sent back to King Hoshea in disgrace. The Assyrians would surely interpret that in a favorable light."

"I don't care about the Assyrians. I've decided to join with Israel and Egypt and gain our independence from them."

"But we couldn't possibly break free from Assyria, even with Egypt's help. Don't you understand? Jerusalem will end up just like Damascus."

The more desperately Uriah pleaded the more it amused Ahaz, but he soon grew tired of the game. He needed a rest.

"Uriah, I'm sick of listening to you. If you can't support my policies, then maybe I'd better look for a new palace administrator." He smiled and closed his chamber door in Uriah's face.

Uriah returned to his own chambers feeling stunned and sick. Why would a king who had been a docile puppet for so many years suddenly abandon all reason and commit political suicide? Because that's exactly what Ahaz had foolishly done. With this one rash act, Ahaz had pronounced a death sentence on his entire nation. The royal dinner tomorrow night was just the final knot in the noose that Ahaz had already slipped around Judah's neck.

Uriah paced around his chambers, trapped in a pit too deep for escape, cursing Ahaz and his impetuous decisions. How had Uriah suddenly lost control over him? And how could he gain it back? He had run the nation for years without any interference from Ahaz, and life under the Assyrians had been safe and predictable, even if it had been financially crippling. Why had the king picked this moment to suddenly decide to take control again?

The king had refused to listen to reason, and Uriah knew that if he continued to plead with him he was certain to lose his position in

the court. But if he didn't talk him out of this alliance, Ahaz's partic-
ipation in the rebellion would bring dreadful consequences on his
nation. The Assyrian retaliation would be swift and ruthless. King
Ahaz and all of his officials would be tortured to death, and Jerusalem
destroyed. Why couldn't Ahaz see that? It was up to Uriah to save his
nation from annihilation—but how?

He spent the rest of the morning carefully considering every possible solution to his dilemma and examining all the implications. He
could try to reason with Ahaz again and risk being fired—or worse.
He could get the support of Ahaz's other advisors and maybe his army
commanders—and risk being accused of conspiracy. He could go
behind Ahaz's back and send the delegation away in disgrace on his
own—and risk execution for treason. But none of those risks could
compare to what the Assyrians would do to him. Either way, Uriah
faced a death sentence. And why should he be the one to die when
King Ahaz was the fool who had placed the nation in such terrible
danger?

In the end, Uriah knew that only one solution remained: He
must place a new king on Judah's throne, one who would refuse to
join Israel's conspiracy, one who would appease Assyria before it was
too late. Ahaz had to be eliminated—permanently.

Uriah felt confident that if Prince Hezekiah were to inherit the
throne suddenly, he would allow Uriah to continue as palace administrator. Then he could influence Hezekiah to reject the Israeli alliance. But first he had to get rid of Ahaz.

Uriah's decision made sense to his rational mind, yet another part
of him drew back in horror at the idea. For over an hour, he paced
his room in frustration as the battle raged between the voice of reason
and the vestiges of his conscience. It was a fight between the two sides
of himself—the powerful palace administrator and the almost-forgot-
ten high priest of Yahweh.

He was contemplating murder. His conscience recoiled at the
thought. How could he have degenerated into a murderer? When did

the process start? Was it when he turned his back on Ahaz's idolatry, or when he helped sacrifice those children to Molech? Had planning the first murder made this one a little easier?

But there had been no choice back then. Ahaz had chosen to murder his sons, and Uriah had only participated in order to gain the king's confidence. And it had been a worthwhile decision, enabling him to do a great deal of good for the nation all these years. And he had no choice now. This alliance with Egypt would bring disaster. Assyria would certainly retaliate. Ahaz was jeopardizing everything they had worked for, and Uriah had to act before the alliance went any further. He was the only one who could save his nation.

But what about Yahweh? Wasn't his nation in Yahweh's hands? Or didn't Uriah believe that anymore? His beliefs didn't matter anyway. King Ahaz wasn't going to suddenly start trusting Yahweh after all these years. He was placing his trust in a new alliance, just as he had foolishly trusted Assyria.

So maybe Zechariah had been right years ago. He had warned Uriah that he would change if he compromised his beliefs. And in his heart, Uriah knew that he had changed. He had wanted to stop the king's idolatry, but instead he had become a willing participant in it.

No. Uriah dismissed that thought with an angry shake of his head. Zechariah was an embittered, defeated alcoholic who didn't know what he was talking about. And the king was an irresponsible fool. Without Uriah, Ahaz would have destroyed this nation long ago. It was up to him to stop Ahaz now.

But was killing him the only way to stop him?

It was written in the Torah, *You shall not murder*. But didn't the Torah also say somewhere that it was permissible to take a life in order to save a life? In this case, Uriah was saving millions of lives, the entire population of Judah. Certainly the Torah would sanction that. It might even be considered self-defense.

And it also might be considered the just punishment Ahaz deserved for all the murders he had committed. His helpless children.

His innocent wife. Ahaz had murdered Abijah, and in God's eyes—
and Uriah's—that was reason enough to execute him. *An eye for an
eye—a life for a life.*

Gradually, Uriah's frantic pacing slowed and his steps became
more firm and assured. His worry relaxed into quiet resolve: King
Ahaz must die.

The only thing left to decide was *how*. The king would have to
die in a way that would throw no suspicion on himself. It was important that Uriah remain in power to deal with the political crisis. And
Ahaz had to be killed immediately. The dinner with the Israelite
envoys tomorrow night must never take place.

Uriah reviewed every moment of Ahaz's daily routine, searching
for the precise time, the exact place when Ahaz was most vulnerable.
One thread ran through the fabric of the king's daily life with unwavering consistency—his dependence on the drugged Assyrian wine. He
was rarely without a glass of it close at hand. As his priest, Uriah had
access to those drugs. He also understood that too much could be
fatal.

Convinced of what he must do, Uriah went to find the king's
royal cupbearer.

# 17

HEZEKIAH DRUMMED HIS FINGERS on the banquet table. His father often arrived late for his meals, sometimes staggering in drunkenly, but he had outdone himself tonight. Ahaz had invited all the men who took part in his trade delegation to join him for dinner, then kept his guests waiting for over an hour. Hezekiah had watched in disgust as the steaming platters of meat grew cold and the bloody fat congealed into hard puddles on the plates. The servants who had carried the huge meal into the banquet room stood evenly spaced like mute statues around the perimeter of the table, waiting.

It seemed to Hezekiah that he had spent the last several months waiting for Ahaz. After making the trip to Tyre six months ago with his new father-in-law, Hezekiah had waited in vain to be offered a position in Ahaz's government. The trade agreement had proved worthless, just as he had predicted, and Ahaz hadn't sent for him again until tonight's mysterious dinner.

Gradually the polite conversation around the banquet table dwindled into anxious silence. The guests eyed the food and each other nervously, but no one dared begin the meal without the king. Hezekiah stopped drumming his fingers. He slapped the tabletop with his open hand and motioned to the nearest servant.

"Why have we been kept waiting? Where's the king?"

"I don't know, my lord."

"Well, has anyone bothered to find out?"

"We know that he's in his bedchamber. We've knocked repeatedly on His Majesty's door but he doesn't answer. We were afraid to disturb him."

"He probably got drunk and passed out cold," Hezekiah muttered to Shebna. He hoped his assumption was true so he could return to his room and forget about the dinner. It was ruined anyway, and so was his appetite.

"The king has never been this late before," Shebna agreed, shifting his position and flexing his long legs.

Hezekiah signaled to Uriah, who sat across the table from him in stony silence. He had said very little in the long hour they had been waiting, and even now he showed no trace of impatience as he stroked his gray-flecked beard.

"Do you know what could be keeping my father?" Hezekiah asked him.

Uriah shrugged. "I haven't seen the king since this morning. He returned to his chambers after holding court, and I believe he ate lunch there, as well."

The hall fell silent again, and Hezekiah heard someone's stomach gurgle with hunger. He looked around and saw Jonadab, captain of the palace guards, turning red with embarrassment. "Pardon me," the captain mumbled. Shebna passed him a platter of date cakes, but he shook his head. "No, thank you. I'll wait for the king."

"This is ridiculous," Hezekiah said, motioning again to the servant. "Send the king's personal valet into his chamber. Tell him to see what's keeping King Ahaz. I'll take the blame for disturbing him."

"Do you think that is wise?" Shebna asked in alarm.

"I don't care, I'm tired of waiting. Go ahead," he told the servant. The man slipped from the room. Several minutes passed, the silence broken only by Hezekiah's drumming fingers and the rumblings of Jonadab's stomach. Suddenly the king's valet burst into the room, pale and trembling.

"Somebody come quick! The king . . . the king!"

Uriah leaped to his feet with surprising swiftness and strode from the room. For a long moment, the other dinner guests sat frozen in their places. Then Hezekiah stood and stopped the frightened valet before he hurried away behind Uriah.

"What's wrong with the king?" he asked. The valet shook his head. He seemed unable to speak. "Show me, then." Hezekiah took the trembling man by the arm.

Hezekiah had no idea what to expect as he hurried down the covered walkway to his father's chambers. The valet was in such a state of shock that the sight of his blanched face made Hezekiah's nerves tingle with dread. Uriah had already gone inside the king's bedchambers by the time Hezekiah arrived, and he quickly emerged again to stop Hezekiah at the door.

"Don't go in there, my lord."

Hezekiah pushed past him. He wasn't prepared for what he saw.

King Ahaz lay sprawled on the floor, his back arched in agony, his limbs twisted in grotesque angles from his body. His fixed eyes stared, and his mouth gaped wide as if in a scream of anguish. Hezekiah wanted to look away but somehow was unable to move.

"The king is dead," he heard Uriah telling the others behind him. His voice sounded very far away.

Hezekiah refused to believe what his eyes told him was true. He squatted down and touched his father's hand, curled against the carpet. His stomach rolled over at the feel of his cold flesh. It was true. Ahaz was dead.

Hezekiah stood, and the room seemed to grow smaller and smaller. Then it began to spin so dizzily that he had to shut his eyes. He shook himself, as if he could wake up from a bad dream, and drew a deep breath. When the dizziness passed, he opened his eyes.

Uriah stood in front of him for a moment, then dropped to his knees, bowing to him. "Long live King Hezekiah!" he said.

Hezekiah glanced around and saw Captain Jonadab and the other men following Uriah's example, falling to their knees and touching their foreheads to the floor, murmuring, "Long live King Hezekiah!" He stared at the prostrate men, struggling to comprehend their words.

His father was dead. He was the king.

Hezekiah turned to stare at his father again. He felt no grief for Ahaz—only shock and surprise. Until today Hezekiah's life had been neatly ordered and scheduled, with few changes and very few surprises. He hadn't dared to hope that he would reign for many more years. But Ahaz was dead. And now he was the king.

The news spread quickly through the palace, creating a hum of noise and confusion in the hallways outside the room. But Hezekiah remained immobile. He continued to stare at his father's body as if it would help him comprehend the utter finality of death. At last, Uriah stood up and gripped Hezekiah's arm, squeezing it until the pain broke the spell of his shock. The priest pulled him toward the door.

"Your Majesty, there's nothing more you can do in here. You should leave now." He pulled Hezekiah all the way into the hallway and closed Ahaz's door behind them. "I know that this tragedy has come as a great shock to you, Your Majesty, but there are several urgent matters of state that must be dealt with immediately. In order to ensure an unbroken command of power, I ask for your permission to take care of them right away."

"My permission?" Hezekiah repeated. He wondered how it was possible that an hour ago he had nothing more important to worry about than dinner, and now he was in command of the nation. He felt Uriah studying him, his eyes bold and challenging, and Hezekiah had to resist the urge to look away. Uriah knew much more about running the kingdom than he did, but Hezekiah had always disliked him, without knowing why. Perhaps it was because, as far back as Hezekiah could recall, the imposing priest had always hovered close to his father. But in spite of his instincts, Hezekiah decided to let Uriah remain in control for now—for the good of the nation. He would need time to learn his new role as king.

"You may continue with your duties as you did under my father," Hezekiah said at last.

"Thank you, Your Majesty." Uriah's steely features never changed. Hezekiah sensed his strong will—so unlike Ahaz's—and he knew who had been running the nation.

"First, there is the matter of the emissaries," Uriah said. "It is imperative that they be sent back to their own country immediately."

Hezekiah had no idea what Uriah was talking about. It seemed to require a great effort to make sense of Uriah's words, let alone their importance. The hallway tilted as Hezekiah nodded his assent. "I will have to trust your judgment, Uriah, until I can be briefed."

"Good. I'm sure you'll want to meet with your father's advisors as soon as possible. Would tomorrow morning be too soon?"

"No, that's fine," Hezekiah replied. He needed at least that long to recover from his shock.

"Also, there are the details of King Ahaz's burial for me to attend to."

At the mention of his father's name, a question came to Hezekiah's mind. "How did he die, Uriah?"

"He was alone, Your Majesty. We may never know."

"Well, I intend to find out. I want to interview all his servants, all his concubines. It's obvious that he died in agony. And it's hard to believe that no one heard him, much less came to his aid."

Uriah's features hardened. He pulled Hezekiah away from the door as if worried that Jonadab or one of the others might overhear him. "It can only tarnish the king's memory to dig too deeply. I already know what you'll discover." He paused, and his voice softened slightly. "You're well aware that your father drank too much. What you may not know is that he also misused the ritual drugs from Assyria. I tried to discourage him, but he demanded more and more.

He was the king. How could anyone refuse him?"

"Are you saying that he took a lethal dose by mistake?"

"I'm certain that's what you'll discover, but I'll look into his death for you if you wish." Once again Uriah stared at him defiantly, and Hezekiah's deep distrust for the priest resurfaced.

"I guess there would be no point," he said at last.

"Then if I may be dismissed, I will take care of these other matters and begin the preparation for your coronation immediately."

"You may go," Hezekiah mumbled. Uriah seemed to vanish.

Hezekiah walked slowly down the hall, oblivious to the flurry of excitement all around him. Ahaz's life had ended. And Hezekiah realized that the sheltered life he had always lived had also come to an end. From now on, he was responsible for the entire nation. He knew that Ahaz had often tried to evade that responsibility, and for a brief moment Hezekiah thought he understood why. He only wished he had been given more warning; that he'd had more time to prepare for his new role. But the time had come for Hezekiah to be king, whether he was ready or not.

———

At first Hephzibah thought King Ahaz's death was only a rumor; gossip was plentiful in the palace. But when she heard the high-pitched mourning cries coming from the king's harem and saw Ahaz's wives and concubines draped in black, she knew it was true. King Ahaz was dead. And she was married to the new king of Judah.

Within days the palace servants prepared to move Hephzibah, and all of Hezekiah's concubines, out of their crowded quarters near the prince's chambers and into the lavish apartments of the king's harem.

"Wait until you see your new suite, Lady Hephzibah," her handmaiden, Merab, told her. "The rooms are the finest in the palace, except for the king's. They have tall windows that overlook the courtyard on one side, and there's a view of the whole city from the balcony on the other side."

For as long as Hephzibah could remember, Merab had taken care of her like a second mother. She had nestled as a baby on Merab's lap and been carried around on her broad hips. Merab's hands had soothed Hephzibah's tears and her smile had greeted her each morning of her life. Now the servant had come to the palace with her as a wedding gift from her father. Merab loved her like her own daughter, and she was Hephzibah's only friend and companion in her new home.

Hezekiah's concubines had refused to accept Hephzibah into their midst. At first, it was because they resented her superior position over them as his only wife. Then, as the months passed and Hezekiah called for one of them night after night instead of Hephzibah, they began to taunt her, making certain she learned of it whenever he slept with one of them. Merab had done her best to shield Hephzibah from their mockery and try to lift her spirits, and Hephzibah knew that was what the servant was trying to do now.

"My lady, the concubines will go to the harem, but you'll have the most beautiful suite of all, the one that's reserved for the king's favorite wife."

Hephzibah smiled to try to hide her pain, but she knew the truth. She was Hezekiah's only wife, but not his favorite. "Here, I don't want those clumsy servants to carry these," she told Merab, handing her the ivory box that contained her wedding jewels. "Will you take them to our new apartment for me?"

"With pleasure, my lady." Merab strode from the room, carrying the box like a treasure.

A few minutes later, when the palace servants returned for another load of Hephzibah's things, she suddenly decided to see her new suite for herself. But as she entered the outer sitting room, she heard Merab's voice in the bedchamber, arguing with someone.

"My lady will *not* live with the concubines! She's the king's *wife*! She'll live here, in the wife's chambers!"

"I'm in charge, and I've already decided," the harem eunuch

replied. "The wives' quarters are only for King Hezekiah's favored wives, the ones he's pleased with. Your lady goes in the harem with the rest."

Hephzibah felt as if she'd been slapped. She stifled a cry and leaned against the wall to keep from falling over.

"How dare you insult my lady?" Merab cried.

"The prince spent his wedding week with your lady and hasn't sent for her since. It's been more than six months. Does it sound to you like she's a *favored* wife?"

Hephzibah covered her face, wishing she could hide from the ugly truth. As the eunuch continued to argue with Merab in the next room, his words struck Hephzibah like the lashes of a whip. "He never asks for her—that speaks plainly enough to me. Besides, she failed to conceive his child. She'll go into the harem until he sends for her again. I'm not going to clutter up the finest suite in the harem with a wife he doesn't want. Now that he's the king, he can choose any woman in the nation for his wife. And the one he chooses will live here."

Hephzibah sank to the floor, weeping. The eunuch ignored her as he swept out of the room, but then she felt Merab's arms around her, soothing her, and she knew by her trembling voice that Merab was crying, too.

"Don't cry, baby. It's okay."

"No, it isn't, Merab. My husband doesn't want me. He doesn't love me."

"Shh. Don't listen to that hateful man. It isn't true."

But Hephzibah knew that it was true. She hadn't pleased Hezekiah and he had rejected her. No matter which room she lived in, Hephzibah would spend the rest of her life alone in the king's harem with no husband and no children. She would have no other purpose in life except to be a decoration at banquets and feasts. She was barely eighteen years old, and her life was over.

"What am I going to do, Merab? I don't want to be imprisoned here until I die. Why doesn't my husband love me?"

"I don't know, baby," the servant said, rocking her. "He only spent a week getting to know you. It's so unfair."

"Why couldn't Hezekiah be an ordinary man instead of the king? Then I could encourage him when he wakes up each morning and comfort him at night. I would always be by his side to take care of him, entertaining important guests for him, and raising his children. I want to love him like a real wife and have him love me in return. Why can't it be that way?"

"Let's go home, baby—back to your father's house. This was a terrible mistake."

"No," Hephzibah cried. "We can't go back home!"

"But why not? Your father loves you. He'd rather die than see you this unhappy."

"I can't go back. I don't want anyone to know that I'm a failure."

"But you're not a failure."

"Merab, I heard what the eunuch said just now. My husband wasn't pleased with me. That's why he didn't send for me again."

"But he's hardly given you a chance."

"Besides, if I go home in disgrace, Papa will never be able to find a husband for Miriam. Oh, what am I going to do? I can't live like this for the rest of my life!"

Merab drew her closer and they wept together. Hephzibah stayed in her arms for a long time, pouring out her sorrow. She loved Merab like her own mother, but there was one thing she would never be able to confide in her, one thing she hadn't shared with anyone because it was the most painful irony of all: She loved Hezekiah—more than she loved her own life. She would stay in the harem until the day she died as long as there was hope that one day he would remember her and send for her again. She could never love another man as much as she loved him.

She remembered the way he stretched when he rose from their bed in the morning and gazed out of the window at the hills surrounding Jerusalem as if they were his nourishment. She loved the way he held her face in his hands when he kissed her and how he buried his fingers in her hair. She had studied him by moonlight each night as he slept beside her, and she could trace by memory every line and plane of his face. She could recall his every movement, every gesture, every word that he'd spoken to her in their one short week together. She had to—because her memories of him were all she had left.

# 18

THE SUN HAD ALREADY SET when Micah squeezed inside Isaiah's home with the other disciples, curious to learn why the prophet had called this meeting. He hadn't seen Isaiah and the others since returning home to Moresheth last spring to tend his crops, and he took a moment to greet his fellow prophets, embracing them warmly.

"Thank you all for coming," Isaiah said, speaking loudly to quiet the gathering. "I know that many of you traveled a long way to be here, and I'm grateful. Please, make yourselves comfortable so we can begin." He stood near the hearth while his wife continued cooking behind him, and the air was fragrant with the smell of onions sizzling in olive oil. The single-room home served Isaiah as a kitchen, bedroom, and study, as well as a classroom, but it had few furnishings. Micah found a place to sit on the stone floor with the other disciples and leaned forward, listening intently.

"Most of you have probably heard the news from Jerusalem," Isaiah began. "King Ahaz is dead, and his son Hezekiah will succeed him as king."

Micah stared at him in surprise. "No, Rabbi, I hadn't heard. I guess it takes a while for news to reach Moresheth. How did he die?"

"It was very sudden," Isaiah said, shrugging. "No one will say what happened."

"It was Yahweh's judgment on an evil king," one of the others said. Micah nodded in agreement.

"The next few weeks will be critical ones for our nation," Isaiah continued. "We don't know anything about the new king, Hezekiah—whether or not he worships idols as his father did. But I'll be returning to Jerusalem tomorrow, and I'm asking for your prayers. I believe that Yahweh wants His voice to be heard again."

"I agree, Rabbi," one of the men said, "but maybe you should wait. Suppose the new king is as evil as King Ahaz was? You'll be risking arrest." The others murmured in agreement.

"I understand your concerns," Isaiah said, "but we've all been praying for a spiritual revival in our nation, and maybe it will begin with this new king. I must take advantage of this opportunity to prophesy to King Hezekiah in Yahweh's name."

Micah shared Isaiah's excitement. The rabbi was right—they had all prayed for an end to the moral decline in their nation, and this new king could bring change. If only someone could convince him to listen to the Word of the Lord.

"I think it's too dangerous for you to go," the man beside Micah said. "King Ahaz had orders to arrest you if you tried to prophesy again. Besides, you're too valuable to us here."

"I'm not afraid—"

"We're not questioning your courage, Rabbi, but what about Uriah? He's still the high priest, and for all we know, he may still be the palace administrator, too. He knows who you are, and he knows that you oppose him. He'll never allow you to speak to the king."

"It's a chance I'll have to take," Isaiah insisted. "Yahweh's Word must be spoken now, while there's a transition of power."

"Then I'll go for you," Micah said, rising to his feet. "No one knows me in Jerusalem. I'll prophesy to the king."

Isaiah took a moment to consider his offer, regarding him with a look of deep respect. "I have no doubt that you're able do it, Micah. I saw the Lord's calling on your life the first time we met. And as different as we are, you're like a brother to me. But I have access to the palace and to the king. I'm a member of the royal family—"

"And that's exactly why you shouldn't go," Micah cut in. "You're too well known. Someone will recognize you as soon as you walk through the city gates. But if I go, I'm just a simple farmer from Moresheth, coming for the king's coronation like hundreds of other farmers."

"He's right, Rabbi," one of the men said. "Let Micah go in your place."

As Isaiah looked around at the roomful of men, Micah glanced at them, too. He saw by their expressions that he had their support. And he knew he would be in their prayers. "Let me do it," he repeated.

"Are you sure you understand the risks involved?" Isaiah asked. "We don't know how King Hezekiah will react to a prophecy from Yahweh."

Micah nodded, as he took his place on the floor again. "I could be arrested or even killed. But I still want to go."

Isaiah sank onto a stool near the hearth. "I don't know. . . . We'll need to help you think of a way to get close enough to prophesy. If Uriah is still the palace administrator, you'll have to get past him, somehow. You can't exactly stroll up to the palace and talk to the king. Public street prophecy may not be possible, either. The crowds will be enormous, and I imagine that the new king will be very heavily guarded."

"Rabbi, would any of your relatives in the palace help us?" someone asked.

Isaiah thought for a moment, then shook his head. "No, I've been out of touch with them for too long. A great deal of political intrigue takes place with a change of administration, and most of the nobility wait to see who's really in power before they take sides. I'm afraid I can't trust any of my blood relatives to risk their lives for one of Yahweh's prophets."

"What about the priests and Levites? Would they help us?"

"Maybe . . . My friend Zechariah had the courage to stand up to King Ahaz, and he was arrested for it. He's King Hezekiah's grandfather. You could try to contact him—if he's still alive."

Micah nodded, but it seemed improbable that King Ahaz would have allowed any of his opponents to live.

"What about the palace guards?" one of the young prophets asked. "Might one of them help Micah get close enough to speak to the king?"

"I have an uncle in the palace guard," someone offered. "But he's assigned to a sentry post at the Water Gate, not the palace."

Isaiah stroked his beard thoughtfully. "Hmm. It's a possibility. . . ."

"Or how about one of the servants at the palace? Could Micah trade places with one for a day and get close to the king that way? Maybe while he dines?"

"Does anyone have a contact among the palace servants?" Isaiah asked.

No one answered.

"What if he sold some of his produce to the palace kitchens and made his own contact? A pretty serving girl, perhaps?"

"It's a good idea," Isaiah said, "but I'm afraid it would take too long. He'll have to act quickly, within the next few days, if possible. I think that the new king will be most receptive—if he's receptive at all—while he's still gathering his advisors and deciding how he will begin his reign. Once Uriah and his supporters manage to gain Hezekiah's confidence, it will be too late."

The room fell silent except for the crackling of the fire and the sound of Isaiah's wife stirring a wooden spoon in an earthenware pot. Micah had felt a range of emotions from hope to despair as they'd tried to formulate a plan. A prophecy from God could turn the king's heart—and the nation—back to Yahweh. But how would Micah ever get close enough to do it? He tried to picture himself walking up the steep road to Jerusalem, climbing the hill to the palace, standing before the king—and he suddenly saw the solution.

"I know what I must do," he said quietly. Everyone turned to him as he rose to his feet again. "Isaiah said it at the very beginning. I will simply walk into the palace and speak to the king."

Stunned silence fell.

"Listen," he continued, "the king will probably announce a feast day to celebrate his coronation, right? I'll wait until evening, when the eating and drinking has gone on for a while and everyone has relaxed his guard. Then I'll walk boldly into the palace as if I belonged there and speak to the king. Isaiah can draw a map so I'll know my way to the banquet hall. After that I'm in Yahweh's hands."

Isaiah studied him, his brow furrowed in thought. Micah felt everyone's eyes on him. His plan was simple but outrageously daring. He waited. At last, one of the other prophets spoke. "You can't possibly attempt such a foolhardy plan."

Micah's temper flared. "I suppose you would have called David foolhardy when he went before Goliath, armed with only a sling," he said, turning on him. "Or maybe Joshua was foolish to think he could conquer Jericho by marching around blowing trumpets? I can't question the way Yahweh chooses to work. I simply obey Him. I feel compelled to go to Jerusalem, compelled to walk into the palace and prophesy to the king. And if I'm wrong, if I am acting foolishly, then maybe I was never called to be His prophet in the first place."

Isaiah stood to embrace Micah, and his eyes shone with respect. "May Yahweh bless you, my friend, for your courage and faith," he said. "And now it's time for the rest of us to pray."

---

Micah left before sunrise, following the winding mountain road through the Judean hills to Jerusalem. By the time he reached the Valley Gate on the city's southern wall, he was hot and tired, and his legs ached from the strain of his steep climb.

He stopped to rest at the Shiloah Pool, cupping his hands to sip the cool spring water. He felt out of place in this bustling city where everything seemed to move at a breathless rate. He studied the unsmiling people hurrying past, longing for a familiar face, but no one acknowledged his greetings. Rich and poor, priest and slave, they either regarded Micah and his simple peasant clothing with contempt or else ignored him altogether. And he realized that this was their attitude toward Yahweh, too. They either hurried through life, ignoring Him, or they regarded Yahweh and His commandments with contempt.

As Micah looked down the valley to the west, he saw the jagged cliffs that marked the entrance to the Valley of Hinnom. Isaiah had described the sacrifices that took place at Molech's shrine, but it seemed almost unbelievable to Micah that parents would offer their children to idols. He knew that a clump of spreading oaks nearby marked a sacred grove for worshiping Asherah, and all along his journey he'd seen altars to Baal in every clearing and hilltop in Judah. How had these changes come so quickly? A few years ago, Micah had journeyed to the northern kingdom of Israel and prophesied against that nation's idolatry, but he'd believed that there was still hope for his nation. Now he saw that her wound was incurable, too. The scourge of idolatry had come to Judah, reaching the very gate of his people, even to Jerusalem itself.

Weariness and depression settled over Micah as he recognized the hopelessness of his mission. It was too late for his nation. His was only one voice, shouting against thousands of others. What could he possibly hope to accomplish? No one would listen to a poor peasant farmer—including the king. Isaiah was an educated man of royal blood, and the king hadn't listened to him. What was Micah doing here? This was useless. Stopping evil was like trying to hold back the waves of the sea.

He stood, convinced that he should turn around and go home to his farm in Moresheth without even bothering to enter the city. But then he remembered how fervently Isaiah and the others had prayed for him throughout the night, and he knew that they would continue praying for him until he returned. They were relying on him to be their spokesman, to remind King Hezekiah of Yahweh's covenant with the nation. If the new king would repent, maybe the whole nation would repent, as well. It might be too late, but Micah knew that he had to try. He pushed his weariness and depression aside and walked through the crowded gate into the city.

The sun stood directly overhead, and Micah's shadow looked nearly invisible beneath his feet as he started walking through Jerusalem's streets. In a few more hours he would watch the coronation at the Temple and then the feasting would officially begin. After that he would wait until everyone at the king's banquet had his fill of wine. Then he would go inside and speak Yahweh's words to King Hezekiah.

Micah saw the golden roof of Yahweh's Temple shining on the hill above the city, and he started walking in that direction. He hadn't made a pilgrimage to Jerusalem in years—ever since learning that Ahaz had closed the sanctuary doors and set up the Assyrian altar. Micah could scarcely remember a time when the holy festivals of Passover and Tabernacles had been celebrated.

The city had seemed beautiful years ago when he was a boy and King Jotham reigned, but now as Micah made his way through the steep, narrow streets, Jerusalem seemed dirty and decayed, cloaked in rags of poverty. He knew how greatly he and the other Judean farmers had suffered under the burden of taxes to Assyria, but all around him he saw proof of how much the city dwellers had suffered, as well. Jerusalem had been a magnificent city once, but now her walls and houses seemed to be tumbling down, and many merchants had boarded up their shops altogether. Beggars of all ages sat in the dust, pleading for alms from everyone who passed by. At least in the country the people could grow food to eat.

When he reached the royal palace below the Temple Mount, Micah saw thousands of people already gathering in the outer courtyard, even though the coronation wouldn't begin for three more hours. He wondered what drew them. Did they hope for a better life under a new king, with renewed prosperity and peace? Micah longed for those things, too, but he knew that they couldn't come from an earthly king, only from God.

He scanned the thousands of faces he passed in the crowd, but no one seemed happy, in spite of the drinking and laughter. For a brief moment he saw them the way Yahweh did—like sheep without a shepherd—and he knew that Isaiah had been right. The time had come for Yahweh's prophets to speak His message once again. God loved these people, and He longed for them to return to Him. But as badly as Micah wanted to proclaim God's Word to them, he knew it was still too soon. He had to wait until tonight at the coronation feast.

He sighed and leaned against the wall of the courtyard, away from the crush of people, and took out the sketch of the palace Isaiah had drawn for him. He had studied it every spare moment along the way to Jerusalem until he had memorized it. Now he compared the drawing to the actual palace in front of him, trying to decide which route he would take to the banquet hall. He didn't know exactly what he would say to King Hezekiah, but Yahweh would provide the words when the time came.

As Micah watched, a squadron of palace guards, armed with swords and spears, pushed the crowd back, then assembled in a protective circle around the perimeter of the palace stairs. He hadn't realized that there would be so many guards, and he wondered how he could get past them. He also wondered what would happen to him after he prophesied—would they let him quietly walk away and return to his home in Moresheth or would he be imprisoned or even killed? To his surprise, he felt no fear. He would listen to the voice of Yahweh and speak the words He gave him—what happened after that didn't matter.

As the restless crowd pressed in on him, Micah decided to go someplace where he could be alone with God and prepare himself for his task. He folded the map once again and pushed his way out of the palace gates, feeling in the folds of his cloak for the silver pieces that Isaiah had given him. He wanted to use some of them to purchase a dove for a burnt offering of purification, and he climbed the steep steps to the Temple Mount—God's dwelling place.

But as soon as Micah entered the men's court and saw the huge Assyrian altar, he stopped short. Isaiah had warned him that Ahaz had erected a pagan altar in Yahweh's Temple, but Micah hadn't been prepared for the overwhelming sense of violation he felt. The idols carved around the altar's base seemed to mock God in His own Temple. Yahweh's altar of burnt offering had been pushed aside, just as He had been pushed aside in men's hearts to make room for their false gods. Micah wanted to cry aloud at this outrage. Instead, he turned and fled from the Temple. He could never offer a sacrifice to Yahweh in this place. God no longer dwelled here. No wonder His nation was suffering.

Micah plowed through the winding streets, not caring where they led him. The crowds jostled and buffeted him, but he was too numb with anger and grief to feel it. He hurried blindly down the hill and found himself in the marketplace, where the noise and activity brought him back to the present. Voices assaulted him from all sides as shopkeepers hawked their wares, competing with each other for customers. Micah was still dazed when an idol merchant stepped into his path.

"Come over here and look at these," the man invited, pointing to his booth. "I sell the finest household gods in the city. See? I have olive wood, gold, ivory . . . What'll it be, friend? Baal, for good crops? Only thirty shekels."

"Leave me alone." Micah tried to push past him, but the merchant grabbed his arm.

"You won't find any gods better than these. For you—twenty-five shekels."

"I don't want your filthy idols!" Micah wrenched free of the merchant's grip, shoving him backward a little harder than he intended to. The man lost his balance and stumbled, knocking over some of the images on his table.

"Hey! You can't push me around! Come back here!"

Micah elbowed through the crowd, hoping the man wouldn't follow him. He didn't know how he had ended up in the market district, but he wanted to get away from here as quickly as possible. He looked around for the street that led to the Valley Gate, but he couldn't see past the jostling people.

Suddenly, someone gripped his arm. Micah spun around, expecting to see the idol merchant, but faced an older man instead. "You're not from around here, are you?" the man said. "Came to the big city for the celebrations, huh? Listen, I can give you a good deal on incense for the gods. It's imported stuff—only ten shekels."

"I don't worship idols," Micah said, prying the man's hand off his arm. He tried to walk away but a woman stepped smoothly into his path. She wore no veil or head covering but approached him immodestly, face-to-face, her eyes painted with kohl.

"Is that old toad bothering you?" she asked Micah, pointing to the incense merchant. "Want me to cast a spell on him?"

Micah couldn't reply. To speak to such a shameful woman was improper.

"Maybe you have a departed loved one you wish to speak to?" she asked, smiling. "Why don't you come home with me, honey, and I might even conjure up King Ahaz for you." She tossed her long black hair over her shoulder and laughed.

Micah turned away and dove into the crowd, shoving people out of his path. He felt shaken and contaminated with the filth of idolatry. But in his haste to leave the marketplace, he unwittingly stumbled into a gathering of Asherah worshipers. The cult prostitutes stood on a small raised platform while an eager group of men bartered for their services. As Micah burst through the mob into the open space in front of the platform, the bartering suddenly stopped. Everyone stared at him as if waiting for him to explain the interruption.

Micah began to tremble as the power of Yahweh flowed through him. Once again he saw the people through God's eyes—saw that His grace was strained to the limit and about to run out. Yahweh's wrath and righteous judgment loomed above the whole nation because of their sins, yet the people were blind to their peril. Micah had to warn them. They needed to know. He leaped onto the platform, shoving the prostitutes into the street.

"Listen to me!" he shouted. "All of you, listen! The Lord in His holy Temple has made accusations against you!" As Micah's voice carried across the marketplace, the chattering and bartering stopped. A hushed silence swept through the crowd.

"Look! Yahweh is coming from His dwelling place to tread the high places of the earth. The mountains will melt beneath Him and the valleys will split apart, like wax before the fire. All this is because of your sins! 'In that day,' declares the Lord, 'I will destroy your witchcraft and you will no longer cast spells. I will destroy your carved images and your sacred stones from among you; you will no longer bow down to the work of your hands. I will uproot from among you your Asherah poles and demolish your cities. I will take vengeance in anger and wrath upon the nations that have not obeyed me. Zion will be plowed like a field, Jerusalem will become a heap of rubble, the temple hill a mound overgrown with thickets.'"

Micah leaped off the platform and overturned a table of carved images, dumping its contents into the street, smashing all the idols that lay in his path. "Yahweh will pour Jerusalem's stones into the valley and lay bare her foundations. All of her idols will be broken to pieces!"

As he paused for breath, Micah looked around at the people, wondering if they would heed his warning and repent. But before he could continue his prophecy, a gang of drunken youths decided to follow his example and began overturning tables of fruit and vegetables, smashing jars of olive oil and ripping open sacks of grain. The crowd went wild, scrambling to loot the smashed booths, and the marketplace erupted into a riot.

"No, wait! Stop!" Micah shouted. "You don't understand!" He had never intended for this to happen. He watched as the violence raged around him, feeling as if he'd stepped into a nightmare.

Suddenly the idol merchant stood in front of him, brandishing a club. Micah tried to step back and realized that angry merchants swarmed all around him, armed with bats and sticks. His heart pounded with fear. This couldn't be happening to him. He had to get away. He had to prophesy to the king tonight. He tried to run, but there was no place to go.

The idol merchant swung at him, and Micah dodged, only to catch a blow from behind. He tried to defend himself, but the force of their attack was overwhelming. Clubs struck him from all sides with unrelenting pain. He raised his arms to shield his head and felt a sickening crack as a bone in his left arm fractured, leaving it limp and useless. They meant to kill him.

"Help me . . . Yahweh, help me!" he cried as he struggled to get away, to keep from collapsing. A violent blow smashed into his forehead and pain ripped through his skull. He staggered forward as blood poured into his eyes, blinding him. Another blow knocked him to the ground, and the angry merchants closed in on him, kicking and beating him until everything went black.

# 19

HILKIAH WATCHED IN HORROR from his booth in the marketplace as angry merchants surrounded Yahweh's prophet and began beating him. Hilkiah had thought that the dark-bearded man was just another peasant who had come to Jerusalem for the festivities—he had the calloused hands and brawny arms of a man who wielded a plow behind a team of oxen. But then he'd begun to prophesy, and Hilkiah recognized the powerful voice of Yahweh that had been silent for so long. But what came next happened much too fast. One minute Hilkiah had listened spellbound to the prophet's warning vision, and the next thing he knew, the merchants were attacking the man.

"Stop, stop—you'll kill him!" Hilkiah cried. He raced from his booth into the street to save the prophet, but before Hilkiah could get there, his son Eliakim grabbed him from behind.

"Abba, no. Don't go out there."

"Let go of me, Eliakim! Let me help him! They're killing him! They're killing God's prophet!" He struggled to break free, but his son was taller and stronger than he was. He wouldn't let go.

"They'll kill you, too, Abba. Stay out of it. It's none of your business."

"Let me go! God of Abraham—somebody! Help that man!"

Hilkiah felt each blow that the angry men rained down on Micah, but he couldn't break free as Eliakim dragged him back to his booth. Suddenly he heard the sound of horses as a squadron of soldiers from the palace guard thundered into the marketplace.

"Oh, thank God—thank God," Hilkiah breathed.

"That's enough!" the captain shouted above the chaos. "Stop where you are! All of you!"

The mob quickly backed away from Micah, dropping their clubs. All over the marketplace, the destruction and looting suddenly stopped as people scrambled to disappear and avoid arrest.

"Spread out," the captain ordered. "Arrest anyone who moves." He stood with his sword drawn, gazing at the destruction all around him. "What's going on here? Who's responsible for this?"

"Let me go!" Hilkiah begged. "Let me explain it to him."

Eliakim tightened his grip. "No, Abba. Stay out of it."

One of the angry merchants pointed to the prophet's motionless body. "He's the one who started it all. He destroyed my booth, and he has to pay for it."

"Are there two other witnesses who can confirm your testimony?" Jonadab asked.

"Yes—I'm also a witness," another merchant said. "The man claimed to be a prophet of Yahweh."

"A prophet?" the captain repeated as he studied the man's bloody peasant clothing.

"Yes! Yes! A man of God!" Hilkiah tried to step forward, but Eliakim pulled him away from the door.

"Shh! Abba, please. Don't get involved!"

"Let me go! Let me explain!" His arms ached from Eliakim's grip.

The crowd murmured as Captain Jonadab paced the length of the street, surveying the damaged booths. Then the captain walked back to where the prophet lay.

"Whoever wants to press charges should bring witnesses before the judges at the city gate. If the prophet lives, he will have to pay for the damages. In the meantime, I'm placing him under arrest at the guard tower. As for the rest of you—go about your business or I'll arrest you, as well!" He signaled to his soldiers, and they lifted the prophet beneath his arms and dragged him away.

Hilkiah sagged against his son as he watched the soldiers leave. When Eliakim finally loosened his grip, Hilkiah turned on him, angry and frustrated. "What is the matter with you? That man was God's prophet. Why didn't you help me instead of stopping me?"

"Abba, I helped you the best way I knew how—I kept you out of it. That mob was out of control. They would have killed anyone who helped him, including you."

Hilkiah sank onto a stool, shaking his head. "I can't understand why you don't share my outrage. Do you even see the evil all around us, or have you grown so accustomed to it that it no longer bothers you?"

"Abba, I stopped you because they would have killed you, too, and—"

"You were so young when it started creeping in that you probably can't even remember when our nation still worshiped the one true God. I wonder if there are any good men left in the world, or if you and I and this prophet are the only faithful followers Yahweh has left?" He sighed in frustration. "It's been so long since I've heard the Eternal One's prophets speak. You probably can't even remember them."

Eliakim rested his hand on his father's shoulder. "Yes, I do, Abba," he said quietly. "I once met Rabbi Isaiah—remember? I went to warn him for your friend, Zechariah."

"The prophets are the only hope for this nation," Hilkiah said sadly. "They're our only hope."

"We have a new king now, Abba. Maybe things will be different."

Hilkiah shook his head as he stared out into the street, watching the merchants sweep up the remains of their damaged booths. "No, I don't think so. Each new king that has come and gone has been worse than the one before him: Uzziah, Jotham, Ahaz . . . O God of Abraham, what can we do?"

"Come on, Abba. I'll help you close up for the day. It's almost time for the coronation."

"Yes, I suppose we may, as well."

"At least they didn't damage your booth," Eliakim said.

Hilkiah stood and began rolling up the colorful bolts of cloth he had placed on display, stacking them inside his shop for the night. The more he thought about Yahweh's prophet and what he had suffered for his faith, the more Hilkiah's thoughts grew into a pressing conviction of what he must do. He walked over to where his son was stacking cloth and took the bolt from his hands, careful to conceal his sense of urgency.

"The coronation will start soon, Eliakim. Why don't you go on ahead and pick a good spot where we can watch it? I'll close up the booth and meet you there in a little while."

"You'll finish faster if I help."

"No, no, no. You go, son. I'll be along shortly."

"Are you sure?"

"Yes, yes! 'Are you sure?' he asks. Of course I'm sure. Go, already!" He motioned for Eliakim to leave, then turned his back and continued rolling up bolts of cloth and straightening the piles with deliberate patience.

"Okay, then. I guess I'll see you later," Eliakim said.

Hilkiah busied himself with his goods as his son set off up the street toward the palace. When he was certain that Eliakim was out of sight, he hurried over to the idol merchant's booth.

"Shalom, my friend," he said cheerfully as he bent down to help him pick up the remnants of his booth. "What a mess—what a mess!"

"Lousy religious fanatics," the merchant grumbled. "I hate them! They're bad for business."

"Yes . . . yes . . . I see what you mean." Hilkiah prayed for God's forgiveness as he gathered up the smashed idols. He helped the man clean up the debris and repair some of the damage, then stood back to survey their work. "So—how much do you figure it'll cost you to make things right again?" Hilkiah asked, idly jangling the silver pouch that hung at his waist.

The merchant eyed him suspiciously. "What do you mean?"

Hilkiah hung his thumbs in his waist belt and patted the money pouch. "It's a holiday, and my business has been good. I was lucky that none of my goods were destroyed, so I'm willing to help you out a little. That way we can both forget this whole nasty mess as quickly as possible and get back to business."

"What's in it for you?"

Hilkiah laughed. "'What's in it for me?' he asks? Look at this mess! It's an eyesore. It's bad for business—yours and mine. And a lawsuit at the elders' gate will be even worse."

"But why would you want to help that filthy peasant?"

"I'm not helping him—I'm helping *you*. Besides, the poor beggar has suffered enough, don't you think?"

"Yeah, we did get him pretty good," he said, smiling.

"Precisely. You already got more justice than the elders at the gate will ever give you. Why bother with a lawsuit? Besides, I'll wager that fellow hasn't a shekel to his name."

"That's probably true."

"Of course it's true." Hilkiah clapped the man's shoulder and pointed him toward the inn down the street. "So—why don't we drink a toast to the rebuilding of your booth? It'll be my treat. We'll round up some of these other merchants and they can join us."

By the time Hilkiah bought a third round of drinks for the idol merchant and his allies, he knew that the prophecy in the marketplace had long been forgotten. And even if they suddenly did remember, they were much too drunk to testify. Hilkiah smiled, pleased with his afternoon's work, and quietly slipped out of the inn.

Uriah watched as his servants prepared his bath, and for the first time in days he started to relax. He had taken a great risk when he'd gotten rid of King Ahaz, but the risk had paid off. The emissaries had been sent back to Israel, avoiding a disaster that would have destroyed his nation. And so far, Hezekiah hadn't pursued the cause of Ahaz's death.

The new king had not only allowed him to continue as palace administrator, but in a few hours Uriah would preside over the coronation wearing the mitre and ephod of high priest. The crisis was over, and Uriah had remained in power.

"Your bath is ready, my lord," a servant announced.

But before Uriah had a chance to undress, Captain Jonadab arrived at his door. "Forgive me for disturbing you, sir, but you wanted to stay informed on all aspects of security for the coronation."

The captain's worried expression made Uriah uneasy. "Yes—what is it?"

"Well, a short time ago my soldiers and I broke up a riot in the marketplace. Now, that's not too unusual, considering that this is a festive occasion and the people are starting to celebrate, if you understand what I mean. In fact, people are coming into the city from all over the countryside, and the feasting and drinking are well underway, and—"

"Get to the point," Uriah said.

"Well, sir, I know how much trouble his kind has caused you in the past. . . ." Jonadab eyed him nervously, as if afraid that Uriah might blame him for bringing this bad news. "You see, the fellow who started the disturbance claimed to be a prophet of Yahweh."

Uriah shouted a curse. He might have known this would happen. He should have expected Isaiah to return—and he should have been better prepared. If he had sent his men to watch the gates, he could have arrested him before he entered the city.

"Was it Isaiah?" Uriah asked.

"No, sir. He was younger than Isaiah and dark-haired—a peasant from the countryside, to judge by his clothing."

Uriah knew that if a prophet of Yahweh were in Jerusalem, he would try to reach King Hezekiah, perhaps by disrupting the coronation ceremony. Uriah could never allow that to happen. "Where is he now?"

"I arrested him," Jonadab said, "and took him to the guard tower. The mob beat him pretty severely during the riot, and he was nearly dead by the time I arrived to break things up. He's still knocked out cold."

Uriah felt only slightly relieved. But he knew better than to forget the incident. "I want this prophet brought to me as soon as he regains consciousness so I can question him. And since there may be more than one of them, I want you to double the number of guards at the coronation ceremony."

"Yes, sir. I'll take care of it right away."

"Understand this," Uriah said, waving his finger in Jonadab's face. "These men are a great threat to King Hezekiah!"

Jonadab bowed and left the room.

The news left Uriah shaken. Yahweh's prophets had been silent for so many years that he had dared to believe that the last of them was finally gone. If they reappeared now, competing with him for King Hezekiah's confidence, they could destroy everything that Uriah had worked to build. He was proud of the reforms he had made in the strict Jewish religious system, reforms that Isaiah and his followers would call too liberal. He had centralized the state religion at the Temple with himself as high priest. These prophets, with their narrow-minded, outdated views opposed all that Uriah had worked for—and they also opposed him. In their opinion, Uriah's religious tolerance deserved the death penalty.

"Do you still wish to bathe, my lord?" Uriah's servant asked.

Uriah nodded, but as he eased himself into the warm, scented water he was unable to relax. Instead, he reviewed all the plans he had made for the coronation ceremony, alert for any security flaws. He couldn't risk the possibility that these men might influence the new king. He had to make sure they never reached Hezekiah.

Zechariah shaded his eyes, squinting in the glare of the afternoon sun. He stood with the other Levites on the Temple porch, waiting for the coronation to begin. But even when he craned his neck he still couldn't see the king's platform. When he'd learned that Hezekiah's coronation would take place in the Temple, he'd begged one of the friendlier guards to allow him to sing in the Levites' choir so he could watch his grandson being crowned king. Now, as applause thundered from the huge crowd assembled in the courtyard, Zechariah pushed forward for a better view. The Temple guard rested his hand on his shoulder and drew him back.

"Please, Zechariah—you promised me that you'd keep quiet. That's the only reason I agreed to let you watch today."

"But I can't see. Please let me move a little closer. I'm not going to disturb the ceremony."

His friend Shimei, who stood nearer to the front, turned around. "Here, let him trade places with me—it's his grandson, after all. You haven't missed anything yet, Zechariah. The nobles and king's advisors are making their entrance."

"Very well—go ahead," the guard agreed. "But remember: Uriah will murder both of us if you cause any trouble."

"I'll be silent, I give you my word."

Shimei quickly traded places with Zechariah, giving him an unobstructed view of the king's platform in the center of the Temple courtyard. The nobles and advisors leading the procession had taken their places near the Assyrian altar. In a moment, Hezekiah would come forward to be anointed King of Judah. Zechariah had never dreamed he would live to see this day.

The trumpeters, assembled on the wall surrounding the Temple, sounded their fanfare. The gates to the courtyard slowly swung open.

Zechariah held his breath. The crowd caught their first glimpse of their new king, and their cheers nearly drowned out the trumpets.

Hezekiah carried himself with the posture and bearing of a soldier as he strode to the platform to take his place. He wore a sword strapped to the belt of his royal tunic. He was tall and broad-shouldered, and his curly brown hair and beard had an auburn luster in the sunlight. Zechariah's vision blurred as tears filled his eyes. Hezekiah still looked the same to him. He was older and taller, but he still looked the same. Zechariah remembered the curly-haired little boy who had run through the rain-washed streets to the Temple, splashing his feet in all the puddles, and he longed to hold him in his arms as he had so long ago.

Hezekiah acknowledged the wildly cheering crowd, then held up his hand to call for silence. His other hand rested casually on the hilt of his sword. The noise slowly subsided.

"Men of Judah and Jerusalem," he shouted. "I am Hezekiah ben Ahaz, rightful heir to the royal house of David. I lay claim this day to the throne of my father, Ahaz ben Jotham."

His deep voice spoke with authority, and he reminded Zechariah of King Uzziah.

"My reign will be equitable and just—and absolute," Hezekiah continued. "When I sit in judgment over this kingdom, you may expect my decisions to be impartial. And in return, I will expect the honor and tribute that is due me by virtue of my position as king and heir to the throne of Judah."

A roar of approval went up from the crowd and the trumpets sounded their fanfare once more. Uriah stepped forward, wearing the mitre and ephod of the high priest. Hezekiah sank down on one knee as Uriah anointed his head with oil.

"May your reign be blessed with peace and prosperity," Uriah said, "by all the gods of Judah."

"No!" Zechariah gasped. The priest's words struck him like a fist in his stomach. *All the gods?* Hezekiah knew there was only one

God—why would he allow Uriah to pray that way?

But even as Zechariah watched, the priests were slaying the king's sacrifices, carrying them up the ramp of the Assyrian altar, offering them to pagan gods. Zechariah's pain was greater than any he had ever known. All his years of waiting, all his prayers had been in vain. Hezekiah no longer believed in Yahweh. Zechariah fought back tears as his hope withered.

Where was Isaiah? Where were all of Yahweh's prophets? If only one would prophesy to Hezekiah—maybe he would listen and remember. Zechariah scanned the huge crowd, hoping to see Isaiah pushing his way to the front to prophesy as he used to do in the days of King Jotham and King Ahaz. But no one challenged the double ring of guards that stood at the base of the king's platform.

Maybe he should go forward himself—surely Hezekiah would remember him. But Zechariah glanced over his shoulder and saw the Temple guard watching him carefully. He had given the guard his word.

Uriah finished his prayer, and a scribe stepped forward from among the Levites to present the manuscript scroll that contained the Divine Law for Kings. If only Hezekiah would read it. Maybe it would help him remember everything that Zechariah had taught him. But by now, Uriah had probably altered the Divine Law to conform to all the other changes he had made to the Torah.

Another priest walked forward, carrying the royal crown of Judah. Zechariah watched with a mixture of pride and pain as Uriah placed the crown on Hezekiah's head. The new king rose to his feet, his chin held high, while the crowd roared, "Long live King Hezekiah!"

Zechariah gazed at his beloved grandson, standing with strength and dignity, the crown of the kingdom on his head, and he remembered all the other kings he had known—Uzziah, Jotham, Ahaz. They had once stood here, too, so full of promise like Hezekiah. Now they were dead—and his hopes for Hezekiah were dead, as well. Zechariah thought his heart would break.

"O Lord . . . he doesn't believe in you," Zechariah murmured as he gazed at Hezekiah. "He doesn't believe. . . ."

He could no longer hold back his tears. As Hezekiah laid his hand on one of the animals that would be sacrificed to an idol, Zechariah covered his face.

"Come on, my friend," Shimei said, taking his arm. "Let's get out of this hot sun. The coronation is over. Let's go inside."

"Yes, it's over," Zechariah said. He walked across the courtyard to his room without looking back.

---

Uriah sent all his servants away and sank onto his couch, exhausted and greatly relieved. The coronation had gone smoothly, without any disturbances. Perhaps the prophet in the marketplace today was the only one left. He could enjoy the ceremony now, in retrospect. Hezekiah had made a striking impression and the crowds seemed pleased with their new king. Uriah smiled to himself and felt his good mood return. But just as he began to relax, Captain Jonadab arrived, alone, looking even more worried than the last time.

"What's the matter?" Uriah asked him. "Where's the prophet? Is he dead?"

"No, sir. He didn't die . . . yet. But I don't have him."

"Why not? Didn't I order you to bring him to me?"

Jonadab cleared his throat. "When I got back to the guard tower, he was gone. While I was overseeing the extra security measures you ordered for the coronation, the guards released him."

"They did *what*?"

Jonadab spread his hands. "None of the merchants showed up with witnesses to press charges. When a man came and paid the prophet's fines and for all the damages in the marketplace, we had to release him. He was gone when I got back to the guard tower."

"You *fools*!"

"How could we hold him if no one pressed charges?" Jonadab asked.

"Who paid the prophet's fines?"

"I don't know. My men didn't ask his name."

*"Fools!"* Uriah repeated. He hoped that his anger would conceal his deep fear from Jonadab. Someone had redeemed the prophet from prison—which meant that he wasn't acting alone. There were more of them, and they would probably try to reach King Hezekiah unless Uriah stopped them.

"I don't think you understand how dangerous these men are," he told the captain.

"With all due respect, my lord—I don't see how the prophet could be a danger to anyone. He was beaten nearly to death during the riot, and he still hadn't regained consciousness when the soldiers released him from the guard tower. It will be a miracle if he even lives." Jonadab was silent for a moment, then added, "I will resign my position if you wish, sir."

"I don't want your resignation, I want you to find the prophet and the men who are helping him. Now!"

"In a city that's jammed with visitors? You're asking the impossible."

"Then do the impossible. They're a threat to King Hezekiah. Don't you understand that? I want to be notified the minute you have them in custody, and this time guard them well. Is that clear? Do it right this time!"

Jonadab lifted his chin. "Yes, sir. I understand."

---

Hezekiah sat in his former study on the bench he had occupied for so many years as Shebna had tutored him. His coronation ceremony had ended a few hours earlier, and he still wore his royal robes, but he was too preoccupied to think about changing them. Scrolls littered the table in front of him, and he pored over them, feeling hopeless, his stomach knotted with dread.

If only he'd had more time to prepare, to learn to handle the reins of government gradually instead of having them thrust into his hands without warning. He felt like a passenger in a driverless cart, racing down a mountain road out of control.

He picked up a ledger from the top of a pile and read the title, "Annual Assyrian Tribute Payment," then skimmed over the long list of items that followed and tossed it aside. The next ledger contained the following year's payments, and its list of tribute was even longer, the financial demands much greater. He crumpled it between his hands and threw it on the floor. Suddenly the door opened, and Shebna walked in.

"Your Majesty!" he said in surprise.

"What do you want, Shebna?" For a reason he couldn't explain, Hezekiah felt angry with his tutor for the first time that he could recall.

"I am sorry for disturbing you. I came back for some of my things, but I did not expect to find you here. I assumed my tutoring duties were over now that you are the king." Shebna's wide grin and the look of pride on his face made Hezekiah angrier still.

"You haven't finished your job, Shebna. In fact, I'd say that my real education has just begun!"

Shebna's smile faded. "I have tutored you since you were a child. You have exhausted all of my knowledge."

Hezekiah stood, knocking the bench over backward. "But everything you taught me is worthless knowledge. It has nothing to do with real life."

"What do you mean? I do not understand."

All the frustration that Hezekiah had stockpiled exploded in anger. "I'm the king of a nation that's in ruins! My kingdom is in shambles—my reign is a joke. *That's* the reality. And you never taught me what to do about any of it."

"Your Majesty, you have been king for only a short time. You will learn what you need to learn quickly. You have a sharp, clear mind, and you learn so fast—"

"Oh yes—I learn very fast," Hezekiah cut in. He knew it wasn't fair to use Shebna as an outlet for his frustration, but he couldn't stop himself. "Do you want to know what I've learned in the few days since my father died? I had my first briefing with Uriah and my other advisors this morning. Do you want to know what I learned? First of all, that my father's advisors are all worthless! Uriah's the only intelligent one of the bunch, and I don't like him. I also learned that our nation is bankrupt!"

"That cannot be true." Shebna righted the toppled bench and sank down on it.

"But it is true," Hezekiah said. "While you and I sat in this room and studied all these useless scrolls, my father and his advisors sold Judah into slavery to Assyria. Sure, you taught me that Judah has a treaty with Assyria, but never the fact that this treaty makes us their slaves! Look at these tribute demands!" he said, shoving one of the ledgers into Shebna's hands. "And the lists get longer every year."

Shebna looked shocked as he scanned the list. "I am sorry. I did not know. . . ."

"Our nation's territory has shrunk to half the size it was fifty years ago," Hezekiah went on. "The Philistines, Edomites, Israel, Aram—everyone has carved out his share. We have no seaport, no fortified cities except Jerusalem, and even these walls are crumbling down around us. The national treasuries are empty. There is no surplus in the storehouses. Everything our people labor to produce goes to Assyria."

He paced in front of Shebna, tugging his beard in frustration. "I have no real power. Judah is one of dozens of puppet states in the Assyrian Empire. I have no army, no defensive weapons, and I can't afford to raise an army because we're bankrupt."

He stopped pacing and leaned against the table, shaking his head. "I never dreamed I'd be king so soon—or that I'd inherit such a mess.

I'm supposed to preside over a banquet in a few minutes, and I've never felt less like feasting in my life."

"I am truly sorry, my lord," Shebna said softly.

"You know what infuriates me the most? The fact that I sound just like my father did with his lousy temper. No wonder he never wanted me to learn about running the government. He's made such a mess of it."

"Well, it certainly explains why he drank so heavily," Shebna said.

"I don't want to escape from responsibility like he did. I want to find a solution. The question is, *how*? The more our country produces, the more Assyria takes. And the chronicles tell what happens to any nation that tries to rebel. None of them has ever succeeded. How did Judah get into this mess? And how am I going to get us out of it? I've been poring over all the records, trying to figure it out, but I haven't found any answers."

Shebna was silent for a moment before saying, "At least you have the support of the people. At your coronation today the crowd loved you. I never saw them that supportive of King Ahaz."

"Is that supposed to make me feel better?" Hezekiah asked, turning on him again. "They expect something of me. They're counting on me to solve all the problems my father created. And I don't have any answers. I don't even know where to begin. How popular will I be a year from now if things aren't any better? Or if things are worse?"

He remembered all the hopeful faces gazing up at him from the crowd, and he felt sick. He longed to do something to help them, to repay their loyalty and hard work with renewed prosperity. But he didn't know how. Several moments passed and neither man spoke.

Finally, Shebna said quietly, "I have failed you, my lord. I am sorry."

"Sorry!" Hezekiah shouted. "Sorry? I don't need your apologies, Shebna. I need your advice!" He grabbed a pile of scrolls from the table and waved them at Shebna before throwing them down again. "Where are the rules that tell me how to govern? Where are the instructions for kings to follow? Where is the order in all this chaos?" Hezekiah turned to the shelves and shoved a pile of scrolls onto the floor with a sweep of his hand. Then he dropped onto a bench, staring at the littered floor.

"I care about my country, Shebna," he said at last, "every rock-strewn, sunbaked acre of it. It's been entrusted to me." He gazed out of the window at the hills surrounding the city and realized how very much he did love his country. Then he bent down and began slowly picking up the scrolls.

"You do not need to do that, Your Majesty," Shebna said. "I will call a servant."

Hezekiah didn't reply as he continued gathering up the scrolls. When he finally spoke, his throat felt tight. "I don't know what I'm going to do, Shebna. But I'm the king of this beautiful, pitiful little nation. And I will find a solution."

# 20

MICAH OPENED HIS EYES and pain exploded through his head. He moaned and fought the urge to sink back into unconsciousness to escape the agony. He tried to move and couldn't. Every part of him ached, and he felt as if a huge stone rested on his chest, making it difficult to breathe.

*Help . . . I need help.*

He tried to cry out, but all that emerged from his swollen lips was a hoarse rattle. He saw the flickering light of an oil lamp drawing closer, then a woman with soft hazel eyes peering down at him. She disappeared as quickly as she had appeared, and Micah heard her calling, "Master, Master—come quick! He's awake!" When she returned, she set the lamp on the table beside him.

Again, Micah tried to speak, to move, but the woman gently placed her fingers on his lips and shook her head. "Stay very still," she urged.

Micah felt too weak to struggle. He heard footsteps, then a plump little man with a jovial face appeared. A small skullcap covered his balding head. "Well, my friend—we've been quite concerned about you," he said. "We weren't sure if you would live through the night or not."

*Through the night?* Could it be night already? How long had he lain unconscious? *Please, God, don't let it be too late.* Micah moaned and tried to sit up.

"Steady, my friend. Take it easy," the little man soothed when he saw him struggling. "It's all right—you're among friends. But you've suffered a terrible beating. In fact, I'd say it's a miracle that you're alive at all. You need to lie still and rest until you're well. I'll have my servant mix one of her concoctions to ease the pain and help you sleep." He nodded to the woman, and she slipped from the room.

Micah felt desperate. He had to get to the palace. He couldn't let them drug him into unconsciousness. "No," he moaned. "No . . ."

"Shh. No one's going to hurt you," the man said, sitting down on the edge of Micah's bed. "You're probably wondering where you are and what happened, aren't you? Just lie still, and I'll tell you the whole story. My name is Hilkiah, by the way, and I'm also a follower of the Holy One of Israel—blessed be His name. But unlike you, I don't go around causing riots in the marketplace—my son won't allow it." He smiled slightly. "Anyway, I'm a merchant, an importer of fine linen and dyed cloth, and I heard you prophesy today. I watched the whole ugly riot from my booth. Such a beating you had! Terrible, terrible!" he said, shaking his head.

"After the soldiers carried you away and things calmed down a bit, I had a talk with the merchants whose stalls were destroyed. Now, I don't blame you a bit for what you did. I agree that their idolatry is an abomination to the God of Abraham—blessed is He. And I can see that you're a true prophet of Yahweh. So I helped the merchants forget their grievances with a little wine. Then I went to the guard tower, paid your fines, and here you are." He smiled again. "As I said, we weren't sure if you'd live through the night or not."

*Night? Please, God, don't let the banquet be over!* Micah summoned all his strength in an effort to speak. "Night . . . is it. . . ?"

"What's that?" Hilkiah asked, leaning closer.

"What . . . hour. . . ?"

"You want to know what hour it is?"

Micah nodded.

"I don't know—it must be close to midnight."

"No!" Micah groaned and closed his eyes, praying for strength. Why hadn't he kept silent in the marketplace? How had everything gone so wrong? Maybe he could still make it to the palace if he left right away—if the palace wasn't too far. He had to try.

"I've got . . . to go . . ." he whispered, and he struggled to get up, fighting against his pain and the dead weight of his body. It was no use. His head pounded violently, and something sharp stabbed his chest with every breath he took. The throbbing ache in his left arm was agonizing. He began to cough from his efforts to move and tasted blood.

"Now listen, my friend," Hilkiah said with concern. "You've got to take it easy. What is it that's so important? Are you supposed to be someplace else?"

"Yes," Micah breathed. "The king . . ."

"Just lie still a minute," Hilkiah soothed. He looked up at the servant who had returned to the room. "Our friend seems anxious to go somewhere, and he's quite determined in spite of all his injuries. Can you bring him a little broth to sip for strength?"

She nodded and hurried away as a young man in his late twenties entered the room. He was tall and thin, scholarly looking, with a high forehead, tousled black hair, and a beard. His deep brown eyes had the same warmth as Hilkiah's. "What's going on, Abba?" he asked. "Has the prophet recovered?"

"Yes, he's conscious now. This is my son Eliakim," Hilkiah told Micah. "And I still don't even know your name."

"Here, Abba—let's help him sit up," Eliakim suggested.

The two men stood on either side of the narrow bed and gently lifted Micah to a sitting position, propping him up with pillows. He cried out in pain as they moved him and coughed up more blood, but his breathing seemed to ease once he was upright, and he found it easier to talk.

"I'm Micah . . . of Moresheth," he said.

"Okay, Micah. My servant has some broth for you, and it should give you a little strength. Then maybe you can tell us what it is that's so important."

The woman had returned with a small bowl of chicken broth, and she sat on the bed beside him to spoon it into his mouth. Micah felt like a helpless child as some of it trickled past his swollen lips and ran down his beard. Again, he blamed himself for his failure. But he hadn't eaten since leaving Isaiah's house early that morning, and the warm soup renewed his strength. He ate all he could, stopping several times to cough. Each time, the piercing stab in his chest dug deeper.

"I think his ribs are broken," the woman said, gently feeling Micah's chest. "Can you move this arm?"

Micah tried in vain to raise his limp left arm, sucking air through his teeth as the throbbing pain increased.

"Yes," she soothed. "It is broken, as well."

"Oh, dear," Hilkiah said. He turned to his son. "Can you fix it for him, Eliakim?"

"I'm an engineer, Abba, not a physician. Buildings and roads I can fix. But people?" He shrugged helplessly. "He needs a physician."

Hilkiah sighed. "We'll have to wait until morning to send for one. Will you be all right until then, Micah?"

He summoned all his strength and shook his head. "I have to leave . . . now."

"What must you do that's so important, my friend?"

"I'm on a mission . . . for the prophet Isaiah."

"Isaiah?" Hilkiah repeated. "Isaiah is still alive?"

Micah nodded.

"God of Abraham, thank you! We were afraid he was dead. They've kept my friend, Zechariah, locked up all these years for speaking out against King Ahaz—he'll be happy to know that Isaiah is safe."

"Zechariah's alive?" Micah asked. "The king's grandfather?"

"Yes. He's under house arrest at the Temple, but I know one of the guards, and he allows me to visit him once in a while."

Micah closed his eyes, thanking God for at least one more ally in Jerusalem. But he couldn't waste another minute, no matter how painful it was to move, to breathe. "I must go to the palace tonight. I must prophesy . . . to King Hezekiah."

Hilkiah looked at Micah with awe. "No wonder you're so anxious! Eliakim, we have to help our friend get to the palace."

Eliakim spread his hands. "What? You can't be serious, Abba. He can't even sit up by himself. How can he possibly go to the palace? Listen, Micah, you'll have to wait until you're stronger. You're in no condition to prophesy to anyone."

Micah shook his head. "No. It must be tonight. . . . I won't get a second chance. Help me."

Eliakim stared at him as if unable to comprehend his determination. "Okay, then," he finally said. "Let's get him ready to go."

Micah was grateful when Eliakim took charge. "You can't wear these bloody clothes," he said, "so we'll dress you in one of my father's robes. And we'll have to bind your ribs to ease the pain. Maybe we can bind your broken arm, too."

"Just hurry, please," Micah begged. "There's not much time."

The servant worked swiftly and gently, binding Micah's throbbing ribs with long strips of cloth soaked in a fragrant mixture of aloe and balm. He nearly fainted when she and Eliakim realigned the bones in his arm, but once they were finished and his arm was tightly wrapped in strips of cloth, the throbbing eased. But as Eliakim was helping Micah get dressed in one of Hilkiah's robes, someone pounded on the front door.

Eliakim looked at his father. "Who can that be at this late hour?"

Micah's stomach tightened with dread. "They're searching for me," he said.

"Who is?"

"I'm not sure, but they probably found out about my prophecy in the marketplace. I can't stay here. I've got to get to the palace." Micah was angry with himself all over again for bungling the task that Isaiah had entrusted to him.

Someone pounded on the door again, and an angry voice cried out, "Open the door, or we'll break it down!"

"Please," Micah begged. "I need to leave."

Outside the door, Captain Jonadab's patience was diminishing with every second. If someone didn't open the door soon, he would tear it from its hinges. He was tired and hungry, and he'd grown more anxious and irritable as the day had progressed. The prophet still hadn't been found. And if he posed a threat to King Hezekiah, then he must be found.

Jonadab had retraced every step the prophet had taken since he'd arrived in Jerusalem that morning. He had interviewed everyone who'd witnessed the riot in the marketplace and had forced the soldiers to relate every last detail about the man who'd paid for the prophet's release.

With every hour that passed, the witnesses had become more incoherent as the coronation festivities and the drinking had escalated. And Jonadab had grown more apprehensive at the thought of facing Uriah again without the prophet. He could never hope to make him understand the difficulty of finding an ordinary peasant in a city that was teeming with them.

Then, just when Jonadab had been ready to give up, one of the merchants remembered the name of the man who had paid for his damaged booth—Hilkiah. And he remembered that Hilkiah was a cloth merchant who also had a booth in the marketplace. Jonadab and his men had painstakingly searched for Hilkiah's house, and now, close to midnight, they had finally found it. The prophet had better be inside.

Jonadab couldn't wait any longer. "Break it down," he commanded.

---

Inside, Eliakim took charge. "Abba, get a couple of servants to help you with Micah. Go out through the back. I'll stay here and stall as long as I can. Hurry! Go!"

"How will I ever thank you?" Micah asked.

Eliakim looked at Micah's swollen face and twisted left arm, and it seemed as if the prophet would collapse to the floor if the servants let go of him. He would need a miracle to be able to prophesy.

"You need to thank Abba, not me," Eliakim said. "Now hurry. And God go with you."

The pounding on the door intensified. "I'm coming!" Eliakim shouted, then waited as long as he dared, holding his breath. But they were no longer pounding—they were trying to break it down.

"Who is it?" he shouted again. "What do you want?"

"Captain Jonadab of the Palace Guards. Open the door or we'll break it down!"

Eliakim lifted the oak bar and opened the door a crack, hoping to stall for a few more minutes. But as soon as the soldiers saw an opening, they kicked the door wide, and it slammed into Eliakim's head, nearly knocking him off his feet.

"Are you Hilkiah, the merchant?" the captain shouted.

"No, I'm his son Eliakim." The blow had stunned him, and he rubbed the bruise on his forehead.

"Where is Hilkiah? And where is the prophet?"

"My father isn't here," he said, trying to stay calm. "And I don't know anything about a prophet."

"Liar!" Jonadab shouted. Without warning, he drew back his arm and punched Eliakim in the jaw, knocking him to the floor. "Your father and anyone else who is helping this man are enemies of the king!"

Eliakim lay on the floor, cradling his jaw, hoping it wasn't broken. It throbbed painfully and he tasted blood. He was furious with his father for getting him into this mess, for always sticking his nose into other people's affairs and trying to help. When he saw the look of angry determination on Captain Jonadab's face he was tempted to tell the truth. But he loved his father, and this situation was serious. He didn't care about Micah, but he had to get Hilkiah out of trouble somehow.

"Search the house—he must be here," Jonadab commanded. Then he grabbed Eliakim by the arm and yanked him to his feet. "Where is your father? Tell me, or I swear I'll beat it out of you."

Eliakim never doubted that he meant it. He wiped the blood from his lip, stalling as he tried to think up an answer. But before he could reply, a soldier emerged from the room where Micah had been, carrying his bloody clothes.

"Captain, look . . . the prophet's clothing. He was here. And this looks like some sort of map."

Before Eliakim could react, Jonadab unsheathed his sword, and in one smooth, swift movement he grabbed Eliakim from behind and pinned his arms to his sides, then held the blade to his throat.

"Where is he?" he demanded.

Sweat ran down Eliakim's forehead and into his eyes. "Y-you mean the peasant who owned those clothes? He's d-dead. My father tried to save him, but he was too badly hurt. He died several hours ago."

Jonadab pressed the sword to Eliakim's neck and drew it across his throat until a ribbon of blood ran down the blade. Eliakim cried out in pain. He was going to die.

"Are you telling the truth?" Jonadab breathed.

"Yes! It's the truth!"

Jonadab lowered his sword and cursed, pushing Eliakim away. "If the prophet is dead, then he's no longer a threat to the king," he told one of his men. "But Uriah won't be content until he sees his dead body—and Hilkiah's."

One by one the soldiers returned with no other sign of Hilkiah or the prophet. From what Eliakim could see, they'd left the house in shambles from their search. He sank down on a bench by the door, badly shaken, and pressed the edge of his robe against the wound on his neck to try to stop the bleeding. They had nearly slit his throat. He was still trembling with shock when Jonadab turned to him again and placed the tip of his sword below Eliakim's breastbone, applying just enough pressure to make him wince.

"Where did you bury him, and where is your father?" he demanded.

"My father has property outside Jerusalem. He left hours ago to bury the man there—in the tomb of his ancestors."

"Then you'll show us where this property is," he said, hauling him to his feet. Eliakim wished he were a better liar.

"Listen, it's a long, difficult journey over the mountains, especially at night. I'll gladly take you there at dawn."

"We can't wait until dawn. Let's go."

"W-where are you taking me?"

Jonadab didn't answer. He ordered two of his men to stand guard at Hilkiah's house, then shoved Eliakim ahead of him into the street.

———

Hephzibah sat at the women's table across the banquet hall from Hezekiah, watching him, waiting for his gentle smile to light up his face. He'd been crowned King of Judah today. This was a festive occasion, his coronation banquet. But her husband's face looked strained and somber. He hadn't smiled once throughout the entire evening, and she wondered why. She wished she could go to him and say something to make him smile or even laugh out loud again. If only she could make him love her. But he didn't love her. And tonight was the first time she'd seen him since the week of their marriage.

At the table beside Hephzibah, the concubines ignored her as they enjoyed the feast, drinking cup after cup of wine. Hephzibah had barely touched her food. She was surrounded by hundreds of people at a banquet that honored her husband, but she could barely contain her grief.

She had obtained everything she wished for all her life—until now. And she was powerless to change her situation. Merab had won her the right to live in the wife's suite until Hezekiah chose a new wife for himself. But like kings everywhere, he would probably marry many wives besides Hephzibah, even the daughters of foreign kings. Hezekiah would never belong to her alone. She would never be the love of his heart. Kings didn't love their wives as other husbands did. She was only one of many women whose job it was to bring him pleasure and provide heirs for the kingdom.

She had known this truth ever since the day she had overheard the eunuch talking and had wept with Merab. But Hephzibah had never accepted the truth in her heart until tonight, until she had watched her husband from a distance and seen him for what he was— a stranger who had never once looked her way.

Soon the banquet would end, and the eunuch would escort her back to the harem. Months or even years might pass before she saw Hezekiah again. Now that he was the king, all hope that he would ever love her had to die.

Hephzibah wanted to bury her face in her arms and weep in despair. But she would have plenty of time to mourn in the days to come. Tonight, she would gaze at her husband in his royal robes for every second that she could. But she couldn't help wondering what he was thinking and why he looked so sad.

———

Hezekiah refused the servant's offer of more wine. It wouldn't

help to lift his spirits. He had longed to return to his rooms all evening, but duty obligated him to preside over his coronation banquet.
His guests showed no signs of leaving, even though it was well after
midnight. Maybe he should set the example and leave first.

He hadn't enjoyed the feast. His talk with Shebna about the state
of his kingdom had drained him and left him feeling sick at heart. All
around him, the banquet tables were heaped with empty plates and
platters of discarded bones, but Hezekiah hadn't felt like eating. He
was much too aware of the true state of his economy and the poverty
that most of his people suffered.

He leaned toward Uriah, seated at his right, to tell him he was
leaving. Uriah seemed to know a great deal about running the kingdom, as well as who all the noblemen were and what roles they played
in Ahaz's administration. Hezekiah relied heavily on him for advice,
although it frustrated him to do so. But just when he got the high
priest's attention, the musicians began to play again.

"Never mind, Uriah," he said. "I was going to leave, but maybe
I'll stay a little longer to hear the music."

"In that case, have more wine, Your Majesty." Uriah signaled to
the servant.

Micah paused halfway up the flight of stairs and leaned against the
wall to keep from fainting. *Please, dear God. Only a little farther.* He
knew from memorizing Isaiah's map that this was the last flight of
stairs he had to climb. He was almost to the banquet hall.

The guards outside the palace gates hadn't stopped him as he and
Hilkiah had boldly strode past them, dressed in Hilkiah's expensive
robes and accompanied by his servants. So far, they hadn't seen any
guards inside the palace, and the few people they'd passed had ignored
them. Once Micah had gotten his bearings, he had told Hilkiah to
wait for him in the courtyard; he didn't want to endanger the little
merchant's life any more than he already had. Micah was concerned

about Hilkiah's son, too, wondering what had happened to him after he and Hilkiah had left. Micah whispered a prayer for Eliakim, then summoned all his strength to climb the stairs.

By the time he reached the top he felt dizzy and nauseous with pain. He forced himself to keep moving and turned down the hallway to the left. Suddenly Micah halted. Two palace guards stood in front of the banquet room doors, looking directly at him. He closed his eyes to keep from blacking out. He didn't know what to do. When he opened his eyes again, one of the guards was walking toward him.

*Help me, Yahweh! Help me!*

The guard smiled. "You look as though you could use some help, my lord," he said to Micah. "You've been celebrating a bit heavily, I see. They must be serving good wine. Would you like help getting back to your table?"

"Yes . . . thank you." The soldier took Micah's left arm to steady him, and Micah moaned in pain.

"And you'll probably feel even worse tomorrow," the soldier said with a grin.

The second guard opened the door for them. Micah gazed at the hundreds of people who packed the enormous room.

"Do you remember which table is yours, my lord?" the guard asked.

Micah spotted the head table on a platform at the front of the room. King Hezekiah was still seated there, wearing his royal robes and a golden crown on his head.

"You can leave me now," Micah told the guard. "I know where to go." The guard bowed slightly and closed the door behind him.

As Micah limped up the long center aisle toward the king's table, he put all his mistakes and all the disasters of the day behind him. His goal was within reach. He began to praise God, and he felt His presence and power surging through him. Micah's pain was forgotten as he concentrated on the words that Yahweh spoke to him.

The musicians finished their song. Hezekiah rose from his seat to leave—then halted. A man stood below the platform, staring up at him. The intensity of his gaze made Hezekiah's heart beat faster. He was certain he had never met the man before, yet something about his piercing gaze seemed familiar.

"What's wrong?" Hezekiah asked. "What do you want?"

"Listen, all you leaders of Judah," the man said. "You're supposed to know right from wrong, yet you're the very ones who hate good and love evil. You skin my people and tear at their flesh. You chop them up like meat meant for the cooking pot—and then you plead and beg with Yahweh for His help. Do you really expect Him to listen to your troubles? He will look the other way!"

Uriah leaped to his feet. "Guards!" he shouted. "Take this man out of here!"

"Wait," Hezekiah said, holding up his hand. "Let him finish." He didn't need this stranger to tell him how much his people were suffering. And seeing the remains of the feast all around him filled Hezekiah with guilt. Maybe this stranger had answers. The hall gradually grew silent as the guests noticed the confrontation.

"Why are you here?" Hezekiah asked.

"Yahweh has filled me with the power of his Spirit, with justice and might. I've come to announce Yahweh's punishment on this nation for her sins."

"Yahweh?" Hezekiah repeated. "One of Israel's gods?" This all seemed like a dream he'd once had, and he had the peculiar feeling that this had happened before. Something about the man seemed familiar to him. He tried to remember but couldn't.

"Listen to me, you leaders who hate justice—you fill Jerusalem with murder, corruption, and sin of every kind. Your leaders take bribes, your priests and prophets only preach or prophesy if they're paid—"

"Your Majesty, tell the guards to take him out of here," Uriah pleaded. "This man is either drunk or insane."

The banquet hall was dimly lit, and although the man's face looked bruised and swollen, as if he'd suffered a beating, he didn't appear drunk or insane to Hezekiah. He turned to Uriah and noticed that all the color had drained from the priest's face. He was glaring at the stranger with a mixture of hatred and fear. Hezekiah had the eerie feeling that his elusive dream involved Uriah, too. He turned back to Micah.

"You've made some serious accusations. I think you'd better explain yourself."

"My judgments are not my own. I'm here to plead Yahweh's case."

"All right," Hezekiah replied. "Let's make this a formal hearing. You may present Yahweh's case." He sat down to listen, and Uriah sat grudgingly beside him.

"Listen, O mountains, to Yahweh's accusation," the man shouted. "Hear, O earth, for Yahweh has a case against his people. He will prosecute them to the full: 'My people, what have I done to you? How have I burdened you? Answer me. I brought you up out of Egypt and redeemed you from the land of slavery. I sent Moses to lead you, also Aaron and Miriam. My people, remember what Balak king of Moab counseled and what Balaam son of Beor answered. Remember your journey from Shittim to Gilgal, that you may know the righteous acts of the LORD.'"

"I've studied our nation's history," Hezekiah cut in. He'd hoped to learn something that would help him, but he was growing impatient. "What does Yahweh want?"

The stranger's tone changed suddenly as he switched roles, pleading the case for the people. He dropped to his knees. "How can we make up to God for what we've done? Shall we bow down before Yahweh with burnt offerings and yearling calves? Will Yahweh be pleased with thousands of rams, and with ten thousand rivers of olive oil? Would He forgive my sins if I offered Him the fruit of my body? Shall I sacrifice my firstborn?"

*Sacrifice my firstborn.*

Suddenly the floodgate burst open, and the memories poured into Hezekiah's mind. The rumble of voices and trampling feet. *"Which one is the firstborn?"* The priest's hand had rested on Eliab's head. *"This one."*

He remembered the column of smoke in the Valley of Hinnom and the pounding drums. He remembered the heat and the flames; the monster's open mouth and outstretched arms.

*Molech.*

Hezekiah began to tremble. "Yahweh," he whispered.

Now he remembered—he remembered everything. And above all, he remembered his terror as the nightmare returned. But it wasn't simply a childhood dream. The sacrifices to Molech had really taken place—his brothers, Eliab and Amariah, had burned to death. And if it hadn't been for Yahweh, he would have burned to death, too. He felt shaken, unable to speak.

Micah rose from his knees and approached him, his voice quiet and soothing. "He has shown you what is good—and what does Yahweh require of you? To act justly and to love mercy and to walk humbly with your God."

*Yahweh is God—Yahweh alone.*

Hezekiah's heart pounded as he remembered another piece of the puzzle. "My grandfather . . ." he murmured.

"He's alive," Micah said with a nod. "Your grandfather, Zechariah, is still alive."

"He's. . . ?" Hezekiah shook his head to clear his thoughts, then stood. "Take me to him."

# 21

IT WAS NO USE. ZECHARIAH couldn't sleep. He threw back the tangled bedcovers and groped in the dark for the oil lamp. Once it was lit, he put on his robe and sandals. There had been many nights like this when he couldn't sleep, and he'd learned over the years to bring his questions to God. It was the only way to find peace in his heart and soul. Tonight Zechariah couldn't stop thinking about Hezekiah's coronation and reliving his bitter disappointment when Uriah had prayed, *"May your reign be blessed by all the gods of Judah."*

Hezekiah never would have allowed such a prayer if he still believed in the one true God. All the long years of waiting, all of Zechariah's prayers and hopes had been in vain. Hezekiah had turned his back on Yahweh.

Zechariah walked down the deserted corridor to the Temple library. Like Job, he would bring his complaint to God, hoping to find comfort—and answers—in His Word. Zechariah loved this room and the scrolls that lined its shelves. He loved to pray here, feeling somehow closer to Yahweh when surrounded by His Word. He lit the oil lamps that were mounted on the walls, then scanned the shelves, trying to decide what to read. He finally chose the fifth book of Moses—the scroll he had read from the day he had brought Hezekiah here—and he sat down wearily at one of the tables. But tears blurred his vision. He was too heartbroken to open it.

Hezekiah knew there were no gods except Yahweh. God had helped Zechariah teach him, he knew the truth! Zechariah remembered the day they had walked to the spring and they had recited the Shema together for the first time. *"Louder, Grandpa! Make the goats bellow!"*

Zechariah cleared the lump from his throat and recited the words aloud: "'Hear, O Israel! Yahweh is God—Yahweh alone. . . .'"

He couldn't finish.

But from the darkness behind him a voice continued to recite: "Love Yahweh your God with all your heart and with all your soul and with all your strength."

Zechariah leaped from his seat. Hezekiah stood in the doorway.

At first Zechariah thought he was dreaming, but in the next moment he felt Hezekiah's arms around him, hugging him fiercely, and he knew it was real. They held each other, without saying a word, for a long time.

Hezekiah had remembered his grandfather as tall and strong, but the man he held in his arms now seemed very different. He finally released his grasp and gazed at him. He saw the familiar kindness and love in his grandfather's eyes and was ashamed that he could have forgotten this man he had loved so much as a child, the man who had comforted him and assured him of God's protection.

"I'm so sorry, Grandpa—"

"No, son. It's not your fault. Everything happens according to Yahweh's will."

"I haven't thought about Yahweh for many, many years," he said softly. He felt the need to apologize and to explain himself to his grandfather. He groped for words. "My father insisted that I have the very finest education, the very best tutor. And I loved learning. I couldn't get enough of it—languages, history, literature. But my tutor didn't believe in any gods, and my father worshiped hundreds of them."

Hezekiah hadn't realized until now why he'd always hated his father. But that memory was coming back, too. Ahaz had sacrificed Hezekiah's two brothers—and he had intended to kill Hezekiah, as well.

"I hated my father," he said. "And I hated his idolatry. I didn't want any part in it. When he moved his idols into Yahweh's Temple—and when you didn't come back—I guess I discarded Yahweh, as well. In time, I forgot all about the things you taught me. After a while, even the sacrifices to Molech seemed like only a fairy tale or a bad dream I once had as a child. I haven't thought about Yahweh in years—until His prophet spoke at the banquet tonight."

"Forgive me, Yahweh," Zechariah whispered, leaning against the table. "Forgive my unbelief."

Hezekiah reached out to support him. "Are you all right? What's wrong?" He helped Zechariah sit down, then pulled up another bench facing him.

"Tell me about the prophet. Was it Isaiah?"

"No, his name is Micah, from Moresheth."

"What did he say?"

"He told me that Yahweh had a case to plead against Judah, and he reminded me of our history and everything that Yahweh has done for the nation. When I asked what Yahweh required in return, he said, 'Shall I offer my firstborn?' And I suddenly realized why he looked so familiar to me. He reminded me of the prophet I met in the Valley of Hinnom. And that's when I realized that it wasn't a dream." Hezekiah closed his eyes for a moment as the memories returned after all these years.

"I remember being so afraid—the sacrifice of the firstborn—and I was the firstborn after Eliab died. I knew I was going to die, just like he did. And then, when it seemed there was no escape, the prophet spoke: 'When you pass through the fire, you won't be burned . . . for Yahweh is your God.' And they sacrificed Amariah instead of me."

It was a few moments before he could continue. "I remember being so afraid that it would happen again, that my father would order a third sacrifice. Then you came, and you promised that Yahweh would protect me from Molech." He stared at Zechariah for a moment. "But one thing you never told me . . . I guess I never asked you . . . *Why?* Why did Yahweh save me?"

Zechariah could barely speak. "Because He loves you, Hezekiah." He shook his head. "But why?"

"King David wondered the same thing: 'When I consider your heavens, the work of your fingers, the moon and the stars, which you have set in place, what is man that you are mindful of him?' I don't know the answer, son, but I do know that He loves us."

"But I haven't done anything to deserve His love. Why would He save me?"

"Whether we deserve His love or not is irrelevant. Of all men, I'm proof of that. I sinned so greatly against Him. . . . but He forgave me, and I know that He loves me."

Hezekiah still couldn't comprehend what Zechariah was saying. "But why me? Why didn't he save Eliab or Amariah?"

"Because Yahweh has chosen you," Micah said, interrupting. He had been waiting in the hallway with Hilkiah, but he suddenly stepped into the library to join them. "Forgive me, Your Majesty, but Yahweh is urging me to speak, and I can't keep silent any longer. Yahweh has chosen *you* to lead this nation back to Him."

Another memory stirred in Hezekiah's mind. The other prophet had told him the same thing a long time ago, in the Valley of Hinnom: *"Yahweh has ransomed you. He has called you by name. You belong to Yahweh."*

"God still loves His people," Micah continued. "And He remembers the covenant He made with them. But we've broken that covenant and disobeyed all His commandments and worshiped idols. So, like a loving father, Yahweh punishes us, giving us over to our enemies until we turn back to Him again. Everything has happened just as the Torah said—if your heart turns away and you bow down to worship other gods, you will certainly be destroyed."

Hezekiah stared at Micah. "Wait a minute. Are you saying that our nation has been conquered and impoverished because we broke our covenant with Yahweh?"

"Yes."

Hezekiah expected a lengthy debate from the prophet, but he had replied with bold conviction. Hezekiah exhaled slowly.

"I'm sorry, Micah, but your reasoning is too oversimplified to take seriously. Judah isn't an isolated nation living quietly with our God. The Assyrian Empire is slowly conquering the entire world—and that's a reality I can't ignore."

"Nevertheless, it's true, Your Majesty. Yahweh's wisdom often seems foolish in man's eyes."

Hezekiah looked at his grandfather in surprise. "You taught me that once, with the story of David and Goliath."

Zechariah smiled.

"Your Majesty," Micah continued, "Yahweh doesn't simply observe mankind from His heavenly throne. He's actively involved in the affairs of men—in the affairs of *all* nations. He's using the Assyrians as an instrument of His wrath, and when He's through judging our nation, they will be judged also. Yahweh is sovereign over all."

"If you believe that Yahweh saved you as a child," Zechariah said, "why is it so difficult to believe that Yahweh could save our nation?"

"I don't know," Hezekiah said, rubbing his eyes. "I've been reviewing our nation's history trying to see how Judah got into this mess and looking for a way out of it. But I haven't found one. Now you're saying that Yahweh is the missing key?"

"Yes," Micah replied. "Didn't our nation achieve great power and prosperity under King David? And David loved Yahweh with all his heart."

"Judah hasn't seen peace or prosperity since King Uzziah's days," Zechariah said quietly. "And Uzziah also worshiped Yahweh—until his pride destroyed him. When Uzziah died, the people slowly turned away from God, and Judah has declined, as well."

"My father was the worst idolater of them all," Hezekiah said, remembering Molech's blazing image. "And Judah has been reduced to poverty and slavery under his rule." Micah and Zechariah were offering him the solution he had struggled to find. Yet he hesitated, his rational mind refusing to believe in a supernatural answer.

"Can you prove any of this?" he asked. "Perhaps some kings were better equipped to rule than others. Or maybe it was the era in which they lived. I can't rest the fate of our nation on a superstition. I have to believe in things that can be proven in a tangible way. Can you show me proof that this link between idolatry and poverty isn't just a coincidence?"

Micah shrugged. "I don't have the kind of proof you're asking for. I believe it by faith."

Hezekiah sighed. "I wish it could be true. I wish I could renew this covenant with Yahweh and see my kingdom miraculously restored, but—" He shook his head. His mind refused to believe it. He felt torn between his seeds of faith in Yahweh and his sense of reason. He turned to his grandfather, pleading wordlessly for help.

"Belief in Yahweh doesn't come with your mind, Hezekiah. It comes with your heart. When you only believe in things you can see with your eyes and touch with your hands, it is idolatry."

Zechariah's words stunned him. "Then I'm an idolater, too?"

"To have faith in Yahweh is to know that there is a realm of the spirit beyond the comprehension of our minds," Zechariah said. "Trusting in Molech, as Ahaz did, or trusting in your own wisdom and intellect—there's no difference in God's eyes. It's all idolatry."

Hezekiah stared at him. "Then in God's eyes I'm as guilty as my father?"

Zechariah nodded.

"But I hate idolatry—the ridiculous statues, the orgies in the sacred groves, the innocent children burned to death. It's repulsive!" He felt shaken to discover his own guilt, that in God's sight he was as much a sinner as Ahaz.

"What does Yahweh want me to do?" he asked quietly.

"The Torah says that if you seek Yahweh your God you will find Him if you look for Him with all your heart and soul. When you are in distress and you return to God and obey Him, He will be merciful. He won't abandon you or forget the covenant He made with our forefathers."

The room fell silent as Hezekiah struggled. His grandfather told him to accept it by faith, but nothing Shebna had taught him prepared him to do that. The one certainty in his life was that Yahweh had saved him as a child. Nothing could change that conviction. His belief seemed small compared to Micah's unshakable confidence, but perhaps it was a place to start.

"I want to seek God," he finally said. "I want to get rid of all the idolatry and renew our nation's covenant with Him. I want to ask Him to heal this land."

"Who is a God like you?" Micah cried, lifting his uninjured arm in praise. "You pardon sin and forgive the transgressions of your people. You do not stay angry forever but delight to show mercy. You will have compassion on us once again. You will tread our sins underfoot and hurl all our iniquities into the depths of the sea!"

---

Uriah sat with the banquet guests in stunned silence for a long time. The king had left with the prophet so abruptly that most of the people had no idea what had happened. But Uriah knew. He had seen Hezekiah's face when the prophet spoke of the sacrifice of the firstborn. It was only a matter of time before he remembered that Uriah had presided over that sacrifice.

He had expected to be arrested then and there, but instead Hezekiah had asked to see Zechariah. Uriah regretted not having killed him years ago, when Ahaz had first given the order. Now Hezekiah would learn about his grandfather's long imprisonment. Yes, Uriah knew that his days of power—and probably his life—were over.

At first he felt resigned to his fate. But as the banquet guests shook off their surprise and slowly began to leave, Uriah began shrugging off his resignation. Anger replaced it. He had ruled the nation of Judah for King Ahaz for years. Why should Uriah give that power to Hezekiah simply because he was born to the house of David? What did that matter? A descendant of King David hadn't ruled the northern tribes of Israel for centuries. The throne belonged to anyone who had the power and strength to grab it.

Uriah rose from his seat, determined to fight to the death for what he deserved. Many government officials hated Ahaz as much as he did, and they owed more loyalty to Uriah than to Ahaz's son. With his persuasive power, Uriah could easily convince them to revolt. And Hezekiah had no sons yet. Once Uriah got rid of him, there would be no heir to replace him. But he would have to act quickly.

He strode across the banquet room, fighting the urge to run. Two palace guards stood outside the main doors, and he ordered them to follow him. They hurried to keep pace as he strode down the hall.

Uriah knew that he couldn't remain in the palace, but he needed to get a few things from his private chambers first. He hadn't decided where he would go or exactly how he would start the rebellion against King Hezekiah, but he knew that he had worked too long and too hard to give up now.

When he reached his rooms, Uriah ordered the guards to remain outside. In spite of his nation's poverty, he had carefully saved a small sum of gold for himself, stolen over the years from the tribute he had gathered for Assyria. He would use it to buy the support of his nation's top officials, including Jonadab, captain of the palace guard. The guards would serve as Uriah's army. Hezekiah would be defenseless.

Uriah quickly gathered the stolen gold and tied it in a bundle. He didn't bother to pack many personal things, assuming he would return to the palace again as king, if everything went according to his plan.

With his bundle tied securely, Uriah scanned the room to see if he had forgotten anything. He spotted the short, sharp dagger he had used to slay the sacrifices when he was a priest, and he tucked it securely into the belt of his tunic, hidden beneath his outer robe—just in case.

Spotting the knife had helped him decide where he should go first. He was still the high priest, and he knew that most of his fellow priests and Levites would support him. He would go to the Temple and gather as many loyalists as he could find. He tucked his bundle inside his robes and strode from the room.

"Find Captain Jonadab," he commanded the two guards. "Tell him to meet me in the Temple council chamber at once."

———

For the first time since Ahaz had died, Hezekiah was eager to begin his reign. Zechariah and Micah had offered him hope that his nation's staggering problems could be solved.

"I'll need your help," he told Zechariah. "Tell me where to begin."

"We'll begin here," he said, motioning to the shelves of scrolls. "With the Torah, Yahweh's divine law. Let it guide you in everything you do."

Hezekiah liked the prospect of studying under Zechariah again, but at the same time he was puzzled. "Why did you stop coming to the palace to teach me?" he asked.

"I wanted to come, but I was held prisoner here."

"By my father?"

"Your father wanted to kill me because I spoke out against his idolatry. Instead, Uriah kept me here."

"All these years?" Hezekiah shuddered when he realized how much time had passed since he'd last seen his grandfather. Then, as he thought about his father and Uriah, he suddenly recalled something else: it was Uriah, dressed in the high priest's robes, who had placed his hand on his brother's head, marking him as the firstborn.

"Uriah led that sacrifice to Molech!" Hezekiah said. "He was the one who came for my brothers and me!"

"Uriah's sins against Yahweh are very great. His life was consecrated to God, and he was in a position of leadership, but he led many, many people into idolatry."

"What's the punishment for that? What does Yahweh's Law say?"

Zechariah slowly walked to the shelves of scrolls and pulled one down from its place. He searched for the passage he wanted, then began reading in a quiet voice: "'If a man or woman living among you . . . has worshiped other gods . . . take the man or woman who has done this evil deed to your city gate and stone that person to death.'" He paused and looked up at Hezekiah.

"Is there more?" Hezekiah asked. "I need to hear it all."

"'Any Israelite . . . who gives any of his children to Molech must be put to death. The people of the community are to stone him.'" Zechariah looked up again, and his eyes were filled with sorrow. "You can't stone every man in Judah who is guilty of idolatry. We'd all be guilty—even me."

"Maybe so. But Uriah was the high priest of Yahweh. When he led the sacrifice to Molech, the people blindly followed him. And he also silenced the truth. It's more than a matter of revenge. Before I can start any reforms, I have to get rid of the evil. Uriah has to die."

Hezekiah didn't know how much time had passed since he left the banquet with Micah, but he suddenly realized that he had given Uriah more than enough time to appreciate the danger he was in and make his escape. "I have to find him," he told Zechariah.

He strode from the room and hurried through the unlit hallways, anxious to return to the palace. But he forgot to take an oil lamp, and he could barely see where he was going as he tried to retrace his steps to the outside. He traveled a considerable distance through the maze of hallways before realizing that in his blind haste to capture Uriah, he had lost his way. Frustrated, he decided to turn around and find someone who could lead him out.

When Hezekiah came to the end of one hallway, he heard the faint mutter of voices and saw a shaft of light glowing in the darkness under a closed door. He was about to knock on it and ask for help when he recognized Uriah's voice. The high priest was shouting, arguing, and someone seemed to be answering him in a low mumble. Hezekiah couldn't make out what they were saying.

He realized the frustrating dilemma he faced. He had found Uriah, but he didn't have any guards to help him make an arrest. He knew there were men in the room with Uriah, but he had no idea how many there were or if they were Uriah's supporters. Hezekiah couldn't even go for help because he was lost in the maze of Temple passageways. A trickle of sweat rolled down his neck. He wished he had worn his sword to the banquet.

All at once the door burst open, and he stood face-to-face with Uriah. The priest seemed as startled as Hezekiah was, and they stood motionless for a moment, staring at each other. Then Hezekiah said, "You're under arrest, Uriah. You sacrificed my brother to Molech. The Torah condemns you to die."

Uriah stared at him coldly. "And the Torah also says that this Temple is a place of refuge. No one can touch me here."

Hezekiah had no idea if Uriah was telling the truth or not. He hesitated, reluctant to violate the Torah. While Hezekiah paused, Uriah thrust his hand inside his robe and drew out a dagger.

Hezekiah saw the glint of metal and reacted swiftly, his reflexes trained by years of military instruction with Captain Jonadab. He grabbed Uriah's right arm with both hands to stop him from plunging his dagger and threw all his weight at the high priest, knocking him off balance. But Uriah recovered quickly and locked his other arm around Hezekiah's neck, slowly squeezing off his air supply.

Hezekiah twisted around, trying to break Uriah's hold and using his legs to kick him, but his efforts were useless. Uriah seemed rooted to the ground. The priest's grip tightened with each of Hezekiah's movements.

Moments passed as Hezekiah struggled to break free, prying with one hand at Uriah's arm, to keep from choking to death, and holding the knife at bay with the other. As his air supply decreased, darkness circled around the edge of his vision. He needed air! He had never imagined that Uriah was so strong.

Hezekiah's arms quivered from exertion. The dagger, only inches away, was slowly moving closer to his heart. If Uriah found a reserve of strength, Hezekiah's life would be over. Uriah only needed to close the circle of his arm and plunge his dagger.

Stars of light appeared as Hezekiah's vision shrank. He strained to pull air into his lungs. Why wasn't the priest showing signs of fatigue? Instead, Uriah was slowly tightening his death hold as he brought the dagger closer. Hezekiah's lungs felt as if they were about to explode. Why didn't someone help him?

In a few more seconds his air supply and his strength would give out. Uriah was going to kill him. And Hezekiah didn't want to die. He wanted a chance to reign, a chance to renew his nation's covenant with Yahweh. In his last moment before darkness closed in, Hezekiah prayed, *Yahweh—help me!*

Suddenly Uriah cried out in pain and released his grip. The dagger fell from his hand and clattered to the floor. The priest staggered forward and fell against Hezekiah, knocking him down and pinning him to the floor.

For a few seconds Hezekiah lay beneath him, stunned, gulping deep breaths of air, amazed to be alive. Then he pushed Uriah off and sat up, looking to see who had saved his life. A knife protruded from Uriah's back.

Hezekiah's grandfather stood over him, holding out his hand to help him up.

# 22

As THE MORNING DAWNED cold and gray, Hezekiah felt the strength returning to his exhausted muscles. He slowly rose from the bench where he'd been resting and found that his legs would hold him. Except for a dull pain behind his eyes, he felt all right. But he was weary of this stuffy building and needed some fresh air.

Uriah's body lay in the hallway where he had fallen, covered with a robe. The atmosphere was still tense after the night's startling events, and the priests and Levites moved about in tight little groups as if afraid of being alone. Everyone seemed dazed, and talked in whispers. Zechariah was the only one who seemed unshaken, as if what he had done had been inevitable.

"Would you do something for me?" Hezekiah asked him. "Gather all of the priests and Levites who are left and meet me outside in the courtyard in a few minutes."

Hezekiah found the door that led from the building and walked outside into the fresh air of the new day. The cool morning breeze made him shiver. He was still dressed in the clothes he had worn to the banquet, now stained with Uriah's blood.

The eastern sky was growing light, but clouds hung over the city obscuring the sun. He walked across the courtyard to the east side of the Temple, out of the cold chill of the shadows. The only sounds were the chirping of swallows and the slap of his shoes against the paving stones as he walked.

When Hezekiah reached the middle of the courtyard he stopped and looked around, seeing it as if for the first time. The Assyrian altar that Ahaz had erected dominated the space, covered with images of idolatry. Nearby, the giant Bronze Sea sat on an improvised base, and he remembered Zechariah telling him that Ahaz had sent the original base to Assyria. A tall brass pole stood nearby, with a serpent draped in a coil around it.

No wonder Yahweh had turned His back.

Hezekiah slowly walked to the sanctuary porch and looked through the grating. The doors had been boarded up with planks of wood that appeared to have been in place for many years. The once-beautiful building looked decayed, neglected. He stood between the pillars that flanked the Temple door and remembered Zechariah teaching him their names. Hezekiah strained to recall what they were; it seemed important that he remember. One was Boaz—*in Him is strength*. And the other was . . .

Hezekiah shook his head and turned away. He tried to recall how the Temple had looked on the day he had watched the sacrifice with Zechariah, but nothing seemed the same.

After several minutes he heard the sound of approaching footsteps. The priests and Levites had come out of a side door and were silently crossing the courtyard to meet him. Hezekiah was surprised to see that only about thirty men had come.

"Aren't there more men than this in the tribe of Levi?" he asked his grandfather.

"All of Uriah's supporters fled when he died," Zechariah said. "But the majority of the Levites stopped serving in the Temple years ago, either because they disagreed with Uriah's changes or because they no longer could support their families on the meager tithes. The handful of us who remained, did so out of loyalty to Yahweh and a desire to preserve the Temple buildings and the sacred books."

Hezekiah looked at the forbidden images engraved on the Assyrian altar, then surveyed the handful of faithful men standing before him. He felt as if he were beginning a long journey up a steep mountain. He knew the time had come to take the first difficult step.

"Listen to me, Levites. I want you to consecrate yourselves and clean all the trash and idolatry from Yahweh's Temple. Our forefathers have sinned and have defiled His Temple, turning their backs on God. They boarded up the doors to the Holy Place and put out the flame that was always supposed to burn. The incense hasn't been lit, and the burnt offerings haven't been given for many years. Therefore, God's wrath has fallen on Judah and Jerusalem. He has made us the object of contempt in the eyes of other nations."

The Levites seemed to come alive at his words, and their faces reflected their amazement and joy. Hezekiah felt a smile slowly spread across his face, as well.

"But now I want to make a covenant with Yahweh so that His anger will turn away from us. Don't neglect your duties any longer, Levites, for Yahweh has chosen you to minister to Him."

A shout went up from the men, and they rushed forward to thank him and to pledge their support.

"I'm Mahath, son of Amasai."

"Joah, son of Zimmah, and this is my son, Eden."

"I'm Shimri, from the descendants of Elizaphan."

"Mattaniah, from Asaph, the musicians of Yahweh."

"Shimri of Heman, and my brother Jeiel."

"I am Uzziel."

The last one who came was Zechariah. "We'll send word to all the priests and Levites who have scattered to come back to Jerusalem," he said.

"Good. And take the gold that Uriah was carrying and use it to make repairs to the Temple."

"We'll begin reconsecrating ourselves and the Temple today."

"Let me know as soon as everything is purified," Hezekiah said. "We'll renew our covenant with Yahweh, beginning with a sacrifice."

Zechariah went back inside with the other Levites, leaving Hezekiah alone in the courtyard. He walked over to the huge Assyrian altar, standing where Yahweh's altar should be, and he studied the forbidden idols that decorated it, running his fingers over the intricate carvings. These were gods you could see and touch. But they were as cold and lifeless as the brass they were carved from. Yahweh, whom he couldn't see or touch, was a *living* God.

"'Hear, O Israel! Yahweh is God—Yahweh alone!'" he recited softly. "'Love Yahweh your God with all your heart and with all your soul and with all your strength.'" Yahweh required nothing less than a total commitment. And that was what he had promised.

A misty rain began to fall, chilling Hezekiah. But it seemed to him that the rain washed the city clean, cleansing away the defilement. He left the Temple courtyard through the main gate and walked slowly down the hill alone, back to the palace.

Hezekiah was twenty-five years old when he became king, and he reigned in Jerusalem twenty-nine years. His mother's name was Abijah daughter of Zechariah. He did what was right in the eyes of the Lord, just as his father David had done. In the first month of the first year of his reign, he opened the doors of the Temple of the Lord and repaired them.

———

2 CHRONICLES 29:1–3 NIV

CHRONICLES OF THE KINGS—Book 2

# Song of Redemption

*Song of Redemption* begins with Judah's nationwide spiritual revival led by King Hezekiah. As he grows in faith and seeks to obey God in every aspect of his life, Hezekiah discovers that the Law forbids him to marry multiple wives. He must then decide whether or not Hephzibah—whom he has ignored for so long—will remain part of his harem.

Hezekiah's reforms promise to bring God's blessings and renewed prosperity to the nation, but his brother and many other officials oppose these changes and conspire against him. The situation reaches critical proportions when the Assyrians threaten the northern nation of Israel. This nation's plight is dramatized through the story of Jerusha and her family, who must find a way to escape the ensuing Assyrian holocaust.

As Hezekiah is challenged by enemies on every side—even in his own household—his newfound faith in God is put to the ultimate test.